SPIRIT SIGHT

The Spirit Song Trilogy | Book One
Volume One

ROSS HIGHTOWER

Black Rose Writing | Texas

©2023 by Ross Hightower
All rights reserved. No part of this book may be reproduced, stored in a retrieval system or
transmitted in any form or by any means without the prior written permission of the
publishers, except by a reviewer who may quote brief passages in a review to be printed in a
newspaper, magazine or journal.

The author grants the final approval for this literary material.

First printing

This is a work of fiction. Names, characters, businesses, places, events, and incidents are
either the products of the author's imagination or used in a fictitious manner. Any
resemblance to actual persons, living or dead, or actual events is purely coincidental.

ISBN: 978-1-68513-027-5
PUBLISHED BY BLACK ROSE WRITING
www.blackrosewriting.com

Printed in the United States of America
Suggested Retail Price (SRP) $24.95

Spirit Sight is printed in Garamond

*As a planet-friendly publisher, Black Rose Writing does its best to eliminate unnecessary waste to
reduce paper usage and energy costs, while never compromising the reading experience. As a result,
the final word count vs. page count may not meet common expectations.

No one knew the small story I wrote years ago would be the seed that grew into my first novel. I certainly didn't. For my partner, Deb, who kept the faith even through my first fumbling attempts, I'll be forever grateful. You made the emotional roller coaster a thrilling ride. You have the patience of a saint and the boundless energy of a hummingbird. I would be lost without you. Thanks to my early readers, whose inspiring words and meaningful feedback helped me believe in the story. You know who you are. Finally, thank you to Kathie Giorgio, friend, therapist, and coach. You helped me learn how to tell a story.

Maps

You can find maps and more at rosshightower.com/argren

SPIRIT SIGHT

Chapter 1

Minna

Minna stood on a hill above Fennig, the village where she lived her entire life. She faced the mountains that cradled the village, lifting her face to the sun's warmth. A gentle breeze, whispering of the coming winter, ruffled her hair. She inhaled evergreen, damp earth, the musty scent of dry leaves, and sighed it out with a smile. For many, familiarity steals the wonder found in simple things. Not for Minna.

Opening her eyes, she searched the nearby trees. The forest, a patchwork of autumn colors, held secrets only she knew. She found them flitting playfully high in the deep green branches of a spruce. Whenever she focused on them, they paused, hovering, as if waiting. Though they appeared to her as small balls of light, she had the distinct impression they watched her. Her father told her they were the *lan'and*, the land spirits, though, like everyone else, he couldn't see them. They were familiar companions. She concentrated, her brow furrowing, calling to them, and they answered, swooping down to swirl around her. Laughing, she lifted her hands and wiggled her fingers, though she couldn't touch the ephemeral orbs.

If these were the moments that defined her life, she would be content. But they were not.

With a sigh, she lowered her hands and sent the *lan'and* back to their games among the trees. It was time to get it over with. From her vantage atop a hill west of the village, she could see the market that appeared in the square every sixth day during the summer and early fall. It was a surprisingly busy scene for such a small community. One would think Fennig would struggle, being so isolated against an unexplored wilderness, but in fact, the opposite was true. The plains below the village were fertile, and isolation shielded it from the troubles found elsewhere in the Vollen Empire.

Though the day was warm, Minna pulled the hood of her cloak up, retrieved her basket, and carrying it in front of her, she descended the hill and stepped onto the Imperial Highway where it entered the village. As she approached the square, she edged over to hug the buildings along the side of the road, pausing in the shadow cast by a large house that bordered the square. The atmosphere in the market buzzed. The fall brought an abundance of early harvest produce, and excitement at the approaching harvest festival was in the air. If she were quick, she might complete her errand unnoticed.

She slipped into the crowd, weaving in and out, keeping her head down, careful to avoid contact with anyone. Still, she noticed some people glancing her way. The problem with living in a small village was everyone knew everyone else. People recognized her, and word spread quickly. To her horror, the crowd parted, clearing a path ahead of her. She hunched her shoulders and hurried on, ignoring the stares. No one was ever openly belligerent, but that mattered little. Their intent was clear enough.

She approached Agatha's stall. Agatha and her husband owned one of the larger farms below the village and offered the most diverse selection of produce. Minna hated buying from them, but her mother insisted. Agatha was the center of much of the gossip circulating in the village, especially the gossip concerning Minna. The proprietor was facing away from her when she arrived, chatting with Mabel, one of her co-

conspirators. Minna stopped several paces away, trying to look small and ignoring the pressure of the crowd's attention on her back.

She was considering how to get Agatha's attention when Mabel noticed her. The woman squinted Minna's way, leaned toward her friend, whispered and nodded toward Minna. Agatha stiffened and turned. When she saw Minna, she winced and said, "Yes, Minna, what can I do for you?"

An unaccustomed flash of irritation colored Minna's cheeks, but instead of retorting, she pressed her lips together and lowered her eyes, reciting the list her mother had her memorize. She lifted the basket and stepped forward with her hand extended. Even though Minna was careful to move slowly, Agatha startled and took a small step back, wincing and peering at the basket, as if she feared it would leap at her. Minna stood with her arm extended, feeling ridiculous, until Agatha, keeping a wary eye on her, shuffled forward and snatched it from her hand. Minna tried on a small conciliatory smile, to no avail.

She couldn't say she wasn't used to it, and even though she expected it, it still hurt. She had happy memories of running through this very market, laughing with the other children. Agatha once slipped her a plum when her mother wasn't looking, a rare treat that earned her a warm place in Minna's heart for years afterward. Now, watching the woman's back as she filled the basket, the memory watered Minna's eyes. Everything changed in her eighth summer, the year the *lan'and* appeared. Now at thirteen, she had endured the villagers' enmity for five years but understood it no better than the day she fled home in tears, chased by her friends' taunts.

She returned from her memories to find Mabel peering at her through narrowed eyes. A flush rose along Minna's neck, and her anger, so near the surface lately, flashed. She sucked in a breath. Anger was an emotion she couldn't allow herself. Squeezing her eyes shut, she took long slow breaths, willing her racing heart to slow and her mind to clear. Mabel's pinched face peered at her from the darkness, stirring the first breaths of the storm behind her eyes. *No, please, not now, not here.* But a hot, rebellious part of her, unfamiliar and unwelcome, gleefully trampled her carefully tended serenity. What did she do to deserve this woman's disapproval?

Nothing! The stirring in her mind gusted fitfully, then surged, becoming a howling gale in an instant. Unprepared for the sudden onset, Minna gasped as pressure erupted behind her eyes, pulsing with the whooshing beat of her heart. Her long, slow breaths came shorter and shallower until she was panting. Squeezing her eyes shut, she lowered her chin to her chest and clenched her body against... whatever would happen if she couldn't contain it.

In that moment, with her entire attention focused on her inner struggle, a presence flickered amid the formless roar. Something altogether alien, something other, something else sharing her mind. And it reached out to her. She clung on against the pressure, willing herself to hold on, extending her perception into the torrent, searching. As she probed the storm, unmindful of how she might appear to others, her face lifted, eyes closed, her hands groping before her, as if feeling her way in the dark. There! A fleeting presence, almost beyond her perception, as distinct from her as Agatha or Mabel, but inside her mind, sharing her thoughts.

A crash and a woman's squeal brought her back. Her eyes flew open to find the *lan'and* swirling around her. Her surprise at finding them in the village chased her anger, and the pressure drained away in an instant, leaving her trembling with relief.

The spirits spun away, and Minna lowered her gaze. Mabel lay on her back behind a crate of turnips, legs in the air, struggling frantically to rise. Agatha pressed against the back of her stall, staring with wide eyes, the basket held in front of her like a shield. Minna took in the scene, open-mouthed, until her gaze settled on Agatha's frightened face. "How much?" she asked.

When the woman didn't respond, Minna pointed at the basket and said again, "How much?"

Agatha flinched, but thrust the basket toward Minna.

Minna fumbled a coin from her purse and set it on the counter. Moving slowly, she reached for the basket and took it. "Thank you," she mumbled, and hurried away.

The women's excited chatter and the mutters of the crowd chased her across the square. As she approached the edge of the square, she heard Agatha's voice rise above the wordless murmur. "WITCH!" The crowd hushed and hurried out of Minna's path. Minna glanced up at a sea of frightened faces. Shrinking within her cloak, she dropped her eyes to the cobbles in front of her and quickened her pace.

Scurrying up the hill, she hugged the buildings as before, until she reached the summit, where she stopped and glanced over her shoulder. No one followed her. She stood motionless, gazing, unseeing, at the mountain peaks, heart thudding, breath as fluttery and delicate as a butterfly's wings. Images of what just happened crowded her mind until she saw the shocked and fearful faces turned her way when Agatha's accusation rang out. She clamped her mouth shut against the sob that fought its way out of her, convulsing with the effort. After long moments, the crisis passed, she took a shuddering breath.

Minna endured the villagers' hostility for years, but it was never this bad. Even on the worst days, she was never frightened. After all, she'd known these people all her life. She knew their names. Many of them welcomed her into their homes when she was young. Everyone knew Agatha was a gossip. She would spread that rumor to anyone who would listen, but would they believe her? No, of course they wouldn't. It was absurd. Wasn't it? She glanced over her shoulder again.

Was she a witch? It was a question she only allowed herself to consider late at night, in the moments before sleep took her. Safe in her bed, with the comfort of her sister sleeping next to her, her parents in their room nearby, the notion carried the menace of stories of witches she heard as a child, too fanciful to be truly frightening. But if she asked herself that question, surely others did as well, and the fear she sensed in the market wasn't from a story. It was real. She peered up at the spirits, back among the branches of the spruce. What else would explain the fact she alone could see them, or the discomfort others felt in her presence? What could explain the rushing wind in her mind, the pressure, the sense of filling up? It happened when she became angry, but it had always been a whisper before, easily dispelled. This time, it was a howling gale, filling her up with a sense of... potential, like the tension in a bow before the arrow is loosed. And there was that presence in her mind, like someone, or something, trying to get her attention. What was happening to her? She squeezed her eyes shut against a prickle of tears. What would Mama say if she couldn't go into the village anymore?

Taking a deep breath, she sighed it out, letting it take the tension with it. She looked up to the lone remaining *lan'and*. "What were you doing in the village?" The little spirit bobbed once and disappeared into the forest.

She watched it go and returned her gaze to the mountains. She couldn't allow herself to lose her temper. It was as simple as that. If she could stay calm, nothing bad would happen, and before long, people would forget about today. The rebellious voice, having done its damage, had no comment. Closing her eyes and lifting her face to the sun, she swayed, taking deep breaths and letting her heart slow.

"Minna, are you causing trouble again?"

Minna's heart leapt, and despite what just happened, a smile curved her lips. Jason always had laughter in his voice. She pushed her worries aside for the moment, unwilling to let them ruin a rare chance to spend time with her only friend. She looked over her shoulder to find him watching her with that smile that filled her heart. Minna glanced at the market. No one was coming, and it didn't appear Jason saw what happened.

"Are you shirking your duties, Jason? Your father will not be pleased."

"It's midday," he said, crossing the road to join her. "I'll have you know I'm missing midday meal so I can walk you home, Minna. I would think you would appreciate it." He gave her a stern look, reaching out a hand.

"A whole meal? I think you may waste away, Jason." She handed him the basket, but plucked out a carrot and held it up, cocking an eyebrow.

"That is funny, Minna." His brow furrowed. "When did you get funny?" Minna snorted and started walking. "No really, is this something new?" Jason asked, a smirk in this voice. He fell in beside her, bumping her shoulder.

Minna lived a league west of the village, far enough that, most days, she could pretend she was a normal girl, living a normal life. They strolled, enjoying the autumn weather and making the most of their time together. She usually relied on Jason to carry the conversation, but today, he was uncharacteristically reserved. The distant honking of geese high above, making their way south, drew her eyes upward. Peeking at Jason, she found him staring at his feet, his lips working as if he were talking to himself. Curious, she said, "You're awfully quiet today. What's got you so serious?" She could swear from the blush that appeared on his pale cheeks, he was flustered, but that couldn't be true, not Jason.

He gazed at her for the space of two heartbeats, then seeming to come to a decision, he said in a rush, "Are you going to the harvest festival?"

Minna's mouth fell open. She dropped her head, hiding her suddenly warm face behind her hair. The shadowy remnants of the cloud cast by her trip to the market parted, and for a moment, she saw herself wearing a traditional dress, flush with excitement, dancing with Jason in the square, the smiling faces of the villagers whirling by. She could feel his anxiety as he waited for her response, but she needed to gather herself, not wanting to shout when she told him yes.

And then Agatha's scowl swam up in her mind, crying, "WITCH!," leaving the fantasy in tatters. She could never attend the festival with Jason. He didn't deserve that. It was bad enough he suffered for being her friend. Still, not wanting to hurt his feelings by saying no, she made it a joke. Gesturing expansively with her arms, she said, "Oh yeah, Minna shows up at the harvest festival and the town riots. Children scream. Fires break out." She dropped her arms, forced a small smile onto her face, and peered up at him out of the corner of her eye.

To her surprise, Jason laughed. "Tell you what, Min. I'll pack a meal. Maybe I can even steal some of my father's mead." He nudged her with his elbow and winked before continuing. "We'll have a picnic on the hill above the village. Just you and me." He stopped, taking her arm and pulling her around to face him. "What do you say, Min? It'll be fun."

Minna looked up at him, his pale blue eyes taking her breath. They had always been friends, despite everything, but something changed recently. He made her feel... well, she didn't know how he made her feel, but she found herself thinking about it frequently. Gazing up into his open, smiling face, she saw herself for a moment as he saw her, and not what others said she was. Jason didn't think she was a witch. The wall she'd constructed between herself and a normal life trembled.

"Are you sure?" she asked. "You'll miss the festival."

"Yes, I am, and I won't miss anything I care about."

Her eyes found a *lan'and* swooping by behind him. Jason glanced back, and in the moment's respite, the rebellious voice whispered, "Don't I deserve some happiness?" When he turned a puzzled expression back toward her, she said, "I would like that very much, Jason."

His eyes widened briefly, then the cocky smile returned. "Well, of course you would. I knew it." She scowled, punched him on his arm, turned and walked away. After a few steps, she glanced over her shoulder and slowed, allowing him to catch up.

Minna slowed their pace, amused to see Jason back to his normal self. The spirits glided along beside them, as if listening to his steady patter. Minna always enjoyed hearing about his work in the smithy, and though she was excluded from village life, she laughed at his humorous take on the latest town gossip. But as slow as she walked, eventually her house came into view. Her father sat on a bench the porch, fletching arrows. When he noticed them, he called out, "Ho, Jason!"

"Ho, Hera Hunter. How's the hunting?"

"Funny every time, Jason," Minna's father said with a smile.

"Hi, Papa. Are we going to the falls tomorrow?" Minna asked and gave her father a kiss on the cheek.

"Of course, Minnow. First thing in the morning."

Minna's sister, Alyn, burst out of the front door, blond hair trailing behind her. "Min, Min, guess what—" Catching sight of Jason, she came to an abrupt stop. "Oh... Jason." She stood, wide-eyed, then turned and fled back into the house.

Jason and Minna burst out laughing.

"Hush, Jason. She'll feel awful if she hears us laughing," Minna said, trying to suppress her laughter. Jason leaned over to peer into the door where Alyn disappeared, then straightened, his smile faltering. Minna sighed and turned around. "Hello, Mama."

Her mother stood on the porch, her lips drawn into a tight line. Though it was subtle, Minna noticed her mother wince when she looked at her daughter. "Minna, take those vegetables inside. We have to get started on supper."

Minna dipped her head and said, "Yes, Mama." She took the basket from Jason, giving him a small smile and disappeared into the house.

"Morning, Jason," her mother said, before following Minna.

• • •

Supper and chores done, Minna sat next to her father on the front porch, the late afternoon sun ceding the day to autumn's chill. She pulled her cloak tighter, idly watching the *lan'and* flitting through the trees across the Imperial Highway. She thought back to the day, five years ago, when her life fell to pieces.

For an eight-year-old, the world is still so full of surprises that the spirits' appearance didn't seem odd to her at all. She was so excited to share her discovery, she ran all the way into town to tell her friends. They surrounded her with the warm familiarity of children who knew each other their entire lives. She bounced on the balls of her feet, describing the spirits and pointing them out among the trees. At first, they peered into the forest in amused bewilderment, but as she persisted, they shifted away from her, casting confused grimaces her way.

When it became clear, they couldn't see the lights, she abandoned her efforts to convince them and tried to join them in their usual games. But whenever she approached, they backed away, baffled expressions on their faces. Eventually, she stood alone, surrounded by accusing stares. Only Jason and one other boy, as confused as she was, stood with her. When the confrontation threatened to become physical, she fled, ashamed, though she didn't understand why.

She ran to the one place a child thinks of in such moments, home. Arriving in tears, the story spilled out of her in a jumbled rush. When he understood what happened, her father, who should have been her refuge, crumpled. The devastated expression on his face frightened her more than anything else that happened that day. He sat on the ground, took her in his lap, and wept. His tears in her hair remained a vivid memory. Later, after the tears, he told her the spirits were real, and he told her their name, but he said little else she remembered. It was Jason, appearing at her front door later, who rescued her. Though she was old enough now to recognize her father's response as coming from a place she didn't understand, he inadvertently planted the belief she was at fault.

She rarely mentioned the *lan'and* to her father, afraid of his response, but her experience in the market that morning left her with questions, and she needed answers. Her father busied himself fletching arrows, humming softly. Looking back at the spirits, Minna asked, "Papa, how do you know about the *lan'and*?"

When he didn't answer, she glanced at him again. He was staring into the distance, eyes glistening. She watched him for a few seconds. When he didn't respond, she sighed. "I'm sorry, P—"

"A long time ago, before the Empire came, the *Alle'oss* had very different beliefs," her father said, a wistful note in his voice.

Minna held her breath, afraid to move, lest she interrupt him.

His hands rested on his lap, and he gazed at something Minna couldn't see. "We believed the world was full of spirits. Not just the *lan'and*. There were spirits of the forest, the air, the water... many more. Most people couldn't see them, but there were women called *saa'myn* who could see them and talk to them." He gave Minna a sad smile. "When a *saa'myn* came to the village, we celebrated. There would be a feast, and people would gather to ask her questions for the spirits."

He paused and Minna, desperate to keep him talking, asked, "What kinds of questions?"

"Mostly questions about the future. What will the harvest be like next year? Will my baby be a girl? Who will I marry?"

Minna's brow furrowed. "So... I'm a *saa'myn*?" She held her breath while he considered her question. She didn't know what a *saa'myn* was, but no one celebrated when a witch came to town.

He was quiet for a long time, then nodded. "I think you are, Minnow. Or at least, you would have been if you were born long ago."

Minna stared at her father. If she was a *saa'myn*, maybe people would be happy to see her. She turned to gaze at the spirits. "How do you ask them questions?"

"No one remembers."

Minna pursed her lips, disappointed. Still, maybe she could find a *saa'myn* to teach her. "What happened to the *saa'myn*?"

"The Empire came. They made it a crime to even talk about the spirits. They said the *saa'myn* lied about the spirits and, because no one else could see them, people believed them." Her father hesitated, cut his eyes to her and finished, "The Empire hunted them down and killed them."

"They *killed* them?"

He nodded and sighed. "Some people tried to hide them and keep the old beliefs, but, eventually, the *saa'myn* were gone and most people forgot."

Minna knew about the Empire, but, as remote as Fennig was, it seemed a vague, abstract thing. "How long ago did the Empire come?"

"Oh, maybe a hundred years ago."

Like most children, Minna had only a vague idea of her father's age, but she knew he wasn't that old. "How do you know about the *saa'myn*?"

"Your mo—" His eyes flicked to his daughter. She was about to speak when he rushed on. "There was a *saa'myn* named Beadu, who lived in Fennig when you were born. She was probably the last *saa'myn*. Some said she had over a hundred summers when she died." His eyes dropped to his hands, fidgeting with a goose feather in his lap.

Minna sat quietly while her father picked up the arrow he was fletching. He held it for a moment, put it down and stared into the failing light.

"Papa?"

"Yes, Minnow."

"Did people hate the *saa'myn*?" She heard her father sigh and chewed her lips, waiting for his answer.

"People fear what they don't understand, Minnow. But no, I don't remember people hating Beadu."

Minna watched the *lan'and* in silence. She loved her father, but she couldn't help feeling if he told her this that day so many years ago, her life would have been very different. The *saa'myn* might be gone, but if they knew how to talk to the spirits, she could learn how to do it. Somehow. If she could ask the spirits questions for people, maybe they wouldn't call her a witch.

Chapter 2

Agmar

The village tavern was always busy on the evenings of market days, particularly so close to the harvest festival. Ale and cider flowed, and the crowd was boisterous, singing local songs, laughing at old jokes and exchanging comfortable insults. Erik, the village's lore master, held forth at the hearth, recounting the tale of Wattana and the faerie lights, a perennial favorite.

Normally, a warm tavern on a cool fall evening was one thing Agmar liked best about Fennig, but tonight he wasn't in the mood. While he wasn't in the market when it happened, his mother, Agatha, told him that Minna girl tried to hex her. He could believe it. That girl made him feel wrong, and his mother knew about such things. He gazed around the tavern, disgusted. How could these people celebrate when such a menace was allowed to run free? The girl skulked around the village, giving people queer looks. Planning something evil, she was, and she nearly done something evil to his mother. He wasn't sure what stopped her, but it didn't matter. His mother was at home now, refusing to come into town at night. It was time to do something about it. He hunched over his ale, brooding, when a snippet of conversation penetrated his gloom.

"That little girl didn't do anything to Agatha!" A woman's voice. He turned and wasn't surprised to find it was Marie. She defended the witch before. To his chagrin, no one at her table contradicted her and two of them were nodding their agreement.

Agmar pushed away from the bar, jostling his mug and spilling the contents across the counter. "What do you mean, she din't do nothin?!" he shouted.

The discordant note in the genial atmosphere brought nearby conversations to a halt. Marie turned in her seat still smiling, but when she saw him, her face fell into a grimace. "It's never your mind what I said, Agmar." She turned her back, dismissing him.

Blood rushing in his head, Agmar took an uncertain step forward. He was a big man for an *Alle'oss*. Taller by half a head than any other man in Fennig, and he had a towering temperament to match, as fiery as his unruly mane of crimson hair and bushy beard. He shoved his way past the people gathered around the bar and found himself standing in a clear space among the tables in the center of the room. Ignoring the others, he focused his attention on Marie. "That's fine for you! It weren't your ma that was almost hexed by that witch!" The room hushed. Suddenly the center of attention, he glared around at the faces turned toward him. To his surprise, he found, though some nodded encouragement, there were more who frowned their disapproval.

Agmar knew he wasn't the smartest man in Fennig, but having had more than his share of trouble, he understood how the wheels of village justice turned. The villagers lived uneasily with Minna's presence for years. The incident that morning merely brought the topic to a head, sparking heated debates throughout the day. No one was surprised at Agmar's accusations, and everyone recognized it for what it was. Though Minna would have no opportunity to defend herself, her fate hung in the balance, and her jury waited in silence for her accuser to make his case.

Agmar took a deep breath and blew it out in a rush, trying to clear his head. When he was ready, he held up a finger, emphasizing each word. "Now, you all know there's somethin' wrong with that girl. When she comes around, it makes you feel…" He put his hands to the side of his head and screwed up his face, searching for the right words, and settling on, "All wrong!" A few more nods and hesitant frowns greeted this declaration. "You all heard the stories. I say the girl's a witch and it's time we did somethin!"

The silence that followed was as a held breath, full of shuffling feet and uneasy glances. The accusation made, someone would have to take up her case, or Minna's guilt was assumed. Agmar waited, glowering a challenge to anyone who would contradict him.

After a long moment, Marie rose and turned to face him. The jury greeted her with a collective exhalation. The farmer towered over the diminutive woman, but she put her hands on her hips and smirked up at him. "Agmar, you believing the stories the bards tell now?" She waved a hand toward Erik, and said, "I suppose next, you'll have us taking to the mountains to hunt for fairy gold." There was more than a hint of relief in the chuckles that greeted her jest, and Erik tipped his hat to her.

Agmar stepped closer, so he loomed over her, scowling. "Course I don't believe in fairies." He swept his arm wide and addressed the room. "But you heard the tales about witches. They look like normal people when they're little. It's only when they get older it starts. The first sign's when they start makin people unhappy and *sick*." He extended his arms out to his sides, having delivered indisputable proof. "It's a sign, a warnin."

More people were nodding now and someone at the bar said, "That's right."

"That *is* right," Agmar said. He peered down at Marie and said, "And, Marie, once they get their power, that's when it's too late. They hex people... and the killin starts." He emphasized the last few words, confident in the verdict.

The tavern was silent, save for uncomfortable shuffling as attention shifted to Marie. Into the hush, Marie threw back her head and laughed. "Oh, Agmar." She turned slowly, appealing to people who had been her neighbors all her life. "Now you all know Thomas Hunter. There's not a kinder, more generous man in this village."

There were general nods of agreement at this. Minna's father was one of the most respected people in Fennig, since long before Minna was born.

Marie continued, "That man dotes on his daughter. Do you think Thomas would care so much for his little girl if she was a witch, even if she was his daughter?"

"She's hexed him, is all!" Agmar scoffed.

Marie turned a skeptical frown on him and said, "But you said the hexing comes after the witches get their power when they're older. Her pa didn't just start loving that girl, so it couldn't be because she hexed him."

Agmar's mouth opened, but no words came to him. Glancing around and sensing the tide turning, he blurted, "Didn't you see what she nearly done to my ma? She's got her power now!"

"I was there this morning," Marie said. "I didn't see anything like what you're talking about." She turned away from Agmar again, lifted her hands to her sides, palms up, and said, "What I see is a little girl who gets treated awful by everyone here. I don't know what I would do if it were me, but I can tell you this, I wouldn't be the sweet, gentle person Minna is." She jabbed herself in the chest with her thumb and said, "If *I* were a witch, I'd let you know if you looked at me funny." She smiled at the laughter that greeted this and turned to a large man sitting at a table near the wall. "Gunther, your boy Jason, has been friends with Minna for a long time. Has she ever done anything makes you think something is wrong with her?"

Gunther started at being addressed, studied his mug for a moment, then lifted his gaze to expectant faces. Clearing his throat, he met Marie's eyes. "No, I haven't." Marie nodded, encouraging him to continue. After a moment, he said in a firmer voice, "She makes me feel a little funny, that's sure, but what Marie says is true; she ain't done nothin to deserve what she gets." He paused, sat up straighter, and gazed around. Thrusting his chin forward, he said, "My Jason is growin up right. He'll be a good man. He thinks the world of that girl and that's enough for me."

Agmar scowled, but noticing others nodding in agreement, he growled, "The girl's a witch. She's got—"

"The girl's no witch. She's a *saa'myn*."

The whispered conversations that started after Gunther's declaration died instantly. Agmar whirled around, searching for the source of the voice, finding Egan, Gunther's father, glowering back at him.

Before Agmar could assemble the scattered words of a response, Marie asked, "A... sa... sah men? Egan, what are you talking about?"

Egan took a swallow from his mug and wiped his mouth on the back of his hand, drawing out the tension and letting the few whispered conversations fade. He gazed around and said, "You young people don't know, but you go ask your elders. They remember." He paused, focused on Agmar, and finished, "There was a time we'd feel lucky to have that girl here."

Agmar couldn't make sense of what the old man was talking about. Most of the others seemed as uncertain as he was. Only the oldest were nodding grimly, whispering to one another. Not sure how the argument got off track, he glanced at Marie and found her staring at Egan, her brow furrowed.

When she noticed him looking, her eyes narrowed, and she asked, "What are you talking about, Egan?"

"I ain't sayin no more," the old man said. "You go ask your ma, Marie. She'll tell you."

Marie hesitated, nodded, and turned away. The whispering died down again as everyone turned their attention to her. Familiar with the ritual flow of justice, they could sense the crucial moment had arrived. "I don't know why she makes people feel the way she does, but as far as I can see, she's done nothing to deserve whatever Agmar is considering." Marie turned back to Minna's accuser. "Go home, Agmar. You've had too much ale. Go home fore you do something you'll regret." She turned away and returned to her seat.

Agmar didn't understand everything that happened. All he knew was he was being dismissed. Shaking with rage, he cast about for support, but found only stony stares. A few people shook their heads and turned away.

The verdict rendered, there was a rush to gather around the eldest among them. A tentative song started, and people joined in.

Agmar turned on the spot but found no one would meet his eyes. Growling his frustration, he stumbled to the door, threw it open, tripped on the threshold and landed on his hands and knees on the cobbles. "They'll be sorry someday," he mumbled.

The door opened, and a moment later, the legs of two people appeared beside him. Someone gripped his arms and lifted him to his feet. It was Jesper and Loden, friends of his who owned farms at the edge of the wilderness.

Agmar swayed on his feet and peered blearily at the two men. They exchanged a look and Jesper said, "There's some of us who are of the same mind with you when it comes to that Hunter girl." He glanced at the tavern door and continued, "We think it's time we take matters into our own hands. Those others won't do it and, like you said, it will be too late soon enough. The few have to act to protect the rest."

Agmar smiled and said, "That's all I'm sayin." He lifted a finger before him as he spoke, stumbling into the other men.

Jesper caught him and said, "Come on, Agmar. Marie's right about one thing. You need to get home." The men each took an arm and led Agmar across the square.

Loden said, "We'll get some boys together. No need to tell everyone. We'll meet next market day, make some plans."

Agmar smiled. "Yeah, we'll make some plans."

Aron

By the time Aron heard an inquisitor and his escort passed through the Imperial city of Hast, the news was a week old. He and Zaina searched frantically for a week before they were lucky enough to encounter a traveling tinker who had seen them. After catching up to the small party, they followed them to a village called Illiantok. It was one of the many small hamlets dotting the upper foothills in northern Argren. It was the perfect place for an ambush. Tucked away in a small box canyon, there was only one road leading away from the village. The road narrowed as it climbed out of the canyon and six-foot high shoulders limited avenues for escape. Their green cloaks blended with the feathery fronds of ferns that crowded the space between widely spaced evergreens, maples and oaks.

They didn't have to wait long. Regardless of what else the Inquisition was, they could be counted on for their efficiency. Squinting into a misty rain, he spotted them topping a small hill, their hoods drawn up to fend off the weather. There were five of them, an inquisitor and his four guards, brothers of the Inquisition, a religious order tasked with enforcing the edicts of the Vollen Church. They were mounted, and the reason for their incursion into Argren sat in front of the sergeant of the inquisitor's escort. The child, shackled and wearing a leather hood, looked tiny in front of her captor. The horsemen, unaware of their impending deaths, laughed as they recounted their encounter with the villagers. Careless. The Inquisition had not yet learned its lesson.

Aron stared at the prisoner, allowing Ella's face to swim up from his memory. For a moment, he let the anguish and helplessness he felt that day long ago loose from where he horded it like a precious treasure. He didn't want to forget, didn't want time to steal from him what he owed Ella. In the years that followed, he used those memories to forge a hard, cold anger, stiffening his resolve when the task he set himself threatened to overwhelm him. Though it would never be enough, each child they saved was a small redemption for his failure to save his friend.

Aron peered across the road and found Zaina looking back at him. Her expression was serene, but her crystal blue eyes, glittering like two gems against her pale complexion, shone with anticipation. Aron returned her nod. Careful to remain hidden, he drew out an arrow from the quiver propped at his feet and nocked it on the string of his longbow. Trusting his companion to be ready, he took aim at a brother at the back of the line, knowing Zaina would target the one in front. They waited.

"So, I said, 'Don't worry, you have another'," one of the men said, drawing laughter from the others.

Aron and Zaina loosed their arrows almost at the same moment. The sharp twang of sinew, the wet thunk of the arrows striking home, followed by a moment of surprised silence. Aron and Zaina nocked two more arrows before the remaining brothers realized something was amiss. The two brothers fell, and chaos erupted. The horses spooked, the ones in the middle shying away from the bodies laying in the road. With nowhere to run, they bunched together, making easy targets. Two more arrows killed another man and wounded the inquisitor.

The child in front of the fourth brother made a bow shot risky, so Aron dropped to the road and pulled his sword. The brother was attempting to turn his horse, but the girl struggled. In the narrow lane, with the other horses milling about and one arm wrapped around his prisoner, he was having a hard time controlling his mount. Aron grinned as he weaved through the nervous horses.

When the brother saw him coming, he shoved the girl sideways. She fell, lost in the hood's darkness, and landed awkwardly on the hard ground. With two hands on the reins, the brother finally turned his frightened mount. As he urged it forward, he threw a triumphant smile over his shoulder.

Aron smirked. So much better this way. He focused on a spot behind his eyes, the spot where his spirit met the spirit realms. With a slight mental nudge, he groaned as a door to *annen'heim*, the realm of the dead, opened, flooding his mind with euphoric waves and allowing him to step through.

The wails of the spirits, the *sjel'and*, protesting his intrusion into their realm, met him. Drifting in their dark world, the spirits jealously regarded the living, covetous of the life they left behind. He was not welcome here and would have to hurry. The realm of the living, *thala'heim*, appeared to him as if through a gauzy curtain wafted by a gentle breeze. Unlike the living, whose time in *thala'heim* was but the flicker of a firefly, the dead measured time in eternities. To Aron, the rider appeared frozen, his face not yet registering his surprise that his opponent vanished.

He strode forward until he was standing beside the sergeant's horse and stepped back across the boundary. To the brother, it appeared as if he crossed the distance in an instant. Before he could react, Aron thrust his blade into his side, under his ribcage, and into his heart. He let gravity pull his blade free as the brother fell from the horse.

Leaving Zaina to tend to the girl, Aron turned toward the inquisitor, who was scrabbling at the steep shoulder at the side of the road, an arrow protruding from his side. Once again, Aron thought back to the day six years ago, when an inquisitor came for Ella. Killing a single inquisitor would cause but a ripple in the vast evil that was the Inquisition, but it was no less satisfying for that fact. The inquisitor rolled onto his back, panting and staring at Aron with fearful, uncomprehending eyes. He was older than was usual, his black hair going gray at the temples. He had been about this business for a long time.

"You got your uniform dirty," Aron said, taking in the mud on the man's knees. "You know how the Malleus feels about that sort of thing."

"You can't kill an inquisitor."

Aron gazed down at the man, then drove his sword into his eye. "Huh, turns out… I can." He pulled the sword free with a squelch and wiped it clean on the inquisitor's white uniform jacket.

Zaina was removing the girl's shackles with the key she found on the sergeant's belt. She had already removed the hood, and the girl gazed at him with eyes glassy with shock. They saved her life, but her suffering would linger because of what they did to her this day. Taking a deep breath, he sighed, then hitching his most reassuring smile onto his face, he approached and knelt to put her at ease. "*Lehasa. Ērtsa Aron. Kisu Alle'oss da* (Hello. I am Aron. Do you speak Alle'oss)?"

A small, worried furrow appeared between her brows.

Few people spoke their language now, but it was worth a try. "Hello, my name is Aron. This is Zaina. What's your name?"

Her eyes focused, and she answered, "Eaven," in a quiet voice.

"Like the flower?" Zaina asked.

She nodded, her gaze shifting to Zaina. A small tremulous smile threatened to break through her shock, like a ray of sun through dark clouds.

"How old are you, Eaven?"

"I have eight summers."

Zaina sat back on her heels. She was smiling, but her bunched jaw muscles hinted at the anger within. Zaina's stoic exterior fooled most people, but Aron knew she harbored a volcano inside her.

The girl looked from one to the other and asked, "Can I go home?"

This was the hardest part. He gave her a sympathetic smile and said, "I'm sorry, Eaven, but you can't. These men..." He gestured to the bodies, "... they take girls like you to a very bad place. If you go home, other men like them will come again. Next time, they may hurt your family." He paused, making sure he had her attention before continuing. "We'll take you to a place where there are other girls like you. They'll take care of you and teach you. You'll be safe there." When she nodded vaguely, he said, "Can you ride a horse, Eaven?"

The girl nodded, her eyes searching. She looked up at Aron and asked, "Can you tell my mother where I'm going?"

No, they couldn't. It was too dangerous for everyone involved. As tragic as it seemed, the informant was sometimes a member of the girl's family. Still, she didn't need to know that now. "Yes, we'll tell her." Maybe a day would come when all the children could return to their homes.

Of course, they could have saved her this trauma. They could have killed the brothers on the road to the village. But the Inquisition knew about Eaven, or they would not have come to such a remote place. Killing the brothers before they arrived would only delay the inevitable. Next time, they would come with more men and sisters of the Seidi, and maybe Aron and Zaina wouldn't find them. Although they might have been able to arrive at Illiantok before the brothers, after much debate, they decided it was too soon to show themselves. The Inquisition would learn what they were doing from their informants. The *Alle'oss* resistance in this part of Argren was yet too fragile to survive the Empire's full attention.

While Zaina wrapped Eaven in her cloak, Aron rounded up the horses.

"Mother, save us," Zaina muttered while they disposed of the bodies. When Aron only grunted in response, she said, "You'd think they'd learn."

"We're just a pinprick to them, hardly noticeable," Aron answered. "Not yet."

Chapter 3

Minna

Minna lay awake long after her parents went to their bed. She'd grown accustomed to the callous disregard of her neighbors, and even outright rudeness from some, like Agatha. As unpleasant and dispiriting as it was, it never occurred to her that someone might try to harm her. But the thrill of fear that rippled through the crowd when Agatha called her a witch changed that. In her panicky rush to escape the market, she felt real fear. She pictured the faces turned toward her when they heard Agatha's accusation. There was Hans, the butcher, and his daughter, Hilda. Giselle and her husband, Erik, who owned the stable. Their son, Ulf, was peeking out from behind his mother. She knew them all, and despite the way they treated her, they were good people. Now, in the safety of her own bed, she was embarrassed, imagining what she must have looked like, fleeing the square.

Minna rarely considered her future, as there didn't seem any point. In many ways, village life was a small life. People's lives followed a comfortable rhythm, governed by unchanging social customs and the slow turning of the seasons. Still, it was a life enriched by family, community and hard, rewarding work.

Minna ached for such a life. In her secret heart, she imagined herself as Jason's wife, the mother of his children. In the silent house, with thoughts of the harvest festival in her mind, she brought out the fantasy, cradling it gently. They would build a small log house, cozy and warm, set away from the village, among the trees. They would have a son and a daughter, both blond and blue-eyed, like their father. She saw their small family walking to the harvest festival, their son riding Jason's broad shoulders, their daughter on Minna's hip. A familiar burning prickled her eyes, and she let her tears flow, moistening her pillow.

She rolled onto her back, wiped away the tears, and laid her arm on the pillow above her head. That would not be her life. This morning only reinforced what she already knew; they would never accept her in Fennig. Jason would tell her they could manage, that he wouldn't mind living within the constraints their neighbors imposed on them. He loved her, Minna was sure, and he would sacrifice for her. But Jason lived a blessed life and saw only the good in people. His buoyant optimism was one thing she loved most about him. As popular and respected as he was, it would never occur to him people would hold marrying her against him. But she wouldn't take that chance. What kind of life would their children have, the spawn of a witch? She tucked the fantasy away, a precious treasure.

Minna would spend her entire life in her parents' house. She would care for them as they grew old and grow old herself, here, in this house. Alyn would visit with her family, and maybe Jason would allow her to be part of his life. A small life made smaller by her neighbors' fear. She never considered another alternative. Until now.

That she might be a *saa'myn*, descended from women with power and respect, ignited a flame of possibility in her heart. She nurtured the flickering hope protectively from the uncertainty threatening to smother it. If all the *saa'myn* were dead, who would teach her what she needed to know? How would she find them? Would she have the courage to leave Fennig? Would she need to go alone? How would she make her way in the wider world? And most dismaying of all, where did her father, Jason and Alyn fit into such a life? She had no answers. Still, she nurtured the flame, and for the first time in her life, she considered the world beyond her small space.

The revelation that the Empire destroyed the old ways and killed the *saa'myn* barely registered as a concern. She wasn't really a *saa'myn*, and the Empire was a remote and abstract thing in Fennig. Her father told her the villagers worked hard to keep it that way, to stay out of the Empire's troubles. She might as well worry about fairies coming for her.

Alyn moaned in her sleep, snuggling closer. Minna rolled onto her side, draped her arm over her sister and breathed in her familiar scent. The house was silent but for the mournful songs of a pair of owls. Her father told her if you ventured into the forest at night and were lucky enough to find an owl, you could ask three questions about your future. She smiled into Alyn's hair. Maybe the owls were the spirits of the *saa'myn*, and she could ask them her questions. It was fall, and they would leave the mountains soon. When the owls fell silent, Minna's mind relented, allowing her to sleep. She drifted in that strange place between awake and asleep, following the owls through the forest, desperate to know her fate.

• • •

Minna woke early the next morning before sunrise. The only thing visible of her sister was a tangle of blond hair, the same color as their father's. Her mother's hair was the red so common among the *Alle'oss*. Minna's was black. In fact, she was the only person in Fennig with black hair. When she was young, she thought perhaps that was the reason the other children hated her. If it were only that simple.

The early morning was brisk. She burrowed further under the covers until she remembered she was going to the falls with her father today. Throwing off the quilts, eliciting a protest from Alyn, she leapt out of bed and dressed quickly in the chilly air.

The falls were high in the mountains, the hike to get there rugged, so they didn't go often, but it was beautiful, and game was plentiful. Other hunters rarely made the trip, so they would be alone, and best of all, they would have to stay the night. They would roast whatever they caught over a roaring fire, singing and telling stories. It was a chance to be with her father, away from her mother's icy disapproval. She already knew the spot where they would camp. There was a pool below the falls, so clear and still, it was a perfect mirror. At night, she called the *lan'and* to marvel at their soft glow darting among the stars, above and below. This time, she would share it with her father.

Making her way into the dark kitchen, she stoked the fire and started breakfast. By the time it was ready, her father sat at the table, organizing provisions for the trip. They ate in silence, though Minna was nearly bouncing on her seat with anticipation.

She finished quickly, then sat still, trying to be patient, but she couldn't help stealing glances at her father's plate. He chewed slower, gazing at the wall behind her. She knew what he was doing, but it exasperated her all the same. "Um… Papa, you know, it's a long walk to the falls. If we leave now, we'll have the afternoon to hunt." She feigned nonchalance, but she couldn't hide the frustration in her voice.

"You're right, Minnow, but we can't go yet. We have something we have to do in the village before we go, and it's a bit early."

"What do we have to do?"

"Just a quick errand. We'll be on our way in no time."

Minna huffed and sat still with her hands in her lap. Her father chuckled before taking one last bite and standing.

She sprang up, gathered the dishes and carried them to the well to clean them, ignoring her father's smirk. Patience was not one of Minna's virtues.

Her preparations done, she sat on the porch, tapping her foot, leaning back, her arms crossed tightly over her chest. When her father emerged and started across the yard, Minna sprang after him as if shot from a bow.

Dawn grayed the trees as they made their way to the village. The whisper of winter on the breeze of the previous day had become a murmur during the night, forcing them to pull their cloaks tight as they walked. Night in the forest would be cold, but the sky was clear and the sun peeking over the horizon promised a warm day.

As they approached the village, Minna searched for anyone who might be out and about early. Much to her relief, there was no one. So intent was she that, when her father veered from the highway, it caught her unaware and he took several steps before she noticed. Hurrying to catch up, she asked, "Where are we going, Papa?"

"Patience, Minnow. You'll see soon enough."

As they made their way around the southern edge of the village, and it became apparent they were headed to the blacksmith, Minna's heart beat a fluttery, breathy rhythm. Soot, hot iron and the ping of hammers rode the breeze, even at this early hour. The smoke, smell and din were the reason the smithy was on a small rise, a hundred paces beyond the boundary of the village.

Minna didn't mind the smells. She would forever associate them with Jason. They clung to his clothes, somehow blending with his own scent in a way she found distracting. Jason's father was the blacksmith, and his son would follow in his father's footsteps. A truth of living in a place like Fennig was most people knew the path of their life from an early age. For some, that chafed, but Jason was not one of those people. He loved the heat, the fire, and the hot iron.

The sun cast the clearing in front of the smithy in a golden light by the time they arrived. *Lan'and* swirled above the building. They gathered in certain places, and this was one of their favorites. A few responded to her arrival by swooping down to swirl around her and her father. Minna ignored them, glancing at her father, resisting the urge to flap her arms to shoo them away. He couldn't see them, but she worried anyway.

Jason stood at the entrance to the smithy, wearing the leather apron that protected his clothes from embers, his shirt sleeves rolled up to his elbows. When he saw them coming, he waved, ducked inside, then emerged holding a bundle. He greeted her father, then they turned mysterious smiles on Minna.

She froze, looking from one to the other. "What?"

Jason held the bundle up. "It was your father's idea. He asked me to make it this past summer. I would have finished it sooner, but I had to work on it on my own time."

Minna looked at the old horse blanket, then at her father, who gestured toward it. She hesitated, then reached over and drew the edge of the blanket back to reveal what appeared to be a bow unlike any she had seen. Her father's longbow was long and flat, assuming a graceful curve when he strung it. It was taller than Minna and she hadn't the strength to draw it. He taught her to shoot with the small bow children use, and though she spent long hours practicing, it lacked the power and range to bring down any but the smallest game.

She lifted the new bow from the blanket, turning it this way and that, trying to make sense of it. It was shorter even than her small bow, with a pronounced curve. "Is it a bow?"

"Of course, it's a bow," Jason said.

"A small bow," she said, frowning at it.

"It's Minna-sized," her father said.

"It's a compound bow," Jason explained. He ran his finger along the belly. "That's Ibex horn, and the back is layered with elk sinew. They let you get the same power from a shorter bow."

Minna ran her hand along the arm. When she reached the curve near the end, she looked at her father.

"It's a recurve bow." She watched his hand as it traced the curve. "These curves give you leverage so you can get more power with a lighter pull."

Minna raised glistening eyes to her father's face, her mouth open.

Jason laughed. "Are you just going to stand there all day gawking, or are you going to try it?"

She took a length of sinew and affixed a loop to the nock on one end. Her father talked her through stringing the unfamiliar bow. She put the tip against the inside of her boot, then leaned on the opposite end, slipping the sinew over the tip and into the nock. She never had the strength to string her father's longbow. Plucking the string produced a pleasing twang.

"Here," Jason said, offering a blunted arrow. "I set a hay bale over there to try it out." He pointed down the hill, away from the village.

Minna nocked the arrow, lifted the bow, and drew the string. The pull was hard, but manageable, and once it reached a certain point, it became easier. She loosed the arrow and was rewarded with a muffled rustle as it disappeared into the hay. Jason and her father cheered while Minna gazed at the bow in wonder. She looked from Jason to her father, tears flowing down her cheeks. "It's wonderful!"

She leapt into her father's arms. "*Tok, tok, tok* (Thank you, thank you, thank you)." Extricating herself from her father's hug, she took a step toward Jason, and stopped short. Dropping her eyes to the ground, her cheeks suddenly warm, she said, "Um..."

Jason laughed, stepped forward and wrapped her in a tight hug, lifting her onto her toes. Minna drew in a sharp breath. She hesitated only a moment, then hugged him back and rested her head against his chest, eyes shut, lost in the sound of Jason's heart thrumming in time with hers. After what felt like an eternity, her father cleared his throat. Startled, she stepped back, grinning up at Jason from lowered eyes.

"Yes, well, I have to get back to work. I'm glad you like the bow, Min. I hope it will bring you luck."

Minna's smile nearly split her face. "Thank you, Jason, it's beautiful." She left her child's bow in Jason's care, resting her hand on it, looking into his eyes. "Take good care of it."

As she and her father walked away, she turned and looked back. Jason stood in front of the smithy, his father standing next to him. Minna returned their waves before hurrying after her father. The troublesome, rebellious voice sang its joy, and for once, Minna agreed. Maybe they could find a way to build a life together. Light and quivery, bouncing with each step, she lifted her arms to the cloud of *lan'and,* who always seemed attracted by her good moods.

When she looked up at her father, he was watching her, a small smile on his face. "If that smile gets much bigger, your face will get stuck like that. Everybody will say, 'There goes smiling Minna, the happiest girl in Fennig.'"

A small shadow flitted through the back of her mind. It was unlikely the people of Fennig would call her anything but witch. But the light blazing in her heart banished the shadow. Today, she would be in the forest with her father, with her new bow. She lifted her face again, and the warmth she felt was not entirely from the early autumn sun.

Chapter 4

Deirdre

Malefica Deirdre ascended the stairs in the Seidi tower, heart hammering as much from her meeting with the Seidi council as from the climb to the top of the tower. She promised herself she would not let the sisters on the council get to her this time, but it was an empty promise. While the Empire teetered, the sisters engaged in pointless arguments, couched in religious dogma. Today's meeting was a perfect example; a wasted afternoon trying to convince the zealots on the council that unrest among the Brochen poor in the city was more important than declaring Sister Edithe an official martyr, 300 years after she died. Too often, she found herself the lone voice of reason. She needed allies, but where would she find them? Her strongest supporters were at the front, paying the price that allowed the council members to indulge their petty whims.

One of the more troubling aspects of the Empire's wars was that it was obvious to all who were paying attention how weak the Seidi was. No one was sure when it started, and it happened so gradually no one noticed during a period of relative peace. A series of competent emperors who were reluctant to share their glory allowed the sisters to keep their secrets. But that changed with the coronation of the current emperor, Ludweig II.

Vain and ambitious, Ludweig was determined to emerge from his predecessors' shadows. Deciding prudent management of an empire at peace wouldn't earn him the glory he craved, he cast about for lands to conquer. Unfortunately, his options were limited. He had neither the patience nor the imagination to look across the oceans that hemmed in the Empire to the north and west. To the east, beyond the Eastern Mountains, a trackless wilderness offered few opportunities for conquest. So, the emperor turned south, and forgetting history's lessons, he provoked the Kaileuk. The barbarians responded with a fury, and this time, they weren't content to bloody the Empire's nose. When the war turned against him, consuming more and more of the Empire's resources and young men, Ludweig was forced to turn to the Seidi for help.

Deirdre entered her office and slowed to a stop, staring at her portrait on the wall behind her desk. She lay awake most nights, worried for the sisters at the front, the few powerful enough to keep the Kaileuk at bay, dreading the inevitable moment when their strength gave out. Looking down, she found her fists clenched. She forced her fingers to open and gazed at the angry red crescents in her palms. What was she going to do?

A furtive movement drew her eyes to her balcony. Her assistant, Nia, stood at the rail, looking down into the Imperial Gardens. Something about the way she was standing, tense, her head moving as if she was tracking something, caught Deirdre's attention. Engrossed in what she was watching, Nia didn't notice Deirdre's approach, until she was within arm's reach and said, "What do you see, Nia?"

The younger woman whirled around, her hands behind her, eyes wide. "Nothing, mistress!"

"Such a pretty blush for someone looking at nothing." She stepped up beside Nia, resting her hands on the rail. Spirits flitted through the gardens below, spirits the Empire denied. According to the Vollen Church, the Seidi sisters' gifts were an expression of the essence of their god, Daga. It did not admit to the existence of spirits or any realms beyond the Otherworld where Daga presided. To claim otherwise was a heresy punishable by death. Yet here before her were spirits. Only a few sisters had true spirit sight, and most of them were away from the capital, helping

33

to fight the emperor's wars. Most sisters saw the spirits as a shifting luminescence, easily explained as Daga's essence.

Nia joined her at the rail, stiff and staring into the distance.

Deirdre knew Nia had spirit sight. She chose her to be her assistant, in part, for that reason. But Nia proved a frustrating enigma. Her timid formality had so far been an insurmountable obstacle to knowing her heart. Until today. "How old were you when they brought you to the Seidi, Nia?"

"Ten, mistress."

"Nia, you've been with me for six months," Deirdre said, exasperated. "You should know by now you don't have to be so formal. Call me Deirdre."

"Yes, mistress."

Deirdre snorted. It was well-traveled ground, but she wouldn't be deterred this time. "When they brought you and tested you for spirit sight, what did they find?"

When Nia didn't answer, Deirdre turned to look at her. Nia stood stock still, biting her lips, a rabbit caught by the fox. Deirdre sighed. "Nia, I've followed your progress since you arrived at the Seidi. I do with all the girls who come here, of course, but in you, I saw such promise, I followed you more closely than others."

Nia peeked at her, sunlight sparkling in tears caught in her eyelashes. The tattoo on the left side of her face that showed her rank and accomplishments stood out stark against her pale skin.

She was so close. All she needed was permission. Deirdre gazed across the garden to the palace. "I dreamed of being Malefica since I came to the Seidi." She smiled, remembering how naïve and optimistic she was. "I thought... such power... I could make the changes I thought were necessary. To right the wrongs I saw." Her smile fell away. "Now that I am Malefica, I find the power I sought was an illusion. I have little influence, many enemies... and I am alone." The last words were a whispered invitation. Deirdre held her breath, and after the space of two heartbeats, Nia whispered her confession.

"I see them." She waited, her lips pressed tight, but when Deirdre didn't respond, she continued in a rush, "I try not to, but it's exhausting. I'm sorry." She sagged, dropping her chin to her chest and wiping at her tears.

Deirdre put her arm around her assistant, pulling her close. Nia let out a small gasp and stiffened. Deirdre was less surprised by Nia's fear than by her ability to overcome it. When young girls, who showed ability, arrived at the Seidi, the sisters isolated those with spirit sight and *cleansed* them. It was a brutal and humiliating experience that left many with lifelong scars. They were taught the techniques to suppress their sight and were allowed to join the other initiates only after they mastered them. Deirdre shuddered at the memory. It was possible to suppress spirit sight, but it required great discipline and Nia was right. It was exhausting.

Fortunately for Deirdre, soon after her cleansing, Ragan came into her life. It was Ragan who urged her to reject the self-loathing the cleansing instilled in her and reclaim her spirit sight. How deliciously rebellious they felt, watching the spirits in this same garden. There were others like her. Some, like Nia, hid the truth out of religious zeal or fear. But some, like Deirdre and Ragan, shared the sinful secret. It was no coincidence most of those women were at the front; they were the only truly gifted sisters remaining.

She thought back to a night fifteen years before, to a breathless, furtive meeting with Ragan. Afterwards, they held hands while they walked in these gardens, watching the spirits and sharing whispered speculations about what they might be. How light and happy she felt, sneaking back into the novices' dorm in the wee hours, still full of future possibilities.

Ragan left that night. She and five other novices. There were investigations, accusations, interrogations. But in the end, there was no explanation. A familiar ache settled on her, and she caught herself shaking her head, as if she could deny it, even now. She'd relived that night countless times in the ensuing years, pillaging her memories for some clue, something she should have seen. Despite the joyful time they spent together, she was now sure there was something sad in Ragan's eyes when she whispered goodbye. She wanted to tell Deirdre something, but they parted with the secret unspoken. Their time together in the garden that night was her farewell. What did Deirdre do that her friend couldn't confide in her?

She shook herself out of her memories. It was 15 years ago for Daga's sake. Nia was peeking at her with an expression Deirdre knew meant she had a question she was afraid to ask. Removing her arm from Nia's shoulders, she said, "Nia, what do you want to ask?"

Nia blushed again and nodded toward the spirits. "What are they?"

When Deirdre became Malefica five years ago, she gained access to the Seidi's restricted archives. What she read about the *Alle'oss* rocked her to her core. There, she found the answers to her and Ragan's questions. "Do you know of the *Alle'oss*, the people of Argren?"

"Yes, mistress."

Deirdre smiled at the formality, suddenly finding it not so irritating. "Before the Empire rooted out the old beliefs, the *Alle'oss* called these spirits the *lan'and*. It means land spirits in the *Alle'oss* language. I've found documents in our archives that mention other spirits as well." She paused, waiting for Nia to look at her. "One of them are the *fjel'and*, spirits of fire from a realm they called *fjel'heim*."

Nia sucked in a breath.

Deirdre smiled. "Yes, Nia."

Deirdre sensed Nia opening herself to the spirit realms. Her assistant lifted her hand, and a small flame appeared, dancing in the air above her palm. "Fell ahnd," Nia murmured. They watched the spirit as Nia lifted her arm, allowing the flame to coil around it, looking for all the world like a living thing. "I always sensed them. I can't use my magic without them." She turned her palm out, and the flame arced over the garden before guttering out. "I never understood how anyone could use magic without seeing the spirits."

"Do you remember the story of the sister called Ione?"

"Yes, of course," Deirdre said.

"What class did you learn that story in?"

"Myths of the Seidi."

"Yes!" The relief at saying out loud what she surmised animated her whole body. She made a cutting gesture with her hand. "People regard the tales of the great sisters of the past as legend and myth, too spectacular to believe." She looked up at the Seidi Tower rising above them and spread her arms upwards. "The truth is, the sisters of the distant past were powerful beyond imagining." Lowering her arms, she cupped her hands in front of her, and said, "When the small group of gifted women founded the Seidi, the restricted histories say a single sister held the fate of armies in her hands." She slammed her palm down on the balcony rail, and asked, "How else could the small tribal nation of Vollen carve an Empire from must larger lands?"

Seeing Nia's alarmed expression, Deirdre took a slow breath before continuing in a more measured tone, "The most gifted sisters living today are a faint echo of those of the past. I don't know for sure how most sisters perceive the spirits in their mind. It's a delicate subject, obviously. But we know what they teach us, and we can guess what it's like for them." She gestured to the spirits. "They *see* them as a shifting luminescence, what we call Daga's essence, so I assume they *perceive* the spirits the same way. What do you sense?"

Nia's brow furrowed. After a few moments, she said, "I can sense them... the spirits. There are individual... presences. I never knew what they were, but it's like they know me. Not like a person would, but they remember me, like they're happy to see me." She laughed. "I always thought that was silly."

"It's the same for me." Deirdre laughed with Nia. "I think those without true spirit sight must *perceive* the spirits the way they see them. They sense a shifting presence, not individuals as we do. That's why it's called Daga's presence. We're told we are sensing god." She continued, almost to herself, "Is it any wonder so many of them are the first to cry heresy? They believe they are communing with God himself."

The documents in the archive were brief and lacked detail. However, the descriptions of the spirits coincided so much more closely to her own experience than the Empire's doctrine, she couldn't deny it. Growing up a member of the upper Volloch caste, her wealthy, if distant, parents shielded Deirdre from the harsh realities outside her small world. When she joined the Seidi, she was even more cloistered, finding in her sisters a tight-knit family. It wasn't until she attained the rank of novice, and the Seidi sent her into the world, she learned what the Empire was like. What she saw led her to an inescapable conclusion: the Empire's vengeful god and their religious doctrine were lies, justifications to enforce a rigid caste system and elevate a privileged few. They had to be. The proof was drifting among the trees below her. It was no wonder the Inquisition persecuted the *Alle'oss* so ruthlessly. They couldn't allow the Brochen to discover the power they possessed.

"The sisters of the past, those with real power, they had spirit sight?" Nia asked, breaking into Deirdre's thoughts.

"Hmmmm? They must have, if they were as strong as the histories say." Deirdre shook her head at Nia's unasked question. "Unfortunately, the histories make no mention of what they thought of the spirits. I've combed the archives and found nothing. No mention of spirits, but no mention of Daga's essence, either. Nothing. The only reasonable conclusion is that someone cleansed the histories at some point."

They stood, silent, watching the *lan'and* in the failing light. Nia sighed. "Thank you, mistress."

"You know, Nia, you cannot speak of this to anyone."

"Of course not. I would never."

"There are those who would use you against me, if they knew."

"You mean Briana."

Briana was the leader of her opposition on the Seidi council. Magically weak, but politically well-connected and religiously zealous, her faction suspected sisters with true power. The only reason they made Deirdre Malefica was a moment of desperation, when they believed the appearance of the barbarians at their walls was imminent. It was a moment they came to regret. When Deirdre remedied the situation by elevating the gifted, the council forgot their fear and returned to their puritanical ways. What they would do when the Seidi's strength, such as it was, failed, she didn't know.

"Briana has many eyes and ears," Deirdre said. "It's best to assume everyone is suspect."

The long shadow of the tower lay across the garden, pointing an accusation at the Imperial Palace, where Deirdre assumed Emperor Ludweig was plotting his next misadventure. She believed in what the Seidi once was but was revolted by what the Empire had become. Briana and her followers were content to hide in their tower, ceding power to the emperor, and relying on the Inquisition's atrocities to protect their privileged status. She thought again of the sadness in Ragan's eyes that night so long ago. Did she draw the same conclusions as Deirdre, but make a different choice? Deirdre chose to use her considerable gifts to try to change the Empire. Ragan, who gave Deirdre the courage to reject the Empire's stifling religious dogma, chose escape. She hoped Ragan found the happiness that eluded her.

Chapter 5

Harold

If you ignored what you knew of the city, Brennan was almost pretty at night. Darkness hid the smoky haze and the grimy, soot-stained buildings. The only thing spoiling the illusion was the smell, a miasma of coal smoke, garbage and human waste. Still, the upper-class neighborhood Harold lived in was a far cry from the squalor of the Fallows where he was born. On a good day, with the wind just right, it was quite pleasant. From the balcony of his apartment, Harold could see the Imperial Palace dominating the city from atop its plateau. The Imperial District was dark this time of night, but there was a light in the highest window of the Seidi tower. Malefica Deirdre was working late, as usual. To his right, he could see the squat fortress of the Inquisition. Although he couldn't see Malleus Hoerst's office, he assumed he was up late as well. The two of them, leaders of the Seidi and the Inquisition, were undoubtedly plotting against one another. Harold made it a point to stay far from that tangled relationship.

He thought of the witch he allowed to escape the week before. It was foolish. Three of the brothers in his escort had been with him for years. He chose them for their lack of religious zeal and knew what they would tolerate and what they wouldn't. But someone in authority assigned a new brother to his escort, without explanation and against his wishes. The man was quiet, taciturn even, but from what little Harold could glean, he was a zealot. Harold didn't trust him. He could see in the man's eyes, he didn't believe a word of Harold's explanation for the witch's escape.

Harold would prefer to get rid of him. Unfortunately, he felt the Malleus' hand in the appointment. He doubted he could simply replace him. Of course, there were rumors of growing unrest in Argren, of attacks on Imperial representatives. Perhaps this interloper might run afoul of the *Alle'oss* resistance.

He sensed Karl padding onto the balcony from their bedroom, stopping near enough that Harold could detect his familiar musk and feel his breath caressing his hair. Harold was about to say something when he felt hands on his shoulders. Karl stepped forward to press against him. He was still naked. "Karl, you're incorrigible."

"Yes," Karl whispered. He pulled the thin robe from Harold's shoulders and let it drop. Fingertips, feather soft, trailed down Harold's arms, raising goosebumps. Karl nibbled the muscle at the base of Harold's neck.

Harold dropped his chin to his chest and whispered, "I have committed abominable sins." His burden was not for the few he let escape, but for the many he didn't.

"Yes," Karl whispered again, and kissed the back of his exposed neck.

The confirmation left Harold feeling hollow, though he knew he deserved it. The kisses along the nape of his neck would normally have derailed his self-pity, but not tonight. "I'm afraid my soul is irretrievably condemned."

Karl paused, whispering, "Why don't you quit?"

Harold lifted his head and chuckled softly. "One does not simply quit the Inquisition. Especially when one is an inquisitor."

"It has always surprised me that someone who rose to be an inquisitor could have a conscience," Karl murmured, so close his breath caressed Harold's neck.

Harold stared into his memories. Why did he join the Inquisition? He was young and naïve. Born in poverty, a member of the Volbroch caste, a half-breed, son of a Volloch father and a Brochen mother. Though, officially, his caste elevated him above the Brochen, it made little difference to a poor, starving boy living on the streets. Having few prospects, he was forced to frequent the missions in the Fallows to eat and hide from the gangs. The price for a meal was a sermon, the message invariably being his position in life was his own fault and part of Daga's plan.

When they detected in him a sensitivity to Daga's essence, rare among the Volbroch, they offered him hope. Considering the life he could expect to have on his own, joining the Inquisition was an easy choice. He was elated when it happened. They fed him three meals a day and gave him a warm, safe place to sleep. He grew strong and healthy, and he associated that with the benevolence of the Inquisition. They sent him to school. Unlike most of his peers on the streets, Daga blessed Harold with a keen and curious intellect. He soaked up everything they taught him. And swallowed every lie. It was easy for them. He had an insatiable desire to prove himself. Smarter and more sensitive to Daga's essence than his Volloch classmates, he reveled in their resentment. Smiling sadly, he mourned that ambitious, gullible young man. Dropping his chin, he allowed Karl to resume his kisses.

Early in his indoctrination, they shielded him from the horrors the Inquisition perpetrated, only slowly exposing him to the violations of human dignity that were the tools of their trade. His entire education was designed to excise his humanity and make him a compliant tool.

Still, it was one thing to work for the Inquisition in one of the hundreds of clerical positions, adjacent to, but not involved in the atrocities. It was another thing entirely to become an inquisitor. To go into a family's home, snatch a child, drag her back to Brennan and hand her over to the torturers. It was an act of evil. No amount of rationalization could explain away that sin. Then why did he do it?

In the beginning, he was proud of his talent, of being special, and he was eager to repay what the Inquisition gave him. That feeling didn't last long, but he didn't quit. The truth took much longer for him to admit. He was a coward. He saw what happened to those who grew a conscience, so he shoved the discordant thoughts into a dark part of his mind and locked them there. That was until three years ago.

The little girl in Fennig was sitting on the porch of her small home with whom he presumed was her father. The scene was idyllic, the two of them talking animatedly and laughing as they worked at some task. It was the first time his conscience stayed his hand. Why that time? The simple answer was he could let her live without risk to himself. The more nuanced answer was his self-loathing finally outweighed his fear. Since then, he let some live and condemned others to death. Each time he condemned some child to death, he felt the weight of his sins grow. Yet, he couldn't save them all or he would find the Inquisition at his door.

"If you can't quit, why don't you do something about it?" Karl whispered.

Harold lifted his head, pushing Karl from his neck. "What would you have me do?"

"Well, you are part of the Inquisition, on the inside, and highly placed. You know how they operate. I don't know what you can do, but if anyone can, it would be you." His voice was soft, but he was no longer whispering. There was a tension in his voice Harold never heard before. He thought back to the girl in Fennig again. It was the first time he allowed a witch to live, but it wasn't the first time he considered it. It was impossible to recall a specific event that shifted his perceptions, but if he had to choose when it started, it would be when he met Karl.

He turned around. Karl took a step back. The gentle smile Harold loved was gone, in its place a flat, cold stare.

"Do you remember the day we met?" Karl asked.

Harold frowned. The question, so close to his own thoughts, caught him by surprise. He thought back. It was a cool, sunny day in Brennan. A young girl accompanied Karl, a girl who, Harold later learned, was his sister. They were laughing, and their happiness drew Harold in. Karl glanced his way, catching his eye. When he looked back, his gaze lingered, an invitation. Harold spent a carefree day with Karl and his sister, and a passionate night with Karl. A week later, Karl moved in. Harold's attention returned to the present. He focused on his lover, nodding. "Yes, you were with your sister. We all spent the day together."

Karl shook his head. "She wasn't my sister."

Harold felt the ground shift under his feet. "What…" He shook his head and tried again. "What do you mean? Who was she?"

"An inquisitor took my sister when she was nine." Karl paused, allowing Harold's confused mind to catch up. "You took her."

Harold heard the words but could attach no meaning to them. He stood frozen, his world falling away around him.

"It was in the summer, nine years ago. A small village on the border of Argren. Her name was Erika. She was a bright, funny child. Full of life. I'm sure you don't remember her." Karl stared at him, a question in the lift of his brow, but he was right, Harold didn't remember. Karl's expression hardened. "I came to Brennan to kill you. I followed you for weeks, waiting for a chance."

Harold, still unable to grasp what was happening, gestured to their bedroom and asked, "Why?"

Karl's gaze grew distant. "I nearly gave up. Living on the streets in Brennan is… difficult, especially for a naïve boy from a small village." He focused on Harold's face again and said, "A woman found me. She showed me the way."

Harold shook his head, brows drawing together. "A woman?"

"She told me a lot about you. She said, despite what seemed obvious to me, there was some humanity left deep inside you. She said killing you would do you a favor, that there were worse things than death." Karl shook his head. "I didn't believe her, but I listened." He laughed softly. "What choice did I have? She took care of me, taught me what I needed to know and, eventually… I agreed to do as she asked."

Despite himself, Harold was drawn into the story. "What did she want?"

Karl didn't answer, cocking his head and gazing at Harold.

"The little girl… your… sister," Harold said. Karl nodded. Harold thought back, sifting through his memories. Karl, kneeling in the market, handing sweets to the delighted children of an *Alle'oss* family. Karl, insisting they attend the winter festival and making Harold play the bringer of gifts for the children. Karl, always bringing his attention to the children who lived on the same streets Harold left. The trip to Argren to visit Karl's large, happy family.

"Your family?"

Karl shook his head.

Family. Harold never experienced the warm embrace of family, having grown up in the streets before entering the cold, competitive world of the Inquisition. By slow steps, Karl taught him what it meant to have a family. It awakened an unfamiliar longing in him. He grimaced as he thought of that happy time in Argren with Karl's family. How surprised and delighted he was when they welcomed him, despite knowing what he was. An elaborate fiction designed to exploit his longing. How foolish was he?

If Karl's family was a lie, what else was? The younger man was watching him, allowing him to put it together. The questions. Initially, there were innocuous questions about the Vollen Church and the Inquisition. Karl's lack of religious education amused Harold, and he happily lectured him on the finer points of the church's doctrine and the Inquisition's interpretation of that doctrine. Over time, the questions became more pointed and uncomfortable. Karl always seemed to accept his explanations, but Harold often replayed the conversations during long days in the saddle, worrying at them like a dog with a bone.

When he focused on Karl's face, he understood. It was so obvious. Yet, even now, part of his mind was screaming at him it couldn't be true, that the last six years of his life couldn't be a lie.

He whispered, "It was you. You planted this seed in my heart."

Karl's expression didn't change, and for a moment, he didn't respond. But then he shook his head. "No, but I nourished it, gave it life. I couldn't have done it if you didn't want it. She showed me how."

"What did she want?"

This time, Karl answered. "What happens to the girls?"

Harold, surprised by the change in direction, took a moment to organize his thoughts. "They're killed."

Karl gave a small nod, smiling, as if this was the answer he expected to hear. "Are you sure? Have you seen it?"

Harold started to say yes but hesitated. In truth, he didn't want to see what happened to them. Not seeing it made it less real. The contempt in Karl's expression shamed him, and the tears in his eyes fell.

"She told me to tell you to find out what happens to them," Karl said. He gave Harold one more searching look, then turned to go.

Panicked, Harold's hand reached out of its own volition and grasped Karl's arm. He wasn't sure what he wanted to say, but when Karl looked back, he found himself asking, "Is there no redemption for me?"

Karl hesitated before answering. "No, it's too late for that. Your sins are too great." After a moment, his expression softened. "But each day, you can make a choice. Regardless of what happened in the past, you can choose what you do today. What kind of man do you want to be? Trust your heart, Harold." He looked down at the hand on his arm until Harold let go, then turned before pausing and saying, "Don't follow me." Then he disappeared into the bedroom.

Harold allowed him to go, undisturbed, waiting, listening, not breathing, unable to decide to sit down or cover his nakedness. When he heard the door open and close, something broke inside him. He gasped, squeezed his eyes shut, and clenched his body against the scream that fought to escape his throat. After a long moment, he relaxed, took a deep breath, and opened his eyes. The balcony was as it was before, yet would never be the same. He stared about at nothing familiar. The vast void of his pain yawned inside him. Too enormous for him to grapple with, it left him numb. Without thinking, he entered his room, threw on some clothes, and left his apartment.

Chapter 6

Minna

In the crisp, cold air high in the mountains, the aspens gloried in their golden mantels. Here, near their home, the elms, hickories and maples enthusiastically embraced the change of seasons with gaudy displays of yellow, orange and red. Only the oaks, ancient and hoary, begrudged fall's arrival, and as if resentful of the spruces' serene permanence, stubbornly held on to their summer cloaks.

It was cool, but there was a noticeable difference in the temperature as they descended to lower elevations. Minna loosened her cloak while she walked, describing her encounter with the turkey for the third time. She gestured with her hands, glancing up at her father to ensure he got the full picture. Although he was present during the event, he smiled, nodded and asked questions at just the right points in the story.

"I thought it heard me and was getting ready to fly, so I loosed even though it was still far away," she explained, her frown conveying the seriousness of the decision.

"It was a good shot, that's for sure."

"Yeah, yeah, it was," Minna said, a satisfied smile settling on her face as she relived the moment. The first hunt with her new bow and she shot a nice, fat turkey. Her eyes kept returning to the bird which hung down her father's back. Her mother would be happy. Turkey was one of her favorites. "Do you think Jason should come over when we cook it? It's just because I used the bow he made me."

Her father grinned down at her and said, "Let's ask your mother."

"Yeah, we should ask her," Minna said. They walked for a while in silence, before Minna launched into the story again. "Do you remember when we heard them? I thought they were too far away, and we would never catch up."

The *lan'and*, reacting to her excitement, whirled through the trees above them. The spirits seemed tuned to her moods and would gather in great numbers when she was especially happy. She grinned up at them, imagining them spreading the word, "Minna is happy. Let's go see what it's about." They were a comforting and familiar presence. But what happened next was completely unexpected.

The spirits, which normally flitted about seemingly at random, began, as one, to spiral down toward her. Her voice trailed off, she slowed to a stop, and let her father walk ahead. In a moment, she was at the center of a swirling cloud of glowing orbs. Smiling, she extended her arms to her sides and twirled slowly. In the shadowy forest, spirit light bathed her in lambent luminescence, like sunlight playing across the turbulent waters below the falls. When her father came back into view, he was staring at her, a worried frown on his face.

"Minna?"

Minna beamed at him, laughter bubbling up unbidden.

And then there it was. The presence in her mind, the same one she felt in the market. She hardly thought about it in the past two days, having decided she imagined the fleeting sensation amid the turbulence of her anger. But this time, there was no storm to mask it. Squeezing her eyes shut, she concentrated on the spot behind her eyes. Fluttery and insistent, like the beat of a butterfly's wings, it was not her imagination. Perhaps it was only because her father so recently told her about the *saa'myn*, women who could talk to the *lan'and*, but she had the inexplicable feeling they were trying to get her attention. It could not be a coincidence the only other time they exhibited such odd behavior, in the market, she felt the same presence in her mind. It must be the *lan'and*. But how could she answer? Maybe if... She focused on the restive presence in her mind, furrowed her brow and called.

Her mind exploded into a whirling maelstrom. She stood stock still, eyes open but unseeing. It was them, the spirits. She was sure of it. There was the same sense of otherness, of a presence that was not her own, sharing her mind. They swirled as they did in the trees when she was happy, but somehow, they were sharing her consciousness. And she felt their joy. In the intimate closeness of her mind, the *lan'and* responded to her happiness, reflecting it back to her and filling her up with their exhilaration. She laughed again.

Her father knelt in front of her, gripped her arms and shouted her name. She focused on his face and said, "Papa, the *lan'and*, they're talking to me!"

Brows knitting, he searched her face, and asked, "They're talking to you? What do you mean? What are they saying?"

Minna closed her eyes and tentatively extended her awareness into the whirlwind. Talking was not the right way to describe what was happening. It was more like she was sharing their emotions. Now that she was paying attention, she realized it was more nuanced than simple joy. It was a boisterous celebration of relief and triumph, exuberant and unruly. And heedless of her presence. A growing disquiet stole over her, a sense of being buffeted and jostled in her own mind. And suddenly, it was too much.

She opened her eyes, searching for her father's reassurance. "Papa?" she asked in a quavery voice.

He gripped her arms, shook her gently and asked, "Minna, what's happening?"

And just like that, the spirits were gone. She sagged into her father's strong grip, closed her eyes and let him guide her to sit on the forest floor. The storm left behind utter silence, as if the spirits scrubbed her of all thought, making her mind a clear, mirror-smooth pool, like the pond they sat next to the night before. In that stillness, a ripple appeared, as if a pebble disturbed the surface. And in the center of the ripples, she found her father. Her eyes flew open. Reaching out, she touched his stubbly cheek. Yes, the ripple was his, she was sure. She could sense his presence in her mind. And there was another ripple.

She gave her father a puzzled look, then fought free of his grip to stand. "There's someone I don't know there." She pointed ahead. "I think they're at our house."

Her father gave her a blank look. "Are you sure?"

She nodded and said, "I can feel him."

"Him?"

Minna nodded, peering through the trees.

"Come on, let's go see who it is," her father said. Minna let him take two steps before following.

They paused among the trees across the Imperial Highway from their house. Their home was set back from the highway on a low rise, and in the large yard, twenty men were preparing to camp, tending to their horses, pitching tents and preparing a meal. Most of them wore the same clothes, green shirts and pants tucked into knee-high boots. Beside the fact Minna had never seen any of them, and they dressed unlike anyone she knew, there was something else odd about them. They all had black hair.

"Who are they?"

"Imperial soldiers," her father answered in a flat voice.

The only outsiders Minna had seen visit Fennig were *Alle'oss*. That here in her front yard were flesh and blood representatives of the Empire, so soon after her father's revelations was disquieting. The Empire, such an abstract thing two nights ago, was suddenly real. But more disturbing than the soldiers was her father's reaction to them. His face was grim, and his grip on her shoulder was uncomfortably tight.

She shook his hand off and edged behind him, fascinated despite her wariness. Two of the men were talking to her mother on their front porch. While she watched, her mother caught sight of them and pointed. The men turned to look.

When they started walking in their direction, Minna's father sighed. He knelt in front of her and got her attention. "Wait here, Minna." He glanced over his shoulder. "In fact, it might be better if you went back into the forest a bit. You know where to go, don't you?"

"Yes."

"Wait there until I come for you, okay?"

Peering over his shoulder, she nodded absently, but didn't move. The two men were crossing the highway.

"Minna! Now."

Minna's attention snapped back to her father. With one last glance at the soldiers, she headed back the way they came. She knew she shouldn't, but when he turned to go meet the men, she stopped where she could still see what was happening. Meeting the men at the edge of the forest, her father listened, hands on his hips. She was too far away to hear what they said.

Laughter drew her gaze back to the other soldiers. They seemed happy, joking and laughing, the mood at odds with the dangers she imagined. She relaxed a bit, scanning the scene until her eyes settled on a tall man who stood alone near the corner of the house. Unlike the others, he wore all white. She could tell instantly the ripples she sensed were his. Though she was sure she was far enough into the trees, he couldn't see her, he was staring in her direction. She edged behind a tree and peered around it. He was still there, still staring.

Minna ducked behind the tree and stood with her back to the trunk, heart racing. When she peeked again, the man was speaking to a soldier and pointing toward her. The soldier glanced at the men talking to her father, then spoke. The man in white stood erect and leaned forward until his face was inches from the other man's face. He spoke quickly, clearly angry, then pointed back along the highway to the west. The soldier's head dropped, then he turned and jogged toward the horses. When Minna turned her attention back to the man in white. He was looking in her direction again, a small smile on his face.

She wasn't sure why, but he scared her. She ducked behind the tree again, hesitated, then headed farther into the forest.

•   •   •

Evening was descending, and Minna, worried and alone, was still waiting for her father. Even the spirits vanished after they *talked* to her. To distract herself from what might be happening back at her home, she pressed her palms to her eyes and tried to make sense of her experience with the spirits.

Was this how the *saa'myn* talked to them? If so, she wasn't sure how she could ask a question. She'd imagined the little spirits floating around her as she talked to them. She even wondered what their voices would sound like or how they might make a sound. It didn't appear that was how it worked. Could they understand her thoughts? Even if it was possible, how would they answer? All she felt was their emotion. And how were they sharing her mind? She tried to remember if she saw spirits outside herself while it was happening, but all she could remember was her father's concerned expression.

The bigger questions were why they wanted to communicate with her, and why now? Minna decided the *lan'and* taught her to recognize the ripples. It was only in the stillness they left in their wake, she recognized them for what they were. She had become so used to them, she no longer paid attention. They were just part of what was familiar about some people. Jason and Alyn had their own characteristic ripples. What did that mean, and why did the spirits *teach* her about the ripples now?

Though she didn't know what it all meant, the possibility the spirits might have been concerned for her well-being overwhelmed her last defenses. A sob of gratitude fought its way past her closed lips, and tears moistened her palms. She always considered the small spirits companions. They were her secret, something no one could take from her. That they might return her affection made her feel, suddenly, less alone in the world. She leaned forward, hugging herself, gave in to her emotions and wept.

• • •

She felt her father coming before he appeared. Her tears had dried, but her anxiety had not diminished. When he came into view, she jumped up and said, "What's happening, Papa?"

Her father sat on the log where Minna had been sitting and patted the space beside himself. "Sit, Minnow."

She sat still, hands in her lap, looking up at her father's face.

When he spoke, it was devastating. "The soldiers are going into the wilderness tomorrow. They've never been east of the mountains, much less into the wilderness. The man I was speaking to is their captain, their leader. He asked me to be their guide."

It took a moment for Minna to work through everything he said, but when she got to that last part, she asked in a small voice, "Guide?"

"They want me to show them the way, so they don't get lost."

"But why you?"

"I'm one of the few people who has been into the wilderness and returned. Someone in the village told them about me."

Normally, that news would have unleashed a flood of questions, but the vast chasm opening inside her swallowed any thoughts she might have on the subject. "But you're not going, are you? They can't make you go?"

He sighed, and said, "Yes, they can make me go. The emperor and his men are not forgiving people. You can't say no to them."

Minna's heart thudded. "What would they do to you?"

Her father turned to look down at her, his eyes hidden in shadow. "You can't say no to the Empire, Minna. I have to go."

Minna was young, but she knew how precarious her situation was and how important her father was to her. Her life revolved around him. He was always there, picking her up when she needed it, making her laugh and teaching her woodcraft. She also understood it was his reputation in the village that shielded her. The prospect of facing the villagers alone scared her. She threw her arms around his chest, tears streaming down her cheeks. "No, Papa, no! You can't go. I'll be alone."

"I have to go, Minna. You'll be alright."

"How long will you be gone?"

He pulled her away and looked into her eyes. "They said it would be a month, at the most. I'll be home before you know it." Shadows hid his face, but she recognized the smile in his voice.

Minna leaned on his shoulder and sniffed. "You'll miss the harvest festival."

Her father chuckled and put his arm around her shoulders, holding her until Minna ran out of tears.

"Papa?"

"Yes, Min?"

"There was a man with the soldiers. He was wearing all white."

Her father's voice carried a tense note when he said, "Yes, I saw him. What about him?"

"He was the man I felt when we were coming home."

Her father shifted around and lifted Minna's face to his. "Are you sure?"

"Yes, I'm sure. He was watching me. I went into the forest like you said, but when I turned back, he was watching me. He scared me."

"What did he do, Minna?"

Startled by his sudden urgency, Minna blinked. "He talked to a soldier, and then the soldier left on a horse."

"Back toward the mountains?"

"Yes."

Her father thought for a few minutes. "Minna, I want you to be careful while I'm gone. You can see Jason, but don't go into the village by yourself."

"Why, Papa?"

"Just be careful. If you see anyone come to the village you don't know, or if you… feel someone you don't know, I want you to go into the forest and stay until I come back. Have a pack and your bow ready. If someone comes, go to the falls. Do you understand?" Her father was speaking in a low, urgent tone.

"Why, Papa? Who's coming? Why do I have to hide?" She paused, swallowing, and asked the next question, though she knew the answer. "Is it because I'm a… *saa'myn?*"

He didn't respond at first. Finally, he said, "Minna, I hoped I wouldn't have to explain this. It should have been…" He shook his head and laughed softly. "I guess I… I don't know what I was thinking." He nodded and said, "You need to know."

Minna held her breath. "What, Papa? What do I need to know?"

"This is too difficult to explain when I'm leaving in the morning. We're both tired and it's been a difficult day. I'll explain when I get back." He nodded, staring into the distance, and then turned to Minna. "We'll go hunting at the falls and I'll tell you everything. Promise me, if anyone comes to the village or you sense anyone like you did today, you'll go to the falls."

She frowned, opened her mouth, then shut it again. She looked into the shadows, then began again. "Papa…" She wasn't sure what she wanted to say, torn between curiosity and fear at what he wanted to tell her. Suddenly, the events of the day settled on her, leaving her exhausted.

"Minnow, promise me."

"I promise, Papa."

The carefree elation she felt that morning seemed such a distant and foreign thing.

• • •

They slept in the forest that night, eating the remains of the provisions they took on their hunting trip, speaking no more of troubling things. Instead, they made plans for hunting trips they would take when he returned. With her father's encouragement, Minna once again related her encounter with the turkey, though more soberly than before. A shadow had fallen between them. A shadow cast by her father's secrets and Minna's sense that she stood on a precipice. Whatever her father wanted to tell her would change her life, irrevocably, she was sure.

The next morning, their farewells were brief, but tearful. He hugged her at the edge of the forest and Minna whispered in his ear, "Please come home, Papa."

He smiled, ruffled her hair and said, "Of course, Minnow. I'll be home before you know it." Then he turned and walked down to join the soldiers.

Minna caught sight of the man in white as he mounted his horse. He only glanced her way, but she didn't like the smile that appeared on his face. As they left, her father looked back and waved before disappearing around a bend in the highway. He was gone.

Minna stood among the trees, pondering the events of the previous day. She watched her mother and little sister, standing in the middle of the highway. Her father and mother were devoted to one another. His leaving would be difficult for her. Minna always tried to love her mother, even though her mother had been cold and distant toward her for years. Whatever caused the people of Fennig to hate her also affected her mother. She turned her attention to her sister, who was watching her. When their eyes met, Alyn smiled, waved, and skipped toward her.

Forcing a smile onto her face, Minna stepped out of the trees. The spirits had returned, drifting idly as if enjoying the warm fall morning. She closed her eyes and lifted her face to the sun. Maybe she would go see Jason today.

Chapter 7

Aron

Aron closed his eyes, relishing the contrast between the sun's warmth on his face and the chill wind as his back.

"*A ali ērtsa ot'skumeos, isto ērtsu lisameos* (If I was an imperial, you would be dead)."

Aron smiled and turned to watch the newcomer approach. "*A ali ērtsu ot'skumeos, isto ali rimenga aku skūsitan* (If you were an imperial, I would have smelled you coming)."

Zaina snorted.

"I knew it was you. Saw you when you left the forest."

They sat on their horses, comfortable in their silence, gazing down at the Imperial city of Hast. Hast sat astride the Odun river on the plains below the foothills of the mountain range the *Alle'oss* called *na'lios* (our home) and the Imperials called the Eastern Mountains. The bridge in Hast was the only way to cross the river this far south on the way from Argren to the imperial capital in Brennan. From their position on the bluffs next to the Imperial Highway, they could see the fort from which soldiers made forays into Argren.

"How's Eaven?" Aron asked.

"She's adjusting. Better than the others, I'd say. They'll be leaving for *Helela* (Sanctuary) tomorrow."

"That's good. Someday, they will be a new generation of *saa'myn*."

"So why am I here?" Zaina asked.

"I have something to do in Brennan."

"Ah, yes. Another mysterious errand for *her*."

Aron glanced at Zaina, a small frown flickering across his face.

Zaina lifted a brow and asked, "Do you ever tire of being her messenger boy?"

"You know, Zaina, has anyone ever mentioned what a cynic you are?"

"Many, and better people than you." When Aron showed no sign of answering her question, she asked, "Well? Do you?"

Aron shrugged. "Her ways appear mysterious, but she knows what she's on about." He met her eyes. "You may not trust her, but I would think you would trust me by now."

They watched each other for a few moments, then Zaina said, "She's spooky."

"Spooky?"

She ignored his teasing tone and searched his face. "You trust her?"

"She's like a mother to me."

"That's not an answer."

Aron faced forward and considered. "Trust. Let us say I trust her goals are worthy, and she knows better than most how to achieve those goals."

"That is an awfully slippery answer for a yes or no question."

Aron gave her a small smile and said, "I trust she has our best interests at heart."

Zaina studied his face, then turned to look down on the city. "Why am I here?"

"You're my wife," he said with a wide smile. When Zaina scowled at him, he said, "It's easier to move through Imperial territory that way. A man by himself, very suspicious, but these imperials tend to underestimate women who don't have a tattoo on their faces."

Zaina's expression smoothed, and she looked down at Hast. "What's our story?"

"Registering our business on the tax rolls."

"Have you ever been to Brennan?"

"Many times. Don't worry, it's big, dirty, smelly and crowded, but we'll be safe. Just don't stick out, don't look anyone in the eye. Act humble… if that's possible."

Zaina's brows shot up. "That's the pot calling the kettle black."

Aron laughed and nudged his horse forward.

Harold

A footstep in the shadows, at the edge of his hearing. If he wasn't so drunk, they would never have gotten so close. Still, he should have known better. After all, he grew up on these streets. He slid his sword from its scabbard, lifting the tip toward the shadow, a glint of moonlight on a pair of eyes, the only evidence someone was there. Harold motioned with his sword toward the other end of the alley and watched the man slink away. Dangerous out here, especially without his uniform on. He backed toward the entrance to the alley, watching the gloom for sudden movements, stumbling when his heel caught on a loose cobble. Steadying himself, he leaned on his sword for support, gazing around at the misty street.

Soon after he fled his apartment, he was drinking in the sterile, but safe taverns of his upper-class neighborhood. People there knew who he was. What he was. They were cordial, even friendly, to his face. But a slight hesitation when they saw him, a certain tilt of their heads when they greeted him, gave them away. They tolerated his presence because he protected their privileged positions and sheltered them from the Empire's truths, but they would never accept a monster in their genteel society.

Harold let his head drop back, smiling bitterly. When he first moved into the neighborhood, after leaving the Inquisition's academy, he naively accepted his neighbors' false platitudes as genuine. The poor orphan grew up to make good. It was Karl's scathingly witty dissection of their social niceties that disabused him of that romantic notion. Still, as long as he had Karl beside him, whispering his biting commentary, Harold found himself amused by the pampered elites' discomfort. Alone, he was defenseless against their contempt, a mirror into his own self-loathing. Rather than lash out, he fled into the night. How many nights ago was that?

With all their usual haunts off limits, he wandered, searching for unfamiliar drinking establishments. Eventually he found himself here, on the perilous streets of the Fallows. The desolate neighborhood barely tickled his memories, but even on this cool, breezy night, the stench churned up echoes of the fear and despair that ruled his childhood.

Few people were out in this part of the city at this hour. The only light on the street was moonlight and a greasy, yellow glow leaking from the crusty windows of an alehouse. The muted sound of a fiddle playing a lively jig was so incongruous to the gloomy setting and his bleak mood, Harold squinted at the sign above the alehouse door. The Monk's Habit. He knew this place.

He whirled around, stumbled, and nearly fell. The mission. His refuge as a child, where a compassionate monk named Xander rescued him. Alone among the missionaries, Xander recognized his promise. Using a personal connection with the Malleus at that time, he set Harold on his current path. Could it be his drunken wandering brought him to this place, drawn by the memory of that young, hopeful version of himself? Before he became the man he was. Perhaps the old monk was still there. Harold took a step, then stopped. What would he say to his savior? How would the kindly old monk judge the man he became?

He turned unsteadily and entered The Monk's Habit. There were more people than he would have thought at this late hour. Then again, there were few safe places to drink in this part of town. The room was as he remembered it, as if the passage of years couldn't be bothered with the small alehouse. He glanced up at the shadowy ceiling behind the bar where he once squeezed through a gap below the eaves. He hadn't wanted to, but a group of older boys dragged him here. They needed someone small enough to fit through the narrow opening. He had no choice. Bodies of forgotten children turned up in the Fallows so often they were barely noted. After squeezing into the empty alehouse, ripping his only shirt in the process, he dropped to the floor behind the bar and crouched, panting like a frightened mouse.

Only the angry urging of the leader of the small gang coming from above got him moving. The room was dark, lit only by the dying embers of the fire in the hearth, forcing him to creep among the tables and benches. After finding his way to the door, he hesitated, hand on the latch. He pictured the owner arriving the next day and finding him there alone. He would explain what happened and the man, being grateful, would take Harold in, let him work, feed him, give him a room to sleep in. A safe room.

It was only a momentary fantasy, interrupted by a loud bang on the door and an angry shout from outside. Memories, if not lives, were long in the Fallows and he would never be safe again if he betrayed the gang. After letting the older boys in, they vented their anger at his delay on him before searching the small business for valuables. Forgotten, Harold slipped away and arrived bloody and beaten at Xander's doorstep. The monk took him in, saving his life in more ways than one. The fiddle was now playing a slow, melancholy reel, so close to his own mood that Harold chuckled while tears welled in his eyes.

"Hey, no swords drawn in here."

Harold looked toward the voice. A burly barkeep glared at his sword, still dangling, forgotten, from his hand. Fumbling it back into its sheath, he dropped into a chair at a table near the door.

A barmaid made her way over to him. "What'll you have, mister?"

Harold lifted his hand with a flourish. "Your best brandy, if you please, dear."

"Brandy?" she asked, her brows lifting. "You're in the wrong part of town for that." She hooked her thumb over her shoulder toward the bar. "We have wine and ale." She leaned toward him conspiratorially. "I'd get the ale. If you ask me, the wine has gone over."

Harold leaned over and peered at the bar where the barkeep was watching them suspiciously. "What's your name?"

"Brandy."

Harold looked up to find the barmaid smirking down at him. Laughter burst out of him, shouldering aside the black weight of his gloom on its way. He collapsed back in his seat, his laughter trailing off, taking with it the numbing shroud he'd drawn over his emotions. He lifted misty eyes to her and said, "Your best ale then, Brandy."

She returned with a tankard of a dark ale. While he fished a coin from his pocket, she studied him. "You're not from around here. Least I haven't seen you before. A bit dressy for this crowd."

Harold handed her the coin. "Actually, I am from around here." He gestured vaguely around. "At least I grew up around here. Grew up listening to the sermons at the mission across the street, as a matter of fact."

"Been awhile since you were here, though, I'm guessing."

"Too true," Harold said. Glancing around, he added, "Can't say it's changed much."

She twirled a lock of hair, glanced over her shoulder, then leaned forward. "I get off in an hour. You want to buy me a drink?"

Harold chuckled. "I'm sorry, Brandy, you're lovely, but..." *You're not my type.* "... I just want to have a drink and think."

Brandy shrugged. "Okay, seem kind of sad. Might be a little company would help. If you change your mind..." She turned and wove her way through the tables.

Harold gazed at the ale, trying to piece the last few days together. He squeezed his eyes shut, but opened them again when his head swam. Not much was clear since he left his apartment. For most of that time, he hadn't felt capable of thinking beyond his next drink. Once the initial shock waned, he indulged in bitter recriminations over what he should have said. His imagined conversations swung from angry condemnations, ending with him throwing Karl from his apartment, to desperate pleas for another chance. But instead, he stood numb, allowing Karl to lead him through his revelations. Why? Shock and confusion certainly played their part. But the real reason was he was ashamed. Only moments before, wallowing in self-pity, he confessed his sins to a man who knew better than most the consequences of his crimes. Karl's expression, when Harold couldn't recall his sister, shamed him into silence, rendering any defense he might offer hollow.

His ruminations on the actual encounter on his balcony saved him from having to confront the emotional catastrophe it left in its wake. He knew, instinctively, it was a wound from which he would never recover. But alcohol, fatigue, and Brandy's good humor finally dulled the raw edge of his pain enough for him to approach the topic. He tilted his chair back, rested his head against the wall, and let the lilting music of the fiddle sift through his memories. So many special moments. Were they all so carefully orchestrated he couldn't see past the facade for six years? Was that all it was? He didn't, couldn't, believe that. What kind of man could pull that off? No one. That Karl felt nothing for him, that it was all manipulation for some unknown reason, was an idea he couldn't entertain. His mind shied away from it as if it might burn him.

Yet, how much worse was his betrayal if it wasn't all an act? If Karl loved him, he must have known how much Harold adored him. If that were true, and he was still willing to do what he did... Harold sagged, giving into the pain, an ache so great it was almost physical, letting his tears fall. He hadn't had many lovers in his life, but he had enough experience to know his own heart. Each day he would wake, and there would be a moment before he remembered, a moment when he felt normal, before the pain, a crushing weight, would bear him down anew. He would drift through each day, dreading the night when he would be alone, defenseless against his demons. Each night, he would pray for the relief of sleep and fear what he would wake up to the next morning. It may be true that time was the great healer, but that assumed time was given the opportunity to work its magic. He just wanted it to end... now... somehow.

He dropped the front legs of his chair to the floor with a bang, jostling the rickety table and splashing beer across its top. Enough! No matter what Karl's motivations were, to manipulate someone's emotions, exploiting their deepest vulnerabilities in such a calculated way, was a staggering betrayal. What kind of person could do that? He lifted the tankard to his lips, paused, set it down, and pushed it away. He hadn't survived his youth by giving into despair, for Daga's sake, and he wouldn't give into it now. Anger, hot and righteous, cleared his mind, allowing him to pull a veil over his memories.

He turned his mind to the much safer puzzle of the woman who put Karl up to it. Who could have known so much about him she could orchestrate the last six years of his life? What could she want from him that would warrant such an effort? It crossed his mind Karl made her up, inventing an excuse for leaving. But the memory of Karl's face when he laid open Harold's life disabused him of that notion. He didn't look like someone who needed such a preposterous fabrication to justify himself. He was left with the inescapable, bewildering conclusion all of it — the time, effort, money, his and Karl's lives for six years, the devastating betrayal — all of it was for that single cryptic hint; find out what happens to the witches? No matter how he turned it over in his mind, he couldn't make sense of it.

Movement at his shoulder drew him from his thoughts. Brandy gazed down at him, a wistful smile on her face. "You change your mind about that drink?"

Harold smiled sadly. "I'm sorry, Brandy. I recently lost someone. Maybe another time."

"Yeah, another time, maybe." She hesitated. "Word of advice from someone who knows. Best to look forward. Nothing good comes from looking back."

Harold met her eyes. "Thank you, Brandy. Those are wise words."

She nodded, turned and joined a boisterous group near the fiddle player, glancing back as she sat.

Look forward. To what? He stood abruptly, stumbling against the wall, and pushed through the door into the street. Gazing at the mission, he considered his options. Brandy was right. Looking back would only lead him to where he had been the last few days: drunk and nursing his misery. He could continue with his life, fulfilling his duties as an inquisitor. The thought sickened him and would lead him, eventually, to the same place. He could rail against the injustice of it all, letting anger cauterize the wound, until numb and apathetic, he drifted through life. He didn't know if he could muster the strength to face these or a half-dozen other equally bleak futures.

But there was another path. One which offered the smallest glimmer of hope. Just before Karl left, Harold chose to believe he allowed a glimpse of what was truly in his heart. It was a moment Harold knew he would cling to in the days to come. And Karl told Harold what to do; follow his heart and decide what kind of man he wanted to be. What kind of man did he want to be? He walked to the center of the street, looking west to where the Inquisition fortress glowed softly in pale moonlight. From his vantage on the highest point in the Fallows, he could make out the upper floor of the prison complex peeking over the curtain wall. *What does happen to the witches?*

Chapter 8

Minna

It had been a week since Minna's father left. Her pack and bow sat in her room next to the door, ready for her to leave at a moment's notice. She watched for travelers on the road, and exercised her newly understood awareness, searching for approaching strangers. She confided in Alyn she might have to leave, but kept it from her mother. She was ready for... whatever she was waiting for.

The house was empty and silent. Alyn's familiar presence was the only one she sensed. Her ripple, strong and steady, indicated she was likely standing out front, next to the road. She was probably waiting for their mother, who was in the village, running the errands that were usually Minna's. Minna waited impatiently for this opportunity ever since her father told her about the *saa'myn*. She slipped into her parents' room. Not that they would object to what she was about to do, Minna just wanted to be alone when she did it.

She stood on tiptoe and slid two books from a shelf above her father's bedside table. Sitting cross-legged in a patch of sun on the old hook rug at the foot of the bed, she settled the books in her lap. Among all the things in Minna's home, these were the only evidence there was a world outside Fennig. Everything else either came from their own industry or from others in Fennig. There were, of course, occasional visitors to the village, most of them tinkers or bards. Minna and Alyn always rushed out to watch them passing on the highway. Those were ephemeral curiosities, passing by and then gone, with only a wave to acknowledge her presence.

But Minna could hold these in her hands, and the fact they belonged to her father was a tantalizing and irresistible mystery. What secrets did they contain, and why did her father own them? Whenever she asked, he deflected her questions, turning them into a joke about his mysterious past. She gave up asking him years ago. Even though she'd known about the books for years — her parents were used to finding her in exactly this spot — the riddle of their origin grew in her mind after the revelations about the *saa'myn*. She waited for this moment, to be alone with the books, to try to understand why.

She held them up, one in each hand, looking from one to the other, though she knew every inch of them. They were both encased in black leather, about the same size, and both were handwritten. But in many ways, they were very different. She placed one on the rug and held the other in her lap. This was the *new* one. It wasn't actually new, but Minna thought of it as new because it showed little wear. The runes on the pages within were carefully written, the text organized into straight lines and regular blocks. Whoever wrote them was very precise. She ran her fingers down a page, enjoying the slightly rough texture of the paper under her fingertips.

She never learned to read. She and Alyn hadn't been allowed to attend the small school for years. It was one of Agatha's friends who ran the school, and Minna and her sister were not welcome. Her mother and father, like many adults born before the school opened, couldn't read Vollen. She remembered what some runes were called and what sounds they made. There was ansuz and othalan. She touched the runes, uttering their sounds, as if she could absorb something of the meaning in the words they formed.

She swapped the books, placing the new one on the floor and picking up the *old* one. It was worn, the back broken, as if it was handled often. When she rested it on her lap, it fell open and lay flat. The writing was less regular, sometimes sloppy, the lines unevenly spaced and tending to slope upwards as they traveled across the page. She could more easily imagine someone writing this one, perhaps hunched over with the book balanced on her knees. It fascinated her. Every page was full. Who could have so much they needed to write? She flipped through the pages until she found one of her favorites. The runes were especially ragged, as if the person was rushing to record her thoughts. She ran her fingers down the page, trying to imagine, not for the first time, what thoughts were so important someone felt the need to write them down in such a hurry.

Suddenly, Alyn's familiar presence surged, stronger even than if she were in the same room. Minna hadn't heard her enter the house. Alarmed, she looked up, eyes narrowed, concentrating, sweeping her head from side to side. Her sister was still out front.

"Minna!"

Minna dropped the book and rushed to the front door. She stepped cautiously out onto the front porch, not sure what she would find. Alyn stood at the edge of the road, staring into the trees, her arms held rigid against her sides. Minna ran toward her, stopping when she came near. Her sister was so focused on what she was seeing, she didn't notice Minna's arrival. She stood still, gazing toward the trees, her head tracking back and forth. Minna followed her gaze, a sinking sensation in the pit of her stomach. The *lan'and* flitted in and out of the forest edge.

Minna was eight when she first saw them, so when Alyn was eight, Minna watched for signs, anxious to make sure her first experiences with the spirits were happier than Minna's. In the two years since, she gradually relaxed, and began to hope her sister would have a chance at a normal life. Like Jason, Alyn suffered because of Minna. There were those, like Agatha and Mabel, who held being Minna's sister against her. Being excluded from school was just one example of the price she paid. But in most ways, Alyn's life was like any other happy, intelligent girl. She had friends in the village, had started noticing boys and their mother doted on her, sharing all the mother-daughter moments she couldn't with Minna.

Minna stepped up beside her sister. Alyn's eyes were following the little spirits, her expression difficult to read.

"Alyn?"

Alyn startled. She glanced at Minna, then turned back and pointed. "Minna! Look. What are they?"

"Alyn, what do you see?"

Suddenly uncertain, Alyn bit her lip and frowned.

Minna rested her hand on her sister's shoulder. "Do you see little lights up in the trees?"

Alyn's face lit up. "Yes, yes! You see them too? What are they?" She was so excited, she was bouncing. "Where did they come from?"

Watching her animated, smiling face, Minna saw herself, five years ago, running to the village to tell her friends the exciting news. Her life was going to change, and the changes would be difficult, but as she watched her, Minna decided she would not let the same thing happen to Alyn that happened to her. At least, not today.

She reached out and took her hand. "Come with me."

They ran across the road and slipped into the forest. Minna led her to a small glade, one of her favorite places in the world. She came often. It was far enough into the trees to be hidden from the road, but close enough to home she could visit it when she only had a few minutes. In the small grassy patch, she could be alone with the spirits and her mother could relax without her near. Sunlit dapples, set dancing by the wind in the trees, mirrored the *lan'and* above them. Minna led her sister into the middle of the glade, then turned to face her, taking both of her hands. Alyn was watching her, a small smile playing across her face.

Minna smiled, glanced up, then looked at her sister. "Watch this."

She looked up at the spirits and got their attention. They paused, hovering and *watching* her.

An expression of delighted surprise lit up her sister's face. "What did you do?" she asked.

"Watch." Minna concentrated and called. The spirits responded, swooping down and swirling around them.

Alyn gasped, a wide smile stretching her face. She pulled her hands free, extended them out to her side, fingers splayed and twirled. Her laughter rippled through the glade. When she turned back to Minna, she said, "How did you do that?"

"I called them."

"How? Can I do it?" She was bouncing again, her hands clasped under her chin.

Minna shrugged. "I don't know. You just… call them." Alyn frowned her disappointment and Minna added, "I was eight the first time I saw them. It took me years to learn how to call them."

"Teach me!"

Minna gazed up, chewing her lips. She didn't know how she did it, she just did. It was like shooting a bow. She had done it so many times, her body just did it without needing her brain to intervene. If she wanted to tell someone how to do it, she would have to slow down and think through the steps so she could tell what her body was doing. She watched the *lan'and* enjoying themselves and considered. Everything seemed to center on that spot in her mind, behind her eyes. That's where she felt the wind and the fluttery feeling when the *lan'and* were trying to get her attention. That was also where she felt them come into her mind when they talked to her. She closed her eyes, concentrating on that spot, and sent the spirits away. She did feel something, a tiny flicker. She just never thought about it before, or she hadn't for years, anyway. When she opened her eyes, the *lan'and* were spiraling away. Alyn was standing, her back to Minna, watching them go.

She took Alyn by the hand and pulled her around to face her, then pulled her down so they were sitting on the soft grass. She touched Alyn on the bridge of the nose with her index finger. "It's right there, behind your eyes. That's where you feel them."

Alyn's eyes crossed, trying to keep Minna's finger in focus, causing Minna to giggle. Alyn shook her head. "What is it?" she asked, touching the bridge of her nose.

Minna thought for a moment. "Let's call that your center."

"But what do you do?"

Minna looked up at the *lan'and* and thought about what it felt like to call them. "It's almost like you're pulling with your mind."

Alyn stared at her for a moment, then her face scrunched up. "How can you pull with your mind?"

"I don't know, you just do." She thought a minute, then said, "Let's try this. Close your eyes and think about the spot behind your eyes... your center."

Alyn closed her eyes, her face screwed up in concentration.

Minna giggled. "No, relax. You'll hurt yourself."

Alyn's eyes opened, narrowed, then she shut them again, her face relaxing.

"Are you concentrating?"

"Yes!" She opened her eyes, looking up, a frustrated frown settling on her face. "Nothing happened."

"Don't worry, it takes time." Minna tapped her knee, thinking. "Try this. Close your eyes, but don't try to pull. Concentrate on your center. See if you can feel it."

Alyn sat up straight, lifted her chin, and closed her eyes.

Minna watched her and murmured. "Now, try not to think too hard about it. Breathe slowly and feel for that spot."

Alyn took long, slow breaths, visibly relaxing. She sat still for what seemed like a long time. Minna was about to interrupt her when Alyn sucked in a breath, a startled smile appearing on her face. She sat motionless and whispered so low Minna had to lean forward to hear her, "I feel it. It's cool, like the water from the well."

Minna laughed. Now she thought about it, that sounded right. "Now, concentrate on that spot and pull... gently."

A frown flitted across Alyn's face, then she relaxed, letting out a slow breath.

Minna felt something, like a pulse in Alyn's presence, and a momentary flutter went through the cloud of *lan'and*.

Alyn's eyes flew open. "I felt something!"

Minna's surprise mirrored her sister's. "So did I." At Alyn's disappointed scowl, Minna hurried to reassure her. "They felt it too. I saw them."

"They did?" Alyn closed her eyes, her face screwing up again. Minna opened her mouth to say something but decided to let her try. After a minute, Alyn opened her eyes, sighing. "I didn't feel anything that time."

Minna grabbed her by the shoulders and shook her. "You did something it took me years to do. You're probably trying too hard now. Keep trying, but don't try so hard."

Alyn sighed and flopped back in the grass, arms flung wide, her eyes following the spirits as they flitted in and out of the space above the clearing. "How do you know what they're called?"

Minna sat crossed-legged, watching Alyn. She plucked a blade of grass and twisted it between her fingers. "Papa told me."

"Papa? Does he see them too?"

"No, he can't see them. He told me there used to be women called *saa'myn* who could see them and could even talk to them. Papa knew a *saa'myn* who lived in Fennig before we were born." She stretched her arms out, speaking in an animated voice. "The village would have a big festival when they came. People would ask the *saa'myn* questions and the *saa'myn* would ask the spirits the questions."

Alyn sat up. "The samen talked to them? How? Can you talk to them?"

Minna let her arms drop and plucked another blade of grass. "Sah men," she corrected, emphasizing the stop between the syllables. She glanced up and said, "I've only talked to them once."

Alyn whispered, "sah men," to herself, then urged, "Try it now. Let me see."

Minna hadn't tried to talk to them since the day she and her father came back from the falls. She was afraid to. She glanced up at Alyn's hopeful face, thinking back, trying to remember how she did it. She was sure it was the same thing she did when she called them a moment ago. The difference was she was focusing on her center, where she felt that fluttery presence. She almost hoped she couldn't talk to them unless they wanted to talk to her. Still, she couldn't be a *saa'myn* if she were afraid to talk to the spirits. She looked up, getting their attention. They paused, hovering in place. Alyn let out a small squeak and clapped her hands to her mouth. Minna shut her eyes and focused on her center. She had to admit, it did feel cool... and quiet. Taking a deep breath and letting it sigh out, she called. The *lan'and* burst into her mind with the same rush of excited exuberance. Her eyes flew open, and she laughed.

Alyn's face filled her vision, her blue eyes wide and shining. "What? What's happening, Minna?"

"They're talking to me!"

"What are they saying?" Alyn asked in an awed whisper.

"I don't..." Minna closed her eyes and probed the whirlwind. Like before, she found it wasn't a formless maelstrom. She could feel the presence of individuals who, although they were alien, they were also familiar in a way she couldn't describe. When she concentrated on one of them, she sensed an awareness, like it was returning her attention. But, like the first time, it wasn't really talking. She sensed them, and they were aware of her, but she didn't know what else to do. She pulled back, perceiving the multitude, and found herself at the center of a whirling tumult, buffeted about. A stranger in her own mind.

Taking a deep breath, she sighed it out, trying to relax and find her footing. But it was too much. As she started to push against their presence, her perception shifted abruptly. Like the forest illuminated for half a heartbeat by a bolt of lightning on a moonless night, the spirits were no longer an alien otherness. And she was no longer Minna. Instead, she was a small, quiet spirit, huddled against the joyous roar of the *lan'and*.

Panic grasped at her, urging her to escape lest she be swept away. Her body jerked as her mind urged her to flee, but could not tell her where to run. How could she outrun her own mind? In the moment before panic seized her, Alyn's voice penetrated the storm, calling her name. Minna clung to it, letting it bring her back to herself. She *was* a small, quiet spirit, but she was still Minna. Taking a deep breath, she steadied herself against the storm, and when she was ready, she reached for her center and pushed.

One moment, her mind was full of a clamorous rush; the next, it was utterly silent, leaving her feeling empty, alone, and disoriented. She shuddered in relief, sucked in a breath and fell forward, embracing her sister to steady herself. Reaching tentatively toward her center, she found she was just Minna again, and was surprised to find a whisper of disappointment mixed with the relief.

"Minna, are you alright? What happened? What did they say?"

Minna supported herself on Alyn's shoulders, breathing deeply, fighting nausea. She shook her head and mumbled, "They didn't say anything. It's more like you feel what they feel." She sat up and pressed her palms to her eyes, trying to make sense of what she felt. "It's hard to explain. It's like your mind is full. Really full. But I could feel them, each one, and they knew me. It was just... too much. I felt really small... and alone."

When she opened her eyes, Alyn was staring at her, motionless, lips parted. "I don't think I want to talk to them."

Minna wasn't sure she wanted to do it again either, but seeing the uncertain look on Alyn's face, she forced a smile and said, "Come on, we should get back."

When they left the forest, their mother was standing on the front porch, hands on her hips, searching with a worried expression. Her eyes found Minna and Alyn, and she sagged, her hand going to her throat, relief softening her features. Alyn pulled her hand free and ran toward her mother.

"Guess what, Mama! I saw spirits and Minna talked to them."

Minna realized instantly what would happen. She reached for her sister, but only grazed the back of her dress with her fingertips. "Alyn, wait!" She ran after her, but slowed to a stop when she realized she was too late.

As Alyn stepped onto the porch, her mother's eyes widened. She took a step back, raising her hands defensively, as if to keep Alyn away. Alyn slowed and stopped. Their mother backed away, a frightened expression on her face. Her eyes met Minna's as she backed into the open door and stumbled over the basket she set on the floor. Kicking the basket aside, she slammed the door.

Alyn stood still for a moment, her hand out in supplication. She crossed the porch and knocked on the door. "Mama, let me in. What's wrong?" She turned to Minna, her hand still raised, stunned incomprehension on her face.

Minna's heart lurched. She stood frozen, everything fading except her sister's devastated expression.

"Minna... What..." Alyn's voice broke.

Minna stared into Alyn's pleading eyes, shaking her head. Her hand rose, unconsciously, to her hair, memories of helplessness, abandonment and her father's tears locking her in place. She couldn't let that happen to Alyn. She took a step and then stumbled forward, taking Alyn in her arms. "Alyn, I'm so sorry." Guiding her down until they were sitting on the edge of the porch, she pulled her sister's head down to her chest and rocked her gently, stroking her hair, searching for the right words.

Alyn's body shook with her soft sobs. "What happened? Why did she do—" She sat up suddenly, her fingers covering her mouth and her wide, watery eyes staring at Minna. "Oh, Minna. This is why..."

Minna nodded. "The same thing happened to me. I was eight. It was the kids in town, all my friends, the first time." She watched Alyn's face as she grappled with what had happened to her. "It hurts her when we're near. I don't understand why."

Alyn's hands dropped to her lap, and she stared out at the forest where the *lan'and* were drifting in the shadows.

Minna pulled her head down to her chest again and whispered, "Things are going to change. It's hard at first, but we have each other. I'll help you. I'll never leave you alone." Minna brushed Alyn's hair back from her face. "Always remember. We're *saa'myn*, the two of us. Women of power. People don't remember the old ways, but we will."

Chapter 9

Harold

Morning? No, a quick peek at the light leaking through the doors to his balcony suggested it was early afternoon. Harold lay still, like a mouse fearing the cat. He sensed the beast, waiting, lurking in the dark recesses of his mind, smugly confident he must eventually emerge from the refuge of sleep. It chased him from his apartment days ago, and stalked him in the days since, preying on his sanity and feeding on his misery. To hold it at bay just a little longer, he rifled through hazy memories, trying to piece the past few days together. He remembered fleeing into the night, and his first aimless wanderings, but after that, all that remained were fleeting images of taverns, beer halls and dark, misty streets. The last clear memories were—

His eyes flew open. Ignoring the throbbing in his head, he untangled himself from damp sheets and sat on the edge of the bed, eyes slitted, swallowing against a wave of nausea. The beast stirred, but Harold's mind evaded its clutches, latching onto the memory of a barmaid named Brandy and the Inquisition fortress, bathed in moonlight. He pushed himself to his feet, swayed unsteadily for a moment, then stumbled out onto the balcony. Resting his hands on the rail, he shut his eyes and let the chill breeze raise goosebumps on his naked flesh.

How could he go about finding out what happened to the witches? He looked at the fortress. If Karl was correct, and something was amiss, it was a secret kept by some of the most dangerous men in the Empire. Simply walking into the prison and poking around would be fruitless, not to mention dangerous. Who else would know the secret? He let his gaze rise to the spires of the Great Cathedral, the Holy See of the Imperial Church, office of the High Priest. There would be no help from that quarter, even if they were part of a conspiracy.

To the left of the cathedral, a row of stone buildings lined the western edge of Cathedral Square, the beating heart of the massive bureaucracy on which the Imperial edifice rested. Few citizens of the Empire, regardless of their station, escaped the notice of the Empire's machinery. Not even the girls brought to the Inquisition prison.

· · ·

Deep in the bowels of the Imperial Records Office, Harold sat in a small reading room, gazing at a file that lay open on the desk in front of him. It was the file for a girl he and his escort brought to the prison only weeks before. No one recorded her name. She was only a number to the Inquisition's record keepers. Squeezing his eyes shut, he racked his brain for the name, but only her pale, frightened face came to mind. Opening his eyes, he let them trail down the page to the last line, brutal in its brevity, that recorded her execution.

He closed the file and let his gaze travel across the paper piled around him. Initially, he requested only the files of recent arrivals. Though he half expected it, when he found nothing amiss, it came as a blow. Unwilling to give up, he had a very unhappy clerk retrieve the records of every prisoner for the past five years. They lay heaped haphazardly around the small room. Each one depressingly similar; a precise record of the witch's time at the prison, and each ending with the same cold finality. Was Karl wrong? No matter which way he turned it, he couldn't conjure another possibility. What was there left to do? The beast stirred. He needed a drink. Stumbling to his feet, he was forced to pause and steady himself before he could exit the room.

The aggrieved file clerk hovered just outside the door, disapproval etched across his face. "Are you quite alright, Inquisitor?" he asked, attempting to peer past Harold to the wreckage of his charges.

Harold leaned on the doorjamb for support. "No, indeed, I am not. However, there is little to be done about it." He stepped away from the door, waved his hand at the files and said, "I'm done with these."

The clerk nodded, managing to convey contempt and relief at once.

Harold brushed past the man, ignoring his disdainful sniff. He was halfway down the hall when a nagging thought tugged at him. He stopped, eyes unfocused, trying to bring it forward. Something Karl wondered about on a rainy morning not long ago. It was such a peculiar question, one for which Harold had no answer. What happens to the bodies? None of the files recorded burials. He spun around and returned the way he came.

He met the clerk exiting the room, arms full. The man pulled up short, clutching the files protectively to his chest. "Yes?" he asked with a wince.

"I noticed the records don't mention what happens to the witches' bodies."

"Yes, that is correct."

Harold waited, but the clerk simply stared at him. "Well, it seems to me a bit of an oversight, given how detailed the records are about..." Harold waved his hand in the air. "... everything else."

"Ah, well, that is because these are the records of the Inquisition."

Harold waited. "And?"

"Well, the disposition of the bodies is the purview of the Ministry of Sanitation."

Harold smiled, and the clerk grimaced.

The Ministry of Sanitation recorded cremations for two of the prisoners brought in the last month. The first indication something was amiss was there were no records of what happened to the other three, including, he noted with a small thrill, his prisoner. Buoyed by renewed purpose, he reviewed the records of every witch from the past ten years and found an interesting pattern. For the first two years, the files accounted for every witch. Beginning eight years ago, the pattern changed. At first, there was only an occasional omission, but the numbers steadily increased. Given the Imperial mania for record keeping, it was unlikely the missing files were oversights. Something *was* amiss.

Harold closed the last file and sat back. What was he feeling? Amid the swirl of emotions, he was surprised to find relief rising to the top. Karl's betrayal had been personally devastating, but surrounded by the evidence of the Empire's brutality, his own pain paled to triviality by comparison. He lifted two files he set aside. Though he didn't remember her, based on what Karl told him about the timing, his best guess was these files belonged to Karl's sister. Weighing them in his hand, he murmured, "I forgive you, Karl, though I know I don't deserve the same." Rising, he left the room, taking the files with him. There was one more thing he needed to do, to be sure.

. . .

It had been years since he visited the prison. Normally, he let the sergeant of his escort handle the actual delivery of their prisoners. The prison complex was a maze of narrow, dimly lit corridors, and it took him a while before he found the place. Now, standing outside the guardroom, he straightened his uniform, took a deep breath and knocked loudly on the heavy oak door.

A small window opened almost immediately, and bloodshot eyes peered out at him. "Yeah, what do you want?"

Harold's eyes narrowed. Putting as much steel in his voice as he could, he said, "I am Inquisitor Harold Wolfe. You address me as sir, and you ask me politely what you can do to assist me."

The eyes widened, pivoted down toward Harold's uniform, then the window snapped shut. A moment later, Harold heard a key in the lock, and the door swung open with a groan. "Sorry, sir, didn't expect an inquisitor this time of night. Don't get *any* visitors this late, in fact." He glanced at the other guard in the small room. "Not to say you shouldn't be here. If you want to, that is. If you got business, I mean." He stammered to a stop and stood erect, watching Harold warily.

Harold took in the man's rumpled uniform and unshaven face. He walked through the door and stood looking down at him. "What's your name?"

"Hans... sir."

"Hans, I have to wonder, what sort of visitor you get in the dungeons, any time of day, to whom you can show such disrespect?"

"Well... uh... like I said, we don't get many visitors. S'long as we keep the door locked, most of the time, no one seems to care what we do. Sir."

"And yet, if Malleus Hoerst were to come to the dungeons, instead of sending me in his stead, how do you think he would react?"

Hans' eyes widened, and snapping to attention, he said, "Sorry, sir, won't happen again."

Harold stared at Hans long enough the guard began to fidget uncomfortably, then turned away, dismissing him. The room was small, the only furnishing a small table on which two oil lamps provided enough light to illuminate the scattered evidence of a game of cards. A second guard, sitting at the table, watched Harold, tense but expressionless. His uniform, personal grooming, and bearing were the exact opposite of Hans. "And what's your name?" Harold asked.

The man hesitated before answering. "Siegfried. Sir."

"Brother Siegfried, is there something wrong with your legs?"

Siegfried took his time standing, not quite coming to attention. "Sir."

Hans cleared his throat and said, "Sir, Inquisitor Wolfe, that is, what can we do for you?"

Harold stared at Siegfried for a moment longer, then said, "I came to see my prisoner. She would have arrived three weeks ago. She had red hair, wearing a blue dress. I captured her in Marne." He repeated the number he found in her file.

Hans frowned and glanced at Siegfried. "Aye, I know that one, but… I'm sorry, sir, we aren't allowed to let anyone see the prisoners."

Though, after what he had seen in the files, he should have expected it, Harold could barely hide his startled expression. "She's still here?"

Hans smiled, revealing a mouthful of yellow teeth. "Yes, well, see, there's already snow in the mountains, the Northern Mountains, that is. All the passes will be blocked till spring. Likely, anyway. We—"

Siegfried hissed. Hans gave the other guard a guilty look and shrugged. "This here's an inquisitor."

The interruption gave Harold time to gather his thoughts. What could the passes in the Northern Mountains have to do with the fate of the prisoners? He focused on Hans and said, "I need to see my prisoner. Malleus Hoerst requires some information before deciding where she'll be sent."

Hans's eyebrows rose and Siegfried asked, "Where she's sent?"

Harold turned to face Siegfried. "What is your job, brother?"

Siegfried's face froze. "What do you mean? Sir?"

"I asked what your job was. Are you an inquisitor, maybe the Malleus himself, or are you a guard in the prison?"

"I'm a guard."

Harold turned back to Hans and said, "I need to see my prisoner. Now! Open the door and show me where she is."

Hans glanced uncertainly at Siegfried. What would Harold do if they refused? Fortunately, Hans nodded and reached for his keys, while Harold let out a slow breath.

The door on the far side of the room opened into a narrow hallway illuminated by torches in brackets spaced at regular intervals. Most of the cell doors on both sides of the hall were open, the cells empty, but three doors were closed. Hans stopped at one of these and gestured to a small window in the door, saying, "Been a bit of trouble with this one, so we had to dose her."

Not sure what the guard meant, but unwilling to let on, Harold peered into the cell. The only light from a narrow window, high on the back wall, was not sufficient for him to make out any details. He stepped back and said, "Open the door."

Hans looked at something over Harold's shoulder.

"Open it, now!" Hans started, then hurried to unlock the door and pull it open.

Harold took a torch from a bracket on the wall and said, "I'll need a few moments alone with the prisoner. Wait in the guardroom." Hans nodded, the ingratiating smile gone. Siegfried stared at Harold before following Hans.

Harold watched them until they were almost at the end of the hall before entering the cell. The cells in the upper prison were almost luxurious compared to the cells lower down. The stone walls and floor were dry, and the window would provide some light in the daytime. There was a small desk and chair, a sleeping pallet, and a hole in the corner for a privy.

He knelt next to the girl sleeping on the pallet, but she didn't wake. It was her. Though he still didn't remember her name, he recognized her face. He pulled an eyelid open and checked her pupil. Dosing her must mean they drugged her. He examined her arms, hands and legs, but found no sign of torture. In fact, though she lost some weight since she arrived, she appeared to be in good physical condition. Despite where he was, in a cell of the Inquisition prison, with a child who was in peril because of him, he couldn't help feeling a small vindication on Karl's behalf. Her presence confirmed what he found in the records. The prisoners were being held here, unharmed, until the Inquisition could transport them somewhere in the Northern Mountains. But where and for what purpose?

Gazing down at her, watching the hair veiling her face flutter with her exhaled breath, he finally remembered her mother called her Ibbe. While

ROSS HIGHTOWER

he watched, the enormity of what he learned settled on him. If the guards were to tell the Malleus or his stooge, Stefan, he was here, his life would be worth less than the contents of the privy. Even if the two guards were silent, his trip to the Records Office would damn him. It surprised him to find he was oddly indifferent to the possibility. The question was, what was he expected to do with this knowledge? If the woman had something in mind, it wasn't obvious. What could he do against the Inquisition? Nothing.

He needed a drink.

Chapter 10

Stefan

Stefan watched the guard. "Well?"

The brother stepped back from the prisoner, who was hanging limply from manacles bolted to the dungeon ceiling. He shook his head. "He's dead, sir."

Stefan nodded.

"Too bad he didn't reveal the names of the heretics."

"Oh, he didn't know anything. I knew that after the first hour. No one can resist that long."

The brother, only recently assigned to this duty, stared at him blankly, then glanced back at the prisoner.

Stefan sniffed. "Clean this up." He exited his workroom to find his assistant waiting outside. Walter fell in beside him as he strode down the hallway.

"Walter, what news?" Stefan said, pulling his gloves off.

"Two things, sir. We've had a report from one of the Dominicans you placed with the inquisitors' escorts."

"Ah yes, which inquisitor were they assigned to?"

"Harold Wolfe."

"Why am I not surprised? What did Harold do?"

"Our informant believes he let an *Alle'oss* witch escape on purpose."

"He believes?"

"Well, he says either Harold allowed the girl to escape, or he's grossly incompetent."

"Harold has many faults, but I wouldn't list incompetence among them."

"No, sir."

"I want to talk to the informant."

"Yes, sir."

"And the second thing?"

"There is a messenger waiting to see you. It's a soldier from the Imperial Rangers. He was on the expedition into the wilderness east of the Eastern Mountains."

Stefan nodded. "If I remember, the Malleus assigned Inquisitor Zebert to that venture, did he not?"

"Yes, sir. In fact, the ranger has a message from Inquisitor Zebert."

"What was the message?"

"The ranger said Zebert told him to tell no one but you. He's waiting in your office. He smells like he rode night and day to get here."

• • •

"I believe he's asleep," Walter said. The ranger sat slumped in a chair in Stefan's outer office, his legs splayed out.

Stefan held his gloves to his nose. "You were right about the smell." He looked at Walter and nodded toward the ranger.

Walter kicked the bottom of the man's boot. The ranger startled awake and looked blearily around the office. When his eyes found Stefan, he climbed to his feet with a groan, hoisted a lazy salute and said, "Sir."

Stefan stared at him. When the ranger said nothing more, Stefan looked at Walter.

Walter said, "Tell us the message, ranger."

The ranger looked from Walter to Stefan, cleared his throat, and said, "Are you Inquisitor Schakal?"

"Tell me the message," Stefan barked.

The ranger jumped, straightened and said, "Inquisitor Zebert said to tell Inquisitor Schakal he sensed a *powerful* witch in Fennig. He made sure I made it clear he never felt one so strong." He paused, looking from Stefan to Walter, then added, "That was the message."

Stefan stared at him, brows drawn together. "Fennig? Where in the otherworld is Fennig?"

Walter shrugged. "I presume it's somewhere on the way to the wilderness."

They both looked at the ranger. When he didn't speak, Stefan said, "Well? Is Fennig somewhere on the way to the wilderness?"

"Yes sir, that is, it's on the other side of the Eastern Mountains. You head out the Imperial Highway and go through the Breakheart Pass and.... there it is. Pretty little town, you know, as they go." He stopped, his eyes flicking toward the door.

Stefan stared at him until the ranger's eyes began wandering around the room.

Glancing at Stefan, Walter said to the ranger. "You may go."

The man bobbed his head and fled while Stefan pivoted on his heel and entered his inner office. He pulled a map of the eastern Empire off a shelf and rolled it out on his desk. When Walter entered the office, Stefan said, "There's no Fennig on this map."

Walter approached the desk and placed books on the corners of the scroll to keep it open. "I'm not surprised. Argren is full of tiny little villages. Fennig is likely not the only one our map makers missed."

Stefan stood, rubbing his index finger along his upper lip. "Hmmm. He said it was on the eastern side of the mountains. I always assumed there was only wilderness there."

Walter didn't reply.

"I suppose it's possible a powerful witch escaped our notice in such a remote location. Zebert is likely the first inquisitor to travel beyond the mountains."

Walter nodded. "If I'm not mistaken, that was one reason the Malleus assigned him to that expedition; to determine whether there was a need to spread the faith to any who live in the wilderness."

"Yes, that is true, though it seemed rather foolhardy at the time."

Walter waited, then ventured, "The only inquisitor in Brennan at the moment is Wolfe."

Stefan considered, leaning over the map. Finally, he stood, straightened his uniform jacket and said, "That will not do. If she is as powerful as Zebert seems to think, we don't want Wolfe letting her go. I'll go myself." Glancing down, he noticed spatters of blood on his otherwise immaculate white uniform. "That's the second one this month. I really need to get some work clothes." He started unbuttoning his jacket. "We're leaving in the morning for Fennig. Notify my escort and the Malleus." He started to turn away, then said, "And tell the Seidi I wish to have a sister accompany me this time, not a novice. A full sister."

"What about the informant in Harold's escort?"

"Ah, yes. Harold. Well, I've waited this long, I can wait a bit longer."

"Yes, sir," Walter said, and left.

Stefan glanced down at the jacket in his hand and called after him, "And get me another uniform."

Hoerst

"Can I ask what you hope to accomplish by talking to Briana?" Stefan stood before Hoerst's desk in his office.

"Deirdre's spies are already chasing rumors to find out what the emperor is up to. Now, we just need to give her something to think about inside the Seidi." The Malleus signed the last document on a stack with a flourish, replaced his pen, tidied the stack and set it aside, aligning it with the edge of his desk. He ran his hands over the smooth surface. He had it made from mala, a hardwood imported from the farthest western provinces of the Empire. Very rare. For all he knew, the furniture in his office represented the very last of that beautiful species of wood. It was a rich, dark brown with swirls of deep red in the right light. Richly colored tapestries and plush rugs complemented the expensive furniture. Sighing with satisfaction, he leaned back in his chair, steepled his fingers, and continued. "As the leader of the more devout faction in the Seidi, Briana has every right to believe she should be Malefica instead of Deirdre. She's more… spiritually pure. One of many reasons she hates Deirdre. She's perfect for our purposes."

"Spiritually pure may be a bit of an understatement. I've heard her described as a zealot. I'm not sure you'll be able to manipulate her the way you do the emperor."

"On the contrary. The religiously devout are quite predictable. Briana will do what we want her to, as long as she believes it's Daga's will, and who knows the mind of Daga better than the Malleus?"

Stefan hesitated and offered, "The High Priest?"

"Pffft." Hoerst waved his hand. "The Church establishes the doctrine, it's up to me to interpret it." To Stefan's skeptical frown, he said, "The High Priest and I are of a mind on this. The Inquisition serves to insulate the priests from the practicalities of a sinful world. And ensure their income, of course." He stood, straightening his uniform jacket. "Now, is there anything else before my guest arrives?"

Stefan hesitated, lips pursed, and then said, "I took the liberty of inserting one of the Dominicans in Harold Wolfe's escort." Stefan paused and Hoerst could see him bracing for a rebuke, but when it didn't come, he continued. "We've had a report from the man, a very interesting report."

Hoerst smiled indulgently. Stefan hated Harold with a dangerous passion, but despite his best efforts, had never produced credible evidence of his supposed misdeeds. At least not in Hoerst's mind. Wolfe, though a half-blood, was the most gifted inquisitor in the Empire. He glanced at the clock. "Can this wait?"

"Yes, of course," Stefan said, trying to hide his disappointment. "It can wait until I return."

Hoerst fixed his subordinate with a penetrating look and said, "Are you quite sure you should be going to Fennig? Could you not send someone else?"

"The only inquisitor in Brennan at the moment is Wolfe," Stefan said. "Inquisitor Zebert's message indicated the witch is one of the most powerful he's ever sensed. If she's pliable..." Stefan shrugged. "Besides, I haven't been in the field for some time. It will be a welcome change of pace."

Hoerst gazed at him. Wolfe would be the better choice, especially if the witch was anything like what Zebert described. "Who are you taking with you?"

"Sister Keelia," Stefan said, a slight blush reddening his cheeks.

That was a good choice. A rare combination of power and piety, she would certainly compensate for Stefan's deficiencies. "Very well. Go to Fennig, but don't linger and be careful. There are new reports of partisan activity in southern Argren."

"Of course. The village is far from the rebels in the north, but to be safe, in addition to Sister Keelia, I'm doubling my escort."

"Excellent!" Hoerst rounded his desk. "Now, let us prepare for my guest. You know the plan."

"Yes, sir." Stefan opened the door to Hoerst's private rooms.

Hoerst called after him, "And Stefan, make sure Aife understands what I wish of her."

"Yes, sir."

The Malleus crossed his office to where floor to ceiling bookshelves displayed his collection of rare editions. He was standing in front of an ornate lectern on which his most prized possession rested, rehearsing how he wanted the coming meeting to play out when there was a knock at his office door.

"Come."

His assistant opened the door and said, "Sister Briana is here for her appointment, Malleus."

"Ah, excellent! Right on time. Show her in." He turned, careful to place himself between the door and the lectern. Briana was unlike Deirdre in almost every way imaginable. Deirdre was open, engaging, greeting everyone as if they were a friend, quick to laugh, but with a volatile temper. Briana was severe, suspicious, taciturn, and clung tenaciously to grudges.

Gray streaked her short black hair, and she wore the traditional gray robes of a sister of the Seidi, a fashion that was no longer common among her peers. Deirdre would burst into a room, leaving no doubt who was in charge. Briana stepped carefully into the office, studying the room warily.

Hoerst approached her, offering his hand. "Good afternoon, Sister. Thank you for coming all the way to my office. I thought it best we speak here."

Briana turned slowly toward him and nodded, ignoring the proffered hand.

"Please, have a seat." He indicated a chair in front of his desk, shifting sideways to reveal the lectern.

Briana glanced at the chair but didn't move from her position next to the door. She looked back at Hoerst and said, "I would prefer to stand until I know why I have come, thank you." Her eyes shifted to the side and widened. "Is that..." Brushing past him, she approached the lectern.

"A first edition of Necco's biography of Lachlan Olafson? Yes, it is." Hoerst stepped up beside her, but rather than looking down at the illuminated page of the tome, he studied Briana.

"I didn't know any survived the reformation," Briana said in an awed voice. She reached out but pulled her hand back before she touched the page.

"As far as I know, this is the only copy in existence. I won't tell you where I found it."

Briana's eyes cut to Hoerst. "Have you read it?"

"Oh, yes. Many times."

She looked up at him, not even trying to hide her desire. "How much does it say about Abria?"

"There are extensive passages." Hoerst smiled knowingly.

Necco wrote the biography long after the events it described, and Hoerst suspected it was more legend than fact. But there was sufficient corroborating evidence of the most important part, that it was probably close enough to the truth. Abria, the first woman to display the gift, was the only daughter of Lachlan and Illiana Olafson. Lachlan was a warlord of an insignificant clan in the small mountainous nation of Vollen, and would have disappeared from memory had he not recognized the potential in his daughter's gifts. With Abria's growing strength, the clan subjugated the other clans in Vollen. Led by Abria and her daughters, Lachlan conquered the verdant lands to the south and built an empire. Abria and her descendants formed the Seidi to rule the empire. Although Necco's writing style provided little insight into his subjects' personalities, Hoerst often wondered what it said about Abria that she took the unfortunate title of Malefica: witch in ancient Vollen. In any case, as the first Malefica, Abria was revered within the Empire and especially within the Seidi. Briana's reaction was exactly what he hoped for.

Watching Briana staring at the book with misty eyes, he offered, "Perhaps, when time allows, you would like to peruse it?"

Her head snapped around, something like hope or greed flickering across her face, before her eyes narrowed and suspicion closed her expression.

"Yes, well, to business." Hoerst sat in one of the two chairs arrayed in front of the lectern, crossed his legs and smiled placidly at Briana.

She hesitated, then sat in the facing chair, perching on the edge with her hands cupped in her lap, watching Hoerst expectantly.

"Briana, the reason I've asked you here is to confess I have become concerned about the Seidi. Of course, the Seidi is not technically within the purview of the Inquisition. After all, I report to the Malefica. It is not my place to dictate to the Seidi. However, it is my role to interpret the will of the Church, and, as my concerns are religious in nature, I thought it best to approach a member of the Seidi council who could allay my fears… or not."

Briana stared intensely at Hoerst. "Deirdre."

So easy. "I'm afraid you have anticipated me. As you know, there were questions when Deirdre made herself Malefica."

Briana nodded, emotions crawling across her features.

"Now, those questions seem especially prescient."

"What have you heard? What has she done?" Briana asked. If she were trying to hide her eagerness, she failed.

"I'm not prepared to say right now. Not until I have proof. Let's just say, I have reason to question her purity, her devotion to Daga." He gathered together a frown. "I bring it to your attention now, because we have come to a perilous point in the emperor's wars, and a vacuum at the top of the Seidi would be dangerous. We must prepare for a smooth succession. If it proves necessary."

"What do you want, Hoerst?" Briana asked flatly.

"Why, I want only what's best for the Empire."

Briana snorted. "You might think, because I follow the will of Daga, you can lead me around by my nose, but you're wrong. You can keep your insinuations to yourself. I don't like Deirdre, and she doesn't like me. We disagree on almost everything, but she is no heretic. Now, what do you want?"

Right on cue, the door to Hoerst's apartment opened and Stefan entered, followed by a woman. The Malleus watched Briana's reaction from the corner of his eye. Her gaze slid past Stefan with hardly any reaction, but her eyes widened, and she went still when she saw the woman. Hoerst understood her reaction. Aife's presence seemed too large for her diminutive stature. Unmistakably *Alle'oss*, she wore her red hair long, with thin braids that hung in front of her left ear. She wore a tunic and leather pants tucked into the moccasin boots common in Argren. As she entered the room, she let her presence appear, a strong steady pulse that left no doubt she was gifted. Though she had no tattoos on her face like a sister, dark paint encircled her green eyes and appeared to drip down her pale cheeks. She leaned her shoulder against the wall, arms and ankles crossed, staring at Briana appraisingly, a menacing, feral presence. Briana stared at her, lips slightly parted, a slight tick at the corner of her eye.

Hoerst cleared his throat and Briana glanced at him before returning her gaze to Aife. "What I want, Briana, is to return the Seidi to the proper path, a less… unpredictable path. A path that you can ensure. I want you to be Malefica."

Briana tore her eyes away from Aife, a hunger on her face. "The council votes on the Malefica and only in the event of retirement." She paused. "Or death."

Hoerst smiled. "I would suggest you gather your support, Briana, so you are ready should your opportunity arise. All I ask is that, in the meantime, you keep Deirdre preoccupied. Keep her out of trouble."

Briana hesitated, glanced at Aife, then looked back at Hoerst, her eyes narrowing. "An *Alle'oss* witch?"

Hoerst's smile faded. "A very powerful *Alle'oss* witch." The Malleus braced himself and nodded to Aife. Aife's expression didn't change, nor did she move, but the pulse of her presence surged violently. Despite knowing what was coming, it set him back in his chair, wincing and fighting against the sensation of his mind twisting on itself. The Malefica, the most powerful Seidi sister, was fond of using this technique to remind people of her station. However, the difference between Deirdre and Aife was as a drop of water to a lake. While the Malefica could cause discomfort in the close proximity of his office, Aife made him feel as if his mind would be torn in two.

Even though her gifts were marginal, as a sister, Briana should be able to withstand the sensation better than he or Stefan, but her shocked expression and the tension in her hands gripping the arms of the chair revealed she was not immune. He nodded to Aife, letting out a shuddery breath when his mind returned to normal.

He waited until Briana looked his way, taking advantage of the moment to breathe and allow his heart to slow. When she did look at him, shock still troubled her pale features.

"Abria's gift appeared among the *Alle'oss* some years ago," Hoerst explained. "There are, as you know, prohibitions concerning fraternization between the Volloch caste and the lower castes, the Brochen especially. Unfortunately, despite these prohibitions, there will always be those seduced by sin." Briana was shaking her head impatiently. This was not new information to her. When she started to interrupt him, he held up his hand, and she clamped her mouth shut and pressed her lips together. "The Inquisition works tirelessly to eliminate the children, and we have successfully turned the *Alle'oss'* own folk tales to our advantage. Their own neighbors kill many of the children as witches before we can get to them." He paused, letting the silence emphasize his next words.

"However, mistakes happen, and we have discovered, quite by accident, that the *Alle'oss* witches, when they are allowed to mature, are quite a bit more powerful than our sisters in the Seidi."

While Hoerst spoke, Briana's gaze drifted back toward Aife, but on that last revelation, her head snapped back. He watched her face, guessing the moment when she realized the full implications. Briana's venomous hatred of the Malefica was rooted in the vast difference in their gifts. Deirdre would already be out of the Malleus' hair if she weren't so much more powerful than Briana and her followers. "You see, power is all about options," he said softly, drawing her in with a conspiratorial smile. "Those with power have options and those without have few. Do we understand one another?"

"Power." Briana's lips twisted as she said the word. Her eyes narrowed and her head tilted. "If it's power you desire, why do you need me?"

The Malleus waved his hand. "Oh, Aife has no interest in being a sister. She rather despises the Seidi, truth be told." Hoerst picked a bit of lint from his pant leg, dropping it on the floor. "Plus, I rather doubt she has the political acumen required to be Malefica. No, Aife is an elemental creature, a force of nature. What I need from you is to provide the steady leadership the Seidi requires. Aife, and her friends would merely ensure you stay there."

Briana studied Aife, the moments dragging out. When she met his eyes, she nodded slowly. "I think we understand one another."

"Excellent! I think we will find that we work well together. After all, we, you and I, have the same goals. We both want what's best for the Empire, that it glorifies the name of Daga. Right?

Deirdre

When Deirdre became Malefica, she eschewed the ornate office furnishings her predecessor preferred. Instead, she took advantage of the sun streaming through the wide east-facing doors onto her balcony, gathering plants from across the Empire. She chose carefully so that she would have colorful blooms from early in the spring through early autumn. When she arrived this morning, the small sithia bush she found in the remote northwest province of Ferra had finally bloomed. Its small white flowers seemed to shine with their own light amid the scarlet leaves. They were the last blossoms she would see before the following spring.

The only concessions she made to tradition were three portraits. The first was of Abria, the first Malefica. The painting showed her standing on a high precipice, staring out over green prairies far below, preparing to lead Vollen out of the mountains. The painting was one of Deirdre's favorites, because despite the gravity of the moment, the artist captured a certain mischievous glint in Abria's eyes. It was an insight into the real Abria that Deirdre found very appealing.

The second portrait was of Ione, the greatest Malefica. The painting captured her at a critical moment when the fledgling Empire, beset by many enemies, was struggling to find its footing. She stood inside Brennan's eastern gate, alone before an invading horde. Lightning flickered from her upraised hands, illuminating her resolute features in a blue glow.

The last portrait, her portrait, was mounted behind her desk only because tradition required it. She stood, chin slightly raised, her right hand held out in front of her and her left hand pointing down at a copy of the *Seidi Sacramentum*. Deirdre found it revealing that, while the past Malefica were depicted in heroic defense of the Empire, her battleground was the Seidi council chambers. She fought her battles against her fellow sisters, the outcomes largely irrelevant to the fate of the Empire. The irony was that they were only able to engage in such indulgent bickering because of the heresy of a few sisters with spirit sight who held back the Kaileuk in the south. The thought brought her back to the enigma of the woman sitting before her now.

The young woman slouched in a chair, chewing a fingernail, her short, unruly hair bobbing in time to a knee that bounced rhythmically. She wore the leathers and boots so popular among the younger sisters who spent time at the front. What happened to her? Keelia suffered through the cleansing when she arrived at the Seidi, and emerged a shy, devout girl, eager to prove herself. She had a reputation for piety and humility and demonstrated the limited gifts of those who suppressed their spirit sight. Deirdre was having a hard time reconciling this morose, churlish young woman with that girl.

Keelia peeked up at Deirdre, her scowl deepening when she found Deirdre watching.

Deirdre sighed. "I have to say, the tales surrounding your exploits against the Kaileuk are hard to credit. It's true, people exaggerate the exploits of heroes." That drew a snort from the young sister. "But there are so many, I have to assume some of it must be true." Keelia said nothing, only studied her nails. "Keelia, are you sure you don't want to talk about what happened?"

She dropped her hand, straightened in the chair and shook her head. "I told you what happened."

"Yes, you did, and I have the reports of your commanding officers." She gestured to a pile of paper on her desk. "But they tell me only what you did, not what happened to you."

Keelia opened her mouth, but nothing emerged. There was the smallest quiver of her chin, then her mouth snapped shut. She returned to examining her nails and mumbled, "I have nothing to say."

Deirdre sighed again. "Okay, I'm assigning you to accompany Inquisitor Schakal."

Keelia's head shot up, her face a picture of outrage. Deirdre held up her hand to forestall her protest.

The young sister gathered herself, took a deep breath with her eyes closed. After a moment, she opened her eyes and asked calmly, "Stefan?"

"Yes, Stefan. I know he can be a trial, but he has requested a sister and, frankly, I rather suspect you can handle him better than most. Some of the novices are far too easily impressed with him."

Keelia slumped and resumed examining her nails.

"Keelia, I've seen you struggling since you returned. I'm sure it doesn't help that so many people want something from you. You need some time to recover. Stefan's going to Fennig. It's a small village on the far side of the Eastern Mountains. You'll be gone for at least three weeks. Take the time to consider what you want to do. When you get back, we'll find an assignment for you that will give you time to heal. Something far from the war."

Keelia looked up, moist eyes wide. "Really?"

"Yes, of course." Deirdre stood, coming around her desk. When the younger woman stood, Deirdre took her by the shoulders and said, "This is your family. We squabble among ourselves sometimes, but we are family. We'll get through this." The Malefica pulled her into a hug. Keelia tensed briefly before slumping, her head resting on Deirdre's shoulder.

When Deirdre released her, Keelia looked up at her, hesitated as if she wanted to say something, then she gave a small shake of her head and fled the office. Deirdre called after her, "Don't let Stefan get to you, Keelia."

Nia, waiting in the outer office, watched her leave. "Well? Anything?" she asked.

"No, she's still as sullen and silent as she has been since she got back. She's always been a bit shy, but once you got to know her…" She shrugged. "Something happened to her she doesn't want to talk about. Hopefully, she just needs time."

Nia followed the Malefica as she returned to her desk, saying, "Briana won't be happy you sent her away."

"Which is a good reason for her to be away from Brennan. Keelia has always been one of Briana's favorites, and now that she's the only member of her faction with genuine talent, Briana has been waving her around like a banner. I don't think that is helping her."

"Do you think the stories are true?" Nia picked up a report and flipped through it. "I've known Keelia since she arrived. She was just two years behind me. I never saw anything from her like this. I mean, lightning? No one has had that gift since Ione."

Deirdre gazed at the Malefica's portrait. "No. I was afraid I might never see her again when she left for the front. She has always had a hunger to prove herself, and she pestered me until I relented. I wouldn't

97

have sent her, even so, but we're running out of options." Deirdre gestured at the files on her desk. "Yet, she returned a hero. A damaged, desperately unhappy woman, but a hero. She doesn't deserve to be used by Briana. She needs time."

"I hope it helps her."

"Me too. I need time, as well, to think about what this means."

Chapter 11

Aron

Aron pointed at the sign above the tavern door, which read The Monk's Habit in faded gold lettering. "This is where he's supposed to be." In the two days it took them to ride from Hast to Brennan, *Talavir*, the spirit of winter, had roused himself, shouldering aside his sister, *Liāna*, the spirit of autumn. The cold fogged their breath and drew filmy sheens of ice across the moldering piles of garbage that dotted the streets of the Fallows. Aron pulled his cloak tighter and lifted his gaze past the tavern sign to a velvet black sky awash with fiery pinpricks. At least the chilly wind swept away the pall of smoke that usually hung over the city.

"You sure this guy is an inquisitor?" Zaina asked. She was inspecting the seedy tavern with a raised brow. "This place looks like a cesspit. Not at all what I imagine when I think of those guys."

"Funny, this is exactly what I imagine," Aron said, meeting her frown with a smirk.

Zaina's eyes narrowed. Giving her head a small shake, she turned to peer down the hill at the Inquisition fortress. "Have we had dealings with this inquisitor before?"

Aron followed her gaze. "Never." Great fires in braziers, mounted on the crenelated walls of the fortress, cast pools of light that seemed to writhe in agony as the wind snatched at the flames. As they watched, a sentry atop the wall strolled into the light. He paused, holding his hands up to the fire, before continuing along his beat, disappearing into the shadows.

They stood in silence, each with their own thoughts, until Zaina asked, "How are you going to recognize him if he isn't in uniform?"

"I'm guessing an inquisitor will stick out like a wolf among sheep in this neighborhood." Aron turned away from the fortress and examined the small tavern.

"You sure you don't want me to come in with you?" she asked, peering through a filthy window. "Looks a little rough."

"No, this I have to do by myself." Taking in the dark street, he said, "I'm more worried about you, alone, out here."

"Not to worry." She pulled her cloak open, revealing her sword.

Aron pursed his lips. "I'd rather avoid violence, if possible, but if you must, don't let any of them get away. It wouldn't do to have someone running for help."

She lifted an eyebrow. "*Alāli pasisia vehlan* (Goes without saying)."

They nodded to one another, and Aron entered the tavern. It didn't disappoint; dark, smoky and smelling like old ale and worse. It was, however, surprisingly crowded, with several large groups seated at long tables in the center of the room. He didn't see anyone matching the description of the man he was looking for, so he edged around the outside of the room, peering at the shadowy tables tucked against the walls.

He found him sitting alone at a table near the bar. Harold Wolfe. The inquisitor stared into space, finger idly tracing the rim of a tankard on the table in front of him. He was a bit scruffy for an inquisitor, not really what Aron expected, but it had to be him. The description she gave him was spot on, and despite his disheveled appearance, he was a far sight better put together than the rest of the crowd. He wore a shirt of fine linen, open at the neck. Loose sleeves fell away from calloused hands, revealing the forearms of a man used to wielding a sword. As he studied him, Aron felt his heart speeding and a flush rising along the back of his neck. How many families had this man ruined? He took a slow breath, swallowed his anger, and pulled the hood of his cloak back. He just needed to deliver the message and get out of here. If he were to kill him, all her plans would be in tatters.

"Hey, no *l'oss* in here!"

Aron jumped and looked toward the voice. A large man in an apron, standing behind the bar, was glaring at him. Beside him, a woman who appeared to be a barmaid stared open-mouthed, a tankard held, forgotten, in one hand. The shout drew the tavern's attention, and when Aron glanced around, he found a sea of hostile faces turned his way. Better get this over with quickly. He looked back at Harold and found him watching him, his expression unreadable.

Throwing his arms wide and showing all his teeth, he said, "But I just came in to see my friend *Inquisitor* Wolfe." He pointed at Harold, winked, then looked back at the bartender. "Won't be but a minute. Not even long enough to…" He looked around, brow furrowed, brushing at the front of his tunic with his fingers. "… sully your establishment." Throwing the wide smile on his face again, he nodded once, took a stride and dropped into the chair opposite Harold.

Harold

Harold was waiting. For what, he didn't know, but ever since he visited the Inquisition prison, he had been waiting. When he first learned the truth, he expected the Malleus' personal guard to appear at any moment. When that didn't happen, he sank into a malaise, sleepwalking through the days, spending nights in taverns to avoid his empty apartment. Waiting. His only consolation was that contemplating the fate of the witches and the riddle of the mystery woman gave his mind a means of escaping thoughts of Karl. It only made sense that she expected him to do something with the knowledge she paid so dearly for him to have. He considered and discarded, the possibility she expected him to act on his own. If that was her plan, she miscalculated badly. In the end, he decided she wouldn't leave it to chance. She had been too resourceful and clever so far. So, he waited.

"Hey, no *l'oss* in here!"

It took a moment for the words to penetrate his thoughts. When they did, Harold followed the bartender's glare to a man in a travel-worn cloak. He did appear to be *Alle'oss*. Blond hair and the braid by his left ear were unmistakable even in the dim light.

The stranger glanced at Harold, then threw his arms out, saying, "But I just came in to see my friend *Inquisitor* Wolfe." He pointed at Harold and winked.

Harold was instantly alert. His hand dropped to the hilt of the dagger at his belt. This man could be what he was waiting for, but inquisitors who were not careful of *Alle'oss* strangers had brief lives.

"Won't be but a minute. Not even long enough to…" the blond man looked around at the room, frowning, "… sully your establishment." When he started toward him, Harold sat up, drew his dagger and held it below the table. The stranger dropped into a seat across from him and winked again. Harold held his gaze, then flicked his eyes to the table which concealed the man's hands. With a grin, he lifted his hands, palms toward Harold, fingers waggling, then rested them on the tabletop.

Renard, the bartender, appeared with the barmaid at his side. Jabbing a beefy finger at the stranger, he asked, "Is this a friend of yours, Inquisitor Wolfe?"

Harold studied the newcomer, who cocked his head slightly and met his gaze. "Yes, he is," Harold said.

Renard opened his mouth as if to protest, but when Harold turned a steady gaze on him, he huffed, turned and walked away, shaking his head.

The barmaid, who was named Louisa rather than Brandy, slid into his place, her eyes roving over the blond man's hair, face and clothes. "Are you really *Alle'oss*?" she said, mispronouncing the last syllable as ahs.

"Indeed I am." His mocking tone set Harold on edge.

Apparently missing the insult, her eyes narrowed. "I don't know. I've never met anyone from Argren. Prove it. Say something in *Alle'oss*."

"*Pa ërtsa shiki feni sha kuta sūmati* (I'm not a trained donkey for your amusement)." He smirked and glanced at Harold.

Louisa squealed and clapped her hands. "What did you say?"

"*Ērtsi Louisa kut maliri. Pa jaelana tsi kuta vashni* (Louisa is a good person. She doesn't deserve your contempt.)," Harold said. Though the man gained control of his face quickly, it amused Harold to see a blush darkening his pale cheeks.

Louisa laughed. "Well, Harold, you are *full* of surprises."

"He said to bring him an ale, Louisa," Harold told her.

"Of course. What's your name, stranger?"

The man tore his eyes away from Harold. "Aron."

When Louisa left, Aron slouched and gave Harold a speculative look. "You're not what I expected."

"How so?"

"I was expecting a bit more spit and polish, for one thing." His eyes roved Harold's face and hair. "You're looking a little rough, not at all what we're used to."

Aron's face had shown no emotion, but Harold heard its echo in his voice. He nodded slowly. "I find that expectations can often lead us astray." Settling back in his seat, he sheathed his dagger, then lifted his hand onto the table. "They often lead to unwarranted assumptions."

Aron studied the hand for a moment, lips pursed, then gave a small shrug. "Perhaps." Lifting his eyes to meet Harold's, he said, "Though I find in most cases, it's best to assume the worst when your life depends on it."

When Harold didn't respond, Aron said, "You don't look Volloch."

"I suspect I'm Ferolin. At least, in part, though I can't be sure. I've never met a Ferol." One of the few memories he had of his mother was her laughing face as she tickled him, her gray eyes, his eyes, the most vivid part of that memory. What became of her, he didn't know. "That makes me a Volbroch, a half-breed."

Aron hesitated, brows drawn together. "How are *you* an inquisitor?"

Harold chuckled softly. "It's a story that would take more time than we have." He nodded to the bartender, who was watching them. "I'm not sure we can test Renard's patience that far."

"That is a fair point." Aron glanced at the bartender and then studied Harold, who watched him in return. "You speak *Alle'oss.*"

"Learned it at the suggestion of a friend." It was, in fact, Karl who taught him. "Told me I needed to know when I was being insulted."

The corner of Aron's mouth twitched up before something else crossed his expression before being banished.

Up close, Harold could see that his eyes were blue, his fine blond hair worn in the *Alle'oss* fashion, a long with thin braid falling in front of his left ear. He draped himself across the chair, as at ease as in his own home, unfazed by the hostility aimed his way. He wasn't a large man, but he moved with a dancer's grace and his hands wore the calluses of one accustomed to violence. Despite his easy manner, this was a dangerous man. Harold caught himself staring, a flicker of possibilities coming unbidden to his mind. Clearing his throat, he looked over the man's shoulder at the faces still turned their way, then dropped his gaze to his ale. He took a sip and looked up to find Aron watching him.

Louisa appeared with the ale. "Thank you, Louisa," Harold said. "You can put that on my tab."

A small frown crossed her face at the dismissal, but she complied, taking one more lingering look at Aron as she left.

Harold waited, but when Aron didn't speak, he asked, "Do I know you?"

Aron took a sip of the ale, put the mug down and pushed it away, his nose wrinkling. "No, I don't believe we've met. Not in person, anyway. I've heard a lot about you."

"I gathered that. From whom?"

"I'm afraid that will have to wait."

So, this *was* what he had been waiting for. Goose bumps rose along his arms and his heartbeat, already thready, sped up. Forcing his voice to remain steady, he asked, "Why so cryptic? Why can't you just tell me what this is about?"

Aron chuckled. "Funny, that's a question I find myself asking often." He gave Harold a sympathetic smile.

They stared at one another until Harold felt a smile pulling at his lips. Aron cleared his throat and looked down at the table, hiding the blush which began climbing his cheeks again.

"Okay, Aron, I'm assuming there is a reason you came to see me."

"Straight to business, then?"

"Oh, I wouldn't mind getting to know one another. I find myself suddenly short of friends." He waved a hand toward the glowering Renard. "Beyond bartenders and barmaids, that is. However, as we probably don't have a lot of time, and you've come a long way for a reason..." He lifted his brows.

Harold's breath caught when Aron leaned across the table. "You're at a crossroads, Harold, wondering which direction to take." He straightened and lifted his hands, palms up. "I'm sure I don't have to tell you, this is one of those moments in life when the wrong choice could be catastrophic."

Harold flashed back to the night on his balcony, the sensation of his world falling away as Karl told him about the mysterious woman. Once again, he had the feeling that he was being pushed along by forces he didn't understand. He opened his mouth to speak, but Aron held up his hand.

"You need allies," he said, cocking his head slightly. "You have more friends than you know. You just don't remember who you can trust."

"How do you know so much about me?"

"Don't ask. I'm afraid I wouldn't be able to explain, anyway." Exhaling, he said, "Believe me, I know what you're feeling right now. I've found the best course of action is to follow her advice. You can fight it, but... "A faraway look crossed his face and then he focused on Harold again. "She's always right, trust me."

"She?"

"There's a tavern at the corner of Imperial Boulevard and Lachlan Avenue. It's called the Siren's Song. You'll find the answers you need there tomorrow night."

"What answers?"

"What you've been waiting for. Trust your heart, Harold." Aron stood. He glanced at the nearly untouched mug. "Um, you can have the ale." Then he turned and left.

He was nearly to the door before Harold's brain caught up. He jumped to his feet and took a step toward the door when Renard stepped in front of him. "Who was that? You're a good customer, Harold, but —"

Harold tried to step around the barkeep, got tangled in a chair, and stumbled against the wall.

"Whoa, Harold." Renard reached out to steady him. Harold pushed past him, ran to the door, and threw it open. Aron was gone.

Aron

Aron barely saw the faces turned toward him as he rushed to the door. What was he feeling? He reached for the hate he expected to feel for this man, but it slipped away. His breath came in shallow gasps, and his heart thrummed. As he pulled the door open, he heard a clatter behind him. Harold would follow, of course. Zaina was waiting, leaning against the front of the tavern.

Her smile slipped as she saw his expression. "What's—"

He took her arm and pulled her around the corner into the alley next to the tavern. "Shhh, he'll try to follow us." He pulled her into the shadows beneath stairs that climbed to the floor above the tavern. They waited, listening to the door open and the sound of boots on the cobbles. Aron's heart slowed, the familiar presence of Zaina, inches away, calming him. The inquisitor's silhouette appeared at the entrance to the alley, peering into the shadows. Aron's grip on Zaina's arm tightened, and she held her index finger to her lips.

They both sighed in relief when Harold disappeared from view. When they heard the door open again, Aron motioned for Zaina to follow, and they headed down the alley.

"What happened?" Zaina asked.

"I gave him the message."

Zaina peered at him, worry creasing her forehead. "*Ërtsu sesīmi da* (Are you well)?"

I don't know. He turned his smile on her. "*Tia jeōda tia suma lath* (As fine as a summer day)," he said, pulling his cloak closed.

She watched him as they walked. "What was he like?"

"Not at all what I expected, actually. More... human."

She snorted. "A black-hearted bastard of a human."

"That's why I love you, Zaina." He craned his neck around to see her face inside her hood. "You always ground me when flights of fancy threaten to take me away."

She watched him, uncertainly. "Flights of fancy?"

Aron waved his hand in the air. "You know. Flights. Of fancy. It's an expression." He could tell she wasn't satisfied with that answer, but decided it was best not to elaborate.

"What now?"

"We go home." He scratched his neck. "I think that place gave me fleas."

"That's it? We came all this way for that?"

"Tiny nudges."

"What?"

"Exactly!" Back on safer ground, he put his arm around her shoulders as they walked. "The path to greatness is not made up of great moments. It's made up of many small moments, tiny nudges, that seem so innocuous as they fly past. The trick is to know when, where... and what?"

"What?"

"My word, exactly."

"Spooky."

"Spooky, indeed."

Chapter 12

Harold

The Siren's Song was a tidy establishment in one of the safer parts of Brennan. Harold watched people entering and leaving, the sounds of a fiddle and a boisterous crowd spilling out whenever the door opened. Why was he here, if he was just going to stand outside? While he was waiting for what turned out to be Aron's cryptic hint, he almost convinced himself to leave the whole thing alone. Let it be someone else's problem. But then Aron appeared and tossed his carefully constructed rationalizations into the air. He lay awake afterwards, replaying their conversation, searching for meaning in every nuance. In the end, he decided it changed nothing. He would ignore it. Yet, here he was, staring at the door, a leaf buffeted by the winds of forces beyond his understanding.

He scanned the crowded street. Imperial citizens out enjoying a crisp autumn evening, oblivious to the fate of the girls locked in cells a few blocks away. That monstrous knowledge left him isolated, set apart from the trivial cares of most people. No one here would care if he didn't enter the tavern. A spark of anger lit his numb mind. Who were these people — Aron, this mysterious woman… and Karl — to intrude into his life this way? The sounds of the busy street faded behind the whoosh of his own blood. All they offered were cryptic messages, manipulation, and betrayal. They expected too much. Instinctively, he knew if he walked away now, he would be free of it. Their plans were a delicate tissue, too intricate to withstand his refusal to play along. Earlier that day, he heard a rumor of a witch in Ka'tan, a village in the far northern reaches of Argren. Getting there would take at least a month. Long days in the saddle, amongst the beauty of the mountains in autumn, quiet nights around a fire, sharing the camaraderie of his escort. By the time he returned, all of this would have gone away, and Karl's memory would have faded to a dull ache. With one last glance at the Siren's Song, he turned and walked away.

He had only taken a few steps when reality intruded. He slowed to a stop. There would be a family, a mother, father, perhaps siblings. And a frightened, lonely girl, taken against her will to an uncertain fate. All so he could escape this choice. An anguished spasm ripped a sob from him before he could stop it. He clenched his teeth and hugged his body against the convulsions. *What do I do?*

As if in answer, a woman's voice drifted ethereally on the night air, her haunting melody somehow audible over the clamor of the street. He took a shuddering breath, held it and listened, letting the woman's voice slow his heart and ease his tense muscles. And something inside him answered. Another voice, a voice he swore, came from within. When he straightened and turned toward the song, the tavern door swung shut, silencing the voices and leaving him alone again.

He sprinted across the street, dodging traffic, and yanked the door open. The tavern was silent, but for the song. The singer, a sister of the Seidi, stood on a stage at the back of the room. Her eyes met his briefly as he stood in the door. He hadn't imagined it. He heard a voice in his mind, rising from the spot where he sensed Daga's essence, but it was not the sister's voice. The voice in his mind sang a counter harmony, a tenor to her alto, the combined voices so beautiful, they raised goosebumps on his back and arms. He stood transfixed. The voices intertwined, calling and answering one another, and though he didn't understand the words, the melody told a tragic story of love found and lost. She finished on a high clear note, the voice in his mind singing a mournful counterpoint that faded to silence, leaving him empty and alone. The singer stood, waiting in the silence that followed, a beautiful embodiment of the spell she wove. Slowly, the crowd came to themselves, until the sound of weeping broke the spell, and the tavern erupted in rapturous applause.

Harold watched the sister descend from the stage and weave her way through the tables, smiling and acknowledging the audience's adoration. She approached a man standing and beaming at her. "Joseph?" Harold murmured. It was Joseph Weidner, the brother removed from his escort against his wishes. Joseph was one of the few people Harold would call a friend. A friend he forgot he had. How could Aron have known?

As the couple took their seats, Harold made his way over to their table. When Joseph looked up, there was a moment before he recognized his former commander, and then his face split in a smile. He jumped up and wrapped his arms around Harold, pounding him on the back. Something inside Harold gave way, a tense knot he only noticed now that it was gone.

Released, he stepped back, allowing Joseph to look him over. "Harold! It's so good to see you."

"It's been too long, Joseph." Joseph's amiable enthusiasm washed over Harold like a cool breeze, soothing the raw, frayed edges of his tattered emotions. He grinned widely, unashamed of the tears moistening his eyes and the husk in his voice. "What's it been? Must be three months."

"Yes, sir, that's about right." Joseph cocked his head. "Came to visit a couple of times, when I was in town, but we kept missing each other."

"I checked up on you. Heard you had escort duty."

"That's right. Got to make sure the high born don't get hassled when they travel."

"You're looking well and happier than I remember."

"Yes, sir, escort duty is pretty boring work, mostly, but I prefer it." He hesitated and leaned in, speaking in a low voice. "It feels cleaner. You know?"

Harold looked into his eyes and nodded. "Yeah, I think I do."

Joseph glanced around. "Hey, you're alone? Where's Karl?"

"He… uh…. he's away." Harold put his finger on Joseph's chin and turned his head so the light fell on the left side of his face. A thin scar ran from in front of his ear to the corner of his mouth, a souvenir of their last trip together. "The healers did a good job on that cut."

"Yeah, it pulls a bit when I smile, but Nia says it makes me look rugged."

"Nia?"

"Oh, right, Nia." He stepped aside so Harold could see the sister regarding them with a bemused expression.

Harold's first impression was of a beautiful woman, one who, based on the warm smile she gave him, was unaffected by her own beauty. Delicate tresses escaped her artfully arranged hair, falling free to frame her face. He didn't know the specific meanings of the various whorls and dots of the tattoos the sisters bore, but he could tell Nia's marked her as a formidable woman. She had the black hair and eyes of the Volloch, but Nia had secrets. As a Volbroch, Harold was tuned to the often subtle signs of other Volbroch. Carefully applied makeup disguised the slightly almond shape of her eyes. Her skin was perhaps a shade too pale. When their eyes met, understanding passed between them.

Unaware, Joseph continued. "Harold, this is Nia Kelly. She's a sister, as you can see, but Nia's not just any sister. She's the Malefica's personal assistant. Nia, this is Inquisitor Harold Wolfe, my commander for years, and I'm not ashamed to say, like a brother to me."

Harold felt a hitch in his chest and had to glance at the floor to hide his embarrassment. When he looked up, the two were grinning at him.

"Join us, Harold, have a drink," Nia said.

After ordering a brandy, Harold said, "That was you I heard before, the siren song that drew me here."

Nia's laughter, a spontaneous and genuine echo of her song, drew a smile from Harold. "Uh-oh, you better be careful, Joseph."

"Harold can't help himself, but, believe me, it's just talk. Speaking of which…" He gave Harold a speculative look. "Harold, I have to say, without Karl around to keep you straight, you kind of let yourself go."

Nia leaned forward. "He's saying you look like crap."

Joseph laughed. "Something like that. Your clothes look like you've worn them for days, scruffy beard, bloodshot eyes, and I'm guessing this isn't your first drink tonight. You're looking a little rough, is what I'm saying. Is everything all right?"

Harold chuckled. "You're more right than you know, I'm afraid. Without Karl, I've been a bit of a mess."

Nia glanced at Joseph. "Karl?"

"Been together for years," Joseph said. "I have to say, I thought Harold was the steady one in that relationship, but I may have misjudged the situation."

Anxious to steer the conversation to safer ground, Harold said, "Nia, I'm sorry, but when you sang, I——"

"You heard your spir——" Her eyes flicked toward Joseph. "You heard Daga singing a harmony."

"Nia has many gifts, more than most sisters, and she is one of few who has the gift of song." Joseph gestured around the room. "They pack this place on Lachlandis evenings." Turning a wide smile on the sister, he said, "They all come to listen to Nia sing."

Harold gazed around at the crowd. There was an energy to the room he was unaccustomed to. The snooty elites in the establishments he frequented with Karl would never let their hair down in such a crass manner, and the pubs he found a home in lately were an entirely different type of place. "Do they all hear what I heard?"

"Some do." Nia hesitated, started to speak, then stopped and began again. "Those who are sensitive to Daga's essence will hear something similar. Everyone's inner voice is their own, so they wouldn't hear exactly what you hear."

"I didn't recognize the song or the language."

"No, you wouldn't, unless you were a student of languages." She hesitated, focusing on his eyes, before saying, "It's Ferolin." She laughed at his astonished expression.

"Ferolin?"

She nodded.

"How did you learn Ferolin?"

"Languages are one of my specialties. In the early days, the Seidi was fanatical about preserving whatever they could of the cultures the Empire subsumed." She shrugged. "The archive is full of such documents." She smiled knowingly at him. "Would you like lessons?"

"I would... when there is time, but I have to ask — Why Ferolin? It's not as if you would have a chance to use it."

"It's beautiful." Nia shrugged, gesturing to the stage. "Of course, even though the old sisters recorded the phonemes, the pronunciation takes a bit of guesswork."

"I could listen to her all day," Joseph said.

Harold watched them looking into each other's eyes. It looked like love, or at least a deep infatuation. Joseph never seemed the type to settle down, and Harold was sure he didn't know her when last they met. "A sister, assistant to the Malefica, no less, and an Inquisition brother." Though it wasn't unheard of, the ancient animosity between the two institutions, and the antagonism between Deirdre and Hoerst, permeated the ranks and discouraged such liaisons. It was rare enough that Harold couldn't dismiss the nagging thought it wasn't a coincidence, especially given recent events. "How did you two meet?"

"Funny story, actually, it was just chance," Joseph said. "I was shopping in that market down on Schiller Square, you know the one? Anyway, I feel a tap on my shoulder, turn around and there's this *Alle'oss* man. He asks me if I'd seen any honey from Argren in the market. Very rare in Brennan, but so good. I always keep an eye out for it since I don't get out that way anymore. So, I take him over, and," He held his hands out toward Nia. "there she was." He leaned over and gave Nia a light kiss. "The rest is history. Love at first sight. She couldn't resist me, of course, once I turned on the charm."

Harold watched them. "Argren honey, huh?"

Joseph nodded, gazing at Nia. "Yeah."

"The man, describe him."

Joseph turned a blank expression on Harold. "The man?" When Harold nodded, he pursed his lips, the scar puckering near his mouth. "Typical *Alle'oss*, blond, blue eyes." His eyes narrowed. "I don't remember

113

him well. I never saw him again. Funny thing is, I don't remember him buying any honey."

"He disappeared?"

Joseph's smile faltered. "Well, disappeared is a little strong. I might have been distracted."

"Blond, blue eyes. Did he have a single braid in front of his left ear, about this tall?" Harold held his hand up.

"That sounds right. Least, that's what I remember. Course, that could be any number of *Alle'oss*."

"When was this?"

Joseph turned to Nia. "It was, what, about two months ago?"

Nia nodded. "Two months today, in fact."

Harold tried to remember the Schiller Square market. "That Schiller Square market's a small neighborhood market, isn't it?"

Joseph hesitated, glanced at Nia, and said, "It is. It's why I go. I know all the merchants and most of the people who shop there. Reminds me of home."

"Did you ever see this man before or since?"

"No, I can't say I have. Why?"

"Are there *Alle'oss* who shop there normally?"

"No, never. What's going on, sir?"

Harold eyed Nia. "That market is a long way from the Seidi. Do you shop there often?"

"That was the first time. Someone told me they had Argren honey. Deirdre has had a tough time lately. It's one of her favorites, so I thought I'd surprise her."

"Who told you they had it at that market?"

Joseph was looking back and forth between Nia and Harold. "Whoa, whoa, Harold. You're sounding like an inquisitor."

Nia shook her head. "I don't remember."

Joseph waved his hand in front of Harold's face. "Harold, what's going on?"

Aron. There were a lot of blond, blue-eyed *Alle'oss* men, but not in Brennan. What were the odds? The woman pulling the strings obviously wanted the three of them together and wanted Harold to confide in them. He trusted Joseph, but the question was more complicated than that. Even if he played her game, did he have a right to drag Joseph and Nia into it? It wasn't hard to deduce where this woman's hints were leading, and he couldn't see it ending well for anyone involved. Once he told them, there would be no walking away when it inevitably blew up.

He thought back to a rainy day four years before. He and Karl were cooped up in their apartment and Karl was restless, pacing and agitated. Suddenly, he stopped and asked Harold about the Vollen Church's commandment against harboring witches. Ironically, the Church considered allowing a witch to live to be a greater sin than murder. It wasn't the first time Karl asked about Church doctrine, but Harold answered only reluctantly that day, distracted by Karl's uncharacteristic intensity. It was all too clear now. Harold's eyes misted, imagining what Karl was thinking during Harold's half-hearted explanation for that evil. Was he hoping Harold might offer some justification for killing his sister or hoping Harold would validate his hate for him? The conversation stuck in his mind, gnawing at him for days afterward. It was, he realized, when the seeds of doubt were planted. Karl told him to choose what kind of man he wanted to be. It was time to make that choice.

When he came to himself, Joseph and Nia were watching him with concerned expressions. He looked at Joseph and dipped his head toward Nia.

Joseph glanced over his shoulder and leaned forward, resting his elbows on the table. "You can trust Nia. She's sympathetic to the way we think."

"The way we think?"

"About the Inquisition, the witches and all that." Joseph laughed at Harold's surprised expression. "You think we didn't know you were letting those girls go? Thought you were being real clever, did you?"

Harold shrugged, waving a hand. "I guess I... I suppose I thought you must know... I just... didn't want you implicated, in case..."

"We went round and round about it the first time, that time in Fennig, but the sergeant, Henrik, he said to let you make the decisions and shut up. After a while, well, we felt better about ourselves. I haven't told Nia anything, but we've… she thinks like us."

Aron told Harold to trust his heart. "Joseph, what assignments have you had since you started escort duty?"

Joseph hesitated, confusion at the change in subject showing on his face. "Well, it's only been a couple of months. Haven't done much. Been to Ulm a couple of times, escorting some Church official. That's about it, except for kitchen and sentry duty, that kind of thing."

"Anywhere else?"

"No, that's it. Like I said, it's only been a couple of months."

Harold sipped his drink to hide his disappointment. "How about others? Have they escorted any prisoners to the Northern Mountains?"

Joseph leaned forward and lowered his voice. "How did you know about that?"

"Why? Is it a secret?"

Joseph exhaled sharply. "Very secret. Those escorts come from the Malleus's personal guard. The only reason any of us know anything about it is rumors. They have to take prisoner wagons from the livery, so some of it leaks out. You know how that place is."

"Where do they go?"

"No idea. They leave Brennan, they're out of sight. The only ones who would know are the Malleus's guards." He glanced around again and leaned toward Harold. "Those guys are a scary group, bunch of fanatics. I wouldn't go asking any of them if I were you or even let them hear you asking someone else."

Harold sat back, considering.

"What's going on, sir?"

Harold sat forward and motioned them to lean in. "The witches, the *Alle'oss* witches, brought to the Inquisition. What happens to them?"

They looked uncomfortably at one another, and Joseph said, "They're executed."

Nodding, Nia said, "I've read the Malleus' reports."

"That's what we're told, but it isn't true, at least not for all of them. The Malleus transports them somewhere in the Northern Mountains, unharmed, as far as I can tell."

"How do you know this?" Nia asked.

"I've seen the records and visited the prison. The guards told me they would be transported in the spring, when the passes in the Northern Mountains are clear."

"But… why?" Joseph asked.

Harold sat back, sighing. "That, I don't know."

"You need to tell Deirdre," Nia said.

"The Malefica? I'm not sure—"

"No, you have to. Listen, I can't explain everything, but you know the wars are not going well. The Seidi is stretched to its limit. If the sisters on the front fail, the army won't hold."

Joseph cocked a brow at Harold, then cleared his throat. "Uh, Nia? I haven't been up that way in some time, but there sure seemed to be a lot of sisters the last time I visited the Seidi."

Nia shook her head and glanced over her shoulder. "This is in strictest confidence." She waited until they nodded before continuing. "There are only a handful of sisters who would survive a real battle anymore." She waved their responses aside. "We think it started some time before the Reformation. It's hard to be sure, because the Church purged the libraries when the Inquisition was created. Fortunately, Tinue, the Malefica at the time, rescued some of our histories, unexpurgated, and hid them in the Seidi's archives."

Harold took in Joseph's reaction, finding his shock mirrored in the younger man's face. For all its corruption, authoritarianism, and unending power struggles among the elite, the three pillars of the Empire — the Seidi, the Emperor and the Church — had always seemed as solid as bedrock. If the Seidi were to fall, the military, in its present state, wouldn't be far behind. His mind refused to contemplate what would happen then. "But why is this happening?"

"We don't know why, and it has been gradual enough that we could hide it. Until the emperor became entangled with the Kaileuk. Today's sisters have fewer gifts and are weaker than sisters were in the past. Deirdre thinks the Seidi lobbied the Church to create the Inquisition to eliminate competition from Brochen witches." She let that sink in for a moment before adding, "The sisters have kept their secret for 300 years by hiding behind the Inquisition's atrocities."

"I'm sorry, but what does this have to do with me talking to Deirdre?"

"I can't explain what she hopes to find, but Deirdre believes she can find answers among the *Alle'oss*." She met Harold's eyes and said, "If the Malleus is doing something with the witches and is keeping it a secret, Deirdre needs to know."

Harold studied her. What did he know about the phantom woman? He assumed she was *Alle'oss*. Both Karl and Aron were *Alle'oss*, and her sympathies toward that people were clear. Still, he couldn't be sure. He couldn't even dismiss the possibility that she didn't exist. In fact, given the scope of what she accomplished, it was more likely to be a conspiracy than a single person. Deirdre's interest in the witches was, at least, coincidental, if not suspicious. And here was her personal assistant, ready with the answers he was seeking. "Forgive me for asking, but are you sure she doesn't already know about this?"

A flash of anger rippled across Nia's face. "What are you implying?"

"The Malleus reports to the Seidi." Harold shrugged. "I'm wondering if the Malefica already knows what happens to the witches."

"No. Absolutely not. I'm sure of it. I've seen the reports. They say nothing about this. She wouldn't hide something like this from me. She——" She clamped her mouth shut. "You need to talk to her yourself."

Not very convincing. But, really, did it matter? If he was right about their aims, their cause became his when he confided in Joseph and Nia. He would take whatever help they chose to provide, regardless how cryptic. The Malefica would be a powerful ally. "I can talk to Deirdre, but you'll have to introduce me. I doubt she will trust an inquisitor who shows up at her door."

"I'll write a letter. Deirdre's in Lachton. I'd go with you, but things are complicated at the Seidi right now. Deirdre wouldn't want me to leave."

Lachton was in the foothills of the Northern Mountains, near the border of Argren. "I can go to Lachton. Won't hurt me to get out of Brennan." Harold made sure he had their attention before saying, "It goes without saying you can't talk to anyone about this. If the Malleus is keeping it a secret, there's no telling what lengths he would go to. He's a dangerous man. Maybe... just keep your ear to the ground. Don't take any chances. I don't know who else knows, but if Hoerst is behind it, you can bet Stefan, at least, is involved."

Joseph slapped the table. "Oh yeah! Harold, I was thinking of you earlier today. Stefan is leaving for Fennig tomorrow."

Harold gave him a blank look. "What's Stefan going to Fennig for? He hasn't gone into the field for years."

"The rumor is there is a powerful witch there. One of the rangers who went with Inquisitor Zebert brought the news back." He shrugged and said, "Long way to go for just anyone." He cocked his head and gave Harold a significant look. "For some reason, Stefan went himself. Taking extra guards and a full sister with him. That's all I know."

"It couldn't be her." He shook his head, gazing into the space above Joseph's head. "She'd be a teenager now. What are the chances she survived this long?"

"Who? What are you talking about?" Nia asked.

Joseph gave Harold a questioning look and Harold nodded.

"We were in Fennig, what was it, five or six years ago? Some traveling bard brought back a rumor of a witch. Turns out, there *was* a witch there, but Harold let her go." Nia turned to stare at Harold, mouth open. "Wasn't the only one, either, but it was the first one."

Harold sat back, grappling with his swirling emotions. It was unlikely Stefan was going to Fennig for the same girl, but it was possible. They would bring her back to Brennan and, once she was in the prison, there was no telling what would happen to her. Still, even if it was her, she was just one among many. Why did he care so much? He closed his eyes, picturing Karl's expression when Harold confessed to what he did in Fennig.

If he left now and rode hard, changing his mount in the Imperial fort at Hast, he could get to Fennig, catch Stefan, and… What? He would think about that later. When he opened his eyes, he found Nia watching him. Could he wait to talk to Deirdre?

"I know what you're thinking," Joseph said, shaking his head. "Are you sure that's a good idea?"

"No, I'm not."

"Whatever you two are talking about, you have to go talk to Deirdre first," Nia said.

Harold studied her, considering. If they were the puppet masters, Stefan's unexpected trip upset their plans, apparently. Still, the Inquisition did report to the Seidi, and theoretically, the Malefica had the authority to intervene on his behalf. Assuming he caught them before she disappeared into the prison. Even if he rode hard, changing mounts at every Imperial outpost, it would take him eleven days to reach Lachton. It would be hard on him and the horses. If he gave Deirdre one day, he might make it to Hast before Stefan returned. Even though Fennig was closer to Brennan than Lachton, Stefan had a reputation for taking a leisurely pace, and the mountains would slow them down.

"I'll go see Deirdre first. If I hurry, I can catch them on the way back."

"And then what? Stefan will have eight guards and a sister with him."

"One problem at a time."

"Nia, you know the sister," Joseph said. "How do you think she would react if Harold tried to free the girl?"

Nia looked uncomfortable. "There's no telling. Keelia is a troubled young woman and very powerful. You don't want to be on her bad side."

Harold smirked. "I'll try to avoid that."

"Tell you what," Joseph said. "I know a brother going with Stefan. He's assigned to Zebert, but since Zebert is out in the wilderness, Stefan is taking his escort. His name is Eckehart. He's new and having a hard time adjusting. He's a good man. I'll tell him to look after her, make sure she gets to Brennan, at least."

"Yeah, okay, that will work. Tell him to be careful."

"Oh, one more thing, Harold. Sergeant Henrik gave me another message for you. He's worried about you. Says you haven't been around much lately." He waved a hand when Harold started to speak. "He just wanted me to tell you, others have been asking where you are. The guy who took my place…"

"Ivan."

"Yeah. That's the one. The sergeant doesn't have much good to say about him. Thought you might want to know the guy's looking for you."

Harold rested his hand on Joseph's shoulder. "Thank you, Joseph."

"Of course! Well, sounds like we have a plan. Guess you'll have to listen to Nia sing another night, Harold. Nia has a letter to write, and you need to get an early start tomorrow."

Harold returned their smiles. As the others rose, he glanced down at his unfinished drink, paused, pushed it away and followed.

Chapter 13

Minna

The weeks since Alyn first saw the spirits were difficult in the Hunter's home. When their mother emerged from her room, her face had the drawn quality of someone fighting a terrible illness. It was difficult enough for her with Minna nearby. Minna could only guess what she was going through now. To give her some relief, she spent as much time as she could outside, hiking in the woods nearby, or working in her father's small workshop next door. She considered taking her pack and bow and heading to the falls, but she couldn't leave her sister alone.

Alyn eventually gave up trying to talk to their mother and spent most of her time sitting on the porch, wrapped in a quilt, trying to enjoy the last of the nice fall weather. Minna took her to the glade every day to commune with the *lan'and* and give their mother a break. Though her sister tried to participate, she seemed to resent the spirits now.

It was unsustainable. They all knew it. Their mother couldn't live like this. Though no one said it, they all knew they were waiting. Their father promised to be back in a month, and though it had only been three weeks, Minna often found herself staring down the road toward the east. She could barely face Alyn's disappointment each time she returned alone. Minna sometimes found her mother in the distance, an old shawl wrapped around her shoulders, standing in the center of the highway and staring toward the wilderness. She would return to the house, hiding red-rimmed eyes. What her father could do, Minna didn't know, and she suspected they all felt the same. It was just that they didn't know what else to do.

Early one morning, Minna was in the root cellar, organizing the winter larder, Alyn's quiet, sleepy presence in the room above keeping her company. She sensed someone approaching the house and was surprised when she recognized Jason. That she could sense him was not a surprise. She supposed, as with her father, she had grown used to it. But it was unusual for Jason to visit out of the blue. She sat back on her heels, smiling for the first time in days. Even from a distance, Jason's buoyant personality shone through. For a mad moment, she pictured him whisking her away from the gloomy house. To where, she didn't care. Maybe that small cozy house from her dreams. Her smile fell away, and she pressed her lips together. It was just a fantasy. And anyway, she couldn't leave her sister.

When the knock came on their door, she smiled when Alyn's rhythm quickened. It was the first sign of life her sister showed in days. Minna climbed the steps to find the room awash in morning sunlight. Jason stood just inside the door, teasing Alyn about her sleep-tangled hair. Alyn hugged the edge of the door, laughing and attempting to pat her hair flat.

"Minna!" he said when he saw her. "Brought your bow back." He leaned the bow beside the door. "How did your trip to the falls work out?"

"It was… It was wonderful. I shot a turkey with the new bow. First trip." Standing shoulder to shoulder with her sister, she couldn't help grinning at the excited ripples coming from her.

"Morning, Fra Hunter," Jason said to their mother, who appeared and stood with a small smile in the doorway to her bedroom.

"Morning, Jason."

Jason cocked his head and gave Minna a sly grin. "Now, Minna, don't tell me you don't remember what tonight is?"

Caught off guard, Minna exchanged a confused look with Alyn.

"I don't want to hear any excuses. You made a promise and promises must be kept." When she still looked confused, Jason's grin widened. He leaned toward her and said, "The harvest festival is tonight, Minna."

The harvest festival. She completely forgot. She gave Alyn a guilty look and shook her head. "Oh, I—"

"Oh, no, you don't!" Alyn said. "You will not mope around at home when you could go to the festival with Jason."

"But—" Minna started.

"But nothing. What good will it do for you to stay home?"

Jason pointed at Alyn and said, "You should listen to your sister, Minna. She knows what's good for you."

"Are you sure?" Minna asked. "You'll be okay, alone with…" She glanced at Jason, then cut her eyes to their mother.

"Yes," Alyn said firmly. She leaned close and whispered, "It's time me and Mama talk." She gave a little shrug. "Maybe it will be easier if it's just the two of us."

Minna glanced at their mother, a grin slowly wiping the worried furrows from her brow. She looked up at Jason, who was watching the exchange closely. "Okay," she said.

"Excellent! Now, I promised I would bring everything, so just bring yourself."

"Jason, why don't you come in for a cup of tea?" their mother said.

"I would love a cup of tea, Fra Hunter."

Alyn nudged Minna in the ribs, giving her a wide-eyed look as Jason made himself comfortable by the hearth and their mother swung the kettle over the fire. Minna stood with Alyn beside the door, listening to Jason relating the latest town gossip. When he told them about an incident between Agatha and her neighbors over a missing cow, her mother actually laughed. Not wanting to spoil the moment, Minna caught Jason's eye. When he gave her a nod, she slipped out and settled onto her father's favorite spot on the bench beside the door. She hugged herself against the morning chill, watching the *lan'and* drifting through the trees across the highway, breathing the musty scents of autumn. It felt like the first deep breath she had taken in days.

Though he was only there for a short time, his irrepressible cheer was like a ray of warm sunshine in the dreary house. They all felt it. Minna shut the door after he left and turned toward Alyn and their mother. They stared at each other, suppressing grins, until they all broke into giggles. The unexpected reprieve from the prison they made for themselves brought them all to tears. For the rest of the afternoon, Alyn attempted to cajole Minna into letting her dress her and fix her hair. Even their mother became involved, laughing with them and offering suggestions from across the room. In the end, the only thing Minna would relent to was to allow Alyn to wash her hair, brush it out and braid it with a traditional ribbon. The mood in their home when Minna left was lighter than it had been since Papa left.

· · ·

The days were already growing short, and the brightest stars were just appearing when Minna approached Fennig. Arriving at the base of the hill where the road turned before descending into the village, Minna stood in the shadows at the edge of the highway, gazing down into the square, wondering how Alyn and their mother were getting along. Wood smoke and the scent of roasting meat wafted from the center of town. She ran her finger over the ribbon embedded in her braids. It smelled of bayberry.

How many times had she stood here, separate and alone, a voyeur into the lives she imagined *they* lived? The normal people. A desperate longing would sometimes come over her on those occasions. Now she wasn't sure what she felt. She climbed the hill and turned to watch the festive scene in the square below. It wasn't the distance between her life and theirs that changed, it was her perception of that distance. She was not the same girl who visited the market only a month ago. She was still standing apart, looking down into their world, but when she searched for the longing she felt before, she couldn't find it. Instead, what she found was a solidifying sense of purpose.

She was a *saa'myn*. What that meant, she didn't know yet, but she knew she wouldn't find her answers in Fennig. So many things — her father's revelations, the intrusion of the Empire into Fennig, her sister seeing the spirits and their mother's pain — were telling her the time was near. But time for what? An owl, lingering in the mountains late in the season, as if it were waiting for something, hooted mournfully.

Shaking herself, she looked up. The *lan'and* seemed to enjoy the festivities. Though they wouldn't normally enter the village, they gathered at the boundary, dancing among the trees that crowded the back of the hill. What did they understand about humans? Were they celebrating the harvest along with the villagers?

She felt Jason coming and allowed him to approach her unnoticed. He stepped up behind her, close enough that she felt his breath in her hair. Her face relaxed into a smile, and she turned to face him.

"Hello, Min." It surprised her how much taller he was than her. When did that happen?

"Hello, Jason." A flush rose on her throat.

He stepped back, bowed, and offered his arm. She laughed and took it, and they walked up to the crown of the hill. Laughter and the sound of musicians tuning their instruments drifted on the gentle breeze. Jason took a blanket from a basket and spread it on the grass. He pulled bread, cheese, sausage, honey and a flask of what Minna suspected was his father's mead from the basket and arranged them in the center of the blanket. Lastly, he removed a small oil lamp and lit it.

When he finished, he stood and bowed again, gesturing to the blanket with a flourish. "Your highness, your table is ready."

Minna laughed, put her hand to her chest and said, "Oh, sir, I don't know that I'm dressed for such a fancy feast as this." She looked down at herself. She dressed like her father, clothes she made herself, appropriate for traipsing through the forest. She wore a tunic, cinched at the waist by a belt on which she carried her small hunting knife, pants of soft leather, tucked into moccasin boots, and a light traveling cloak. She peeked up at him, her cheeks warming, suddenly shy in front of a boy she knew all her life.

Jason watched her, a curious expression in place of his usual playful smirk. "I wouldn't have you any other way, Min."

Minna lifted her cloak to her sides, attempted a curtsy, and said, "Well then, good sir, I find the accommodations quite acceptable."

Agmar

Agmar was watching the crowd when Loden approached him at a run. After his confrontation with Marie in the tavern, they met and made their plans. Whatever Marie said, he was sure the girl was planning something and tonight, with the entire village gathered, would be the perfect time for whatever it was. Unfortunately, they hadn't seen Minna in weeks, though they took turns watching for her where the road entered the village. Up on that hill where she sat sometimes, brooding. Agmar suggested they go to her house, but Jesper and Loden argued against it. The villagers would not stand for an attack on the family. They could wait for her to come to them.

"She's here!" Loden exclaimed, panting. "She's with the blacksmith's boy at the top of the hill."

Agmar's heart raced. Finally! "Get the boys! And keep it quiet!" It was unfortunate that Jason was with her, but they weren't likely to have a better opportunity.

Minna

Minna sat, tucking her legs under her, expecting Jason to sit across from her. Instead, he stepped across the blanket and sat beside her. Minna's breath caught when their knees touched. She looked up and found Jason's face only inches away, the minty warmth of his breath on her cheek. His usual smile was gone, replaced by an expression that asked a question. Music was wafting up from the square. Minna searched his eyes. A small smile lifted the corners of her mouth, and she gave him the slightest of nods. The smile she loved returned, and Minna let her gaze drop.

Jason stood and offered his hand. "Let's dance."

"What? I don't dance. I don't know how." She looked down the hill where the villagers were dancing. She watched them before, of course, but she never tried the dances, at least not with anyone other than Alyn. She looked up uncertainly at Jason's smiling face.

"Come on, Min! There's no one here but us. There's no reason to be embarrassed."

A smile playing across her face, she took his hand and let him pull her to her feet. She glanced back at the dancers, then looked down at her feet.

"No, up here, Min. Look at me." Jason took her other hand.

She looked into his eyes, resisting the urge to wipe her sweaty palms on her tunic.

"Like this," he said. He dipped his right hand and lifted his right foot.

Minna tried to mirror his movements and, before she knew it, they were off. It was all she could do to keep up, but Jason's touch was sure, and he led her confidently. They spun and skipped around the crown of the hill until Minna was breathless and flushed. As the song ended, they spun one last time, then fell in a laughing, sweaty heap. They lay on their backs, catching their breath, their fingers still intertwined. The *lan'and,* who had joined them while they danced, retreated into the branches.

"Oh ho, what have we here?"

Jason and Minna jumped up, and Jason pulled Minna behind him, forcing her to peer around his broad shoulders.

Figures were emerging from the shadows that obscured the northern edge of the village. Their faces, illuminated only by the shifting light of torches and lanterns, were hard to make out, but Agmar's bulk was instantly recognizable. As they drew near, spreading out and climbing the hill, she recognized Jesper, Loden and other men who had tormented her for years. She squeezed Jason's bicep, pulling him toward the forest. "Jason, we—"

"I heard what you did to my mother the other day," Agmar shouted. Others nodded, jeering and adding their own accusations.

Unaware of Minna's urgency, Jason resisted her pull and asked, "What are you talking about? Minna didn't do anything to your mother. I saw her in the square today."

A spasm rippled through Agmar's frame. He threw his arms out, forcing Jesper to duck away from the lantern he carried. "It's not because she didn't want to!"

Loden pointed and said, "It's time we did something about her before it's too late! Step aside, Jason."

They were after her, not Jason. If she ran, they would leave him alone. Releasing Jason's arm, she turned to flee into the forest when something struck her behind her ear. She cried out, her legs collapsing, leaving her huddled at Jason's feet, arms shielding her head.

"Minna!" Jason knelt, resting his hand on her shoulder. "What happened?"

Minna looked up into his eyes. She opened her mouth to urge him to run, when he dropped to the ground, limp, his legs twisted beneath his body.

"No!" Minna cried and knelt beside his body, cupping his cheeks with trembling hands. "Jason, Jason, wake up!" Feeling something hot and wet at his temple, she lifted her hand and stared at the blood dripping from her fingers. Forgetting the men climbing the hill, she looked up and shouted, "Help!"

Some men stopped, surprise and uncertainty on their faces. A few began backing away. Agmar glanced at Jesper and Loden and said, "Come on, boys, let's get this over with."

Hot prickles sizzled across Minna's skin. For years, she endured abuse from people like these without complaint, never rising to their snubs or insults. She wouldn't even allow herself to become angry, afraid of what would happen to them. Not this time. She welcomed the first turbulent breaths of the storm stirring behind her eyes. The *lan'and* descended from the trees, swirling around her, and in a flash, she knew what to do. Focusing on her center, she called.

The spirits roared into her mind and the storm erupted. Gasping, she fell forward onto Jason's chest, squeezing her eyes shut and focusing on what was happening inside her. Huddled against the gale, she quailed until she *heard* a rhythmic note from her center. She extended her awareness, and found, not the howling entities, careless of her small spirit she imagined the last time. Instead, she sensed curiosity and reassurance. Encouraged, she followed the pulsing note further into the maelstrom. Like a beacon on a dark night, the note drew her on until she emerged into the quiet eye in the center of the vortex. From deep in her center, surrounded by the joyful tempest of the *lan'and*, she finally understood. She *was* a small, quiet spirit. The stillness at the center of the storm was her. The pressure she always felt before was gone, and in its place, an intoxicating potential.

When she opened her eyes, she was surprised to find Jason's lifeless face below her. She touched his cheek, leaving a bloody smudge, then lifted her gaze to the approaching men. There were fewer than before, but those that remained were nearing the crown of the hill. She focused on the man at the center of the mob. Agmar hesitated, his gloating smile faltering. When she lurched to her feet, he startled and took a step back. They locked eyes for the space of a heartbeat, then Agmar drew his arm back and hurled a stone. Minna threw her hands towards him and screamed.

The potential bottled up inside her exploded outward, an immense pressure wave that crashed into the men, throwing them down the slope. They tumbled, coming to a stop in a hollow at the base of the hill. The wave passed over them, spreading outward, driving everything not anchored to the ground before it, until it impacted the sturdy buildings at the western edge of the village. The walls flexed and groaned, windows shattered and doors splintered. The walls held, directing the force upward where it tore at the eaves, before spending its fury in the open air.

Minna saw all this in a horrifying flash as she crumpled and fell over Jason's body.

She drifted in darkness, alone and empty, without the *lan'and*. Slowly, her awareness returned, and she dragged herself awake. The men who surrounded her were scattered around the base of the hill. Some of them were groaning and moving feebly, but many lay still. Evidence of the magnitude of the blast was everywhere. None of the buildings escaped damage. Debris littered the ground. A large wagon lay on its side. The corner of the general store was ablaze.

Feeling slow, as if she were moving through molasses, she took in the devastation. "No," she whispered. Staggering to her feet, she took a stumbling step and tripped over Jason's body, falling into the remains of the meal he so carefully arranged for them. He lay still, the blood smeared across his temple and leaking into his hair, glinting red in the light of the flames. "Oh no, no, Jason." She crawled to his side, her trembling hands hovering above his face. "Jason, wake up." Her tears spattered his face, leaving red tracks down his cheek.

She looked up at a crowd approaching on the road from the village square. "Help!" she called, waving her arms to get their attention.

"Witch! She's a witch! Get her!"

One of the men who attacked her had recovered and was pointing at her.

Minna extended her hands in entreaty, and the men flinched. "No!" she said. "No! I didn't..." Her gaze swept over the scene, settling on the crowd approaching from the festival. She looked down at Jason again and reached for him when the cry of, "Witch! Get her!" sounded again and was joined by others.

Some men, fear and rage on their faces, approached warily. "No," she whispered, then stood on shaky legs and backed toward the trees. Stones struck her on her chest and thigh, and she cried out. With one last look at Jason, she fled into the forest, chased by voices rising behind her as the crowd gathered at the edge of the wood. She ran blind, her arms in front of her face to ward off whipping branches.

She ran without thinking, needing to put distance between herself and Jason's lifeless body, to escape the anger and violence. The voices grew more distant, but she ran on until the branches above became so thick she could no longer see the shadowy trunks of the trees. Still, she ran until she slammed into a tree. She hit the ground hard and lay on the damp forest floor, gasping.

When she could finally draw a breath, she sat up, tense, listening for sounds of pursuit. It was quiet. Not even the forest animals broke the silence. Minna stared into the darkness, and the crushing weight of a despair she held at bay for years fell on her. She drew in a heaving breath, searing her chest where she impacted the tree. She opened her mouth to scream her anguish, but breathless, she could make no sound. Hugging herself, she fought desperately for breath. When the dam broke, a low moan escaped her throat. "No, no, no, nooo!" The memory of Jason collapsing to the ground played over and over in her mind. She wept until she had no strength left and then, mercifully, she escaped through the door of unconsciousness.

Chapter 14

Deirdre

Deirdre flipped idly through the pages of the treatise on the *saa'myn*. She read it so many times, she practically knew it by heart. Yet, she couldn't help hoping, somehow, to find something she didn't see before. It was frustrating, hinting at deeper truths, but omitting the crucial details she needed. She was convinced the answers she needed lay with the *saa'myn*. Perhaps a deeper understanding of the spirits would unlock the secrets the ancient sisters understood.

Unfortunately, she was running out of time. Briana would force a confrontation soon, she was sure of it, and what would she do then? Was she willing to start a civil war within the Seidi? Until recently, Briana and her allies seemed content to allow Deirdre to remain Malefica. After all, it was Deirdre's allies at the front, who were holding the Kaileuk back. What changed? She didn't know, but she felt the emperor's hand in it. She let her head drop, resting her forehead on the back of her hand. When she tumbled into bed late each night, her worries clamored for her attention, troubling her sleep. If she could just rest for a few moments…

A knock at her door jolted her awake. She shook herself and rubbed her face before saying, "Yes, come in."

The door swung open, and the young novice serving as her assistant in Lachton stepped through. "Excuse me, Malefica, but there is an Inquisitor Harold Wolfe who is rather insistent on seeing you."

"Inquisitor? Wolfe?" She shook her head and said through a yawn, "Did he say what he wanted?"

"No. He refused to tell me, but wouldn't let me put him off. He said you would want to hear what he has to say, and he has a letter from Sister Nia."

"Nia? Did he give it to you?"

"No, mistress."

Deirdre closed the book. "Very well, show him in." She stood, gathering herself, trying to shake the fuzziness from her head. A visit from an inquisitor was rarely good news.

The novice entered again, followed by a man in an inquisitor's uniform. Deirdre didn't know what to make of him. She was sure Malleus Hoerst, a stickler for appearances, would not approve. A rumpled uniform, dark circles under his eyes and several day's growth of beard contributed to an overall unkempt appearance. Yet, he entered the room with a casual grace that belied his appearance. His eyes wandered the room with interest, apparently in no hurry despite his insistence on speaking with her. When he looked at her, his pale gray eyes struck her. Too light for the Volloch caste. Now she remembered who he was. He was the Volbroch inquisitor. This was very mysterious. If Malleus Hoerst had official business with her, he would not send this man.

He stopped in front of her desk, nodding a greeting, a small smile at the corners of his mouth. "Malefica, good afternoon. I don't believe we've ever met."

Deirdre watched him, expecting him to grow uncomfortable under her scrutiny, as most people did. Instead, he stood, relaxed, returning her gaze, his smile not faltering. "No, we haven't." He dipped his head in acknowledgment, but remained silent. "I have heard of you, of course."

He lifted his eyebrows, nodding slowly. "Yes, I've heard of you as well."

Deirdre frowned. Something about the way he said it suggested the words meant more than their face value. "Has anyone told you, you don't look much like an inquisitor, I mean, besides the uniform?"

His grin widened. "Indeed, they have. It must be true, as I hear it a lot lately."

Was this a joke? "What can I do for you, Inquisitor? I understand you have a letter for me from Nia?"

"Ah, yes." He fished a crumpled envelope from a pocket and handed it over. "Nia is a delight. Seeing a former member of my escort. What are the odds of that, do you imagine?"

Again, there was an odd note to his voice, but Deirdre, curious about the letter, ignored it. "Yes, she speaks highly of Joseph." She sat and gestured to a chair. "Have a seat, Inquisitor."

He sat, resting his hands on the armrests, right leg crossed over his left. "Please, you can call me Harold, Malefica."

Deirdre turned the letter over, examining it. The handwriting looked right, and it had Nia's seal. She broke the seal and extracted the letter.

Dierdre,

I'm writing this letter to introduce Inquisitor Harold Wolfe. I wish we could speak to him together, but the urgency of his information prevents me from waiting until you return. He can explain it to you. I know we don't know the Inquisitor well, but I don't sense any deception in him, and Joseph speaks for him. You should make your own judgment as to his credibility.

Yours,

Nia

It was frustratingly brief. She looked up to find Harold watching her. "Nia says I am to trust you."

"I assumed as much."

Deirdre looked back at the letter. Nia wrote that she didn't sense any deception in this man. One of Nia's many gifts was the ability to detect lies, but it was one of her weaker gifts and she had been fooled before.

"Does the Malleus know you're here?"

For some reason, this made him chuckle. "Malefica, I'm afraid I don't have a lot of time. How about I just tell you what I came to say, and you can make up your mind?"

"Okay."

Harold took a deep breath. "Nia tells me you have an interest in the *Alle'oss* witches."

Deirdre glanced involuntarily at the book on her desk, alarm bells going off in her head. From most people, this would be a dangerous question, but from an inquisitor... Nia said to trust him. She pursed her lips, then gazed steadily at him and said, "Yes, that's true."

"Can I ask why?"

"You did say you were in a hurry, didn't you?"

Harold nodded. "Yes, I did, didn't I. Malefica, are you aware what the Inquisition does to the *Alle'oss* witches they bring to the Inquisition fortress?"

Deirdre could not have guessed what this man was here to talk to her about, but even so, the question surprised her. No one besides Nia knew of her disgust at the Inquisition's methods. If Hoerst knew, she would expect them to send more than this one inquisitor. But perhaps he was probing, searching for weaknesses. "I am aware of what the Inquisition does in Argren. We get regular reports from the Malleus."

With a small shake of his head, he said, "Forgive me, Malefica, but that sounds like a carefully worded deflection. I didn't ask about Argren. What do those reports say happens to the witches when they arrive in Brennan?"

Deirdre hesitated, allowing her irritation to subside and noting the sudden tension in his face as he waited for her answer. What was he looking for? "They're execute. According to Church doctrine." She winced slightly as she said, "The reports are quite detailed."

She detected the slightest narrowing of his eyes before his face relaxed and he turned his gaze to the bookshelves behind her head. "Yes, that is what everyone believes. That's what I believed until recently." He focused on her face again. "Turns out that is not what happens to them, at least, not all of them."

Deirdre stared at him. "What are you saying?"

"They hold some of the girls in the prison, unharmed, before they transport them somewhere in the Northern Mountains." He shrugged. "Where, I don't know."

"For what purpose? We've heard nothing about this."

A momentary twist to his mouth signaled his frustration. "I'm afraid I don't know that, either. All I know for sure is that Malleus Hoerst is behind it. His personal guard escorts the prisoners, and they are very secretive about it."

"How do you know this?"

"I've checked the records, seen the prisoners and talked to the guards. There is no doubt."

Deirdre's mind whirled. So much of her time and resources were devoted to finding out what the emperor and Briana were up to. Never once did she suspect Hoerst. Not that there was any love lost between them, but she always considered Hoerst a bit of a toady. But what was this man's motivation? An inquisitor, a man she didn't know, came all the way to Lachton to tell her this? What did he want from her? When she focused on him again, she found him watching her, expectation in the lift of his brows. "Why are you telling me this?"

He shrugged, the weary nonchalance back. "Nia said you would want to know."

For a man in a hurry, he didn't seem able to come to the point. "Harold, what is your specific concern? Are you concerned that the witches are escaping justice or are you concerned about what Malleus Hoerst is doing with them?"

The small lines at the corners of his eyes smoothed, and he grew still. "Justice. Malefica, do you think what happens in Argren is just?"

A flash of emotion. That was interesting. "It's the law, is it not? To suggest otherwise is heresy. I would expect an inquisitor to know that."

He looked up at the ceiling, took a deep breath, blew it out, then returned his gaze to Deirdre. "Yes, I know the law. What I'm asking is do you believe it's *just* to steal children from their families, drag them to the prison and kill them... even if it's in Daga's name?"

Deirdre couldn't reconcile what he was saying with anything she knew about the Inquisition. She stared at him. "But you're an inquisitor."

He lifted his hands, palms up, a hint of exasperation leaking into this voice. "Yes, I'm an inquisitor. Witness and accomplice to the horrors the Inquisition perpetrates. I know better than most what I'm talking about." He paused, pressing his lips together, gathering himself. "I'm not asking what the law is or what the Inquisition does." A note of pleading crept into his voice as he asked, "I'm asking whether *you* think what we do is just."

What did he want from her? "Our official position is that the Inquisition is authorized to carry out Daga's will as promulgated by the Vollen Church."

They stared at one another. Deirdre saw disappointment, then resignation cross his features, before the weary mask covered it. He sighed and stood. "I'm sorry to have bothered you, Malefica. I suggest you find out what the Malleus is up to. I suspect whatever it is, will not be good for either of us. Now, if you will excuse me, I have an urgent appointment in Fennig."

Fennig? She stood and called after him, "Excuse me... Harold. Did you say Fennig?"

He paused, turning back. "Yes, it's a small, remote village in Argren. Do you know of it?"

"I've heard of it. Can I ask what urgent business you have in Fennig?"

He gave her a guarded look. "It's of a personal nature."

"So, it's not official business of the Inquisition?"

"No."

"Does it have anything to do with the fact that Inquisitor Schakal recently left for Fennig?"

Harold hesitated before saying, "Indirectly."

It was quick, nearly undetectable, but Deirdre saw an unidentifiable emotion flicker across his face. Was it anger or fear?

Nia said she could trust this man, but the defenses she erected in the years since Ragan opened her eyes were not easily abandoned. If he was an agent of the Malleus, what she was about to say would be heresy, punishable by death. She took a deep breath, a sense of leaping from a precipice speeding her heart. Gathering herself, she said, "No, Harold, I don't think what the Inquisition does is just." She watched his reaction, holding her breath, expecting a look of triumph. What she saw instead was a reflection of her own relief, a recognition of the risk she had taken. She let her breath out, sagged, and said, "When I became Malefica, I believed I could right the wrongs I saw committed by the Empire. Now, it seems there is little I can do to affect anything of importance. I find the Inquisition's actions abhorrent, but I'm powerless to stop it."

"But, by all accounts, you're the most powerful sister in a generation." His eyes roved over her tattoo.

Deirdre's fingers touched the mark of her rank. "Yes, even so, that no longer means what it once might have." Deirdre's eyes fell to the book on her desk. "Inquisitor, you've spent time among the *Alle'oss*. You must know more about them than most. Have you heard of the spirits or the *saa'myn?*"

"Spirits, no, but the *saa'myn* were *Alle'oss* spiritual leaders, branded as heretics. The Inquisition largely eliminated them years ago."

A flicker of hope sped her heart. "Largely? Do you believe any survived?"

He shrugged. "There are rumors, but the Inquisition places little stock in them." He studied her face, perhaps noticing the disappointment she couldn't hide. "Still, although Argren isn't a large place, it is mostly trackless mountain terrain. There is much the Empire doesn't control. I suppose it's possible."

Deirdre stood, came around her desk and pulled the treatise toward her, opening it to the first page. "This is a description of the *saa'myn,* written some years ago by an anthropologist from the Imperial Academy." Harold stepped up beside her, his shoulder brushing hers, leafing through the pages. "How much do you understand about Abria's gift?"

"Only what everyone is told," Harold answered absently. "A thousand years ago, Daga blessed a woman named Abria with the ability to wield Daga's essence. What her specific gifts were is no longer known for sure, but they must have given her tremendous power because her clan descended from the small mountainous nation of Vollen to create the Empire."

"Yes! The Church teaches that Abria's gift is a blessing from Daga to the Volloch caste, his chosen people. Yet, if what the Church says is true, why would Daga bestow this blessing on so many of the Brochen caste? It's the *Alle'oss* now, mostly, but before it was the Ferol and before that the Andian." When he looked at her, she gazed at his eyes and added, "That is one of the reasons why so few of those people remain. Unlike the *Alle'oss*, they rebelled and were crushed."

With only the smallest hesitation, he said, "Well, the official explanation is that Brochen witches don't have Abria's gift. Somehow, they're stealing Daga's essence." When Deirdre snorted at this, Harold smiled and returned his attention to the book. "There are complex metaphysical explanations, but, frankly, if you're expecting the Empire's religion to be logically consistent, you'll be disappointed. The truth the Church established the Inquisition after the Reformation to ensure the Volloch maintain their privileged position."

Deirdre stared at him. It was so close to her own thoughts, it was as if he read her mind. She glanced involuntarily at his white uniform.

Harold, studying the book, didn't notice. "I don't know how your magic works. The Seidi guards its secrets well." He glanced at her, a grin softening his features. "But the *Alle'oss* witches seem as if they are far more powerful than any sister I've met."

"Have you seen them using magic?"

He looked up at the tension in her voice. "No, the Inquisition works hard to capture them while they're young, before they have learned to harness it."

"Then it's only the strength of their presence you're basing this judgment on?"

"Yes. They have no one to teach them to hide themselves, so it's rather easy, usually. For most of us, that is." For some reason, this brought another grin to his face. "It's why the Inquisition worked so hard to eliminate the *saa'myn,* to eliminate that knowledge."

Deirdre placed her hand on the book, unable to hide the eagerness in her voice. "This treatise doesn't mention that the *saa'myn* were powerful, quite the opposite, in fact."

Harold nodded. "That is my understanding as well, though I suppose it would be difficult to tell for sure because the *Alle'oss* people are… were, a peaceful people. The *saa'myn* never used magic aggressively. They were spiritual leaders, healers, seers."

"Then why are the witches you see different?"

Harold looked back at the book and began tapping the page thoughtfully. "I suppose the *saa'myn* came by their magic without Abria's gift, and the Brochen witches we see today are blessed with Abria's gift. Relations between castes are, officially, illegal, but… things happen. Maybe, because the *Alle'oss* are naturally sensitive to Daga's essence, Abria's gift has a greater effect on them."

Deirdre stared at him until Harold looked at her. "Does Hoerst know this?" she asked.

Harold became still. "It couldn't be. The Volloch would never allow such blasphemy. Can you imagine what the Church would make of it? Besides, how could he hope to control the witches? After what the Inquisition has done in Argren, they would turn on him as soon as they could."

"I don't know, but it would explain why he's keeping them alive."

Harold's brows drew together. "Maybe. It seems unlikely, but I suppose it's worth investigating."

"Harold, I'm not sure how much you know about the war in the south and the role of the Seidi there, but it's not going well. The sisters there are nearing collapse, and, without them, the army won't be far behind."

"Yes, Nia mentioned it. Some trick, keeping that secret."

"Yes, well, that is another conversation. But my point is, in the face of an existential threat, religious principles are easily cast aside. If Hoerst offered them a way to maintain their comfortable ignorance, I would imagine the Church could manufacture some justification that satisfied their sensibilities."

Harold hesitated, studying her face. "Are you suggesting that what Hoerst is doing is a good thing... anything to save the Empire?"

"Absolutely not! He's kidnapping these girls from their families and is sneaking them off in the dead of night. Whatever his intentions are, I sincerely doubt they are for the good of those girls, or even for the Empire."

"So, what do we do?"

"First, we find out where they are taking the girls. We can decide what to do about it when we know. Second, I want to talk to one of the *Alle'oss* witches. We need to understand them." It was possible their strength was purely inherent, as Harold believed, but Deirdre still held out hope that part of it was their knowledge of the spirits. Knowledge they could impart to her. In either case, it was better to have powerful allies than enemies.

Harold's grin widened. "I may be able to accommodate you there. Five years ago, I went to Fennig to bring in a witch. When I got there and saw her..." He hesitated, gave a small shrug and then lowered his voice, as if making a confession. "I had a change of heart."

"You let her live?"

"To this day, I couldn't explain exactly why, and she was not the last. She might be exactly what you are looking for. She had the strongest presence of anyone I've ever encountered. If she's still alive, she would be old enough to harness her power. I'm afraid Stefan has gone to Fennig to find her. If I'm not too late, I'll try to bring her back."

"By yourself? Stefan took eight guards with him."

"Yes, well, I was rather hoping you might help with that." He closed the book and faced her. "Technically, you have authority over the Inquisition. You could order Stefan to hand her over to me."

Deirdre shook her head. "Unfortunately, it's a technicality without meaning. You might use my name to intimidate a younger inquisitor, but

Stefan would refuse, and it would raise questions we're not prepared to answer." She could see his disappointment and offered, "I can, perhaps, even the odds. Stefan has a sister with him. A woman named Keelia. I think you might confide in her. I'll give you a message, so she knows we've spoken." She wrote a quick note.

Keelia,

This note is to introduce Inquisitor Harold Wolfe. Harold has my complete trust and is on an urgent mission for me. I don't wish to write the details in the note in case it is intercepted. I would ask you to assist him in any way you can.

Malefica Deirdre

She sealed it with wax and handed it to him. "I'm not sure how she can help, but at least you'll have an ally."

He nodded, took the note, and turned to leave.

On impulse, Deirdre called after him. "Wait... Harold." He paused, and Deirdre hesitated. "You've spent a lot of time in Argren."

"More than most, I would say."

"Have you ever encountered sisters there?" She frowned, gesturing oddly with her hand. "I mean, women who may be trying to hide the fact they are... were... sisters."

"Friends of yours?"

Deirdre dropped her eyes, tidying papers on her desk. "Yes."

"Not personally, though I've heard stories." When Deirdre didn't respond, Harold said, "The Seidi sends sisters and novices into Argren. Have you asked them?"

"I ask everyone who travels in Argren." Deirdre was horrified to hear the tremor in her voice. She cleared her throat and continued. "It's important to the Seidi to determine what happened to them."

"More than a friend, then."

Deirdre met his eyes. "It shows, does it?"

"Let's just say I recognize the signs." Deirdre returned his sad smile. "I'll keep an eye out."

"Thank you. I would appreciate it." She extended a hand and Harold took it. "If you can bring this girl back, hide her and send a message to Nia or me. We'll be in Brennan. In the meantime, Nia and I will try to find out what Hoerst is up to. Good luck, Harold."

He nodded, turned, and left.

Deirdre wiped the moisture from her cheeks, a sense of hope she hadn't felt in weeks swelling her chest.

Chapter 15

Stefan

Stefan watched Sister Keelia's back, swaying in time to her horse's gait, her short black hair bobbing with every step. You couldn't see it now, under the gray overcast, but the sunlight brought out ruby highlights in her hair, lending her a touch of the exotic. She took to riding ahead of the rest of them after the first night. He hoped she would provide a pleasant distraction during the long ride, but unfortunately, she made her opinion of Stefan quite clear. Her short, searing rebuke accounted for almost every word she spoke in the two weeks it took them to get to this Daga forsaken village. He still caught the occasional smirk from the brothers in his escort when they thought he wasn't looking. Apparently, she was too good for a little harmless flirting. It was a shame, really; the sister was quite attractive or would have been without that hideous tattoo on her face. He never understood why the sisters marred themselves in that way. He could tell from the tattoo that she was a full sister of considerable rank. Rumors had it she was fresh from the front, apparently some kind of hero, but his prodding of that experience met a stone wall. Stefan found her morose. Still, the way she swayed in the saddle was pleasantly distracting.

They must be getting close, though there were few recognizable landmarks this far into Argren. It was one long, dreary day after another, plodding through a forest that, to his eyes, never varied. If forced to, he would admit the mountains in their autumn colors held a certain charm, but the leaves had already fallen and without them, the dark silent forest seemed to watch, begrudging their passage. He peered at the low clouds, pulling his cloak tighter. Before he left Brennan, his assistant, Walter, warned him winter would come soon to the Eastern Mountains, blocking the high mountain passes for months. He shuddered at the thought of being stuck on the eastern side of the mountains with only his escort and the sister for company. He barely knew these men, but then he had never developed an easy camaraderie with his escort. Gazing sourly at Sister Keelia, he decided he should have asked for a novice instead of a full sister.

In the old days, before the Malleus elevated him, a novice always accompanied him. Novices were younger, more pliant, easily impressed by his stature as an inquisitor. Among inquisitors, only Stefan insisted on being accompanied by a representative of the Seidi. People assumed it was because he enjoyed a bit of female company during the long days in the saddle and frosty nights by a fire. There was some truth to that, but the real reason was a shameful secret. Stefan had very little sensitivity to Daga's essence. He couldn't hope to find a witch on his own unless he happened to bump into her. That he was an inquisitor at all was because of his father.

Stefan's relationship with his father was complicated. A cardinal of the Vollen Church, Holger Schakal was a pious and domineering man, whose influence within the Empire was eclipsed only by the Emperor and the High Priest. Even by the Draconian standards of the Empire, Stefan had to admit his father held extreme views. As cardinal of the northwestern archdiocese, he authored the 313th diktat, ensuring the extermination of the Ferol after their rebellion. A fact that Stefan relished every time he looked into Harold's gray eyes.

Cardinal Schakal's dream for his only son was to become the Malleus, and he raised him according to the strict asceticism he thought proper for that lofty position. Stefan would forever remember his father's face when his son's deficiency became too obvious to deny. It seemed that Stefan would never reach the heights his father wished for him. But the old man was not one to let reality derail his dreams. He used his influence with the Malleus at the time, a man named Ulvan, to get Stefan into the Inquisition. Once in, Stefan made powerful friends, including the current Malleus, Hoerst. They shielded him from discovery, cultivating him for his current role. Hoerst cared little what gifts Stefan didn't have. He only demanded the blind loyalty, and the ruthlessness required to help him achieve his aims, two traits Stefan's father could instill in him.

The only problem they had to overcome was that Stefan had to operate in the field long enough to justify his promotion by Hoerst. While every brother was required to have a certain sensitivity to Daga's essence, for most, it was only enough to stand in the presence of a witch with minimal discomfort. Inquisitors were chosen for their ability to detect witches. They could, of course, have combed the ranks for brothers who had the required gifts and placed these men on his escort. But it would only have been a matter of time before his secret was out. Gossip and rumor were favorite pastimes among the rank and file of the Inquisition. It was Hoerst who suggested he request novices to accompany him, and it worked. The young women proved easy to manipulate. The trips with Stefan were usually their first times out of the cloistered world of the Seidi. Naïve and eager to prove themselves, Stefan merely had to flatter them a bit, then pretend he was allowing them to demonstrate their abilities.

Although he was sure some suspected, no one let on if they did, especially now that he was the Malleus's fixer. No one except Harold Wolfe. A flush rose along his neck. He could see it in Harold's eyes; he knew. Always so smart, with his clever insults and insinuations. Harold had secrets, he was sure of it, and Stefan would savor extracting them in the most brutal and humiliating fashion he could devise. That snide half-breed wouldn't be so clever when he was done with him. Stefan's horse stopped walking and craned his neck around to glare reproachfully at him. Lost in angry fantasies, Stefan had been twisting the reins with clenched fists. Glancing at his escort, he forced himself to relax and prod his horse back into a walk. Taking a deep breath and exhaling slowly, a satisfied smile settled on his face. He would take care of that thorn in his side when he returned to Brennan.

Keelia pulled her horse to a stop and stood in her stirrups, looking down the road. After a moment, she sat and looked back, scowling. "I sense someone ahead."

Stefan had concluded the scowl was her normal expression. When he drew even with her, he gazed down the highway for what he thought was enough time to show he was considering his options, then he gestured ahead and said, "Excellent, you may take the lead."

Keelia gazed at him longer than was strictly necessary, the scowl slowly sliding into a smirk. "Yes... sir."

Stefan felt himself blushing as he watched her receding back. The woman was insolent. He glanced at his escort, who were looking everywhere but at him, then urged his horse forward.

As they rounded a curve, a small house, set back from the highway, came into view. It was a typical home for the *Alle'oss* who lived outside the cities. On a low rise, nestled in among the forest, it was constructed of logs with a cedar shingle roof. It had a larger middle section, which Stefan knew was a common or family room. It also had two smaller wings on either end, which were likely bedrooms or pantries. A covered porch extended the width of the middle section. A trough sat next to the well's pump handle at one end of the porch. The trees were cleared to the east of the house to make way for a small shed. There were no people visible, but smoke rose from the chimney. Stefan almost forgot how cramped and primitive these people's homes were.

The sister pulled her horse to a stop and gestured toward the house. "She's in there."

Stefan stopped beside her, pulled his shoulders back and made a show of studying the house. Clearing his throat, he adopted the leading tone he found so successful with novices. "Inquisitor Zebert said the witch he sensed was the strongest he ever felt before." He tipped his head so that he was looking down at her. "In your opinion, could this be the one he was referring to?"

She twisted in her saddle and studied his face, brow furrowed as if she wasn't sure what to make of him. But as she watched him, her brow smoothed, and the corner of her mouth quirked up into that infuriating smirk. Stefan was ashamed to feel a blush reddening his cheeks again. She nodded slowly and said, "Could be. She's certainly powerful." After a pause, one eyebrow lifted, and she asked, "What do you think?"

Stefan coughed. "Yes, I quite agree." He nodded to one of the brothers. "Sergeant Ellgar, if you will."

A standard escort for an Inquisitor in relatively safe areas like southern Argren was four brothers, consisting of a sergeant and three companions-at-arms. In northern Argren, where partisan activity was more organized, ten men accompanied an inquisitor. It was only recently that a small number of rebels began causing the Empire trouble in the south. They would pacify Argren soon enough, but in the meantime, the rising violence was the reason Stefan brought two escorts and was forced to put up with Sister Keelia.

The three brothers under Sergeant Ellgar's command, dismounted and approached the house, spreading out and drawing their swords. Ellgar stepped onto the porch and pounded on the door, shouting, "Open the door in the name of the Inquisition!" There was no response. The sergeant looked at Stefan, who nodded. Ellgar stepped back and kicked the door with his heel. Though the door held, the splintering crack was accompanied by a squeal from inside. The door gave way on the third kick, and the sergeant shoved the broken door aside and entered the house. He reappeared after a short time and shook his head. "No one here."

"Then who squealed?" Stefan asked. He smirked at the sister, who rolled her eyes before dismounting and walking toward the house with Stefan in her wake. The common room looked like so many he saw before. In the middle of the back wall, a fire burned in a fireplace surrounded by a stone hearth. Rugs from some shaggy creature and two rustic rocking chairs were arrayed in front of it. A basket with knitting supplies sat in the corner next to a rack with several long bows and quivers full of arrows. In the center of the room was a long trestle table and benches. Everything was tidy, with the exception of one of the benches which lay on its side. A brother exited one of the side rooms and shook his head. Stefan looked at Keelia. She was studying the room, hands on her hips, lips drawn into a tight line. When she caught Stefan's eye, she hesitated, jaw muscles working. It looked, for a moment, like she was going to ignore him. But then she pointed out a small leather strap, difficult to see in the dim light, nailed to the floor where the bench should have been.

"Sergeant," Stefan said.

Ellgar grasped the strap and pulled up a section of the floor, revealing a small root cellar. A woman and young girl huddled in the corner, their pale faces and wide eyes seeming to glow in the shadowy light. As Ellgar started down the stairs, Stefan smiled, intending to congratulate Keelia, but the sister's expression silenced him. Turning her back on the scene, she swept out of the house.

Stefan watched until the woman launched herself at the big sergeant, then followed Keelia, screams and the sounds of a scuffle chasing him out the door. He found the sister standing near the highway, gazing intently toward the trees on the far side. Something about the way she was standing, leaning slightly forward, her arms by her sides, fists clenched, caught his attention. He approached her quietly, searching the trees for what drew her attention. He was almost even with her when she startled, glanced over her shoulder, then strode toward her horse. Was that guilt he saw on her face? He watched her go, then scanned the trees, finding only a stretch of forest indistinguishable from what he looked at for days.

A commotion behind him drew his attention. One of his companions-at-arms exited the house, carrying the witch over his shoulder. The sergeant followed, a thunderous expression on his face and blood dripping from a cut above his eye. The girl kicked, beat the brother's back and screamed. Ellgar grabbed a handful of her blond hair, pulling her head up until she was looking at him, and growled, "Shut up or you'll get what your mother got."

Dropping her next to his horse, the brother withdrew a pair of manacles and a leather hood from his saddlebag. The witch, taking advantage of his distraction, leapt to her feet and dashed toward the forest. She brushed by Keelia, who stepped aside. As she dodged past, Stefan reached out and tripped her. She landed hard on her chest, grunting as the air was forced from her lungs. Still, she tried to regain her feet, but stepped on the hem of her dress and fell again, giving the sergeant time to catch up with her and wrap his hand around the back of her neck.

"I told you to stop it."

When she stopped struggling, he lifted her to her feet by the scruff of her neck and her upper arm. She stood immobile, face screwed up in pain, as the brother attached the manacles and pulled the hood over her head. Just before the hood covered her face, her eyes widened, and Stefan was sure he saw her look toward the forest, mouthing words soundlessly. While Sergeant Ellgar lifted her to sit in front of one of the mounted brothers, Stefan turned back toward the trees. Something was not right.

When he turned back, Keelia was watching him intently. He said the mounted brother sitting behind the witch, "Sergeant Siegleman, take the girl and head back to Brennan. We'll catch up with you." He glanced at the trees again and added, "Sergeant Ellgar, the village should be close. I want to go question the inhabitants. It seems the people of Fennig have been harboring a witch."

"Yes, sir."

Keelia watched him, wearing her usual scowl. Stefan smiled at her.

Minna

Minna woke to the sounds of voices and people crashing through the forest. It seemed the villagers found their courage in the daylight and were looking for her. Some part of her whispered for her to flee, but a deep lethargy weighed her down. The events of the previous night played in her slow mind. Images of destruction, of bodies, people she knew, scattered like leaves by... whatever it was she did. How many did she kill? She rolled onto her back, staring through bare branches, black against heavy gray clouds. Jason was dead. With a great effort, she lifted her hands and held them in front of her face, turning them this way and that, then touching the blood, staining her fingers, to her lips. Her pursuers drew closer. It wouldn't be long now. She wanted them to find her. She deserved whatever they had in mind.

She swiped at the tears moistening her temples and caught something between her fingers. Lifting it, she saw it was the ribbon Alyn used to bind her hair. She stared it, fluttering in the soft breeze. What would become of Alyn if the villagers found Minna? Would she be next? The whispers that were telling her to flee reminded her of the promise she made to her sister. *I'll help you. I'll never leave you alone.* Clenching the ribbon in her fist, she rolled onto her stomach, wincing as her muscles complained. A deep breath earned her a sharp pain in her chest. Breathing carefully, she took a moment to inventory her various injuries, and concluded none of them was serious enough she couldn't walk. She pushed herself unsteadily to her feet, then glanced around to get her bearings. She ran north and west from the village and was at least four leagues from home. With a last glance toward her pursuers, she moved quietly away.

As she walked, she felt her ribs and concluded nothing was broken. Her other injuries, minor scrapes and bruises where the rocks struck and strained muscles she incurred during her flight through the forest were minor. Once she was satisfied she had no serious injuries, she considered her options. She wanted to talk to her father. Though he wasn't here, he told her what to do before he left. She would go to the falls and wait, and she would take Alyn with her. Alyn wasn't accustomed to the forest, but she would adapt. They would wait for their father to come for them. A small voice asked what they would do if he didn't come, but she shook the thought away. The first thing to do was to get away, to get somewhere safe.

She felt them before her house came into view. Recognizing Alyn's presence, but not the others, she approached cautiously, peering at the house from behind the same tree she watched the man in white weeks before. When she saw the horses in the yard, her heart raced, and for a moment, she thought her father might have returned. But the small hope was crushed when she noticed the four men standing in the yard wore white uniforms. These were not the same men who took her father away.

Noticing their front door laying in pieces, a deep foreboding came over her. A woman with short black hair exited, looking back over her shoulder. When her head came back around, Minna had to squint to be sure what she was seeing. At first, she thought the woman was scarred on the left side of her face, but as she approached the road, Minna saw the marks had a regular pattern of swirls and dots, like someone painted them on her face. The woman stopped at the edge of the highway, hands on her hips, scowling at the ground. Suddenly, her head snapped up, eyes wide, mouth dropping open in surprise. She pivoted her head back and forth as if searching, glanced over her shoulder at the mounted men, then stared straight at Minna. Suddenly, Minna felt the ripples of her presence.

How did she do that? It was as if she were invisible, then appeared out of thin air. It was a strong, insistent pulse, more urgent than the lazy ripples she felt from others. Minna felt something like it before, when Alyn tried to call the spirits, but this was much more powerful and continuous. This woman wasn't like Jason or her father, someone who she could sense, but had no control of their presence. She was like her and her sister. Who was she? Could she be a *saa'myn*? Minna was walking toward the highway, questions crowding out her caution.

When a man stepped onto the porch through the ruined door, Minna retreated behind the tree. He wore a white uniform, but it differed from the others, more like the one worn by the man she saw before. Minna couldn't sense his presence at all, not even the dim flicker she felt from the other men. He stopped and peered at the woman, then stalked slowly toward her. Something about the way he watched the woman put Minna on edge. Remembering how Alyn produced the pulse, Minna focused on her center and pulled hard. The *lan'and* reacted instantly, but Minna pushed immediately, and they shot away from her. The woman's eyes widened, then she turned and walked toward the horses.

The man watched her go, then searched the trees, his eyes passing over Minna's hiding place. She wanted to run, but the thought of what might be happening in the house and the mystery of the woman held her. When two soldiers emerged, one of them carrying Alyn, her heart raced. She started toward the house again, calling the spirits, but they didn't respond. She focused on her center and pulled, hard. Again, there was no response. She looked up to find the branches devoid of the small orbs. Choking down a scream of frustration, she stopped. What could she do? When one of the men yanked Alyn's hair and screamed in her face, Minna started walking toward the house again. She was nearly to the thick underbrush that flourished in the light at the edge of the forest when she felt a powerful pulse that stopped her. The woman was staring straight at her, even though Minna was sure she was still hidden. The woman shook her head quickly, then looked at the man with no presence.

Minna watched her sister's attempted escape, trembling with the need to act. As they pulled a hood down over her head, Alyn looked toward her, and Minna felt the small pulse from her she felt before in the glade. The man stared into the trees again. Minna stood frozen. Her dark green cloak blended into the shadowy foliage, and she dropped her head, so her black hair hid her face. When she heard voices, she peeked through her hair and saw them preparing to leave.

She watched them split into two groups and ride in opposite directions. As the men who took Alyn disappeared around the bend, she left the forest and jogged to the center of the highway. She took a few halting steps after them, but stopped. Was she going to chase them down on foot? Then what? She turned back toward Fennig. The other party was disappearing around a bend. The woman had answers she and Alyn needed. She was with these men, but she warned Minna. Why would she let them take Alyn and save Minna? What was she going to do? Looking down, she noticed Alyn's ribbon fluttering like a pennant from between the fingers of her clenched fist. She bit her lips. There was only one choice. She was going to find her sister, but she needed a plan. First, she needed provisions and a horse.

She started jogging toward her house, then remembered her mother and broke into a sprint. The house was silent when she stepped cautiously onto the porch. Alyn's recent change obviously devastated their mother, but Minna was sure if her mother were alive, she would not be sitting silently in the house while they dragged her daughter away. She peeked around the door frame, afraid of what she would find. It appeared deserted. Everything was normal except for the open root cellar. She tiptoed to the opening on wobbly legs, her heart thudding in her chest. Taking a deep breath, she steeled herself and peered over the edge. The sight dragged a groan from her throat. The contents of the cellar, the food carefully prepared for the winter, were scattered across the floor. Visible at the edge of the square of light cast by the open door were her mother's legs. Minna scrambled down the steps, took a step toward her mother, then stopped, waiting for her eyes to adjust to the gloom. Her mother didn't move or make a sound.

"No, no, no, please, Mama," she whispered and knelt beside her. The right side of her face was swelling, a bruise already forming. There was blood on her temple and lips. Minna put her ear next to her parted lips and felt the tickle of her mother's breath. She let out the breath she didn't know she was holding, took her mother's hand and murmured, "Mama, can you hear me?"

Her mother's eyes fluttered opened, then looked wildly around before they settled on her daughter. Minna felt her mother's flinch in her heart. She let her mother's hand drop, sat back on her heels, stood and backed toward the steps. "Mama, are you okay?"

Her mother pulled herself to a sitting position, her back against the wall, and nodded weakly.

"They took Alyn," Minna said. "The soldiers took her toward the mountains." Her mother made a choking sound that might have been a sob and rested the unbruised side of her face in her hand. "I'm going to go get her."

Her mother nodded before dropping her chin to her chest.

Minna watched her for a moment, then climbed the stairs. She went into her room and grabbed the pack and bow she prepared for a trip to the falls. Back in the common room, she stuffed as much food into her pack as she could. She donned her heavy cloak, then hefted the pack and took one last look around the room. She was about to leave when she paused. On a whim, she went into her parents' room and slid the two books from their shelf. She considered them, then replaced the one that was neatly written and put the other in an inside pocket of her cloak.

When she returned to the common room, her mother stood near the door, leaning heavily against the door frame. They stared at one another. Her mother's eye was nearly swollen shut, but she pulled her lips into a tight line and pushed herself upright. She wobbled for a moment, then steadied herself and walked over to stand in front of Minna. She held out a pair of mittens, and said, "You'll need these in the mountains. It'll be cold."

Minna hesitated, staring at her mother's determined face, then took the mittens. "Thank you, Mama."

The muscles around her mother's eyes were tight, but she didn't flinch.

Aware of what this simple gesture cost her mother, Minna's voice softened as she said, "I'll find her."

"I always loved you, Min. Both of you. I just... I'm sorry... for everything." She reached out and cupped Minna's cheek.

Minna's eyes watered, the tears leaking out and moistening her mother's fingers. "I know, Mama. I'm sorry too." She started to go, then hesitated. "Tell Papa where I went."

Her mother nodded. "Go talk to Marie in town. She's been west of the mountains before, and her brother owns the stables."

"Thank you, Mama. I love you," and then she left.

Chapter 16

Harold

It was snowing in Lachton. While Harold was meeting with Deirdre, fat, fluffy flakes began falling. Swirled by a gusty breeze, they had already left a dusting of snow on the cobbles of the small courtyard outside the Seidi house. Harold wasn't surprised. The temperature began falling as he approached the foothills of the Northern Mountains. The day before he arrived, an icy blast rolled down the slopes of the mountains, knifing through his thin travel cloak. To a southerner like Harold, it was an appalling state of affairs, and might have proved deadly if it arrived a day earlier. He left Brennan in such a hurry, he hadn't considered the possibility winter would have arrived in Lachton. The first thing he did when he entered the city was to procure a thick wool cloak and gloves. Now, his mind full of his meeting with Deirdre, he stood on the steps outside the Seidi house, peering up at the sky, and fumbling at the buttons of the cloak. His fingers, trembling with fatigue, wouldn't cooperate, and with a frustrated groan, he gave up on the buttons, clenched the cloak closed, and trudged across the courtyard to the stable.

He barely acknowledged the two novices, who gave him curious looks and broke into whispers as he passed. The novice he handed his horse to when he arrived was nowhere to be seen, so he shoved his way through the stable doors, letting in a gust of frigid air and drawing annoyed whinnies from the occupants. Every horse came to the front of their stalls, curious about the intruder. All of them except the chestnut stallion that carried him over the final sprint to Lachton. Puzzled, he walked down the aisle, peering into the stalls. He found him jammed into the back of his stall, staring balefully from the shadows. Harold decided at the last minute before leaving Brennan to forgo the horses he could requisition from the Inquisition's livery. Instead, he purchased a mount from someone he knew who could keep a secret. An unannounced visit to the Malefica could only raise unpleasant questions, questions he hoped to avoid. Unfortunately, keeping the trip secret meant he could not acquire fresh mounts at the Imperial outposts between Brennan and Lachton. The stallion, which he named *Chak'do*, obstinate in *Alle'oss*, was only the third horse he had been able to procure during the trip.

Chuckling, he said, "Don't worry, I wouldn't do that to you again. Your job is done. I, on the other hand…" His voice trailed away, and they stared at one another. "Maybe one night. I could find a small inn. Get a good night's sleep." *Chak'do* had no comment.

Stefan would be in Fennig by now. If Harold wanted to meet them in Hast, he had to leave now. And there were the four men he glimpsed behind him as he climbed into the foothills. The sight sent a thrill of fear through him. The white cloaks, visible for leagues, marked them as Dominicans. If the Empire was a vast evil, the Dominicans were the black heart at its core. Their mandate was ensuring the Inquisition's spiritual purity. Their appearance was rarely good news, and Harold had more than one reason to avoid them. Wanting as much time as he could in Lachton before they arrived, he pushed himself and the unfortunate stallion hard the last two days, resting only long enough to avoid injuring *Chak'do*. It was a punishing effort at the end of a long, exhausting ride. Though he bought himself enough time to meet Deirdre, he didn't want to linger. The problem was, he wasn't sure he was physically or mentally capable of riding at the moment. Even if he could, the frosty nights could be deadly.

"What do you suggest?"

The horse swung his head toward the open stable doors, and Harold followed his gaze. The Seidi house was on the River Road, which connected the city's southern and northern gates, hugging the western bank of the Odun River. He couldn't see the water, but he could see the walls that hemmed it in as it passed through the city. While he watched, a small barge drifted past. The crew, shouting among themselves, used long poles to maneuver the barge past the narrow section. The bright, clear clang of the vessel's brass bell cut through the city's soundscape. Harold and the horse looked at one another. "Good idea," Harold said. Taking a barge down the river to Hast would shave several days off the trip, and, most importantly, he would have a warm place to rest and recover.

Harold stood in the dim stables, staring at *Chak'do*. "The question is what to do with you." The horse responded by laying his ears back against his head. Harold couldn't take him on the barge, and if he left him in the Seidi stables, someone would eventually remember he arrived with Harold and notify the Inquisition. The best thing to do would be to find a good stable in Lachton and sell him. "Don't worry, I'll make sure you have a good home."

Harold managed to saddle the reluctant horse, though the effort left him winded. Despite his fatigue, he couldn't bring himself to force the horse to carry him, so he led him out onto the River Road and made his way toward the busy port in the northern quarter.

It was Harold's first time in Lachton, but in his short time in the city, he decided it was unlike any other city he'd seen in the Empire. Originally a small *Alle'oss* fishing village, it drew the interest of the Imperials for the same reason it did the *Alle'oss*. Besides the fish, mussels and eels harvested from Lake Vitaeshu, north of the city. The surrounding hills were rich in copper and lumber. Harold didn't know the original *Alle'oss* name of the village, but the name of the lake was a corruption of the *Alle'oss* phrase *vitik jyaeshu* which meant white fish.

His expectations of the city were based on what he knew of Hast, as it was the only other *Alle'oss* outpost outside Argren. Hast had a significant *Alle'oss* population, but they were isolated in a ghetto and had few rights. Even though he heard Lachton was different, it still surprised him to find a large community of *Alle'oss* actively involved in the commercial life of the city. He even heard *Alle'oss* spoken openly. One hundred fifty years before, when Imperial geologists discovered iron and coal in Argren, the Empire took an active interest in the region. Missionaries of the Vollen Church were the first to arrive, backed by the Imperial military. They brought with them edicts designed to impose the Empire's will and enforce the caste system. Foremost among these edicts were those designed to eradicate the local religion and language. Both promoted a sense of shared community that encouraged rebellion. Harold knew that many older *Alle'oss* still spoke their language, at least in secret, but it was rare among the young. At first, parents tried to pass it down to their children, but as the generations passed, the language faded, leaving, in some cases, a corrupted pidgin language of *Alle'oss* and Vollen like the one spoken in Hast. Most citizens of the Empire, like Louisa at the Monk's Habit, were not aware of what the Empire did in conquered regions. It was a mark of Aron's bravery, or recklessness, that he spoke his language at Louisa's request.

Lachton grew prosperous by exploiting the resources in and around the lake and through trade with Argren and the Tituun, in the far north. All of it was shipped south on the river to Hast and the small port of Lubern on the Southern Sea. The honey Joseph and Nia sought in the Schiller Square market undoubtedly passed through Lachton. The relatively cosmopolitan attitudes of the Lachtonians made much of this prosperity possible. Harold wondered if they knew how precarious that prosperity was. The Church and the Inquisition hated the city. It was bad enough, from the Inquisition's point of view, that so many Brochen lived without fear of persecution. It was far worse that they owned property and enjoyed the fruits of Lachton's prosperity. Fortunately for the Lachtonians, the emperor was well aware of the contribution their wealth made to his treasury. Now, with his ruinous wars going so badly, Lachton's importance only grew. That would change, of course, with a less pragmatic emperor.

The first four captains he approached refused his request for passage outright. Disappointed and running short of options, he turned toward the last barge docked alongside the quay with little hope. The man he assumed was the captain stood on the quay, glaring at him as he approached. Small and wiry, he wore a shapeless wool hat, pulled low on his head. A tangled mass of red whiskers rose high on his cheeks, and between that and the ragged bangs that sprouted from his hat, he looked like an ill-tempered gnome peering through a hedge. Before Harold could pose a question, the man let go with a stream of colorful language, leaving no doubts about his opinion of inquisitors. It was a brave or foolish act. Most inquisitors would have had him arrested and his barge confiscated for such insults. Harold decided he liked him.

He looked down at himself. Wrapped in a non-regulation cloak, his uniform wasn't visible. "What gave me away?"

"Your boots," the captain said. "The rest of you looks like *sheoda*, but no one outside the Inquisition wears boots like that."

Harold glanced over his shoulder and found two of the other captains watching. When he turned back, he found the small man grinning.

Harold laughed. *"Kīzha alālar ta Hast* (I'm trying to go to Hast.)" The captain began to assemble a scowl until Harold pulled out a bag full of silver eagles and jingled it in front of his nose.

"Ērtsu kuta vikīsir ni sheoda. (Your accent is shit)," he said, but added, "Five silver for the ride."

It was an exorbitant price, but Harold wasn't in a position to bargain, and besides, a warm berth in his present condition was worth a lot more to him than five silver eagles. He counted out three coins and promised two more when they left port.

"Name's Taavi," the captain said. "We leave in two hours, with you or without you."

"Harold."

With two hours until his ride left, Harold set out to make arrangements for *Chak'do*. Fortunately, Taavi provided directions to a nearby stable.

Another curiosity about Lachton was the roads. Imperials liked their cities square and symmetric. Where the Imperials controlled the layout of a city, the roads were arranged in square grids. The roads in Lachton climbed up and around the hills on which the city perched. It reminded him of an *Alle'oss* village, except that most of the city must have been built after the Imperials arrived. After wandering for an hour, attempting to follow Taavi's directions, he had to admit, though Lachton had a certain charm, the Imperials may have the right idea on their streets.

When he finally found the stable, the proprietor stared at him suspiciously until he mentioned Taavi sent him. With little leverage, the negotiation was short and decidedly in the stable master's favor. After ensuring *Chak'do* would go to a good home, he headed back to the port.

The return trip was just as confusing. The stable master assured him he knew a quicker route back to the port, but before long, he was convinced the man's directions were intentionally confusing. He knew he would eventually find the river by always heading downhill, but he didn't have time to wander. Judging that he had maybe a quarter hour before Taavi left, he started to jog, every aching muscle complaining. Most of the roads, in addition to winding with the terrain, were narrow. The small two-wheel carts he saw around the city suddenly made sense. He rounded a curve in one of these lanes and found himself on a wide, straight avenue. He stood on the corner, panting, peering up at a street sign. The Emperor's Way. It was one of the few streets in the city he recognized, because it led straight from the River Road to the Inquisition compound. He passed it on his way to the stable. After searching the street for brothers, and finding none, he turned left and headed toward the river.

Glancing uphill for oncoming traffic, he stepped off the curb to cross to the south side of the street. When he turned back toward the river, he nearly tripped. Turning onto the Emperor's Way from River Road were four riders in white cloaks. These had to be the Dominicans who followed him to Lachton. Resisting the urge to turn and flee, he forced himself to continue across the street and duck into a tavern. There were enough people inside that his entrance attracted only cursory glances. He stood at the door, his breath fogging the small round window in the doorway.

"Hey, you just going to stand at the door, or you ordering?"

Harold glanced back at the bartender, whose question focused the crowd's attention on him. He tucked one foot behind the other and said,

"An ale. Whatever's good." Turning back to the window, he wiped away the fog with a gloved hand.

He could tell the Dominicans were approaching before they appeared. Like the bow wave of a boat, the Lachtonians scattered ahead of them, deciding whatever they were about could wait. A pair of men entered the tavern, brushing past Harold and standing nearby, jealously eying his spot next to the only window.

When the riders finally arrived in his field of view, he was happy to see they looked as beat up as he felt, slumping in the saddle and gazing around with hollow expressions. Several day's growth of beard and rumpled hair were so out of place on a Dominican brother, that for a moment, Harold wondered if he might have been mistaken about who they were. But only for a moment. The fat snowflakes, which were now drifting down in still air, seemed to vanish as they fell in front of the men's white cloaks. It had to be the four who were following him. They must have ridden hard to arrive so soon. What was their hurry?

As soon as they passed out of sight, Harold flipped the bemused bartender an iron penny, nodded to the other men hiding in the tavern, and slipped out the door. Now that the Dominicans' backs were turned, the Lachtonians emerged from their hiding places, and expressed the deep-seated hostility the citizens held toward the brothers. A variety of hand gestures appeared, some of them Harold never saw before, though their intent was obvious. An *Alle'oss* man beside him spat into the road. Two brave men walked into the center of the street, aping the haughty manner of the brothers to much suppressed laughter. Harold stood frozen, shocked and amused at the brazen display of disrespect for some of the most dangerous men in the Empire.

Perhaps sensing some of what was happening behind him, one of the riders turned in his saddle and looked back. The brave citizens of Lachton abruptly remembered they had other appointments. Harold watched them disperse, then looked up the hill and locked eyes with the rider. It took Harold a second to recognize him. He never saw him with a beard before, but the streak of white hair that followed a scar running from his left eye to the crown of his head was unmistakable. His heart lurched, and hot sweat beaded on his back. It was Ivan. The man inserted into his escort without his consent. The man his sergeant, Henrik, told Joseph to warn him about. Ivan was a Dominican.

For a heartbeat they stared at one another, not long enough for Harold's hope that Ivan wouldn't recognize him to fully blossom, then a look of triumph appeared on Ivan's face. Harold fled. At the next intersection, he turned south, Ivan's shout following in his wake.

Before he made it to the next cross street, the horses rounded the corner behind him, their hooves on the cobbles deafening in the narrow lane. He turned east onto a road that bent around to the right. Adrenaline numbed the ache in his tortured body, but it couldn't completely compensate for his depleted muscles. Even after a short sprint, he was laboring, and the sounds of pursuit were coming closer. He followed the road as it curved back to the left, then he shot out onto the River Road, cutting in front of a team of draft horses, laboring to pull a large dray stacked with wooden barrels. The horses shied away. The driver bellowed his anger.

He crossed the road, turned south and ran along the wall on the river side of the road. Ahead, he saw his ride pushing away from the quay. Taavi stood on the cabin roof, shouting instructions to his crew, who pushed the barge away from the dock with long poles. Too winded to shout, Harold kept running. Glancing behind him, he found two of the riders negotiating the narrow space beside the dray. Ivan's horse clattered along the walkway across the road, scattering pedestrians. When he drew even with Harold, he swerved into the road. The horse slipped on the slick cobbles, barely staying upright, granting Harold a reprieve.

Harold sped past the berth the barge recently vacated and continued on, passing the slow vessel. Taavi watched him, shaking his head, but making no move to change course. The horses were right behind him. It crossed his mind that if he took a sword to the head, he would never know what happened. One moment, he would be fleeing for his life, then oblivion. No more pain, no more struggle, no more guilt. Even in the midst of the chase, it surprised him to find it wasn't an appealing thought. Somehow, in the weeks since Karl's revelation, something awakened in

Harold. Though he did not ask for this burden, somewhere along the way, he accepted it as his to carry.

Ivan pulled up beside him, hemming him in against the river. Harold was running out of quay. Glancing to his left, he saw he was even with the bow of Taavi's barge. Just as Ivan veered toward him, Harold leapt onto the last barge moored at the quay, stumbled across the crates stacked on its deck, leapt the open stretch of water between the two barges and landed on the bow of Taavi's vessel, where he fell into an exhausted heap. He lay on his back, sucking in deep, painful breaths, too sore and exhausted to worry about how his pursuers reacted.

"Friends of yours?"

Harold opened his eyes to find Taavi peering down at him. He pushed himself into a sitting position and craned his neck to see over the rail. The Dominicans sat on their horses, watching. "I wouldn't call them friends, exactly."

"Ayuh. Was what I was thinking," the captain said. "*Vo, kustak*," he said and spat into the river, forcing Harold to duck. "That was some escape." Harold gave him a small grin. "What are they after you for?"

Indeed, that was the question. Harold gave a noncommittal grunt. The brothers were riding south on the River Road, passing the barge. Harold looked ahead to a bridge in the distance that arched over the river. "Um," he mumbled.

"Ayuh," Taavi said again, following Harold's gaze. "That *would* be a problem." He smiled, showing a mouth full of yellow teeth. "If we were going that way." He turned away and shouted at his crew in *Alle'oss*. Harold could only understand every third word, but he guessed from the tone, they were variations on a colorful theme.

Ivan was pacing the barge on the road, shouting at him. When Harold smiled at him, his entreaties for him to surrender peacefully gave way to cold threats. Harold glanced ahead and saw that the other brothers were nearing the bridge. Curious about what the captain meant, he turned his attention to the crew. At Taavi's command, the crew thrust their long poles into the water on the starboard side and heaved against them. At first, nothing happened, but ever so slowly, the barge drifted to port.

Harold looked to the bank on the left side of the river and found that it forked about twenty paces before the bridge.

The barge was turning so slowly, he was sure they wouldn't make it, but Taavi and his crew knew their business and as the vessel entered the left fork, Harold couldn't resist a wave to the riders waiting on the bridge.

"Bit cheeky, don't you think?" The captain stepped up beside him, gazing at the bridge as it disappeared behind the buildings that bordered the river.

"Maybe, yeah," Harold answered. "Uh, won't they just find another bridge up ahead of us?"

"Aren't any. This opens up onto the river, just up ahead."

Harold frowned at him. "Aren't we on the river?"

"No, the river runs east of the city. This is a canal."

"But it's called the River Road."

Taavi laughed. "Ayuh. Used to be the river ran through the city, but the Imperials came and decided that wouldn't work. So, they rerouted the river, if you can believe it, and built the canals in the city." Taavi grinned at Harold's expression. "It actually makes some sense. Easier to control flooding in the canals, the current is slower, easier to put bridges across."

Taavi went back to screaming at his crew, and Harold leaned out and looked aft. Two of the Dominicans watched the barge drifting away. That Ivan was a Dominican, and he had been placed on Harold's escort, meant someone was spying on him. It had to be Stefan. The question was, what was Ivan doing here? Not that they didn't have plenty of reasons. Inquisitors had significant autonomy in their actions, but an unannounced trip to Lachton, alone, with no explanation, would invite questions. Even though Harold tried to cover his tracks, Ivan obviously found out somehow. Although it was unlikely, they knew he came to see Deirdre, if they learned of it, the questioning would take place in the dungeon. His biggest concern was that they knew about his visit to the prison. If that was the case, Stefan's workshop would be the last place on earth he saw.

And then there was the witch. With an unfamiliar man on his escort, it was a risk to let her escape. But the opportunity arose, and he took it. Someone must have warned the family an inquisitor was coming, because they fled their home and were hiding in a neighbor's barn. They were fortunate Ivan apparently didn't have sufficient sensitivity to detect their daughter. Harold set Ivan and his other two companions-at-arms to searching the forest around their home and visited the neighbor with Sergeant Henrik. He told the father to take his entire family and move to the northern reaches of Argren. The odds were, the Inquisition would find them eventually, but a slight chance was better than none. Remembering the faces of her parents when they realized he wasn't going to take their daughter, he couldn't bring himself to regret it.

Whatever the reason he was here, Ivan's expression when he recognized him was all Harold need to know he was in trouble.

He watched Ivan and the other Dominicans ride north toward the Emperor's Way. If they were as exhausted as he was, he likely had at least a day before they came after him. Still, he had a feeling he would see them again.

His berth turned out to be a hammock in the room shared by all the crew. Despite the odors of men and women who work hard all day, and a variety of improbable snores, it turned out to be rather pleasant. A small stove warmed the room, and the gentle sway of the hammock lulled him into a pleasantly drowsy state. While he waited for sleep to save him from his many aches, he replayed his meeting with Deirdre. If the Malefica was the mystery woman, she was the greatest mummer in the Empire. Her suspicions at his motivations seemed too genuine, the vulnerability she revealed as he was leaving too raw. It was disappointing she couldn't, or wouldn't, intervene with Stefan, but he wasn't surprised.

While it was unlikely Deirdre was the phantom, Nia, on the other hand, seemed the perfect candidate. Powerful, with inside knowledge of the Seidi and the Inquisition, she appeared at the right place, at the right time, and was quick to offer a course of action. And the mystery of how

Aron knew they would be there that night was easily explained if it was
her. He wasn't ruling her out yet.

The captain's stream of colorful *Alle'oss* followed him into his dreams,
where instead of the captain, Aron spoke to him out of the darkness, his
words, while not as angry, were no less colorful.

Chapter 17

Stefan

As remote as Fennig was, Stefan wasn't expecting much. Even in the parts of Argren close to Hast, the villages were small rustic affairs. Buildings were half-timber frame, logs or uncut stone, and rather than clear an area and lay out a sensible plan, the *Alle'oss* built wherever, tucking buildings in among the trees and the terrain so that it was hard to discern where the village ended, and the forest began. There was usually some sort of community space, but after that, Stefan could find no rhyme or reason to them. Only Kartok or Richeleau came close to Stefan's ideal of a proper city, and he put that down to the strong Imperial presence there. But the town that came into view as they rounded a bend in the road surprised him. Although not as large as Kartok, it was larger than most *Alle'oss* villages. As in Kartok, and much of the Empire, the buildings were constructed of half-timber frame and stone or cut stone, and it appeared from his vantage to be laid out in a sensible way. It reminded him of some of the smaller Imperial towns like Lubern.

The road bent around a large hill, then turned to descend into the heart of the village. Stefan halted his men, his attention drawn by what looked to be significant damage to the buildings facing the hill. Windows gaped open, jagged fragments of glass in many of them. Doors were missing, and their shattered remains could be seen scattered across the floor through the openings. Fire damaged the building next to the road, the ashy scent of smoke still strong. A group of men stood nearby, watching the Imperials and whispering among themselves. Judging by the tools and ladders in evidence, Stefan guessed they were repairing the damage, but had made little progress. What happened here?

As they descended the hill into the center of the village, he turned in his saddle and looked back at Keelia. Her sudden decision to ride behind them reinforced his belief that she was hiding something. Each time he looked back, he found her searching the trees beside the road or looking back the way they came. To his annoyance, this time, he found her examining the village with interest, no trace of her typical scowl. Not until she noticed him watching.

The central square was larger than in most villages and was cobbled. It was deserted, which, in his experience, was unusual enough, but there was more evidence that something was amiss. Vendor stalls, normally dismantled or shuttered when not in use, were open, their wares abandoned. There was a hog, still on a spit over a cold fire. In one stall, there were rows of the small pies that could be held in the hand and contained a variety of sweet or savory fillings. Banners in the colors of Argren, flapping forlornly in the chilly wind blowing off the mountains, festooned the square. As he surveyed the scene, a blue ribbon of the type the *Alle'oss* women wove into their hair at festivals, caught by the swirling wind, snaked through the air over their heads. Something was terribly wrong in this village.

Neat stone buildings bordered the square. Four of them appeared to be residences, fronted by tidy gardens enclosed by picket fences. Stefan motioned to the largest of these and said, "Ellgar."

Ellgar dismounted, walked to the door, and knocked loudly. "Open the door in the name of the Inquisition."

After a brief wait, the door creaked open, and a woman's face appeared in the narrow space. "Yes?"

Stefan rolled his eyes and nodded at Ellgar. The sergeant shoved the door open and pulled the woman out of the house by her arm. She let out a frightened yelp and stumbled down the steps, nearly falling until Ellgar steadied her and dragged her over to stand beside Stefan's horse. Short, plump, with graying hair pulled back in a neat bun, she looked around at them with wide eyes until settling on Stefan.

"Who is in charge in this village?" he asked.

"No one is in charge," she stammered. "I'm on the council of elders. Is there anything I can do for you?"

"Do you know who I am?"

She looked confused. "Should I?"

"Ellgar."

The sergeant, still holding the woman's upper arm, backhanded her across her face with his other hand. When she looked back at Stefan, a trickle of blood leaked from her nose, but the fear in her eyes was gone. "Sir, I know you are an inquisitor of the Empire, but I have never met you, as far as I know. How could I know who you are?"

Stefan felt a flush redden his cheeks. He hated dealing with these people. Ignoring the snort behind him, which could only be Keelia, he gestured around the square. "It appears you've recently celebrated a festival."

"Yes, the harvest festival. Last night."

"It's very unlike the *Alle'oss* to leave the square in such a state, even after a festival."

She stared at him.

When she didn't answer, Stefan exhaled heavily and said, "What happened here?"

"Local disagreements and too much drink." She paused and cocked her head. "I'm surprised the Inquisition would take an interest in such small matters."

Stefan's voice rose in volume. "The Inquisition is not interested in your petty disputes. We're here because you have been harboring a witch."

The woman's only reaction was a slight tightening of the muscles around her eyes. "I am not aware of any witches in Fennig."

Stefan smiled, but before he could respond, a man ran into the square, his boots slapping the cobbles. When he caught sight of the brothers, he came to a stumbling stop. His mouth opened as if he was going to speak, then he bent forward, hands on his knees. He glanced up at Stefan, held his hand up, taking deep gasping breaths. He was big for an *Alle'oss*, with a great bush of red hair and a matching beard.

"Agmar, you got no business here."

The woman, no longer restrained by Ellgar, stood with her hands on her hips, her face twisted in anger.

Agmar straightened, leaned back and ran his hands through his sweaty hair, pulling it back to reveal a large bruise discoloring the right side of his face. "Ha! Now we'll get her. The Inquisition is here."

The woman started walking toward him before Ellgar could stop her. "This is your fault, you oaf." Her hand shot out, gesturing around the square. Ellgar caught up to her and gripped her upper arm, bringing her to a stop. "I told you to let it go. We all told you to let it go."

The man froze for a moment, arms extended, face slack, then his expression clouded and his face reddened, nearly matching the color of his hair. "What are you talking about, Marie?" He pointed up the hill. "You saw what she did? Weren't just me, was there?"

"She did what anyone would do with a bunch of bullies throwing stones. And Jason, you saying she did that too?"

For the first time, uncertainty flickered across the man's face, but before he could respond, Stefan raised his voice and said, "Who are you talking about?" The man and woman looked at him, and Stefan directed his question at Agmar. "What did this person you're talking about do?"

Agmar's face lit up. He pointed at Stefan, nodding and smiling triumphantly at Marie. "I told you. The girl's a witch. You'll see." To Stefan, he said, "Come on. I'll show you what she did. That girl, Minna, she nearly killed us all." He started up the hill, looking back and waving them forward. Ellgar gave him a questioning look, and Stefan nodded. "Bring her."

• • • •

Stefan stood at the top of the hill, hands on his hips, staring at the destruction. Agmar was still providing a lurid retelling of the previous night's events, but Stefan was no longer listening. Could this have been the witch they found this morning? He didn't think so. The blond girl was too young to wield such power. "What did she look like?"

Agmar stammered to a stop. "Huh?"

"The witch who did this" he waved his hand toward the village, "... what did she look like?"

Understanding dawned on Agmar's face. "Oh, she's about this high." He held his hand in the middle of his chest. "Got black hair..." His eyebrows rose, as if this bit of information was particularly damning. "... green eyes. Dresses like a boy." His eyes wandered as if he was searching for something, then nodded and looked at Stefan expectantly.

"Black hair?" Stefan asked. "She's *Alle'oss*?"

Agmar nodded enthusiastically.

"How old is the witch?" Stefan asked.

Agmar's face went blank. He looked to Marie for inspiration, but found her staring back at him with narrow eyes. Frowning, he said, "Well, let's see." Lifting two fists, he mouthed numbers to himself as he released his fingers until all of them were extended, then he stared up at the sky before concluding, "She's had maybe thirteen summers?"

Stefan smiled. Another witch. He raised his gaze above the small gathering of people, finding Keelia still sitting on her horse at the bottom of the hill. When she saw him look at her, her expression clouded, and she turned her horse and walked it toward the road. He watched her go and asked Agmar, "How many people died?"

Agmar let a breath rush out through flapping lips. "None, but it weren't cause she didn't try. We were lucky, is all." He pulled one corner of his lips back and shrugged. "All except Loden, I mean. Might be awhile fore he's right."

"You say she ran into the forest, this witch?" Agmar nodded. "Have you checked her home?"

"First thing we checked. She lives up the road toward the mountains. She weren't there."

Stefan pointed in the direction they came to the village and raised his eyebrows. Agmar nodded and Stefan asked, "Where would she go?"

Agmar shrugged. "Don't know. We, me and the boys, we went lookin for her this morning. She and her pa are in the forest all the time. She probably got lots of places she could hole up."

Stefan examined the forest.

"That boy, Jason. He's a friend of hers. He might know. If he lives, that is."

"Jason?" Stefan asked.

Agmar's head bobbed.

Stefan looked up at the heavy clouds, then swept his gaze once more over the destruction. A thirteen-year-old witch who could wield this type of power would be exactly what the Malleus was looking for. Not as powerful as Aife, perhaps, but she was still very young. It would not be easy. They had to find her first. Keelia was slouching on her horse, pointedly ignoring what was happening on top of the hill. It wouldn't be easy if Keelia wouldn't cooperate.

Assuming they could find her, they would have to subdue her, and she was obviously very dangerous. Still, given the witch's age, her gifts would be undeveloped and erratic, and they had ways of controlling witches if they could get close enough. She was older than most of the witches they attempted to condition. There was no way to tell how she would respond. Still, they could kill her later if necessary. He returned his gaze to the men repairing the damage. They were nailing boards over the broken windows while trying to follow what was happening on the hill. For this potential, it was worth the risk.

He would send to Brennan for more men. If they hurried, they might arrive before the heavy snows. A month, at the most. Hoerst would understand. In the meantime, he would see what he could learn from the good people of Fennig. He looked at Marie. "Is there an inn in town?" She gave him a curt nod. "Good, you can move into it. We'll take your house until further notice. Ellgar, help the woman move."

Minna

Minna's mind whirled as she jogged toward Fennig. She needed to talk to Marie, but her house was on the village square. She couldn't get that far into the village without someone noticing. They didn't need to see her, they could feel her, and after the previous night, they would be looking for her. How different would her life be if she could hide herself like the woman with the painted face? Who was she? She couldn't be a *saa'myn*. Minna was sure those men were from the Empire and her father told her they killed the *saa'myn*. That had to be the reason they took Alyn. She assumed these men came because of the man in white, the one who sent a soldier back toward the mountains. But why did the woman warn her when she let them take Alyn? Minna had too many questions and no one to ask. To her annoyance, the *lan'and* were back, pacing her on either side of the road. "Where were you when I needed you?" Another question with no answer.

As she neared the village, she slipped into the forest on the south side of the highway, the side opposite the hill where Jason died. Unable to think of a way to get to Marie's house, she decided to work her way around the village, toward the stables on the eastern end of town. If she were extraordinarily lucky, she would find a way to get to Marie. If not, she would steal a horse. She didn't know where the soldiers took Alyn, but if she hurried, she could catch them before they made it through the mountains. The thought of stealing a horse from the Lothans, who never treated harshly, gave her a sick feeling in her stomach, but what choice did she have? She would make it right when she could.

With her mind full of unanswerable questions, she barely paid attention to where she was, only staying far enough into the forest to ensure no one could see her. A familiar pulse stopped her in her tracks. Another warning, she was sure, but her curiosity drew her to the source. The first person she saw was the invisible man, the man with no presence, standing atop the hill. Agmar stood next to him, gesturing wildly and speaking excitedly. A crowd gathered around the base of the hill, milling about the spot where the bodies of her victims lay the night before. She crept closer, drawn to the spot where Jason died, but also wanting to hear what they were saying. Another pulse stopped her. The woman with the painted face sat on her horse at the base of the hill, looking straight at her. She gave a small shake of her head. Minna crouched, searching for Marie.

If she were in the crowd and lingered after everyone left, Minna might get her attention.

"Is there an inn in town?" The man standing at the top of the hill shouted at someone hidden in the crowd. "Good, you can move into it. We'll take your house until further notice. Ellgar, help the woman move."

He started down the hill with Agmar trailing after him, a wide smile on his face. When the crowd dispersed, Minna glimpsed a soldier leading Marie back toward town. So, they were moving Marie to the inn. Could she get to her there? It wasn't likely. The inn was only one street off the square. She couldn't wait days for an opportunity to present itself. How long would it take for the soldiers to get to Brennan? She didn't know, but she felt a pressing need to leave right away. With one last, lingering look at the hill, she moved deeper into the forest.

A sense of urgency churning her thoughts, she moved mechanically through the forest, head down, not paying close attention to where she was going. When she stepped from the forest debris onto packed earth, she jerked to a stop, realizing where she was before she looked up. She had stumbled into the clearing where Jason's family lived.

"Oh!" The sound escaped her lips before she could clamp them shut. Wrapping her arms around herself, she swayed slowly, cradling the pain next to her heart. Even the smithy seemed to mourn his death. The *lan'and* that normally gathered here were gone, leaving it somehow dull and lifeless. The hammers and bellows were silent, and no smoke rose from the furnace. It was as silent and lifeless as the grave. Of course, it would be. Jason's family was mourning their son. She wanted to go to them and apologize, but what could she say? Her presence would only make their pain worse. She didn't kill him, but it was her fault he died.

"Goodbye, Jason. I'm sorry," she whispered, turned away, wiped away her tears and tucked the empty ache away where she kept the fantasy of their life together.

She made her way around the smithy, staying far enough into the forest that she wouldn't be able to see it, and Jason's family couldn't sense her presence. Once past it, she circled until she was on the eastern side of Fennig, then turned west. The stables were just outside town, next to the road that descended toward the farms below the village. When she detected the earthy aroma of horses, she climbed an old oak to survey the scene. The Lothans' house, a timber and stone construction with cedar shingles, sat in a clearing south of the road. Across the road from the house were the stables, corral, barn, and several smaller buildings.

Marie's brother, Erik, was standing next to the corral, his arms resting on the top rail of the fence, talking to two of the soldiers. While she watched, Ulf, Erik's son, exited the stables, approached the men and stood awkwardly apart from the group. Ulf. Before she changed, she and Ulf were friends. She remembered a quiet, intense boy, whose awkwardness made other children uncomfortable. Minna liked him. Though somewhat eccentric, his idiosyncrasies hid a thoughtful intelligence. From what Jason told her, people didn't like him any better now, though he didn't seem to care. In a way, she and Ulf were kindred spirits. They were both outcasts, shunned for reasons that were not their fault. She hadn't spoken to Ulf in years, and though the Lothans had not treated her poorly, that didn't mean Ulf would help her. But with no other ideas, it was worth a try. She would ask Ulf to bring Marie to the stables.

· · ·

Minna sat on the hard, narrow limb, watching the stables for the rest of the day, waiting for an opportunity to approach Ulf. High in the tree, there was little cover from the wind, which grew colder and stronger as the day passed. She huddled behind the trunk as much as she could, but she had to lean out and watch constantly, lest she miss her chance. She saw Ulf often. He tended and exercised horses, carried bales of hay from the barn, brought buckets of water from the well to the stables, and carted out the soiled hay from the stalls. Unfortunately, there was always another person nearby, or he came and went too quickly for her to catch him. By early evening, with the sun dipping toward the horizon, she was growing desperate. Even in her heavy cloak and wearing the mittens her mother gave her, she shivered violently, and it was getting difficult to hold on to the tree with numb fingers. With thoughts of Alyn getting farther away, she decided to risk knocking on their door.

Climbing down from the tree in the failing light proved far more difficult than climbing up. The cold seeped into her muscles while she sat, leaving her stiff. Every move was a painful reminder of her blind flight through the forest the previous night. Her numb fingers wouldn't grasp the limbs of the tree, and if she stretched her body too far, a searing pain flared in her bruised ribs. It was a maddeningly slow process. Still, she almost made it. Stretching her toe out to the last sturdy limb before a six-foot drop to the ground, her fingers slipped. Her toe caught on the limb, and she pivoted in the air and landed on her back.

She lay in the gathering darkness, hugging her chest, until the pain subsided enough for her to stagger to her feet. Leaving the trees, she limped up the road, until she was standing at the point where the tree line bent away at the edge of the Lothans' yard. The scene was quiet and still. Horse and wood smoke perfumed the air. Just as Minna stepped into the clearing, Ulf exited the house. She froze and watched him cross the road, hop the corral fence, and disappear into the stables.

Keeping an eye on the house, Minna dashed across the yard, slipped through the rails of the fence and jogged to the open stable door. Peering around the edge, she found Ulf tossing handfuls of hay into the stalls. His back was to her, so she slipped through the door and walked quietly toward him. When she was a dozen paces away, he froze, bent over. He straightened slowly, hands hanging limply at this side and his shoulders sagging. "Minna."

Her heart sank at the tone of his voice. "How did you know?"

He turned to face her. Minna remembered him as an undersized, sallow boy, always following after the bigger boys, like Jason. She saw him from time to time since then, but she never noticed how he changed. She hardly recognized him. He was tall, with broad shoulders and the lean, hard build of someone used to physical labor. His red hair, dark with sweat despite the chill, fell to his shoulders and across his brow. It wasn't until she looked closer that she saw the awkward boy she remembered. He tended to slump slightly, one shoulder higher than the other. One arm hung limply at his side, and one hand rested on his hip. His eyes roamed, occasionally finding her, locking on with a discomfiting intensity, before wandering off again. When his eyes found hers briefly, a quick smile crawled across his face.

"You know you make people feel uncomfortable." He shrugged. "It's not so bad for me, but I'd appreciate it if you didn't come any closer." His eyes wandered to the rafters. "Why'd you come?"

"I need to talk to Marie."

He didn't answer at first, appearing to be interested in the bale of hay at his feet. Minna was wondering if she should repeat herself when his eyes shot up and found hers. "She's staying at the inn. The Imperials took her house." His gaze slid off again. "You'll never be able to get to the inn without them knowing it. You want me to bring her here."

"They took Alyn, those soldiers, they took her. They beat my mother." She bit down on the last word, ashamed at the helpless pleading in her voice. A hot, prickly flush rose up her neck and the first gusty breaths of the storm swirled around her center. Who were these men who thought they could come to their home and take her sister? What had she done, other than being born different? Pressure surged, catching her by surprise. She went rigid, bent slightly at the waist, fists clenched at her sides. Her tight muscles pulled at her ribs and her other injuries, the pain throwing fuel on the fire. The *lan'and* streamed through the open doors. Not now! Ulf was staring at her, his usual fidgety awkwardness gone. What must he think? Why would he help her now, after seeing her like this?

But instead of fleeing, he took a halting step toward her, one hand extended. "Minna? Are you okay?"

She was so surprised at this simple kindness, so overwhelmed with gratitude, the storm spun apart, leaving eddies that dissipated and were gone. She gasped in relief, closed her eyes and forced herself to take slow, deep breaths, willing her muscles to relax. When she opened her eyes, Ulf was watching her with the same concern as before. "Ulf, aren't you afraid of me?"

"A little." The quick smile reappeared, but remained this time. He held her gaze for a moment, then lowered his eyes.

Watching him fidget, Minna couldn't stop a small grin from curving her lips. When she spoke, she was in control of her emotions. "I'm going after them, but I need a horse." Ulf's gaze flicked up to her face, then scanned the stalls from which the horses watched. "Mama told me to talk to Marie because she's been west of the mountains."

He nodded, and his other hand rose to rest on his hip. "You can't stay in here. My da might come looking for me. Go wait out past the corral. I'll bring her." With that, he spun around and was out the door on the far side of the stables before Minna could say thank you. She watched the door for a moment, then did as he asked.

Minna waited longer than she thought necessary for Ulf to get to the inn and back. It was dark, and as the adrenaline and purpose that kept her on edge all day ebbed, she resorted to pacing to stay alert. When she heard voices carried by the wind, she edged toward the forest and peered across the yard.

"Minna. I've got Marie," Ulf called.

Minna approached the silhouettes of two people, one much shorter than the other, stopping when she could make out Marie's smiling face in shimmery spirit light.

"Minna," Marie said, walking over and wrapping her in her arms.

Minna sagged against her, squeezing her eyes shut. She disengaged herself from Marie's hug and stepped back when she noticed the strain in Marie's face.

"I'm so sorry… about everything, Minna."

"Thank you. The reason I—"

"The reason you wanted to talk to me is you want to go after your sister. I know, Ulf told me. How can I help?"

"Mama said you've been west of the mountains. I don't even know where they'll take her and I need a horse. They're already so far ahead."

"Have you ever ridden a horse before, dear?"

"Yes," Minna said firmly, then shook her head and added, "It's been a long time, but I have."

"They'll take her to Brennan. How long will it take?" She looked back at Ulf, who was watching his feet. "Ulf?"

Ulf startled. "What?"

"How long will it take men on horseback to get to Brennan?"

"If they're going slow? Maybe two, three weeks."

"The brothers… those men, they work for the Inquisition," Marie said, turning back to face Minna. "They'll take her to the Inquisition in Brennan." She eyed Minna's bow, doubtfully. "If they get her there, there won't be much you can do, dear."

Minna's voice trembled as she said, "I need to hurry."

Marie studied her, then nodded. "Ulf will take you."

Ulf yelped. "I will?"

Marie gave him a stern look and said, "Yes, you will. You've been to Brennan, you know how to get there. Minna will need help."

Ulf started to speak, then caught Minna's eye. Dropping his gaze, he shuffled his feet, hands on his hips. Finally, he looked at Minna briefly before looking up at the sky. "Wait here." With that, he spun around and dashed up the highway toward town.

Minna and Marie watched him go. "There's something not right about that boy," Marie said. She cut her eyes to Minna.

"Is he coming back?"

"I guess. Eventually. He *does* live here."

Minna waited with a growing sense of desperation. Maybe she could steal a horse. She watched her father saddle a horse when she was young. She took a step toward the stables when Marie spoke.

"Do you know what a *saa'myn* is?"

Minna froze. She dragged her eyes away from the stable and found Marie watching her. "My papa told me about them."

Marie nodded. "Of course he did."

"But he didn't know much. He said it was so long ago that people don't remember."

"Your papa was right. Mostly. But there are still some people who know about the old ways. Minna, you need to find someone who knows about these things." She glanced once more at Minna's bow. "You're going to need help to rescue Alyn."

Minna was about to ask who she could ask when Ulf appeared, running toward them with his loose-limbed gait. He skidded to a stop, scattering twigs and pebbles, sweat beading on his forehead and breathing hard. Between breaths, he said, "We can't take the horses through the forest at night, and you can't go through town. You circle around and I'll take the horses through town and meet you on the road." Without waiting for an answer, he spun around, sprinted toward the stables, and disappeared through the door.

Minna smiled. Marie was right about Ulf. There was something strange about him. When she caught Marie's eye, they burst out laughing.

"Well, I guess you better do what the boy says. I'll go organize some provisions for him. He'd take off across the mountains with not a stitch of clothes on if you let him." She looked at Minna and said, "Good luck, Minna. I'll look in on your mama for you." She came forward and gave Minna another hug, then said, "Go on and, remember, find someone who can help you."

"Thank you, Marie. I will." She turned and hurried away.

Chapter 18

Alyn

This isn't happening. The moldy darkness of the leather hood magnified the sound of her ragged breath and the whoosh of blood in her ears. This isn't happening. A blind, unreasoning hysteria fluttered at the edges of her mind, like bats' wings in the darkness. Only her desperate litany held it at bay. This isn't happening. Nothing in her short life prepared her for such naked brutality, and with no way to respond, she sat frozen, panting, clinging to a hopeless wish. This isn't happening.

Someone would rescue her. But who? Her mother was likely dead, and her father was gone, maybe forever. Minna. A flicker of hope pushed the panic back into the shadows, unfreezing her mind for a moment. She felt something. When they dragged her from her home, she felt a pulse, a ripple, in that spot Minna called her center. And something inside her awoke and responded to that call. And before they pulled the hood over her head, she sensed someone else, someone familiar. It was Minna, she was sure of it, without knowing how she knew. Minna is alive. A small sound escaped her throat and her breath sped.

She felt herself slumping in the saddle while the world outside the hood faded into the blackness inside.

"I told you to sit up." Through the thick leather hood, the voice had the detached quality of a shadowy beast from a nightmare. But the vice like pressure on the back of her neck was not from a dream. The hand twisted her head to the side and then released her with a small shove. She fell forward, flinging her hands out and catching herself on the horse's neck. The soldier grasped the back of her dress and pulled her upright. The panic, banished to the fringes by thoughts of her sister, snatched at her and she began panting, clenching her body against the hysteria that clamored for release. She slumped sideways as the world faded.

"I'm not telling you again," the beast snarled. "If I have to, I'll drag you behind the horse."

She had fainted again. She couldn't catch her breath in the musty hood. Gritting her teeth, Alyn tried to take a deep breath, but only brought on waves of nausea and dizziness. She heard another muffled voice but couldn't make out the words. After a pause, the monster spoke.

"If you don't stop breathing so fast, you're going to keep fainting. Calm yourself, we have a long way to go."

Calm herself? The grasping claws of panic scrabbled at her once again. How was she supposed to stay calm? Out of the turbulent whirl in her mind, something spoke to her. Not words. Nothing she could understand. It was there and gone, a flash which she might have dismissed if she hadn't felt it earlier that day, but it was enough for her to regain control. Taking a slow, shuddery breath, she cast about for something to focus on and settled on her mother.

They waited up, she and her mother, anxious to hear about the festival. Though they had to sit as far apart as they could in the small common room, the good mood that prevailed in the house that afternoon swept away the barrier the spirits erected between them, and her mother opened up to her. She described what she felt when she or her sister were near, and how she worried about what kind of parent she could be without their father's support. She wept when she confessed that she never confided in Minna, though she wouldn't say why. Alyn told her there was still time.

As the night dragged on, their mother disappeared into her room, coming out from time to time to wander around the common room before disappearing again. Alyn sat in front of the fire, cradling a forgotten cup of tea. Long before Agmar and some others came early in the morning, Alyn knew something was terribly wrong. When the knock sounded, her mother appeared and shooed Alyn into her room, then met them on the porch. They told a wild story about Minna killing people and destroying part of the village. It made little sense, and Alyn refused to believe it, but it was clear something happened to Minna. Her mother wanted to search for her, but Alyn convinced her that Minna would come home. She told her about their father's plan for Minna to go to the falls if anything happened. So, they waited. Hours later, her mother, who was pacing in the front yard, burst into the house and dragged Alyn into the root cellar.

Alyn refused to dredge up what happened next, but the memories served their purpose. She was thinking again. These men were from the Empire. They wore clothes like the man Minna told her about, the one she sensed who was with the soldiers who took their father into the wilderness. Minna told her the Empire hunted the *saa'myn*. That was why they took her. How they knew about her, she didn't know, but it was the only explanation she could come up with. She also didn't know where they were taking her, but they hadn't killed her yet, and the man sitting behind her said it was a long way to their destination. It didn't make sense for them to go to the trouble of taking her somewhere else just to kill her. It was a small hope, but it was enough. For now.

As the panic subsided, her awareness of her body returned, and the first tendrils of pain began. Before long, every step the horse took was an agony that eclipsed every other thought. Squeezed between the soldier and the pommel of the saddle, with no stirrups, she had no way to support her weight. Every time she shifted around to find a more comfortable position, the beast growled at her to stop fidgeting. Each time she rested her weight on the rider, he pushed her forward. Sitting, unsupported, put a strain on her lower back that accumulated as the day dragged on. It was uncomfortable with the horse walking, but it was when they occasionally broke into a trot, pounding her thighs against the saddle, that the pain began in earnest. She tried supporting her weight on the saddle's pommel, but the impact of the horse's strides transferred up her arms to her shoulders and it wasn't long before her arms buckled. They dragged her from her home without winter clothing, and as they climbed into the mountains, the temperature fell, and she began to shiver.

The day became an interminable battle against pain and despair. It wasn't long after they started, she wished they would stop, if only for a moment, to allow her some respite. Eventually, she wished only that it would end some way. It didn't matter how. She endured one moment to the next, misery crowding out every thought except the need to survive. She was beyond the point she felt she couldn't endure one moment longer when, mercifully, the horses came to a stop.

She sagged in the saddle, unaware she was leaning against the soldier until he shoved her forward so that she was lying on the horse's neck. She felt him dismount, then she was pulled roughly sideways out of the saddle and dropped to the ground. Her mind shut down, overwhelmed by the agony in her legs and back. She lay still, her entire body clenched against the scream fighting to escape her throat. When the pain subsided somewhat, she let out a long breath, listening to the men joking and laughing, oblivious to her misery.

Rough hands closed around her arms and lifted her to her feet, ripping a scream from her. When he let go, her legs collapsed, and she fell. The men laughed, but lost in her own struggle, she didn't care. The man fumbled with the hood, and a moment later, he jerked it from her head. Even evening twilight was blinding after a day in darkness. In the moment before she squeezed her eyes shut, she glimpsed muddy boots inches from her face. She heard the squelch of the man's boots in the mud and felt something brush her arm. When she slitted her eyes, the boots were gone, and she could see the clearing in which they stopped for the night.

Three of the soldiers gathered around a fire, the flames already licking the bottom of a pot suspended above it. Engrossed in their conversation, none of the men looked her way. She pushed herself up to sit, squinting around, absently wiping muddy hands on her blouse. The spot they stopped nestled up against the eastern side of a rocky ridge, but even so, the wind that strengthened while they rode, occasionally found its way over the barrier, plunging down into the clearing, swirling the smoke and raising goosebumps on her exposed skin.

She pulled her legs beneath her dress and examined her surroundings. Though she had been too disoriented to pay attention when they left her home, she knew they must be heading west. The *Alle'oss* didn't call their mountains *na'lios*, our home, for no reason. For Alyn, the peaks she saw from her front door were as familiar as old friends, as fundamental to her sense of place in the world as her parents and her sister. She never needed a map to know where she was. She learned to tell time, not in hours and minutes, but by the subtle interplay of shadow and light on *Shitana's* shoulders. The slow march of snow down *Jibora's* lofty flanks marked the changing of the seasons. Gazing at the unfamiliar mountains visible over the trees across the highway, Alyn felt lost for the first time in her life.

Amid all her aches, the one that brought her back to her immediate situation was a growing pressure on her bladder. She looked over her shoulder at the soldier who removed her hood. He busied himself brushing the horse with a currycomb, humming an unfamiliar tune. After all the humiliations she suffered, it seemed absurd that she was embarrassed to admit such a normal thing as needing to pee to this man. But there was nothing for it. It was either tell him, or wet herself, which would be infinitely worse.

At that moment, the soldier finished with his horse and turned around. Alyn looked down at her hands twisting in her lap. She stared at his boots when they appeared in front of her, face burning. When he bent over her, she looked up. He paused when their eyes met, exhaling sour breath into her face.

"I need to pee," she said.

His nose wrinkled. "You can't stand, you can't pee." She steeled herself when he took hold of her arms, clamping her jaws shut when he jerked her to her feet. Rather than letting go, this time he held onto one arm and half carried her, one agonizing step after another, toward the edge of the clearing, where he leaned her against the trunk of a tree and let go.

"Well? If you need to pee, do it now or hold it. We won't tolerate you stinking all the way to Brennan."

Flushed with embarrassment, she craned her neck to look at his face, but then something caught her attention. The *lan'and* drifted lazily in the trees behind the soldier's head. She stared at them.

The soldier glanced back to see what she was looking at, then turned back, scowling. "Get on with it," he said, then left her to return to the fire.

She watched him go, shifting around to put her back to the tree, then lifted her hands and examined the chain. How was she going to manage this?

"Do you need some help?"

It was a different soldier. When she looked up, his eyes wandered off to the side before settling on his feet. She wasn't sure what to make of him. He was younger than the others, and though he had the same imposing physical presence, he projected none of the others' menace. He spoke softly, and when he glanced up and found her watching him, his cheeks darkened. It came to her he looked embarrassed, but whether it was for himself or her, she couldn't guess. She held up her hands, stretching out the chain and said, "I need to pee."

He gave her a quick nod, turned, and walked away. When he returned, he gestured to her hands and produced a key. "We'll have to replace these before you sleep, but this will make it easier." Alyn rubbed her wrists, and he asked, "Do you want my help?"

Alyn shook her head and said, "Thank you."

He turned without another word and walked away.

It took nearly all her remaining strength to pee, her back against a tree trunk. When she finished, she rolled to the side and put her clothes back in order. She lay shivering, pulling her legs under the relative warmth of her dress, careful to keep her sore thighs from rubbing together, grateful to be breathing fresh air. The *lan'and* circled slowly above her. She reached for her center, as Minna taught her, but with her mind dulled by fatigue and pain, it remained illusive.

She braced herself when footsteps approached, and a hand wrapped around her arm. But instead of yanking her to her feet, he lifted her gently into a sitting position. It was the younger soldier, again. As before, he wouldn't meet her eyes, but he guided a bowl into her hands and left her. She watched him go, then examined the contents of the bowl. It was too dark to see it clearly, but it smelled wonderful. She took a tentative sip and groaned. A rich venison broth, flavorful and hot. Resisting the urge to tip up the bowl and gulp the meager helping down, she sipped it slowly, relishing its warmth. After licking the bowl clean, she cradled it in her lap, a deep lethargy settling over her.

The young soldier returned, took the bowl and supported her while she lay on her back. He wrapped the manacles around a sapling and locked them onto her wrists. As he settled a rough blanket that smelled of horse over her, his eyes flicked to hers and he whispered, "It's most comfortable if you sleep on your back with your head next to the tree."

Even this simple tenderness almost undid her. Alyn watched his retreating back, tears leaking from her eyes and pooling in her ears. The chain on the manacles was just long enough that she could hold her hands together on her chest. Minna promised she wouldn't leave her alone, but what could Minna do against men like these? She was alone, and no one was coming to help her. Exhaustion dragged her into darkness, the spirits orbiting above her, quiet sentinels keeping watch.

Chapter 19

Minna

Dawn was still hours away and Minna was pacing. Back and forth, she trudged across the highway, peering into the dark toward town at every turn. The *lan'and*, perhaps curious about her anxiety, kept her company, swirling above her. A frigid wind, funneled by the Breakheart Pass, plunged down the eastern slopes of the mountains, tugging at her cloak and worming its way into every chink in her winter armor. She swung her arms across her chest, working her fists inside her mittens, letting the pain in her ribs keep her alert. If she stopped, even for a moment, she was reminded how long it had been since she slept. *Where was Ulf?* The soldiers who took Alyn had to stop for the night. She could be making up lost time.

Pivoting at the edge of the road, she paused, arms flung wide. What was happening to her sister? What must she be thinking? Did she know Minna would come after her? She would. Minna made a promise, and she kept her promises.

Where are you, Ulf? And as if in answer to her question, a horse's whinny rose above the wind's mournful moans. She edged toward the brush at the side of the highway and squinted toward the sound. Under the dark overcast, the buildings she damaged at the edge of the village were mere shadows against a black background. Another whinny, closer, then the jangle of the horses' tackle, accompanied by Ulf's quiet encouragement. Minna relaxed and moved into the center of the road as Ulf appeared, his face illuminated by a lantern he held aloft.

"It's about time," she said, when he was close enough, feeling ashamed even before the words were out of her mouth.

Ulf dismounted and held the lantern up so that Minna had to squint and shade her eyes. He opened his mouth, then, catching sight of her expression, he closed it and looked at the ground. When he looked back up, he said, "I couldn't let my parents know. They wouldn't let me go, so I had to be careful."

Minna reached out, then pulled her hand back. "Ulf... I'm sorry. I didn't even think of that." Ducking her head to hide her embarrassment, she asked, "Will they be worried?"

"It's okay. Marie is going to let them know where I went." Minna looked up to find a small smile lifting one corner of his lips. "They won't be happy, but we'll be long gone by then."

He took the bridle of the second horse and led it over to her. "That thing, you know, that makes people feel funny?"

Caught by surprise, Minna could only nod.

"Does the same thing happen to horses?"

"No... or I don't think so. I don't know, let's see." The horse watched her warily as she approached, but showed no signs of distress, and nickered softly when Minna rested a hand on her neck.

"Her name is Edda. She's the gentlest horse we have." He eyed Minna doubtfully. "You said you rode before."

She nodded with only the slightest hesitation. Minna did ride a horse when she was much younger. She remembered something about how to tell the horse which way to go, but that was the extent of her experience. She knew, in theory, how to get on the horse, though in her previous experience, her father lifted her so she could get her foot into the stirrup, then boosted her up into the saddle.

Anxious to allay Ulf's doubts, she tucked her mittens in her belt, took a step back, and studied the situation. The stirrup was too high for her to reach with her foot. Her cheeks warmed at a fleeting image of Ulf lifting her up. Gritting her teeth, she grasped the pommel and the back of the saddle, where it curved down the horse's flank. After a couple of experimental bounces, she hopped and got her left foot into the stirrup. So far, so good. But as she pulled herself up, her right hand slipped, and she found herself hanging onto the pommel, right leg swinging away from the horse. With a mighty effort, she heaved herself up and threw her leg over, landing with a whump in the saddle. That wasn't so hard. She lifted the reins and looked down at Ulf, who seemed to be very far below her. Edda twisted her neck and gave her the same uncertain look that Ulf was. "What?"

Ulf's mouth twisted, and deep furrows creased his brow. He started to speak, but then gave a quick shake of his head and started again. "Try not to squeeze so hard with your legs and don't hold the reins so tight. She won't like that." He looked up at the sky for so long, Minna was thinking he forgot she was there, then he lowered his gaze, shrugged and said, "We'll start walking slow. Really slow."

"We can go faster."

"Not in the dark." He patted Edda's neck and added, "Besides, it'll give you and Edda a chance to get to know each other."

Ulf doused the lantern, stuffed it into a bag tied to the back of the cantle, and climbed into the saddle. The light surface of the road was just visible against the darker brush on either side. Minna lifted the reins and shook them. When the horse didn't respond, she looked at Ulf and said, "Um."

With a small smirk, he turned his mount toward the west and began walking. She watched, but couldn't see how he was doing it. Fortunately, Edda had her own ideas, and as Ulf's horse moved away, she fell in behind. Minna perched on the horse, feeling like a tick on a dog's back. When it became apparent Edda didn't need her intervention, Minna tucked the reins under her thigh, pulled her mittens on and stuck her hands under her armpits.

She felt like she should say something to Ulf. To thank him for taking such a risk, but she wasn't sure what she could say, so they rode in silence. Leaning out as they rounded the bend before her home, she found the house dark and there was no smell of smoke from a fire in the hearth. A vague disquiet came over her. What would her mother do if her father didn't return? Surely the villagers wouldn't hold it against her that her daughters were witches. "Goodbye," she murmured, as the house passed behind them, wondering if she would ever see it again.

The initial nervousness and excitement wore away quickly. It wasn't long before her back stiffened, forcing her to fidget as she tried to find a more comfortable position. Despite the discomfort, the slow sway of the horse's gait lulled her into a drowsy stupor, and she caught herself slumping precariously in the saddle more than once. To keep herself awake, she watched the *lan'and,* who seemed to keep pace with them, flitting to and fro and casting a shimmery light that played across Ulf's back.

• • •

"Minna!"

Minna jerked awake, felt herself sliding sideways and grabbed for the pommel. "What?" The horses were standing beside one another, and Ulf, his face visible in dawn's gray light, was leaning toward her.

"We're going to try picking up the pace," Ulf said and dismounted. He came around and adjusted Minna's stirrups so that her knees were bent slightly. Once he was mounted again, he leaned close enough to her to be heard over the wind. "Let the horse push you up but control yourself on the way down with your legs. It will be easier on you, and easier on Edda." He paused, thinking. "Just try to stay on." Minna nodded, and with that, they started walking again. Edda waited until Ulf's horse pulled ahead before falling in behind.

Ulf glanced back, caught Minna's eye, gave her a nod, then turned forward and urged his horse into a trot. Even with the warning, it caught Minna off guard. The first stride lifted her from the saddle and pitched her forward. Her bottom smacked back down into the saddle as it rose with Edda's next stride. Minna bounced, her feet coming free of the stirrups, and for a moment, she floated above Edda. When she smacked down again, she let go of the reins and clung to the pommel for dear life. Ever more precarious bounces followed each painful impact. At one point, she found herself hanging sideways, one leg across Edda's back and a death-like grip on the pommel, the only things keeping her attached to the horse. Grunting with the effort, her ribs screaming at the abuse, she dragged herself back into the saddle just as Ulf slowed them to a walk. Scrabbling for the reins with one hand, the other locked onto the pommel, she composed her face, grateful he couldn't see her tunic drenched with sweat and hear her heart galloping in her chest.

The wind was howling, so that Ulf had to yell to be heard. "How was that?"

"Fine. We can go faster." But the manic smile she hitched onto her face must have given her away.

Ulf snorted, shaking his head. He glanced down. "Don't hold on to the pommel. Remember, let the horse lift you, but use your legs to keep from bouncing." He pressed his lips together and finished, "If you fall off, scream really loud, so I hear you."

The rest of the morning, they varied their pace. Each time they sped up, Minna fought a grim battle to stay in the saddle. Deciding Ulf's advice wasn't helping, she tried straightening her legs to stand in the stirrups. The first stride nearly threw her over Edda's head. After that, she gritted her teeth and fought to find a way to work with Edda.

Ironically, it was when her strength flagged, and she was forced to stop fighting Edda, that she found a rhythm that worked. Not comfortable perhaps, but at least she was no longer in danger of being thrown. Once the horses were warm, they tried a canter, which, to Minna's relief, was much easier on her battered body. They continued like that most of the day, alternating paces and taking few breaks. Late in the afternoon, it started snowing. The tiny ice crystals, driven by the wind, stung her face and forced her to duck her head inside her hood, trusting Edda to stay on the highway.

It was nearly dusk when Ulf pulled up beside her and yelled above the wind, "We have to stop."

Minna lifted her hand to shield her eyes from the wind and was startled by how much her fingers trembled. She shifted in the saddle, trying to find a comfortable way to sit on her bruised butt, peering up at the clouds. "No, we have to keep going. There's still some light left," she said, though she was relieved when Ulf shook his head.

He pointed ahead. "The horses need to rest, and there's a spot just ahead where we can shelter from the wind. If we're caught out in the open at night in this wind..." He drew his lips into a straight line and held her gaze an uncharacteristically long time. "We have to sleep, or we won't be able to stay on the horses. *You* have to sleep."

She squinted up, again, into the fading light. When she looked back at Ulf, he was watching her, waiting for her answer. She nodded, and Ulf's face visibly relaxed. "We'll stop just up ahead. There won't be any firewood there, so dismount here and gather some wood while you walk. We'll need to keep a fire going all night. I'll get the horses settled."

With a groan, Minna swung her leg over the horse, hovered for a moment, hanging onto the pommel and gathering herself, then leapt backward. She landed awkwardly, letting out a yelp when her momentum carried her backward to sit heavily. The bruises and scrapes she acquired the night of the harvest festival complained, but that pain was forced into the background by the ache in her legs and back. She bent over her outstretched legs, groaning and massaging her lower back. When she looked up, Ulf was disappearing around a bend in the road, her horse in tow. Before he disappeared, he looked back. Something about the way he looked at her struck her as odd. Still, it was Ulf. Everything about him was a bit odd.

Sitting up, she looked around. She'd been so focused on remaining on the horse's back, she hadn't paid attention to where they were. Though she had never been this far from home, by the looks of the mountains, she guessed they were nearing the top of the Pass. It suddenly occurred to her she knew nothing about this area, and her pack and bow, strapped to her saddle, just disappeared with Ulf. Struggling to her feet, she limped across the highway to get a better view around the curve. Ulf wasn't there. She felt the cold sink into her. He left her alone.

No, that wasn't right. The road extended straight for at least a league. She would be able to see him if he left her. Walking slowly, she searched the ground on each side of the highway, finding what she was looking for about thirty paces on; the tracks of the horses where they left the road. Tightly packed evergreens pushed up close to the highway, but the tracks entered the forest through a narrow opening between two spruce trees. If she hadn't seen the tracks, she would not have noticed it. How was he expecting her to find him?

She listened but heard nothing over the wind's howl. Slipping between the trees, she found a path. To Minna's experienced eye, it looked as if someone deliberately tried to obscure it. Fallen leaves and sticks were scattered across the path, but it didn't appear natural, and the ground beneath the leaves was compacted. People came this way often and tried to hide the fact. She peered into shifting shadows beneath wind-tossed trees, but didn't see any signs of Ulf or the horses.

She crept down the path, listening and watching for movement. In the relative quiet among the trees, the sound of her breath rose above the muted howl of the wind. A horse snorted up ahead. She stopped, holding her breath and listening. Were those voices she heard? Sure that something was amiss now, she inched forward until she glimpsed the horses through the undergrowth. They were alone in a large clearing. Who had she heard? She hurried forward and stepped out of the trees just as Ulf exited the brush to her left. He was looking back in the direction he came, saying, "*Pakaliānok tae hemlatha* (Wait until tomorrow)!"

When he turned toward Minna, he froze. It was just a moment. There and gone in a heartbeat. If she weren't already wary, perhaps she wouldn't have noticed, but she thought she saw guilt in his expression.

With a grimace, he gestured over his shoulder. "I've had to go for the longest time." They stared at one another, then noticing Minna's empty hands, he said, "Where's the wood?"

Instead of answering, Minna watched him busying himself with the horses, then examined the clearing. Ulf was right. This was a good spot to spend the night. It nestled against the eastern side of a granite outcrop that arched over the clearing. The rock channeled the wind above them, leaving a relatively warm, snow-free pocket. Clear signs of previous occupants confirmed her sense the path was well traveled. Soot stained the bottom of the stone overhang above a stone-lined fire pit. A pile of wood was stacked nearby. She held her hand over the fire pit, finding it warm. Wisps of smoke escaped the earth, thrown over the remnants of a fire. Ulf pretended not to notice Minna's unease, but she caught him glancing her way.

"How did you expect me to find you here?" she asked.

"Knew you were a good tracker. If you didn't show up, I would have gone looking for you."

Minna searched the trees where Ulf exited the forest. She saw nothing through the tightly packed brush, and the hard, stony ground obscured any tracks. "Who were you talking to?" she asked.

He winced and stared up at the sky. "I wasn't talking to anyone. Sometimes I just talk to myself." He smiled widely, an expression that was so rare on his face that Minna found it unsettling. "You know everyone says I'm a bit odd, right?"

Minna held his gaze for a moment. "*Vehlu sha aku ra Alle'oss* (You talk to yourself in *Alle'oss*)?" Minna didn't know anyone who spoke the old language, other than her family. Her father told her almost no one in recent generations did. He ensured his daughters were fluent, telling them there would come a time they needed it, but cautioned them against ever letting anyone hear them speaking it. To Ulf's astonished, red face, she asked, "*Pakaliāna jīla sha hemlatha sut* (Why are we waiting for tomorrow)?"

"We... have to wait till tomorrow... before we keep going." Turning back to the horses, he said, "Get the fire going. We need to take advantage of the light."

Ignoring his attempt to change the subject, she asked, "Someone has been here recently. Did you see anyone?"

Pausing in the act of lifting the saddle from Edda's back, he turned and said, "People use this place all the time. I didn't see anyone, but someone must have been here earlier."

He turned back to the horses. Minna watched him for a moment, then gazed around the clearing. Something didn't feel right, but what options did she have? She retrieved her pack, then set about making a fire. Rolling out her bedroll so the fire was between her and the clearing. She watched Ulf brushing Edda's back, feeling herself drifting with the slow, methodical motion of the currycomb. Flopping onto her back, she stretched grateful muscles.

* * *

Minna startled awake, pushed herself into a sitting position and stared around. Ulf knelt beside her, looking down at her as if he had just spoken to her.

When she didn't answer, he repeated himself. "Soup?"

She noticed a bowl in his extended hand and took it.

Ulf retreated to the opposite side of the fire and settled down to sit cross-legged, sipping his soup. She ate mechanically, fighting fatigue and watching Ulf, whose eyes wandered everywhere, but never found her. When they finished, Minna took their bowls to clean them, while Ulf disappeared into the forest to collect more firewood.

When he returned, he dropped an armful of small branches, plucked one from the pile, and knelt beside the fire. "What are you planning to do when you find her?"

Minna shook her head. She felt slow, her body ached all over, and she could barely lift her hand to brush the hair away from her face. She looked at her bow laying on top of her pack., then glanced up at the lan'and, remembering the harvest festival. Could she do that again when she meant to?

"Have you ever killed someone?" Ulf was standing now, looking down at her, the branch dangling from his hand. When she didn't answer, he said. "I'm just saying. You're going after your sister, and you don't know what you'll do if we catch them. They're Imperial soldiers and we're... not."

Minna stared up at him. "I'll... you know, what I did at the harvest festival... I'll do that again."

"Can you? Are you sure?" He knelt again and looked across the fire at her. "And let me know when you do it, because I want to get out of the way. From what I saw, no one nearby is safe."

Tears prickle her eyes. "She's my sister. I promised I would always be there. I'll... think of something." She stared into the fire. "Besides, there's nothing for me in Fennig anymore."

When she looked back up, Ulf was watching her, his expression unreadable. He nodded and said, "You best get some sleep. We should start early. I'll take the first watch." When he sat on his blanket, she heard him say in a low voice, "It's for your own good."

Something wasn't right, but Minna finally had to surrender to exhaustion. She lay down, dragging her blanket over her and let sleep take her.

Chapter 20

Alyn

They woke her by ripping the blanket off her in the predawn light, only moments after she finally gave into exhaustion and fell asleep. The snow that dusted the ground during the night melted on contact with her face and hair, leaving her damp and chilled. The blanket was too short to cover her entirely, unless she rolled onto her side and pulled her legs up. With the manacles wrapped around the tree, she couldn't get her hand between her knees to prevent her chafed thighs from rubbing together. It was only when the snow finally stopped that she could stretch out on her back and sleep.

Stiff and sore, she struggled into a sitting position and sat shivering, staring blearily around at the men as they prepared to depart. They gave her some dried meat and a bit of water for breakfast, then replaced the hood and hoisted her onto a horse while she was still chewing. When her thighs contacted the saddle, she gasped, ejecting the contents of her mouth, which slithered down her neck and lodged in the collar of her dress.

Already sore and weak from the previous day's trials, she had no defense against the pounding when the horses picked up their pace. "I can't do this," she mumbled to no one, during a respite while the horses walked. Numb with despair and too many aches to distinguish, a heavy lethargy settled on her. She barely noticed when they slowed to a stop. She heard rough voices, but couldn't rouse herself enough to care what they were saying. The rider behind her shifted, and a pair of hands encircled her waist. Someone pulled her roughly from the horse, carried her a short distance, then hoisted her again into a saddle.

The second time they stopped, the rider gave her a shove sideways and for a moment, she thought she would fall all the way to the ground. Instead, she fell into the arms of someone who guided her carefully to sit. When the hood was pulled from her head, she was squinting at the young soldier. He peered into her eyes, frowning. Tugging a mitten from his hand, he squeezed her fingers in a warm hand, rough with callouses, then dug his nail into the pad of her thumb. She barely noticed the pain at first, then pulled feebly against his grip.

"What's your name?" he asked. Alyn, who was gazing at the other soldiers sitting on rocks across the highway watching the exchange, didn't answer. The soldier took her chin between his index finger and thumb and pulled her face around to look at him. "What's your name?"

"Alyn," she said automatically. Her voice, hoarse and wispy, sounded far away, like someone else answered for her.

He gave a quick nod, pressed something into her hand, and moved off to sit with his comrades. She gazed down at her hand. It was a hard biscuit. She fumbled around her collar for the remains of her breakfast. Not finding it, she let her hand drop and sat, shivering, the biscuit already forgotten.

They stopped at a point where the land fell away to the south. Across a forested valley, snow-capped peaks marched to the south as far as she could see. While she watched, the sun broke through the clouds and set the snow on the mountains glittering. Though she never traveled far from Fennig, her father told her the mountains extended all the way to the Southern Sea. His description of the sea and the ships that sailed it captured her imagination, as so many of his stories did. She dreamed of seeing it one day. Minna would always laugh when Alyn told her of her dreams, but afterward, when she didn't know Alyn was watching, her sister would retreat to some faraway place.

When the young soldier found her still holding onto the biscuit, he took her hand and lifted it to her lips. "You must eat whenever you can."

She took a small bite and chewed absently, watching his face. He still wouldn't meet her eyes, but he lifted a water pouch to her lips and poured a small swallow into her mouth.

"Eat quickly. They will not wait."

"Why—" she croaked.

"Shhh!" He lifted the biscuit again and whispered, "Don't talk, just eat. Quickly." He let her chew for a moment, gave her two more swallows of water, then stood and walked away. When he returned, he carried the hood. He let her cram the last of the biscuit into her mouth and then replaced the hood. She braced herself when she heard a horse approaching, expecting to be pulled roughly onto her feet. Instead, someone lifted her carefully and held her until she was steady. She heard him mounting his horse and then she was lifted into the saddle, sitting sideways, both legs hanging off the left side of the horse. She scrabbled for the pommel to pull herself upright.

"Settle back." A murmur, almost too quiet to hear through the hood.

She tensed, unsure she heard right, wary of some new torture. Then a hand took her right shoulder and pulled her sideways. She fought feebly against his pull, but with no leverage and little strength, she couldn't resist for long. She lay against him, tense, waiting for a blow to fall. He shifted, then she felt his cloak pulled open and drawn around her shoulders.

"I can't button it, so you'll have to hold it closed."

She could tell from his voice that her head was resting against his chest. She felt for the edges of the cloak and pulled them together so that they almost closed.

"Don't do this with the others. Do you understand?"

She nodded stiffly, still not trusting this wasn't a trick.

They began to move, and he spoke again. "Just get through today and tomorrow. You'll get stronger and it will be easier."

Finally, she let herself sag against him, sobbing softly. Though her legs, which chafed painfully against one another, wouldn't let her truly sleep, the gentle rocking of the horse's stride and the warmth of his thick cloak soon lulled her into a drowsy stupor. She startled awake when the horses accelerated into a trot, letting the cloak slip from her fingers and clutching at the soldier's uniform. His arms tightened around her, holding her in place, and though it was uncomfortable, it was infinitely better than what she experienced before.

They moved her twice more before they stopped for the night. Though it was no less painful than it had been during the morning, and the other men were as cruel to her as before, the brief respite the young soldier provided gave her the courage to carry her through the afternoon. Still, by the time they stopped that night, she ached all over and was shivering so violently she couldn't stand on her own.

The soldier she was riding with dropped her roughly to the ground and removed the hood. "Get up," he said, standing over her. She tried to stand but couldn't get her legs under herself.

"She's going to die."

"So, the *l'oss* dies. What of it?"

"The inquisitors expect them to arrive in Brennan alive. If she dies, you'll answer to Inquisitor Schakal."

There was a slight pause and then the first man said, "Fine, you're so worried about her, from now on, she's your problem. Go ahead, coddle her. We'll see what the Inquisitor has to say about that." His boots receded.

Someone threw a cloak around her shoulders. It swallowed her small frame, but it was thick and soft. Hands grasped her elbows and pulled her to her feet, supporting her so she didn't fall. She looked up to see the kind soldier buttoning the cloak at her neck. "Thank you," she said, forcing the words past chattering teeth.

He didn't look at her, but he blushed and said, "Don't thank me."

He led her to a spot near the fire and helped her into a sitting position. The portion of broth he brought was larger than the night before and again she whispered, "*Tok*," as he left.

Chapter 21

Minna

Minna was on the hilltop above Fennig, Jason guiding her as they danced, their laughter exciting the *lan'and* who whirled around them, sharing their happiness.

"Minna!"

Jason faded, his blue eyes closing, his skin taking on a deathly pallor before he vanished, replaced by Ulf's ghostly face.

"Minna, get up. We have to get going."

It was still dark. That was her first thought. Then pain crowded out every other thought. Her back and legs were so stiff, she was afraid for a moment that she couldn't move. With a groan, she stretched, reaching over her head and pointing her toes, then she carefully rolled onto her side and pulled her knees to her chest, stretching her back. Rolling onto her knees, she rested her forehead on the cold ground for a moment. With a mighty effort, she pushed herself onto her feet, then slowly rose until she was upright. She stood, absently trying to tame her tangled mop of hair, watching Ulf saddling the horses.

When he finished, Minna was still trying to loosen tight muscles. He handed her a hard biscuit, looked down at her rumpled bed roll and said, "We have to go."

She managed to organize herself and get her pack and bow strapped to her saddle before remembering her disquiet from the night before. Ulf waited patiently. On impulse, she untied her bow, strung it and slung it over her shoulder. Taking the reins, she started leading the horse to the path.

"Why did you do that?"

"What?" she asked.

"String your bow. Why did you do that?"

She shrugged. "We might catch them today. I want to be ready."

Ulf looked as if he would argue, but then he turned and led his horse down the path. Minna watched him go then followed.

They started out walking, leading their horses, giving all of them time to warm their muscles, a mercy for which Minna was grateful. By the time Ulf had them mount, the clouds behind them were lightening. With thoughts of the previous morning's near debacle in mind, Minna prepared herself. Taking a firm hold of the reins, she flexed her knees and bounced in the saddle several times. She reached forward and patted Edda's neck, whispering to herself, "Let the horse lift you and guide yourself down. Move with the horse. Don't let the horse bounce you out of the saddle." She waited, but instead of immediately picking up the pace, Ulf had them walk. She bit her lip but decided not to press the issue. After what seemed a long time, when she was nearing the end of her patience, Ulf finally urged them into a trot.

She tensed, preparing herself. Still, the initial upward surge nearly threw her from the saddle. Resisting the urge to lunge for the pommel, she forced herself to relax and pay attention to Edda's rhythm. To her surprise, she found herself matching the horse's movements. She was still sore, but she thought it might be manageable. After a time, she became comfortable enough to lift her eyes and look around. Ulf was watching her with the crooked grin Minna decided was his most genuine. She returned his smile, all worries from the night before forgotten.

The snow stopped during the night, leaving a dusting of powdery fluff on the highway. There would be much more snow soon, but by noon, when they stopped for a cold meal, the wind was ushering the clouds to the east, leaving blue skies in their wake. They let the horses forage the narrow shoulder beside the highway and shared lunch.

Minna perched on a boulder beside the road, enjoying the sun's warmth and chewing a tough piece of dried venison. They stopped on a section of the highway that swung north before it turned west again and tracked the northern edge of a wide valley. To her left, a stream descended in a series of cascades and fed a narrow river. Sunlight glittered on mist where the water met the valley floor. Looking west, she followed the path of the river until it disappeared as it descended to the lowlands. She could just make out a sliver of the land beyond. It was breathtaking, as if she were seeing to the end of the world. Most of it looked familiar, the glint of sunlight on the river, the green of evergreen forest, the browns and blacks of deciduous trees in the winter. Far in the distance, though, it changed. She held her hand over her eyes, shielding them from the sun, trying to understand what she was seeing.

"It's the plains. Beyond the forest, the plains stretch to the sea. Brennan is beyond the horizon." Ulf pointed to the southwest.

"Plains?"

Ulf chuckled at her puzzled expression. "The plains are flat lands, with no trees, or, at least, very few trees."

Minna gaped at him. "No trees?"

He laughed. "Yeah, that was my reaction the first time. How could there be no trees?"

Minna looked down into the valley where she could just see the *lan'and* among the trees. What do the spirits do in the plains? She looked back at Ulf, who was watching her, amused. "Is it just dirt?"

He shook his head. "Grass, as far as you can see, and you can see a looong way. Kind of unsettling, at first. You feel sort of… exposed." He gazed to the west. "Now that I think about it, I still don't like it. It's not a good place, Minna."

Contemplating the idea of a place with no trees, Minna decided she didn't want to see it. "We should be getting close, right? They can't be going very fast."

Ulf stood and wiped away the crumbs of a biscuit. "We better get going."

As they readied themselves to leave, Ulf said, "I'm not sure it's a good idea to keep the bow over your shoulder. It digs into the saddle." He pointed to some scuff marks on the back of Minna's saddle. When she looked at him, he gestured down the road. "The highway straightens when it turns west. We'll be able to see them from a long way off."

Minna looked down the highway, considering. When she looked back at Ulf, he focused on his pack. It wasn't a good idea to leave a bow strung when it wasn't in use. She unstrung the bow and tied it behind her saddle. Moments later, they were on their way.

As the afternoon wore on, Minna felt her frustration growing. She didn't know if they were getting closer or falling further behind. She knew the soldiers had a head start, but the excitement of beginning the pursuit blinded her to the reality of the situation. Feeling a renewed urgency, she implored Ulf to speed up. He refused, arguing that the horses wouldn't last all the way to Brennan if they pushed them too hard. Minna countered that she didn't want to make it all the way to Brennan. If they had to go that far, it would be too late.

She was trying to think of a fresh approach to the argument when Ulf turned off the highway.

"Whoa," Minna said, pulling Edda to a stop. "Where are you going?"

He pointed into the forest where Minna could see the first few feet of a path. "This is a shortcut. It will cut leagues off the trip. The soldiers wouldn't take this road, so it will put us ahead of them."

"But you said Brennan is that way," Minna said, pointing to the southwest.

"It is, but you have to cross the Odun River in Hast." He pointed to the northwest. "This road will get us there before them."

It didn't look like a road to Minna. It was barely wide enough for the horses to walk without the branches of trees brushing their flanks. She looked down the highway. Ulf was right. Once they turned west, she could see several leagues ahead, and there was no sign of the soldiers. For all she knew, they were falling further behind. "What are we waiting for, then?

207

Let's go." She might have imagined the relief on Ulf's face before he turned away, but before she could consider what it meant, he was already among the trees. She watched his back for a moment, glanced once more to the west, then followed.

Once they were among the trees, the path narrowed further until the prickly spruce needles brushed her legs. Ulf fidgeted, glancing back at her and peering into the trees on either side of the path. She studied the trees. She was hemmed in, with no room to turn around, and she didn't know how to tell Edda to back up. It was a bad idea to unstring her bow.

The path widened and then opened up into a small grassy glade awash in sunlight. Ulf stopped at the edge of the clearing, turning his horse so that he blocked her from entering. He looked directly at her, grimaced, and said, "Sorry, Minna, it's for the best." Raising his voice, he said, "*Ērtsa jīla Alle'oss (We are Alle'oss)*."

The trees on each side of the path moved as people emerged onto the path. Lifting her right foot over the horse's back, she reached for her bow as she dropped to the ground, but her left foot caught in the stirrup, and she twisted away from the horse. The bow slipped through her fingers, and she landed on her shoulder.

"Minna!" Ulf shouted.

A person in a dark green cloak stepped out of the trees. One hand held a bow, and the other caught Edda's reins to control the shying horse. When he looked down at her, all she could make out in the shadow of his hood were the twin glints of his eyes.

Jerking her foot free of the stirrup, she rolled onto her hands and knees and crawled between Edda's legs, but found her way blocked by more cloaked people. Heart strumming, she dodged the nervous horse's hooves, searching frantically for a way out. They surrounded her.

"Minna!" Ulf shouted again. "It's okay. They won't hurt you."

She tensed, gathering herself to break through the ring when strong hands grabbed her from behind, and dragged her, twisting and kicking, backward. The *lan'and* burst from the trees, whirling among the cloaked figures. She scrabbled at the hands gripping her arms until other hands wrapped around her wrists, pulling them behind her back. Pressure spiked painfully in her center. She prepared to call the spirits, not sure whether she could do anything with Ulf and the horses nearby, but wanting to be ready.

"Stop! *Atuk! Sa...* uh... *Ērtsi sa ni Alle'oss (Stop, she's Alle'oss)."* Ulf leapt from his horse and began shoving people aside to get to her. "*Ērtsi Alle'oss! Ērtsu ku... so... soman wa* (She's *Alle'oss.* What are you doing)?"

When he broke through the ring, someone stepped in front of him and placed a hand on his chest. A woman's voice said calmly, "*Atuk, Ulf. Ērtsi chira ni sha jīlata nalongia* (Stop, Ulf. This is for our protection)."

"Don't scare her! You don't know what she can do." Ulf struggled to get past, but only managed to cast an apologetic grimace over the woman's shoulder.

Once Ulf relented, the woman turned toward Minna and pulled the hood of her cloak back. Her crystal blue eyes, blond hair and pale skin marked her as *Alle'oss.* She studied Minna, her expression unreadable. "*Kisu Alle'oss da* (Do you speak Alle'oss)?"

Minna couldn't seem to get a full breath, but she nodded and said, "*Da.*"

The woman's face relaxed slightly. "*Ērtsu Minna Hunter* (You are Minna Hunter)?"

"*Da.*"

She nodded and said, "*Ērtsa Zaina. Pa ala pajuata jīla aku* (I'm Zaina. We won't harm you). She tugged a black cloth from her belt and held it up. "*Eitu, ērtsi chira ni sha jīlata nalongia da* (You understand, this is for our protection)?"

Minna stared at the cloth. Though she wasn't sure what the woman intended, she nodded.

Zaina turned away, tossed the cloth to another woman with short spiky red hair, and said, "*Paluwok atsa* (Blindfold her)."

Zaina stepped away, revealing Ulf. When he saw her staring at him, he grimaced and said, "I'm sorry, Minna. It'll be okay."

The red-headed woman lifted the cloth, which turned out to be a hood. She held it up for a moment, meeting Minna's eyes and lifting a brow. Minna sent the swarm of spirits spiraling away, then met the woman's eyes and nodded. The hood was wool, long enough to gather over her shoulders and across her chest and left her in total darkness. She heard the rustle of the group moving into the brush, and someone grabbed her arm and guided her off the path. Her legs, weak and trembly, felt as if they weren't part of her. She stumbled and other hands took her other arm and steadied her.

She heard Zaina say, "*Ulf, ērtsu sidey.*"

Ulf stammered, "I..what?"

"You're late."

"I...I know, I'm sorry. She's never ridden a horse—"

"*Kisok Alle'oss eia.*"

"I'm sor... *Ama...* uh...*Sosenga* (Sorry)."

"*Sa'iti, Ulf. Kasok eon'asutā* (No problem, Ulf. Bring the horses)."

"*Da. Tok.*"

In her dark world, it felt to Minna that they walked a long way. The bright, clean scent of evergreen diminished to be replaced by the mustiness of moldering leaves. She tried counting steps, but even with the hands supporting her, it was difficult navigating the uneven, root-covered ground, and she lost count. As they left the path, people spoke in *Alle'oss*. They were quiet and tentative at first, as if they feared being overheard. But when Zaina joined in, the group seemed to relax, and soon, multiple lively, overlapping conversations broke out. Their *Alle'oss* was faltering, often incorrect, and between that and the odd accents, she could only catch bits and pieces of what they said, but she could detect no menace or anger. Her fear faded, but anxiety kept her breath shallow and left her limbs weak. On more than one occasion, she heard her name, and once, she was sure she heard someone say *saa'myn* before someone shushed them.

The first hint they were reaching their destination was the smell of smoke and the indescribably delicious aroma of roasting meat. They stepped into what must have been a clearing, as she no longer felt branches tugging at her cloak. The voices around her rose in volume, their tone happy, and others joined them. The hands on her arms pulled her to a stop, then fell away, leaving her standing silently, listening to what sounded like people exchanging greetings and hugs. The shouts and laughter were cut short when a man's voice rose above the others. *"Zaina, ērtsi atsa? (Zaina, is this her)?"*

"Da, ērtsi Minna Hunter."

There was a pause when all Minna could hear were people shuffling about and a few whispers, then the man said, *"Kasok atsa (Bring her)."*

Hands again took her arms and urged her forward. She could tell from the sounds and smells around her that they were walking through a large encampment. They came to a stop and Minna heard the man say, *"Beadu, ērtsi Minna Hunter. Ērtsa pakaliāna malika ni sha ki ku. (Beadu, this is Minna Hunter. The girl you've been waiting for)."*

There was a pause, then the hood was pulled from her head, leaving her squinting in the sudden light. She stood in front of a small hut. A fire burned in a shallow pit and behind the fire sat the oldest woman Minna ever saw. Despite her age, she sat cross-legged on the ground, a wooden staff across her knees. She hunched over slightly, making her seem somehow shrunken. An unruly cloud of white hair floated around her head in the breeze. Her skin was leathery, and her eyes seemed to disappear into the wrinkles that covered her face. But what caused Minna's mouth to drop open was the swarm of *lan'and* swirling around the woman and her hut. She never saw so many in one place. Their light made everything nearby shimmer.

The woman cackled, her face split by an immense toothless smile. "Minna, stop gawping and sit," she said, tapping a log beside the fire with her staff.

Minna could only stare at her.

Chapter 22

Minna

Minna gaped at the woman until the sound of laughter caught her attention. She spun around and looked out at a small community. Huts, like the one the old woman sat in front of, nestled in among the trees in typical *Alle'oss* fashion. People gathered around fires, preparing evening meals and socializing. More than a few were looking her way. The late afternoon light filtered through the leafless canopy, backlighting the smoke from the fires and setting the trees in sharp relief, lending the scene a dreamlike clarity. The smell of food set her stomach grumbling and flooded her mouth. Zaina was engaged in conversation with a tall man with long, red hair and a maroon cloak. They glanced her way occasionally, and when she caught Minna looking, Zaina gave her a brief smile. Minna turned back to the old woman.

She was watching Minna, grinning. Reaching out, she tapped the log again with her staff.

Minna edged over and sat, studying the woman. "You're the *saa'myn* my father told me about. Beadu."

"Just so," Beadu said, returning Minna's gaze.

"Um… I'm Minna."

"Yes, I know who you are. I knew your mother and father. Was there when you came into the world. Never heard a baby squall so loud."

"You know my parents?"

Beadu nodded.

Minna's mouth opened, but she had so many questions, she didn't know where to start. To give herself time, she looked up again at the spirits.

"Ah, yes," the old woman said. "You have *and'ssyn*, of course."

Minna glanced at Beadu, then returned her gaze to the spirits. "*And'ssyn?*"

"Spirit sight. You see the *lan'and.*" She cocked her head, peering at Minna. "Can you call them?"

Minna frowned up at the swarm. She focused on her center and called. Although she had done it many times before, the sight of so many spirits pausing in their flight was startling. A great cloud of glowing orbs surrounded her and Beadu, and she felt them watching, as if wondering what she wanted.

Beadu laughed. "Just so!" She looked up, and the spirits resumed soaring around the small hut. Minna watched them for a moment. When she looked back at Beadu, the old woman was studying her. "You have done well for one on her own so long," she said.

Minna, still having trouble organizing her thoughts, found herself asking, "Who are all these people?"

Beadu nodded, gazing out across the encampment. "Some are those who have lost their homes to the Empire. Others have lost much more." She paused until Minna met her eyes. "At long last, the *Alle'oss* are learning to fight back."

"They speak *Alle'oss.*"

"Just so. They wish to reclaim the old ways that were stolen from them." Beadu grinned. "That is why I am here."

"Where have you been?"

"Hiding." She cackled. "Didn't want to at first. Thought I would be safe in Fennig, as it is so remote. It was your mother who convinced me to go away and hide. Said I would be needed for this moment. Your mother is not always right, but…" She gestured toward Minna. "… often she is. It was your father who took me to a place I would be safe."

Minna's head swam. Why didn't they tell her any of this?

Beadu nodded, watching Minna's face. "Don't be hard on your parents, Minna. Choosing what's best for your children is no easy thing. They loved you and your sister and wanted to keep you safe." Beadu sighed. "I suppose they thought they needed to keep me safe as well. I am, after all, the last *saa'myn*."

Minna tried to reconcile the parents she knew with what Beadu said. Anger flickered at the edge of her mind and the *lan'and* responded, swirling in tighter circles. She felt a familiar pressure in her mind and closed her eyes, taking long slow breaths until the pressure eased. When she opened her eyes, Beadu was watching her with an expression that was difficult to interpret.

"You have much to learn and too little time," the old woman said.

Minna shook her head. "I can't stay here. I have to save my sister. The soldiers are taking her to Brennan, and they'll kill her when she gets there."

"Just so." Beadu lifted her staff and waved at Zaina and the man in the maroon cloak.

When they approached, Minna stood. "My sister—"

Zaina lifted her hands in a placating gesture. "We know about your sister. Ulf sent a message before you left Fennig to tell us you were coming. He's just told us about your sister. We're sending some people to look for her."

Minna took a step forward. "Let's go!"

"You're not going anywhere," the man said. "We'll have to ride fast, and Ulf told us how well you ride. Besides, you won't be able to help if we catch them." He nodded at Beadu and said, "You can help by learning as much as you can from Beadu, as fast as you can." He turned and walked away.

Zaina watched him go, then gave Minna an apologetic look. "*Sosenga, Minna. Reōmi Torsten ni sesīmi. Āla sinnu kuta mali'sa* (I'm sorry, Minna. Torsten means well. We'll save your sister)." She rested her hand on Minna's shoulder briefly, gave her a quick smile, and followed Torsten.

Minna watched them go, feeling useless.

"Now, sit."

Minna looked back at Beadu, who was tapping the log with her staff again.

When Minna sat, Beadu said, "You have much to learn. It's true, but perhaps this will be enough for today." Minna was still looking at Torsten and Zaina who were standing at the center of a group of men and women holding bows. "Minna!"

Minna turned sharply toward her.

"You must listen to this." Minna was startled to see Beadu's eyes emerge from the wrinkles. They were blue and clear, not what she expected from someone so old. Satisfied she had Minna's attention, she continued. "You are a danger to yourself and everyone here because you cannot hide yourself. Not to mention the fact you make many of them uncomfortable."

Minna's attention instantly focused on the old woman. It had not occurred to her until this moment, but if Beadu was a *saa'myn*, she should have been able to sense Beadu's presence, and she couldn't.

Beadu nodded. "You have suffered much, I am guessing, because you hurt people." She shook her head at Minna's expression. "You could not help it. It was not supposed to be this way."

"How? How do I hurt people?"

"When you call the spirits, where do you feel it?"

Minna, caught off guard by the question, hesitated, then placed her finger on the bridge of her nose between her eyes and said, "In here. I call it my center."

Beadu nodded. "Just so. Now close your eyes and find your center."

Minna did as she was asked, finding her center cool and quiet, forcing the jangly turmoil in her mind into the background.

Beadu spoke softly. "That place, your center, that is the place where your spirit resides."

"My spirit?"

"Just so. We will speak of this soon, but for now, it is enough for you to know you can feel your spirit because you have spirit sight... *and'ssyn.*

For most people, their spirit is so tightly bound by their material essence, they can't feel where one starts and the other ends. They're unable to perceive the spirits in the world around them."

"But why does it hurt other people?"

Rather than answering the question, Beadu said, "Your center connects you to the spirit realms."

Minna frowned impatiently.

"You must understand, the *saa'myn*, we have studied the spirits for a very long time. We are not so arrogant to believe we know the minds of the gods, but we know what we experience and what I tell you now, if not true, suffices for our purposes. Do you understand?"

Minna opened her eyes. "No, I don't."

Beadu smiled, nodding. "What is the color blue?"

Minna looked up at the sky, deep blue in the evening light. She looked back at Beadu and shook her head.

"Just so. It does not matter if we see blue differently or whether something called blueness exists apart from what we perceive. We cannot describe it, but we both know what we mean when we say blue. Yes?"

Minna bit her lip, not completely sure she saw the connection, but nodded uncertainly.

"As it is with the spirit realms. We cannot know the minds of the gods, but we have learned to describe our experience, so we understand one another. I do not know for sure that there is a spirit realm called *luft'heim* because no one has ever gone there, but I know there are spirits we call the *luft'and* and they are not among these." She waved her hand at the *lan'and*. "It does not matter whether this realm, *luft'heim*, exists. We name it because it helps us to understand what we experience. Do you understand?"

"Maybe."

"Good enough! Now, we believed the world is made up of more realms than what we see around us. How do we know this? We see the *lan'and* and they are the *only* spirits we see. But, as I said, there are other spirits. Yes, many other spirits and we cannot see them. So, we say they exist in other realms, the spirit realms."

"How do you know there are other spirits?"

"That is a question for another day." Beadu pursed her lips, then pointed at Minna and said, "Your center is part of one of these realms. A realm we called *mid'heim*, the middle realm. It is, as I said, where your spirit resides, and it connects you to the other realms." She lifted her arms to the *lan'and*. "For you, that connection is wide open. Though your spirit is bound to your body, *mid'heim* extends outward from your center. This allows your spirit to sense the *lan'and* and for them to sense your spirit." She leaned toward Minna and tapped her temple. "It is not your eyes which *see* the *lan'and*. It is more correct to say your spirit senses their presence. Do you understand?"

"Yes! I saw… sensed myself… my spirit, when I talked to the *lan'and*." Beadu sat quietly for a long time, staring at her. "What?"

"You have asked the spirits into your… center, into your mind?"

Minna nodded. "Three times."

Beadu's mouth stretched into a wide smile. "That is very good. Yes, you have done well." She gave a quick nod, leaned toward Minna and said, "Now! Close your eyes and find your center." When Minna was ready, she continued. "For some, it is painful to be near you."

Minna sat frozen, breath thready, feeling as if she was standing on a precipice. How much would her life change if she could stop herself from hurting people? She swallowed, licked her lips and asked, "Why?"

"When you find your center, how do you feel?"

Minna sighed. It seemed Beadu would get to the answer she needed in her own time. "Peaceful… happy. It feels wonderful."

"Just so." Her voice became more animated. "Your spirit rejoices, temporarily freed from the demands of your material essence. Though we are also spirits, like the *lan'and*, our spirits are crippled by our material essences." She reached over and pinched Minna's arm. "Our bodies, our material essence, are subject to the vagaries of the flesh. We become fatigued, hungry. We can be injured or grow sick. We grow old and die. When we are born, our spirit is tightly bound, trapped. It twists and pulls against these constraints, but slowly, so it is barely noticeable. For some, the boundaries relax, freeing their spirit, if but a little. For a very few, the boundary expands beyond their material essence, and they achieve *and'ssyn*. Your spirit calls out to the *lan'and* and to other spirits." She paused before saying softly, "I am sure you remember, as I do, the day your spirit recognized the *lan'and*."

Minna remembered how she felt that day when she was eight years old. Not the anguish brought on by her friends' rejection or the fear and despair she felt at her father's tears. What she remembered was the moment she first saw the small orbs of light. It wasn't fear or caution she felt, as one would expect, but a dawning joy, a bewildering sensation that she suddenly discovered she was not alone in the world. Minna felt her face stretching in a wide grin. Tears leaked from her closed eyelids and spilled down her cheeks.

"Yes, just so," Beadu said quietly. "Now you understand." She waited, allowing Minna a moment. "To understand the effect you have, you must understand that spirits are not solitary creatures. They wither and despair when isolated from their own kind." When Minna nodded, she continued. "For many people, their spirits remain trapped. When they are near, your spirit calls out to them, but bound as they are, they can only pull and twist in an effort to respond. It can be quite painful for them."

"My father, I don't think it hurts him, but he said he can't see the *lan'and*."

"Yes, your father's spirit is free, but only just so. That is how it is for some. Their spirit senses yours and they can respond, after a fashion. They feel a small part of your happiness when they are near you." Minna opened her eyes again at that. "Yes, being near you brings their spirits joy, if maybe just a little bit."

Minna looked up at the cloud of spirits. Did Jason feel her happiness when he was near? The thought filled her with a confusing swirl of emotions. To hide her tears, she gazed out at the encampment. Small groups were gathering around their fires, laughing and talking. What would they think of her when she walked among them? She remembered a crowded market, fearful stares from people she knew and Agatha's shouted accusation: "WITCH!" Turning back to Beadu, she said, "How do I hide myself?"

"You must close your connection to the spirit realms."

"How?"

"Find your center."

When Minna was ready, she nodded.

"Now, everyone has their own way to describe this, but, for me, it is as if I am pushing... gently... against my center."

"Like when I push the spirits from my mind?"

"Just so. When I say push, it is as if you are pushing the spirits from your mind, but much more gentle."

Minna found her center and tried to remember how it felt before. When she was ready, she took a breath and pushed. The cool, quiet place in her mind vanished, leaving her feeling vaguely empty and alone.

"Yes, that is good." Beadu said. "I cannot feel you, and if I cannot, no one will be able to."

Minna opened her eyes and stared, in wonder, at Beadu. "It's that easy?"

"Not quite as easy as that. Already, I feel you. Closing your center is easy. Keeping it closed when you are not paying attention or are sleeping is less so. You will need to practice. At first, it is difficult to stay hidden, but with time, you will learn to do it without thinking."

Her recent trip to the market in Fennig came to Minna's mind again, chased by many other similar memories, and the anger she set aside earlier flashed hot. She tried to slow her breath, but panted, her hands clenched into fists pressing down on her thighs. This time, her anger would not be denied. Someone could have told her. It was so easy. Her mother suffered unnecessarily for years, simply for the sin of having Minna as a daughter. Alyn and Jason suffered as well for being associated with her. The pressure built.

Thwack! Her eyes flew open to find Beadu holding her staff over Minna's head. Although it had only been a tap, Minna screwed up her face in mock outrage. "Ow!"

Beadu replaced the staff across her knees. "You have a right to your anger, Minna, but you are not just anyone. When you were younger, it was one thing, but now you have great power, and when you lose your temper, people will suffer. You must put your anger aside, for now, until you can control your power." She paused, took a deep breath and added in a gentler tone, "Now, find your center."

Minna, rubbing the top of her head, scowled. She closed her eyes and searched for her center. It was more difficult this time, but eventually, she found it. She sighed, letting it quiet her mind.

Beadu spoke softly. "Your mother did not intend to leave you alone. She planned to give you the help you needed, but, as I said, events intervened. You must not judge her too harshly before you understand her. Now, take your anger and put it away. For now."

Minna held her center in her mind until her breath settled into a slow rhythm.

"Very good. That is enough for today, I think. Your young friend is waiting to show you to your hut."

Minna opened her eyes. Beadu was watching her. "*Tok*, Beadu."

"*Ju sa.* Now go and don't forget to practice closing your center. Let your fellow *Alle'oss* ease your pain and come back tomorrow morning."

Minna nodded and stood. When she turned toward Ulf, she saw the anxiety in his face before his eyes wandered up to the trees. Minna marched over and stood in front of him, hands on her hips. His eyes found hers briefly before dropping to his feet. "I'm sorry, Minna."

"You could have told me."

"No, I couldn't." He met her eyes again, wincing, but held her gaze this time.

Closing her eyes, Minna pushed on her center. When she looked at him, Ulf was staring at her, eyes wide.

"What did you do?"

Her irritation melted away in the warmth of Ulf's astonished smile. For almost since before she could remember, the pain she caused other people ruled her life, limiting her world in ways she simply came to expect. The simple act of standing so close to Ulf, without worrying about the pain she caused him, left her nearly breathless. She gazed out at the busy community. A song, one she recognized, started in one corner of the camp and was soon picked up by others. They were scenes she could only watch longingly from afar. Until now. The shadow of her anger flickered in the back of her mind, but she shoved it down. There would be time for that later. She returned Ulf's smile and said, "I'm hungry. Is there something to eat?"

Alyn

The next day, Alyn rode with the young soldier the entire day. He wouldn't tell her his name and rebuffed her attempts at conversation, but she began to think of him as Tomtie, a benevolent spirit in *Alle'oss* folklore, who appeared to aid travelers in trouble. The wind died, and the temperature rose as the day passed. It felt as if they were descending to lower elevations. She felt good enough to consider her situation, but she could think of no plan that would allow her to escape. With nothing better to do in the dark world of the hood, she sought her center.

Bouncing along on top of the horse, in considerable pain, it was much more difficult than in the quiet glade with Minna coaching her. It was a thrill when she found it while they sat by the road for the midday meal, but she found it impossible to concentrate on it for long. Late in the afternoon, she found it again and was able to hold on to it. She began letting it go and finding it again, each time more easily. When she held onto it, it felt as if she were sinking into a cool, quiet pool far from the soldiers, the cold and the pain. The ache in her back and legs retreated to where they were barely noticeable. Though she didn't know how she knew, she was sure this was the home of what awoke inside her and responded when she felt the ripple on the day they took her. When they stopped that night, though she was not pain free, she could walk upright again.

When Tomtie brought her supper, he kept his eyes averted as usual, but when his gaze slid across her face, he stopped and stared at her. Alyn smiled, lifted the bowl cupped in her hands and said, "*Tok.*" He searched her face, his brows drawing together, before nodding and leaving her alone.

The *lan'and* flitted playfully through the bare branches of the maples they camped under. Without thinking, Alyn reached out and got their attention. They stopped and hovered. A slow smile lifted the corners of her lips, and she lowered the bowl until it lay cradled in her lap. On instinct, she sank into her center, and the *lan'and* appeared. Not the small orbs of light she could see with her eyes, but something more substantial, individual presences who she somehow knew were watching and waiting. She called them again and was rewarded when they swooped down and whirled joyfully around her. She felt herself respond to their welcoming embrace and laughed. Leaving the bowl in her lap, she lifted her hands and wiggled her fingers, as if she could entice them to settle into her palms. After Minna's description of *talking* to the spirits, she was reluctant to go further for now, so, with a thought, she sent them back into the trees. Lifting the bowl to her lips, she noticed the four soldiers watching her with stunned expressions. Alyn lowered her bowl, swallowed the warm broth and smiled.

Chapter 23

Stefan

Stefan supposed if he had to spend months on this side of the mountains, it could be worse. The woman's home was surprisingly comfortable for an *Alle'oss* house. The furnishings were not up to the standards of his apartment in Brennan, but they were comfortable and there was plenty of room. The latter was a blessing as he quickly grew weary of his companions. He sent one of his companions-at-arms to Brennan with a message for Malleus Hoerst. The other three gathered in the smallish kitchen, filling the space with their bulk and playing a card game called sabat. The warm, inviting smells of dried herbs and recent meals were quickly overwhelmed by the odor of men who spent days on horseback without bathing. Stefan gave up trying to understand the complex rules of the game and retreated to what passed for a parlor.

He sat gazing into the fire, a healthy portion of the mead they found in the cellar in a wooden cup, dangling from one hand. Yes, it could be worse, staying here, but he desperately hoped he didn't have to. He toyed with the idea of abandoning the search, but after examining the scene of the witch's attack again, he decided it was worth a bit more of his time.

His only solace was that Keelia seemed even more uncomfortable than he did. She spent the day out among the *Alle'oss* and her nights hiding in a bedroom upstairs, more morose than ever, if that was possible. She didn't even share meals with them. He wasn't sure what she was doing to sustain herself, but he suspected she was making friends with the natives. Stefan hadn't said anything, hoping she would glean useful information from the villagers, but she simply shook her head when he inquired.

His own efforts to learn more had been unsuccessful. There were many willing to talk, including that oaf, Agmar who showed up at the door at least once a day, but they offered little that was useful. Some stories they told were so obviously false that he didn't know whether to believe any of it. When his party returned to the witch's house, they found the mother absent and, of course, no one knew where she might have gone. He still held out hope for the boy, Jason; the one everyone said was a friend of the witch. Although he was conscious, his family flatly refused to allow Stefan to talk to him until he was stronger. He would normally order his escort to force their way past the blacksmith into the house, but when he suggested it, Keelia gave him a dangerous look, so he waited. He was running out of options, and the black-haired witch might be far away by now. If only Sister Keelia would cooperate.

She wanted to accompany the brother returning to Brennan, but Stefan refused. She knew something, and Stefan was determined to find out what it was. The trick was how to force a sister to do anything she didn't want to do. He didn't know what her specific gifts were, but he suspected, based on the stories surrounding her exploits in the wars, she was extremely dangerous. The sound of a door opening on the upper floor pulled him out of his reverie. Maybe the time had come. Footsteps descended the stairs. He stood and faced the doorway to the house's small foyer. Keelia appeared, glancing his way before heading to the front door.

"Keelia."

She paused, hand resting on the doorknob. After appearing to gather herself, she turned to face him, her expression guarded and her hands hanging at her sides. "Yes, Inquisitor?"

Stefan forced a smile onto his face. "I would like to speak with you, Sister Keelia."

She gestured toward the door and said, "I was on my way to check on the blacksmith's boy."

Stefan tried a placating smile. "That can wait. We can go together later. Come sit with me by the fire."

Keelia hesitated, glanced at the door, then walked over and sat stiffly in one of the two chairs arrayed in front of the fire. She cocked her head, peering up at Stefan expectantly, the fingers of her left hand tapping the chair's arm.

Stefan sighed inwardly. Would a little civility be too hard? He remained standing, swirling the mead in the mug. "Keelia, it seems we may have gotten off on the wrong foot somehow."

She snorted, the left corner of her mouth lifting in that infuriating smirk. Heat rose along the back of his neck. So much for civility.

"Keelia, you sensed something when we took the blond witch. Something in the forest across the highway."

She stared into the fire, her expression tight, her left knee bouncing in time with her tapping fingers.

Stefan rolled his eyes. "It was the other witch, wasn't it? You felt her in the trees and warned her away, didn't you?"

Keelia turned a wide smile on Stefan and said, "How could that be? *You* didn't sense her, did you?"

He stared at her, his expression frozen, a blush warming his cheeks. He had to suppress an impulse to leap at her, to wipe that smirk from her face, an act that would likely be his last. "Yes, you figured it out, did you, Keelia? It makes you feel so superior to sneer at the inquisitor who can't sense Daga's essence." He meant it to be menacing, but he was ashamed at how petulant he sounded.

Her response was to cock her head, taunting him with an expression of mock surprise. "No, really?"

"You sisters, so smug. Lording it over everyone. Well, you allowed a witch to escape. That's a crime punishable by death."

Keelia rose to stand directly in front of Stefan, her smile sliding into a smirk again. "Prove it."

Stefan's mind went white. "Your time is coming. You, and the whole Seidi. We're going to make sure you know your place."

Keelia's brow furrowed. "What in Daga's name are you talking about? Without us saving the Empire from the emperor's stupidity, the barbarians would be peeling your skin from your flesh to hear you scream." Her eyes narrowed. "Now, get out of my way."

Stefan looked toward the kitchen, preparing to shout for his escort, when he felt Keelia open herself to the Daga's essence. His mind squirmed. She lifted her hand, letting sparks crackle along her fingers. He took a step back, dropping the mug, the sharp tang of ozone prickling his nostrils. Tearing his eyes away from the crackling glow, he looked at Keelia's face.

She showed no emotion, but there was a frightening edge to her voice when she said, "I'll be leaving in the morning. Until then, you and your flunkies stay out of my way. I'm done with you. Now, get out of my way and keep yourself out of my sight when I get back."

Stefan got his trembling legs to move so he could step aside enough to let her pass. When she turned her head toward the foyer, he saw a flash of blue at the nape of her neck. It was the *Alle'oss* ribbon, caught by the wind when they entered the village square. She wrapped it around the back of her neck and tucked the ends into her tunic at the shoulders.

The whoosh of blood in his head drowned out rational thought. Before he knew what he was doing, he snatched the small knife hidden in his belt, reached out, and nicked the back of Keelia's arm as she passed. She whirled around, reaching across her body to the injured arm. When she withdrew her hand, she stared at the blood on her fingers. The shock on her face twisted into a terrifying rage and Stefan felt her open herself again to Daga's essence. This was nothing like what he felt before. He brought his hands to his head, squeezing as if he could stop his brain from twisting on itself. She lifted her hands, blue sparks crawled along both of her arms. He stumbled backward, tripped over a chair, and landed just short of the fire in the hearth. Shielding his head with his arms, he hoped only that it would end quickly.

Nothing happened. The twisting sensation in his mind stopped, and the electrical crackle of Daga's essence went silent. When he peeked at Keelia, he found her swaying on her feet, her eyes unfocused and searching, as if she was watching something no one else could see. His escort burst into the room, swords drawn. Taking in the scene, Sergeant Ellgar raised his sword to strike Keelia down.

"Stop!" Stefan yelled. Ellgar stopped himself, just in time, staring in confusion at his commander.

Stefan clambered to his feet. "Yes! It worked!" He laughed, giddy with relief. A wave of dizziness washed over him, forcing him to lean over, hands on his knees, taking deep breaths. How close was that? He snatched up the knife at his feet and straightened. "Of course, we've tested it thoroughly on the witches, but never on a full sister and it was only a nick." He gestured to Keelia. "I'd call that a successful test."

"Sir? What's going on?" Ellgar asked.

Stefan waved his hand, holding the knife toward Ellgar. "Everything is under control, sergeant." He stood in front of Keelia, studying her wandering eyes, waving his hand in front of her face.

"What's wrong with her, sir?"

Stefan lifted the small knife. "The blade is coated with witchbane. It's a plant that grows in the Northern Mountains. Not what the natives call it, of course." He paused, hand to his chest, taking a moment to catch his breath. "It has hallucinogenic properties. Our sister, here, is lost in her own little world right now, and more importantly, she's completely incapable of accessing Daga's essence."

Ellgar exchanged a look with his two companions. His lips worked as if he were composing a question for his superior.

Stefan ignored him and said, almost to himself, "Unfortunately, she is also incapable of understanding me or answering questions." He started to rub his chin, then remembered the knife in his hand. "And I'm afraid she will be quite unmanageable when she wakes up. Her secrets will have to go to her grave with her." He glanced at his knife, then focused on the sword in Ellgar's hand. "It wouldn't do to make a mess here. We may have to live here for some time, after all. Sergeant, take her out into the forest and take care of her."

Ellgar glanced at the late afternoon light leaking around the curtains in the windows. "Now, sir?"

"No, of course not. Wait until tonight. Late, when the villagers have gone to their beds. Make sure you do it far enough away that she won't be found." He smiled, studying Keelia's slack face. "Pity, she's really quite pretty."

Keelia

Keelia was riding a dragon. A dream. It had to be, because dragons aren't real. Still, it felt more real, more vivid than anything she experienced in life. Sunlight glinted on the overlapping scales on the dragon's neck as it swung its great head to and fro, unleashing lightning bolts into the hordes of Kaileuk. The muscles in the dragon's back rippled beneath her as the massive wings lifted them into a cloudless sky. She extended her arms, thrilling at the wind whipping her hair behind her, confident she would not fall.

A memory. Not from life, but from a small girl's imagination. Borne of her mother's fanciful tales, but no less real than any other memory, even so. But Keelia's mother and her mother's imaginings were long gone. And dragons don't exist. She pushed the nagging thought away, grasping after the vision, but it was too late. It fell away in tatters, leaving only darkness, nausea and a repetitive jarring, as if someone was punching her repeatedly in the stomach.

She opened her eyes. The dream... vision... was gone, but the world retained a bluish tinge and edges twisted and sparkled. In place of the cerulean sky, there was leaf-strewn ground and the backs of a man's legs, clad in the uniform of an Inquisition brother. It took her a moment to understand what she was seeing and feeling. A man carried her over his shoulder. The jarring she felt resulted from the man descending a slope. With each step, she lifted slightly, then crashed down on his shoulder when his leg took their weight. It was dark. The last thing she remembered before the dream, she was in her small room in the house in Fennig. It was the middle of the afternoon, and she was preparing to go visit the blacksmith. After that... nothing. Stefan must have drugged her. She couldn't remember how she came to be in this predicament, but it was clear she was in trouble.

She reached into her mind, looking for her connection to the spirits. It wasn't there. Her heart lurched and cold sweat slicked her back. Without the spirits, she was just a smallish woman, alone with a large man who obviously intended her harm. The fizzy swirl of panic swept through her, threatening, for a thudding heartbeat, to steal her mind. But bitter experience taught her panic was a killer. She bit down on the inside of her cheek, tasting blood and letting the pain anchor her in the moment.

Taking as deep a breath as she could, she considered her predicament. For whatever reason, she couldn't reach the spirits. The man carrying her was a large man, probably Sergeant Ellgar, and there was little chance she could defeat him in hand-to-hand combat. She felt for the small knives she kept strapped to her wrists. They were gone. Now what? Her hand, flopping limply below her as Ellgar descended the hill, brushed against something hard at Ellgar's side. His sword. She could never pull his sword free and use it before he noticed, not in her current position, but... she carefully felt his belt on his side opposite his sword, pulled the dagger he kept sheathed there, and drove it into his side just above his belt.

Ellgar screamed and launched her away from him, down the slope. The hill was steep enough that she fell free, her arms pinwheeling for balance. Her left arm struck something hard, sending the dagger spinning into the night. An audible crack, followed immediately by searing pain, forced a scream from her. She hit the ground, off balance and, unable to stop her momentum on the steep slope, she tumbled violently backwards down the hill. A kaleidoscope of purplish smears forced her to close her eyes as she crashed through the underbrush, bouncing off trees and stones, until she came to a sudden stop against a large oak near the bottom of the hill.

She lay on her side, taking short, shallow gasps through clenched teeth, clinging to consciousness. The sergeant was coming. She could hear him bellowing and crashing through the underbrush as he navigated the steep slope. Unfortunately, the dagger Keelia stuck in his side probably didn't penetrate anything vital, so, apart from gaining her freedom, she only enraged him. She rolled onto her back, cradling her broken arm, jaw clenched against a scream that tore at her throat. She opened her eyes to a swirl of sparkling light among the writhing branches of the tree above her. Her breath caught, but they were not spirits. Just the lingering effects of the drug. The sight roiled her stomach. Turning her head to the side, she retched, filling her mouth with acrid bile.

Growling in frustration, she rolled over onto her knees, supporting herself with her undamaged arm. She gave herself a moment, panting, waiting for the worst of the pain to recede. Blood from a cut over her left ear flowed into her eye and mouth. Ellgar was getting closer. She tried to stand, but her ankle collapsed beneath her. This time, she couldn't hold back her scream. Easing onto her back, she sagged into the sodden mulch-covered ground, eyes shut against the disorienting effects of the drug.

How many times had she cheated death? Keelia couldn't help hearing some of the stories they told about her. Briana was especially fond of them. Some of them even retained elements of the truth. But the problem with all such stories is that people needed their heroes to be pristine, indomitable bastions of courage and honor. But heroes were not made from the truth. Terrifying moments when the heroes wet themselves from fear, when they discarded honor in a bestial struggle to save themselves and their comrades. Yes, she survived. Time and again, but each time, the burden she carried grew. Would they tell the story of how Keelia, the war hero, was taken down by that puffed-up fraud, Stefan? Her executioner approached, but she knew better than most, it could be worse. A moment of terror, then she could set her burden aside.

He was almost here. She only hoped he got it over quickly.

Not wanting to meet Ellgar with her eyes closed, she opened them and found the branches of the old oak full of small orbs of light. Spirits? They sparkled and left bluish smears as they flitted through the branches, but they were not the random flashes that were there before. She reached for her connection to the spirits and found it, a calm oasis in the swirling chaos of her mind. She called desperately, as Ellgar burst out of the undergrowth, and to her relief, the spirits responded, flooding in and sweeping away the last effects of the drug, clearing her vision and sending her agony into the background.

Ellgar's sneering face appeared above her. "Not so high and mighty now, are we?" He squeezed her jaw in a blood-smeared hand. "I'm going to make you pay for this. I think I'll start by cutting that ugly tattoo off." He patted her left cheek and stood, pointing his sword at her face.

Keelia lifted her hand, turning her palm outward. Ellgar flinched and took a half step back, but when nothing happened, he threw back his head and laughed. Leaning over her, he said, "Can't reach Daga's essence now, can—"

Ellgar's leer froze on his face, then dissolved into a panicked grimace. He stumbled backward. "What are—" She could see his lips moving, but the sound cut off as he faded, becoming first insubstantial, then translucent, and then vanishing. In the silence that followed, not even a breath of wind rustled the trees.

The Seidi taught her it was one of Daga's gifts, one not granted to anyone in living memory. The old sister who taught History of the Seidi would say Ellgar was now in Daga's Otherworld, roaming that dark realm in search of Daga's grace, a grace he would not find. She didn't know where he was, but she was sure Daga had nothing to do with it. Her faith in that vengeful deity was one of many casualties she left in the mud and blood of the southern provinces. Daga's essence, it turned out, was no match for the Kaileuk's implacable ferocity. It was, she discovered, why Deirdre only sent the 'bad girls' to the front. The girls who snuck out at night to commune with spirits. Keelia grew up a good, pious girl. But, driven by necessity and fear, she reclaimed her connection to the spirits the Seidi's cleansing stole from her. Before long, she was using gifts she only read about while in the Seidi. She came home a hero of the Empire, hardened by violence and burdened by doubts and guilt. The spirits saved her life, and through her, the lives of countless others. It was undeniable.

But she couldn't shake the shame a lifetime of religious indoctrination ingrained in her.

"You going to lie here, feeling sorry for yourself until you die?" In the silent forest, her voice rang out, breaking the spell. Moving would invite a world of agony, but she was shivering. If she didn't get moving, she would die of hypothermia.

She rolled over and struggled to her feet, supporting herself on the trunk that ended her fall. Leaning against the rough bark, standing on one foot, she took inventory of her injuries. Her arm was broken. The bone wasn't protruding from the skin, but she couldn't use her left hand. She had various cuts and bruises, including the one over her left ear which still bled freely. Her ankle was broken or sprained badly, and a sharp pain in her back must be from broken or bruised ribs. She turned, putting her back to the tree, and gazed around her. An innervating wave of despair settled on her. She was nearly immobile, lost in a forest she didn't know, near a village in which most of the residents had reason to hate her and her only ally was an inquisitor who tried to kill her. She squeezed her eyes shut, refusing to let the tears filling her eyes wet her cheeks.

Stefan's sneer swam up in her mind, and an unreasoning rage gripped her and yanked her out of her anguish. She screamed, welcoming the bright shafts of pain. She did their dirty work, killed for them, paid a terrible price, and this was how they repaid her. She was done with them. Stefan and everyone else in the Empire who perpetrated their evil. She would kill again, but it would be on her terms, and the victims would be of her choosing.

But first, she needed to find some place to heal. Ellgar probably brought her directly from Fennig. Based on the stars she could see through the bare branches, that meant she was south of the village. If she headed north, she would return to Fennig. In the short time in Fennig, she met a few people in the local tavern who might help her. Not many, but a few. The problem was the hostility generated by Stefan's high-handed contempt for the villagers was directed at her as well. She couldn't be sure how they would react if she showed up in this condition. In any case, there was no way she could climb the slope Ellgar threw her down.

If she skirted the village, she might make it to the little house where the witch lived. She could rest there and heal if it was still empty. If the mother returned… well, one problem at a time.

Pushing herself upright, she took a deep breath and carefully tested her injured ankle. No use. It wouldn't hold her weight. She welcomed the spirits into her mind, sighing in relief as the pain ebbed. Unfortunately, while the spirits would allow her to heal faster than a normal person, it wasn't fast enough to help her now. Casting about, she spotted a likely stick nearby, then pressing her left arm protectively against her stomach, she hopped over to it, grunting with each hop.

Using the stick as a cane, she limped from one tree to the next. Even with the spirits' help, it was slow going. It wasn't long before it was obvious her injuries were worse than she thought. Her head swam, and she stopped twice to vomit. More than once, she found herself tangled in the underbrush and was almost too weak to extricate herself. Tears of frustration froze in her eyelashes. Each painful step drew her entire focus. She didn't know where she was or how far she had yet to go. Time passed unmarked in the unchanging forest, and each time she stopped to rest, it became increasingly difficult to rouse herself to struggle on.

She was resting, her forehead pressed to a small tree to still her shivering, when the spirits left her. Pain rushed in to fill the void, but she hardly noticed. A muddy drowsiness blanketed her mind, dulling her thoughts and obscuring her connection to the spirits. Hypothermia. She was going to die.

She opened her eyes and saw a light out of the corner of her eye. Blinking the moisture from her eyes, she lifted her head and peered through the undergrowth to her left. The light was soft and golden, like a lamp or a fire. She stood, swaying on one foot. It wasn't far. Just a few more yards. Then she could sleep.

She came to the edge of a large clearing and saw the light came from the window of a log building. She had been staring at the buildings for several minutes before she realized she recognized them. It was the smithy where the boy, Jason, the friend of the witch, lived. Standing just inside the tree line, she gazed at the house. Spirits swarmed the clearing. Some of them drifted over to investigate the new arrival. She watched them circling overhead, then looked at the family's home.

The light was too bright to be a banked hearth fire. Someone was awake. They had no reason to help her. Stefan treated them harshly, and might even have killed some of their family, in an effort to interrogate the boy. They didn't know she stopped him. But if she explained, maybe they would take her in. While she stood debating, dawn's gray light lifted details from the darkness. What did she have to lose? She would wait until the sun was up, when they were all awake, then she would try to explain. She slid down to the cold ground and rolled onto her side. Pulling her knees to her chest, she wrapped herself around her injured arm. Just a brief rest. Until the sun was up.

Shouts penetrated her murky dreams, and gentle hands rolled her onto her back. Reluctantly, she opened her eyes and found a man's face, haloed by the morning sun, filling her vision. She thought, at first, he was bald, but then realized his head was wrapped in a bandage. The blacksmith's son? She tried to explain, to beg forgiveness for her part in what they did to the village, but though her lips moved, no sound came.

Concern crinkled the skin around his blue eyes, but a smile transformed his face when he saw her eyes open. "You're alive." His face retreated. "Pa, Ma, come help!"

She heard running feet as she slipped back into darkness.

Chapter 24

Minna

Before the riders left, Zaina pulled up beside Minna on one of the compact mountain horses the *Alle'oss* favored. With her hair pulled back and tied at the base of her neck and wearing a hard expression that seemed to transform her entire demeanor, Minna almost didn't recognize her in the twilight. "*Āla tītota jīla lōrna hemdis* (We will return tomorrow morning)," she said, then wheeled her horse around and led the other riders away. There were no smiles among the men and women, no sign of the laughter and good humor Minna saw before. She watched them until they were out of sight.

"They'll bring her back," Ulf said, watching the last of the riders leave the camp. "Zaina can be scary, but my brother said she's the best we have." He glanced at Minna and asked, "You hungry?"

Minna nodded, dragged her eyes away from the spot her sister's rescuers disappeared and fell into step beside him. He steered them toward a group of young people gathered around a fire, laughing and sharing a meal. One of the boys noticed them approaching and shushed the group.

"Mind if we join you?" Ulf asked.

They all glanced at one another, suppressing smiles. A girl about Minna's age with blond hair said, "Sure." Two people scooted over on a log and made space.

Still worrying over her sister, Minna barely glanced at the group until she was seated. When she looked up, six pairs of eyes were looking back at her. From Ulf's furrowed brow, she guessed he was as perplexed as she was.

"This is Minna and I'm Ulf."

"We know," the blond girl said. "I'm Ase." She made introductions, but Minna lost track of the names, distracted by a tall, rangy boy who was staring intensely at her. Ase introduced him last. "And the rude one here is Rab." The boy sitting on the other side of Rab elbowed him in the ribs, but he ignored it.

"*Eesta samen?*" Rab asked.

Minna frowned and glanced at Ulf, who was glaring at the boy. "You... have? *Saa'myn?*" she asked.

The boy smirked and glanced at Ase. "No, *are* you a *samen?*"

"Oh! You meant to say '*Ērtsu saa'myn?*'" When everyone stared blankly at her, she said, "The first sound is eh, not ee, and you hold it longer than the other sounds. There's an rrrr sound before the ta sound and you roll it." She demonstrated the trilled r. "And you were asking about you... I mean me... so you would use *ērtsu* instead of *ērtsa*. Second person. *Ērtsa* s*aa'myn'* would mean you're asking if *you* are a *saa'myn*, not me." Now there were some open mouths. "*Saa'myn* has a stop in the middle, sah men. So... *Ērtsu* s*aa'myn?* Or you could say '*Ērtsu ku* s*aa'myn da?*', which translates, 'You are *Alle'oss*, yes?'" Silence. "Or just, '*Ērtsu saa'myn da?*'"

Smiles slowly grew on everyone's face, even Rab's.

"*Aut da, ērtsa saa'myn* (But yes, I am a saa'myn)."

"Minna is fluent," Ulf said.

She glanced at him, her cheeks warming at the pride in his voice.

Slowly, the group's good cheer drew Minna's mind from her sister's rescue. She spent the evening laughing, singing, and telling stories. When it was her turn to share a tale, she described herself hanging from the side of the horse and was rewarded with their laughter and good-natured ribbing. The group was thrilled to find she was a native speaker, and bombarded her with questions, laughing at each other's attempts to replicate her accent. She was laughing in wonder at this simple, joyful experience, when their cheerful faces twisted into grimaces.

Ulf grabbed her arm, leaned in and whispered, "Minna, I can feel you."

Minna bit her lip, dropped her eyes, and slammed her center shut. Too late. Suddenly, she was eight years old, having run all the way to town to tell her friends about the lights in the trees. Their happy faces twisted in the same way. She stared at her knees, unwilling to meet their eyes and relive that moment. Then Ulf spoke.

"It's a *saa'myn* thing. She's just learning, and sometimes she slips."

Minna's head pivoted toward Ulf and found him casually shrugging his shoulders.

"Oh, a saa'myn thing," Ase said. "Very mysterious."

"*Eetsa sa saa'myn nama,* right?" Rab asked.

"No, you *wota*," Ase said, punching his shoulder playfully. "It's *ērrrrtsa*, like she said."

There were some chuckles, and Ulf threw Minna a small grin.

"It's *ērtsi*, actually," Minna said, returning Ulf's smile. She returned Rab's smile. "Third person. *Ērtsi sa ni nama ti saa'myn* (It's a *saa'myn* thing)."

In the easy silence that followed, a small red-headed girl, who had spoken very little, began to sing. The song was *The Lay of Wattana,* one every child in Argren knew. It was normally sung in Vollen, but the girl sang *Alle'oss* lyrics Minna never heard before. The change transformed the song, the lyrics much more at home with the haunting melody and Wattana's sorrow. As she listened, Minna realized this was not the story of Wattana and the faerie lights she heard growing up. In that story, Wattana was a young woman who lived somewhere in northern Argren. One day, she abandoned her husband and two small children to journey into the high places, foolishly chasing faerie lights. She and her family suffered terribly for her folly. In the end, when she emerged from her madness, she found herself alone and ill from the hardships she suffered at her own hand. Distraught, she climbed a nearby peak and threw herself from the precipice.

In this *Alle'oss* version, Wattana's neighbors banished her to the high places because they believed she cursed them. Abandoned by her friends and family, she struggled against terrible deprivations to understand what was happening to her. At the end, she stood in triumph on the precipice, surrounded by the faerie lights. With a start, Minna realized it was the story of the first *saa'myn*. She gazed around at the dreamy expressions, wondering what they understood.

The song ended on a high, plaintive note, and the group slowly came back to themselves. It was late and Minna wasn't the only one feeling the hour. A warm, comfortable silence settled over them, until the little singer shyly asked Minna, "What does it mean?"

When everyone turned expectant expressions on her, Minna asked, "You don't know?" Her voice came out husky.

"No, I used to listen to my grandpa sing it, but he never told me what it meant."

Minna hesitated, lowering her eyes and wiping the tears wetting her cheeks. "It's not the sad story we all know. Or at least, not in the end." She looked up at their eager faces, opened her mouth, then hesitated. They wanted to know about their own language, their own culture. They would understand, if anyone would. But the thought of explaining Wattana's pain, so much like her own, was too raw, too personal. She closed her mouth and dropped her eyes. The worry and fatigue she kept at bay all evening descended on her like a heavy weight.

Sensing her need, Ulf said, "I'm really tired. Maybe you can tell us the real story tomorrow night."

Minna threw him a grateful smile, and they stood, fending off the good-natured protests. She followed Ulf to a hut at the edge of the camp and followed him inside. Her pack, bedroll, and bow were waiting for her. Crawling under the blanket, she gazed up at the ceiling, marveling at the simple joys of sharing an evening with others. No longer would she stand atop the hill, a voyeur into a forbidden life. "Thank you, Ulf," she said, though she could tell he was already asleep.

As exhausted as she was, she expected to follow him instantly, but her troubled mind would not allow it.

Surely, they would be able to rescue Alyn. The *Alle'oss* knew their mountains, and though she didn't know Zaina very well, the woman made a powerful impression. Ten men and women went to Alyn's rescue, and there were only four soldiers. Still, she couldn't help imagining all that could go wrong. What if they didn't find her? What if Alyn was injured in a fight or the soldiers used her as a hostage?

To distract herself, she replayed her conversation with Beadu, but only brought up thoughts of her parents. She tried to reconcile what Beadu told her about her mother with the woman she knew, but could not make the two fit. What events could have intervened, preventing her from helping Minna? They lived together for thirteen years. Her mother never left. And why was it only her mother that Beadu said could help her? She couldn't escape the conclusion her parents knew more than they told her. How much easier would her life have been if she knew only a small part of what Beadu told her today?

Tossing and turning, she got herself tangled up in her blanket. Taking a hold of it, she yanked, but only wrapped it more tightly around her legs. She took a breath, trying to calm herself, then began kicking, yanking, and flailing at the blanket. When it finally came free, she threw it aside, leapt to her feet and stood, flushed and panting. The storm in her mind gusted dangerously. Anger. She didn't need Beadu to tell her how dangerous it could be. She managed for years with no help, and only once did she hurt anyone.

"Minna?" Ulf mumbled from the other side of the hut. "Are you okay? Are they back?"

"No. Go back to sleep," she said, her guilt calming the storm. Ulf rolled over and was snoring softly within seconds. Minna sat heavily and searched for her center, but with her mind in such turmoil, she found it impossible to settle into it. She sighed, untangled her blanket and lay back down, resigning herself to a long night.

The two concerns, her sister and her parents, took their turns with her, keeping her awake, until her exhausted mind finally relented shortly before dawn.

Chapter 25

Minna

She woke with the sun on her face. Through the hut's open door, she saw people moving about. Throwing the blanket aside, she pulled her boots on, got stiffly to her feet and stumbled from the hut.

Glancing up from tending the fire, Ulf said, "They're not back yet." He handed her a biscuit and said, "Beadu is waiting for you."

Minna looked toward Beadu's hut through the trees. The old woman sat in the same spot as the day before, sipping from a mug cradled in both hands. Minna frowned at the disappointing breakfast, stuffed it into a pocket and trudged toward her hut. When she drew near, Beadu had her face tilted toward the sky and Minna had the impression her eyes were closed, though it was hard to tell. She approached quietly and took her place on the log beside the fire.

"Good, good. I did not feel you coming. That is very good. How was your sleep?"

Minna considered lying, but decided Beadu already knew. "Not good. I barely slept at all."

Beadu smiled. "Just so. You have much to think about." She lowered her face and looked at Minna. "Now… you have questions."

Minna shook her head, as if jangling the many questions that troubled her would shake one loose. "There was a woman with the soldiers who took my sister. Her face was painted, and she could hide herself."

Beadu nodded. "She is a sister of the Seidi, of the Empire. The painting is called a tattoo, and it marks her rank and accomplishments."

"She warned me, when the soldiers were taking Alyn, the… sister warned me away."

"Ah. Yes, I have known sisters who have grown disgusted with their Empire. That there are others is a hopeful sign."

"I felt her. It was very strong."

Beadu nodded.

"Do they… do they have *and'ssyn*. Can they use the spirits?"

"Yes, and no. Some of them have *and'ssyn*, though most will deny it. Their religion considers seeing the spirits a great sin. Though it was not so in the past, today, most of the sisters do not have *and'ssyn* in the same way as you."

"So, those sisters who don't have *and'ssyn*, how do they use the spirits?"

Beadu shook her head, frowning and pursing her lips. "You must understand that we do not *use* the spirits. The spirits may choose to grant us their gifts. *And'ssyn* allows you to commune with spirits, but that does not mean the spirits will grant your requests. It is the spirit's choice, not ours." She waited until Minna nodded her understanding and then continued, "There are those, especially among the sisters, who grasp after the spirits, attempting to bend them to their will. This is not the way of the *saa'myn*." She looked up at the spirits above their heads. "The *lan'and* have decided they like you. That is a good sign. You must meet the other spirits and allow them to come to you, if they will."

Minna followed Beadu's gaze, a smile lifting the corners of her mouth. She always felt an affinity for the little spirits and wondered if they were capable of the same sort of feelings. That Beadu felt the *lan'and* decided they liked her deepened her affection for them.

"The Seidi sisters," Beadu continued, "especially those who do not truly have *and'ssyn*, they are like blind women, feeling their way around in the dark until they find what they want. They must spend years grasping after the small gifts the spirits grant them."

Minna lowered her gaze. "How do you know if the spirits will grant your requests?"

Beadu shrugged. "You cannot know until you ask."

Remembering the chaotic storm the spirits created in her mind, Minna couldn't imagine getting their attention to ask a question. Maybe Beadu meant the other spirits. "You said there are many spirits in other realms, but I only see the *lan'and*. How do you find the others?"

"You could thrash around in the dark for years as the sisters do, or,..." She cocked her head, one brow lifted. "... because you are *saa'myn* and the *lan'and* like you..." Beadu grinned, and settling her mug on the ground beside her, she raised her hand, palm up. One spirit, indistinguishable from the others, swooped down and settled on her palm. She lowered her hand until she held her hands cupped in her lap. The small spirit hovered there, quivering. Beadu lifted her eyes from it and smiled at Minna. "You must find your *and'reoime,* your spirit guide." She lifted her hand, and the small orb flew up her arm, around her neck and down her other arm into her lap again. Beadu cackled.

Minna stared at it. Her interactions with them were always with the entire group, never with a single spirit. "What does it do?"

"It will help you, introduce you to the other realms in its own time. As I said, we cannot know the mind of the gods, but the *saa'myn* believe the gods created the *lan'and* in our realm in compensation for crippling our spirit with our material essence. To show us the way." Beadu shrugged. "I am not so sure of that, but it suffices."

"How do I find a spirit guide?"

"It will find you." She gave Minna an uncharacteristically stern look when she said, "You need only recognize it when it chooses you." She held Minna's gaze until Minna nodded, then she smiled, lifted her hand again and the spirit rejoined the swarm above them. Beadu watched it merge with the others and said, "They are not fond of being away from their own for long." She looked back at Minna. "You have other questions."

"Yesterday, you said I have great power. How do you know?"

"Just so. Although, it would be more correct to say you have great potential. Two things must be true to have power. The spirits, of course, must want you to have the power. We shall see about that, but I am optimistic. Ulf told me about what you did in Fennig."

"At the harvest festival?" When Beadu nodded, Minna opened her mouth, pressed her lips shut, then asked, "What did I do?"

"It is a gift of the *lan'and*." She scrunched up her nose, peering up at the sky. "It is as if someone throws a stone into a still pond." She held her hands up, palms down, wiggling her fingers. "The ripples spread out in all directions. The *lan'and* 'throw a stone' into the spirit realms and it ripples in our realm." She paused for a moment, then shrugged and dropped her hands to her lap. "That is the best that I can do."

Remembering the bodies scattered across the ground, Minna said, "It seems dangerous."

"Yes, that was Ulf's concern, as well." Beadu chuckled. "But you can control it, focus it so that it is more useful, less dangerous."

"How?"

"As is always the answer to such questions, you must tell the spirits what you want."

Minna hesitated, thinking she must be missing something. "How?"

"When you called the spirits into your mind, what did you feel?"

"It was like a storm," Minna said, shaking her head and looking at the fire. "I felt like they would sweep me away."

"Yes, the *lan'and* are excitable, careless of your spirit. You must stand up and show them who you are. Like dogs, really, they are. Show them you are in charge, and they will be happy." Beadu nodded. "But did you feel them, the spirits?"

"Yes, I felt them, and it was like they knew me."

Beadu nodded. "Just so."

Minna stared at her. She opened her mouth to ask what that meant, but with a small shake of her head, she decided to move on. "You said there are two things that determine how powerful a *saa'myn* is."

"Ah yes. The first, again, is whether the spirits decide to grant your request, whether this is a gift that you have. The second is how open you are to the spirit realms." She picked up the mug, still half full with her morning tea, and held it up. "Let's assume this mug is a person, and the tea is the spirit realms." She looked at Minna, an eyebrow raised in question.

Minna nodded.

"Right now, the mug is Agmar."

Minna was watching the mug, but when Beadu said Agmar's name, she looked up to find Beadu watching her.

"Yes, Ulf explained what happened." When Minna nodded, Beadu said, "Do you understand?"

Minna nodded and dropped her eyes to the mug again.

"The tea stays in the mug because there is no opening." Beadu touched the bottom of the mug with her finger. "Assume we used a needle to poke a hole in the bottom so that the tea dripped out slowly. That is your father."

She looked at Minna until Minna nodded.

"We could use a nail to make the hole larger. Even so, it merely drips. That is the Seidi sisters who do not have *and'ssyn*." She waited for Minna to nod again. "If we use an arrow, so that the tea pours out, that is me." She upended the mug, pouring the contents onto the ground. "This is you."

Minna stared at the mug, her mouth dropping open.

Beadu laughed at her expression. "Just so!" Beadu let her think for a time and then said, "But you have not asked the question you wish to ask the most."

Minna looked up to find Beadu leaning toward her, a curious expression on her face. "What question?"

"You have not asked about your parents."

Minna opened her mouth, but before she could speak, a commotion on the far side of the camp drew her attention. The sound of horses arriving at a gallop and shouts brought Minna to her feet. Alyn! Raised voices, their tone angry and frightened, caught at her. She moved toward the voices, then Beadu called, "Minna! You must go, quickly."

Minna looked back at Beadu. Her bright blue eyes held hers for a moment, then Minna turned and sprinted toward the voices. People ran in all directions, frightened, calling frantically to others. Minna swerved to avoid a woman fleeing, a child clasped in her arms. A chill ran through her when she heard the words "Empire" and "Imperials." There were horses on the far side of the camp, not as many as left the night before, and only one had a rider. When she drew even with her hut, Zaina emerged from the chaos running toward Beadu's hut. Minna turned to follow, but Ulf caught up to her, took a handful of her cloak and pulled her to a stop.

"Minna! We have to go." He grabbed her arm and pulled. Minna resisted until Ulf shook her and yelled, "Minna!"

She looked at him, and he put his face close to hers.

"The Empire is coming! The group that went to rescue your sister ran into them. Only a few of them made it back. We have to run."

"Alyn?"

He shook his head. "Zaina said they didn't find her. Come on. They'll be here soon."

Minna stood still amid the chaos. People were streaming past them in one direction now, fleeing the coming Imperials, clutching whatever they could grab quickly. The shouts were reaching a hysterical pitch. She met Ulf's pleading eyes, then turned and ran to their hut. Ducking inside, she snatched their packs and her bow, pausing only long enough to string it. When she emerged, Ulf was waiting for her, dancing from foot to foot, staring at the other side of the camp. Minna grabbed his arm and pulled him toward Beadu's hut.

"What? Where are we going?"

"We have to get Beadu," Minna said, pulling him along.

Ulf stopped, forcing Minna to turn and face him. "Zaina will take care of Beadu," he said, pointing. Zaina and several other people gathered around the old woman, some of them helping her to her feet.

Blood smeared Zaina's cheek. Catching sight of Ulf and Minna, she yelled, "*Kumu ena alālar. Alālok Minna se leosok.* (You know where to go. Take Minna and go)."

Ulf leaned close and asked, "Did you understand that?"

When Minna nodded, he grabbed her arm and said, "Come on, let's go." The twang of bows and the sound of steel striking steel drew their eyes to the far side of the camp. Imperials in green uniforms were emerging from the trees. Ulf shouted, "We have to hurry! They'll try to slow them down, but they won't hold for long."

Minna let him pull her in a direction perpendicular to the fighting. She looked once more at Beadu and found her being led in the opposite direction, as serene ever. As they were nearing the edge of the camp, figures appeared out of the underbrush. Soldiers. Ulf stopped abruptly, and Minna crashed into his back, knocking him to the ground. Minna didn't think. Practiced hands drew an arrow and nocked it. As she drew the string, a flight of arrows came from her right and fell among the soldiers, scattering them and sending some to the ground. Minna adjusted her aim and let her arrow fly. It struck a man crouching behind a tree. He stood upright, hands scrabbling at the arrow protruding from his neck, mouth open in surprise. Minna sucked in a breath, frozen to the spot, unable to avert her eyes. The man took a step back, hand pressed to his neck, then dropped limply on his back and lay still.

She stared at the dead soldier, only dimly aware of Ulf standing beside her. It wasn't until he stepped in front of her, took her arms and shook her, that his voice finally penetrated her numb mind. "Minna, come on."

She nodded, and Ulf pulled her into motion. They ran parallel to the line of soldiers, who were regrouping to face the greater threat of the *Alle'oss* archers. As she ran, the bright sun dappling the ground dimmed. At first, she thought there was something wrong with her eyes, but when she looked around, she realized the forest was filling with fog. Moisture gathered on her skin, leaving icy trails down her back. Ulf slowed, and this time she caught herself before she collided with him.

"What's going on?" she asked. The fog was now so dense, she could only see a few feet in any direction. The sounds of fighting — clashing steel, angry shouts and screams — drifted eerily out of the murk.

Ulf leaned close to her and said, "It's Beadu. She's making the fog. Come on, but be careful."

Minna took his hand and let Ulf lead her, hoping he had a better sense of where they were. Spectral outlines of low shrubs and spindly saplings loomed out of the fog as they neared the edge of the encampment. In the fog, the *lan'and* appeared as diffuse orbs, like moons obscured by high, wispy clouds. They slipped in among the undergrowth and started climbing a slope. The sounds of fighting were diminishing behind them, leaving only occasional shouts. In the silence, the dense fog seemed to magnify every sound they made. She was sure anyone nearby could hear her ragged breath, her hammering heart, or Ulf's clumsy steps.

Minna pulled him to a stop. She leaned close and whispered, "Slow down. You're making too much noise. Let me go first." His hair tickled her cheek as he nodded. Taking his hand again, she said, "Step where I step." His pale face, ghostly in the fog, nodded again.

Minna almost tripped over the body. It was an *Alle'oss* man. He lay sprawled on his back, arms flung wide, eyes staring.

"Sentry," Ulf whispered. "Someone slit his throat." He pointed to the crimson smile across his exposed neck. He stooped and pointed to his sword. "Someone snuck up on him. He never drew his sword." He hesitated, then unbuckled the sword belt and pulled it free.

"Do you know how to use that?"

Ulf, wrapping the belt around the sword, shrugged. "Not yet."

Minna turned to continue up the slope, and Ulf squeezed her hand. "I hear something."

She held a breath and listened. A group was above them, moving slowly, trying to be quiet, but on the steep slope in the fog, they were having a hard time of it. She started to retrace their steps, but Ulf held her up. "We can't go back. The camp will be full of Imperials."

They both looked down at the sword in Ulf's hand, then looked at each other. "Let's try to hide. Maybe they'll pass us," Ulf said.

Retracing their steps, they encountered a copse of junipers. "Hurry," Minna whispered. Ulf got to his knees and borrowed under the prickly branches. Minna followed, and they crouched, faces inches apart, waiting. Minna could feel Ulf's fluttering breath on her cheek.

In a frighteningly short time, a soldier's legs passed by an arm's reach away. Minna glanced at Ulf and found his wide eyes fixed on a spot in the distance.

Then the soldiers were past. Minna let out a breath she didn't know she was holding. She smiled at Ulf and found him looking back at her with alarm.

"Wait! Do you feel that?" A soldier's voice. "Stop! Everyone stop. There's a witch nearby. Behind us."

She closed her center, but the damage was done.

"Come on," Ulf said frantically. "Maybe we can slip away in the fog."

Minna put her hand on his chest to stop him. Finding her center, she glanced up at the *lan'and,* braced herself and called. The spirits answered, erupting into her center with a roar. She shut her eyes, trying to find herself amid the tumult. Show them you are in charge. What did that mean? The soldiers, no longer trying to be stealthy, were crashing through the underbrush on their way back up the slope. No time. Opening her eyes, she found Ulf's face locked in a mask of pain. She ducked down and shimmied under the branches of the junipers, emerging in time to see soldiers appearing out of the fog.

"There she is!"

The soldiers had been approaching the back of the camp, spread out in a line. Minna focused on the four she could see, urgently throwing her awareness at the spirits, telling them what she wanted. Was that a response? She couldn't tell, but she was out of time. Mimicking her actions at the harvest festival, she raised her hands and screamed, imploring the *lan'and* to respond.

And they did. The gathered potential in her center rippled down her arms and exploded outward in an arc. Her center rang like a bell. A high, pure note that produced ripples of euphoria so powerful, she nearly swooned as she had at the harvest festival. This time, though she staggered, she squeezed her fists and clamped her mouth shut, determined to remain conscious and witness the effects of the blast. The wave blew the fog away from her in a narrow arc. The pressure wave caught the soldiers and threw them down the slope along with detritus from the forest floor and branches stripped from trees. In the blast's wake, fog flooded in from the sides, swirling in tight eddies. She stood, slack jawed, the other soldiers forgotten, watching the roiling fog. It worked! The spirits heard her.

Ulf was up, pulling her cloak. "Come on."

Minna let the spirits go, took one last look, then followed. The panicked voices of the soldiers who were still standing followed them into the fog.

Chapter 26

Harold

Harold woke the last morning of his voyage with a nervous energy that kept him on the move, pacing the deck in the predawn light. Now, with the sun peeking between two soaring peaks in the Eastern Mountains, he stood on the bow watching Hast's busy northern harbor emerge from darkness. It was anticipation, he realized with a start. His trip to see Deirdre felt like a detour, and now, watching the wharf through the mist rising from the river, he felt as if he were at the outset of a quest. A quest to learn what *she* had in mind for him and to discover what came of the black-haired witch. The seven-day voyage down the river had been exactly what he needed.

The first two days, he expected his pursuers to appear behind them at any moment. When he wasn't in his hammock, catching up on weeks of lost sleep, he perched on the roof of the cabin, huddled in his cloak, gazing aft. Not that there was anything he could do if Ivan commandeered a faster vessel. As accommodating as Taavi and his crew were, he doubted they would risk the ire of the Dominicans for him. Other than a heroic last stand, his only other option would be to set off across country, a perilous journey on foot with few provisions. One thing he wouldn't do was surrender.

Fortunately, the river behind them remained empty, and on the morning of the third day, he woke feeling more refreshed than he had since the night Karl turned his world upside down. After a brief meal, he tracked Taavi down and asked the captain to put him to work. He asked in *Alle'oss but* repeated himself in Vollen when Taavi stared at him blankly.

"I heard you the first time," the captain grumbled. He tipped his head back, peering up at Harold as if he didn't know what to make of him. Harold waited, holding his gaze. "You want to work. Fine! We can always use an extra hand." His eyes narrowed, and he clambered up onto the cabin, so he was looking down at his passenger. "But I'm the captain." Gesturing to the crew, who were watching curiously, he said, "You want to work, you're no better than any of the crew."

Harold shrugged. "Of course."

Taavi stared down at him for a long moment, then called to a woman whom Harold surmised was his second in command. "Sinta, our guest says he wants to work. See he doesn't get in the way too much." With that, he hopped down to the deck and disappeared below.

Sinta was a tall woman, with short, prematurely gray hair and active green eyes. She, like the rest of the crew, had the leathery skin of people who spent most of their lives in the sun. She watched Taavi go, then gave Harold a skeptical look, as if he were trying to sell her a lame horse. Taking one of his hands without asking, she studied it, rubbing a rough thumb over his callouses. "Alright, you want to work, decks need scrubbing." When Harold nodded, Sinta shrugged and motioned for him to follow her.

After a few days, Harold concluded the diminutive captain ruled his much larger crew through pure rage. He made no exception for Harold. In fact, he seemed to take special pleasure in pointing out all of Harold's faults, almost as if he were trying to provoke him. Since the rest of the crew took his abuse with a blase cheerfulness, Harold guessed it was mostly bluster and ignored it. Besides, he didn't understand half of what Taavi shouted at him at first. Unfortunately, the crew was only too happy to translate. Harold learned more eloquent *Alle'oss* profanity in seven days than he had from Karl in five years.

Unlike many of his peers, Harold trained relentlessly with his sword and expected no less from his men. Even after his recent debauchery, he thought himself fit. He was wrong. Taavi and Sinta took it as a challenge to find his limit, working him to exhaustion each day. He never knew there could be so much to do on a river barge. It was all he could do at the end of the day, to climb into his hammock. He slept dreamlessly for eight solid hours, waking only at Sinta's prodding early the next morning. It wasn't until he found himself scrubbing the same patch of deck for the third time that he guessed their game. But he didn't mind. It was exactly the distraction he needed.

If Harold had learned anything in life, it was that people were dangerous and weren't to be trusted. Until they earned it. He grew from a boy into a young man on the treacherous streets of Brennan and became a man as a Volbroch in the Volloch world of the Inquisition Academy. He survived by keeping life at arm's length, hiding his true self behind carefully maintained walls. A tendency to withdraw within himself, obsessing over potential threats, viewing the world through a veil of suspicion, and cutting himself off from the few who cared for him... well, that was the levy survival required. He never knew it was possible to live any other way. Not until he met Karl.

Karl would not be held at arm's length. To him, Harold's reticence was a challenge to be swept aside, and he would tolerate his lover's black moods only so long before assailing Harold's walls. Over the years, the resulting dance took on the comfortable rhythm of ritual. Now, on the sun washed deck of the barge, scrubbing the spotless planks, Harold danced the familiar steps in his mind. Knowing a direct approach would only invite a surly rebuff, Karl would bypass Harold's gruff exterior and appeal directly to the soft interior only he knew. Harold knew what he was doing, but it was part of the dance, and it gave him the excuse he needed to open up. He would petulantly justify himself, enumerating the roots of his angst. Even Karl would have to admit he had them in abundance this time. On top of the fact that the love of his life betrayed and abandoned him, a mysterious woman manipulated him into a hopeless quest he was unlikely to survive, the Dominicans were hot on his trail, and his bitter rival threatened a young woman who Harold regarded as the symbol of his redemption. It was a daunting list, even for someone with Karl's indefatigable disposition. Harold sat back on his heels on the barge's deck, gazing at the blue sky, trying to imagine Karl's response.

His eyes would narrow thoughtfully, middle finger caressing his upper lip and index finger tapping his temple. Then he would pop his lips and say, "Yes, that *sounds* bad. Certainly nothing to dismiss." Then he would leap to his feet and pace. Harold would watch him, amused. Though Harold would never admit it, truth was, by this point, Karl's work was already done. Harold loved him for always taking up the challenge, regardless of how often Harold needed him to.

Eventually, Karl would say something like, "On the other hand, you aren't alone. You have allies. You couldn't ask for a better friend than Joseph. I always said there was more to him than that oafish exterior would suggest. And you have not one, but two powerful sisters on your side. This Nia is very intriguing and, come on." He would turn, spread his arms and cock his head. "The Malefica?" He would start pacing again, wagging a finger. "And then there's this Aron. A very dangerous man *and* very mysterious. There're possibilities there!" Harold chuckled. Maybe that last part was a bit of an exaggeration. Finally, Karl would sit next to him, rest his hand on Harold's shoulder, and wait until he met his eyes. "Can you honestly say the noble quest, hopeless as it may be, isn't more worthy of you than snatching little girls from their families and throwing them into a dungeon?" Karl never failed to break the spell. Was it all merely an act to keep Harold going until it was his turn to step onto the stage? Picturing Karl's earnest face, searching for just the right words, Harold couldn't believe it was.

Taavi's voice interrupted his fantasy. "Hey, *sheoda sīnuta*, you getting weepy over a little hard work?"

Between the hard, honest work, simple but hearty meals and hours of uninterrupted sleep, Harold felt better at the end of the voyage than he had in a long time.

• • •

"You're an odd man, Harold."

Harold returned from his thoughts and found Taavi joining him at the bow. "How do you mean?"

"You say you're an inquisitor, but you're not what I would expect for an inquisitor." There was something odd about the captain's demeanor. Not exactly nervousness, but an uncharacteristic hesitancy.

"Yeah, I get that a lot." Harold's gaze lingered, noting how the captain fidgeted with the stay that secured the mast to the bow, then turned back to the approaching wharf. "I suppose I should take it as a compliment." He glanced back at Taavi. "You don't believe I'm an inquisitor?"

"No, I believe you, I guess." He spat into the river and wiped his lips with the back of his hand, rested his hands on his hips, and shrugged. "Course, it's a bit odd. You got them others after you, them Dominicans, and, like I said, you're different." He lifted his hands, ticking off the points on stubby fingers. "Not afraid of a bit of hard work, take more abuse than an old mule, speak the tongue... after a fashion." He dropped his hands back to his hips. "More human, I guess. Gives a man pause."

Harold grinned at the man. "I take it you aren't fond of the Inquisition."

"Who would be, I mean, outside the Volloch?" There was no humor in his expression or his voice.

Harold's grin faded. "You knew I was an inquisitor." Taavi turned his gaze down river without responding. "Then why did you take me on? Was it just the money?"

"Ayuh, the money helped." He was quiet for a time. "It occurred to me, from the way you were asking around for passage, that you were on your own. If you were about the Inquisition's business, you'd'a threatened the first captain and that'd be that. I figured no one knew where you were going."

Harold turned to face him, a chill running down his back.

Taavi stared ahead, not meeting his eyes. "Man slips and falls in the river, and no one knows where he is..." He shrugged and looked up at

Harold. "No one comes looking for him." The captain smiled. A smile that revealed more about the man than all his colorful bluster.

Harold glanced ahead to the busy harbor. "A threat like that to an inquisitor. It could get a man killed."

Taavi shrugged.

"Why tell me now?" Harold asked.

Taavi's face screwed up and his mouth worked silently. He shrugged, took a breath and blew it out through flapping lips. "There's many aren't willing to give a man a chance, least wise an inquisitor. There's some who are thinking they've had enough of the Empire. People who wouldn't pass up an opportunity that walked in their door." He looked up at Harold, one shaggy brow disappearing under the fringe of hair protruding from his misshapen hat. "Could be dangerous, wandering around on your own." He looked away and shrugged again. "Me, I'm willing to get to know a man, find out what he's made of."

Harold watched him, surprised at finding himself moved, despite the threat. "Well then, I'm glad I disappointed your expectations."

"Ayuh."

Harold dragged his eyes away from Taavi, and looked back toward the wharf, finding it closer than he expected. "Aren't we coming in kinda fast?"

"We would be, if we were stopping."

Harold's head snapped around to find Taavi grinning at him.

"I thought you said you had cargo to unload in Hast."

"Ayuh, I did, but I expect your friends will arrive near enough, and I don't intend to be around when they do."

"Well... how am I getting off?"

"Same way you got on," Taavi said, laughing. He spun around, giving Harold a parting leer before screaming instructions to his crew.

Harold watched him go, then whipped around to gape at the fast-approaching wharf. He scaled the crates stacked on the deck, sprinted back to the cabin, stumbled down the short ladder and snatched his pack. Vaulting the ladder in one step, he shoved the hatch aside and broke back out into morning sunlight. The barge was passing the north end of the wharf. He ran to the rail and looked down at the river. The gap between the barge and the wharf was too far to jump. He leaned out and peered ahead. The crew maneuvered the barge so that it would pass within six feet of a small sloop moored at the southern end of the wharf. River Witch was splashed across the stern in elegant gold letters. Harold turned back to find the captain standing atop the crates stacked on the deck, hands on his hips, a wide smile stretching his face. Harold clambered up on the cargo and gauged the distance. The sloop's rail was below the top of the cargo, but it would still be a long jump and a painful landing. For a brief moment, he considered denying the cantankerous old captain his fun and simply jumping over the side into the icy water.

"You'll never clear her rail from here. Best if you try to get hold of the rail, then pull yourself up," Sinta called from atop the cabin. The entire crew was gathering for the spectacle. Someone started chanting his name, and it was soon taken up by everyone.

Harold flung one of his newly acquired curses at Taavi, much to his amusement. The bow of the barge was passing the stern of the sloop. He swung his pack in a circle and let it fly, then ducking under the boom of the barge's single mast, he retreated to the port side to give himself room, took a quick breath, blew it out, then sprinted across and leapt into space.

He wasn't going to make it. The overlapping planks on the sloop's side rushed at him, and he was falling too fast to reach the top of the rail. At the last instant, he shoved his arm between two of the posts supporting the rail, and hung on, despite slamming into the side of the vessel and smacking the side of his face. He hung for a moment, gathering himself and listening to the crew's cheers, then heaved himself up and over the rail. Dabbing at a cut on his lip, he glared at the receding Taavi.

The captain swept his hat off, releasing an unruly red bush. "*Jae'ki lessa ti ata, joräela* (Until next time, friend).

Harold spat blood into the river and bent in an elaborate bow.

"Can I help you?"

Harold turned to find one of the sloop's crew watching him quizzically. "Sorry, just passing through." Snatching up his pack, he made his way to the gangplank, ignoring the crew's stares, and disembarked.

Hast was really two cities. The old *Alle'oss* town sprawled north of the Imperial Highway. Its origins were unmistakable. As in Lachton, many of the roads followed winding paths, but while it made some sense in the hills of Lachton, Harold saw no reason for it on the flat plains surrounding Hast other than preference. The Empire's classically symmetrical architecture would be as out of place here as he often felt in Argren. In his short walk, he saw river stone, timber frame and plaster, and even logs, artfully arranged in a variety of architectural styles. Another difference was the *Alle'oss's* fondness for color. In Hast the warm colors of autumn accented the ubiquitous Argren blue. To rigid Imperial sensibilities, it appeared chaotic and ramshackle, but Harold was learning to appreciate the *Alle'oss's* eclectic aesthetic.

Strolling along one of the few wide, straight lanes on which wagons could travel, Harold heard snippets of the strange patois spoken only in Hast. That was until people noticed him. Even disheveled as he was and wearing the cloak he purchased in Lachton, they recognized him as Imperial because of his hair. No one in Hast would dare show open hostility, not with the heavy Imperial presence in the city, but they didn't need to. He felt their animosity. Still, he had only briefly visited this part of the city in the past, and it was a nice day, so he didn't let their chilly disapproval rush him.

The *Alle'oss* district was bordered on the south by the Imperial Highway, which, after crossing the Odun River, ran west through the city before veering southwest as it crossed the plains to Brennan. Emerging from North Hast, Harold took in the grandiose stone buildings of the Imperial District. Fronted by marble columns, they were festooned with statues and friezes that glorified, and exaggerated, the Empire's history. Hast wasn't much more than a small *Alle'oss* town in which a small Imperial presence was tolerated until the Empire took an interest in Argren. That it was the closest Imperial city to southern Argren with a bridge made it the natural place to locate the headquarters of the Imperial

Military District of Argren. Along with the headquarters came various military installations and the Imperial bureaucracy. The Imperial fort in Hast, Fort Ludweig I, was one of the most active in the Empire, outside the war zones. Harold suspected the recent growth of the fort's garrison was due to the scattered reports of resistance in southern Argren.

As the only way to cross the river this far south, there was always heavy traffic on the Imperial Highway through Hast. He dodged a caravan of wagons carrying coal from the mountains in Argren to Brennan. A wretched group of *Alle'oss* slaves followed the last wagon. Officially, they were criminals, but it was more likely they were just unfortunates, whose crime was to be at the wrong place at the wrong time. They looked thin, even for *Alle'oss,* staring around at the city with disinterest. The traffic slowed as it passed through Hast to allow Imperial soldiers and tax collectors to inspect the wagons. It surprised him to see Inquisition brothers, some of them the Malleus' personal guard, among the Imperials. Curious, he paused on the way to the stables to watch them searching the wagons and questioning the slaves. They must be looking for someone.

Unlike his trip to meet the Malefica, visiting Fennig was within his purview, so no one would question him taking advantage of Inquisition resources. Still, with Ivan on his trail, there was no point announcing his intentions. He would slip into the stables and intimidate a stable hand into handing over a horse without the proper paperwork. It wasn't ideal, but no one in North Hast would willingly sell him a horse, and there were no private stables south of the highway. He was in the stables in search of a likely victim when he heard a familiar voice.

"Inquisitor Wolfe! It's about time. Was gonna come looking for you, you took much longer."

Harold smiled, turning to find Joseph and three other men standing in the doorway. "What are you doing in Hast?" The other men were three members of his escort. "Sergeant Henrik, Fenton, Raif. I assume Joseph is to blame for your presence."

"Not entirely my fault. They came looking for you. Said you were making yourself scarce, and they were worried about you." Joseph leaned in confidentially. "I put them off, at first, but they tortured me and plied me with ale. I told them everything."

Harold eyed the three men. "So, you came all the way to Hast to say hello?"

"No, sir. We're going with you," Henrik said.

Harold glanced at Joseph, who had the good grace to look ashamed. "What do you think I'm going to Fennig for?"

"To save our girl," Joseph said. "We, all of us, feel responsible for her. A sort of obligation, as it were."

Harold shook his head. "We don't even know if it's her."

"Well, about that——"

Harold held up a hand to cut him off. "You realize, if you come with me, there may be no going back. And before you answer… I ran into Ivan in Lachton."

"Our Ivan?" the sergeant asked.

"The very same. He's a Dominican." A round of curses met this news. "My guess is Stefan's been spying on us."

They were silent, considering the implications.

"If it is Stefan, he's after me. You could all plead ignorance. It might work." Harold said to Henrik, "Sergeant, you're Volloch. Have you thought about what you're giving up?"

"I'm not Volloch."

They all turned to stare at him. "But I've seen your papers," Harold said.

"Forged. My father was from Styria on the far western frontier. My mother was Volloch. That makes me a Volbroch, like you. I take after my mother. Imperials killed my father during the Styrian uprising ten years ago. My mother knew someone who got me papers when we moved to Brennan. She died last year, and I have no love for the Empire." He shrugged. "I'm thinking I'd like to do some good in the world."

Harold wasn't sure how to respond. They had known each other since Harold was a novice, ten years before. He always knew the reticent sergeant had secrets, and now he knew why. If he were discovered, he would be executed for impersonating a Volloch. Still, he couldn't help feeling a little hurt. Henrik, at least, had the good graces to look guilty. "Why did I never know about this?"

"Never can be too careful. I trust *you*, but the fewer who know, the more likely it stays secret." He shrugged. "If you knew, and it was discovered, you would pay the same price I would."

Harold gazed at him before nodding and looking at Fenton and Raif.

"We're Brochen, the lowest of the low," Raif said. He glanced at Fenton, who nodded. "We just joined to have regular meals. We'd be slopping out the Inquisition's stables if you didn't pick us for your escort."

Fenton added, "Besides, rumor is, it won't be long before we're in the south fighting the Kaileuk. If we're going to die, we'd rather not do it so a bunch of Volloch can stay comfortable."

Joseph smiled and rested a hand on Harold's shoulder. "See, Harold, you've been a bad influence."

Harold met his eyes. "What about you, Joseph?"

Joseph grimaced. "I'd love to come, but I've got Nia to think about. Besides, I'm clean." He wiped his hands and held them up. "I left before Ivan got there. Might be useful to have someone on the inside."

"What are you doing here, then?"

"Hast is my new station. Word came down a few days ago." He gave Harold a broad smile. "You probably noticed the city is full of brothers and Imperials."

"I noticed. Seems like they're looking for someone."

"That's what I was going to say." Joseph and Henrik exchanged smiles. "Looking for some fugitive from Argren. Big operation. Roadblocks, forays into Argren, no stone unturned." He paused. "Word is, Stefan found a witch in Fennig. Very powerful. With black hair."

Harold stared at Joseph's smiling face. "So, it is her."

Joseph nodded. "Sounds like. How many *Alle'oss* you seen with black hair?"

"She got away from Stefan."

The men were silent for a moment, and then Joseph chuckled. Harold joined him, and soon they were all laughing.

Chapter 27

Minna

For the first few hours, Minna and Ulf set aside the question of where they were going and concentrated on putting as much distance between themselves and the Imperials as possible. Occupied with their own thoughts, and needing to save their breath for walking, they spoke little. Minna couldn't help worrying about all the people in the camp. As old as Beadu was, how could they get her to safety? How many of the group who welcomed her last night survived? But it wasn't any of the people that prompted her to speak.

"Edda," she said.

Walking ahead of her, Ulf didn't hear her, so she said it again.

"What? Oh. Yeah." Ulf stopped and looked back the way they came. "I was thinking about that as well. They were good horses. I think... or I hope they'll be okay. No one would kill them. Horses are too valuable." He wiped his hand across his face, then added more quietly, "On purpose, anyway." He turned and started walking without another word.

As the morning wore on, they left the densest part of the forest and entered a more rugged area, interspersed by open meadows covered by tufty brown grasses. They had just crossed one of these meadows and were resting in the shadows of the tree line when they saw their pursuers.

At first, it was the men's white uniforms, like ghosts in the shadows of the forest across the meadow, then a dozen men emerged into the light. Minna and Ulf wormed their way beneath a mountain laurel.

"They look different," Minna said.

"Different?"

"They're all in white. The soldiers that attacked the camp were wearing green."

"Ahh. These are brothers of the Inquisition."

"Brothers?"

"Yeah, it's sort of a religious thing. They're called monks. For some reason, they call themselves brothers." He started to back away when Minna stopped him.

"Who were the soldiers that attacked the camp?"

"Those were Imperial Rangers. They're part of the army."

"But they're on the same side? All Imperials?"

"Yeah."

"So, it was the brothers who took Alyn."

"Yeah. That's what the Inquisition does."

They started backing away, when Minna caught sight of a flash of color among the white. "Who's that one, the one kneeling down? He looks familiar."

Ulf raised up slightly and squinted across the meadow. "It looks like— But it can't be." The man stood and talked to two of the other men. After a moment, he pointed across the meadow toward Ulf and Minna.

"It's Torsten," Ulf said,

Now, Minna remembered the red hair and maroon cloak.

"Why is he helping Imperials?" Ulf asked.

"He's helping them track us. We better go. Hurry."

They put trees between themselves and their pursuers, then ran.

Torsten

Torsten examined the prints the boy made in the loose dirt at the edge of the treeline. This was too easy. They weren't even trying to hide their trail.

He stood and pointed across the meadow. "They went that way," he said to the inquisitor.

Inquisitor Anders, who may have been the most arrogant man Torsten ever met, squinted into the shadows between the trees. "And you said she wasn't dangerous?" he asked.

"Oh, no," Torsten said. "I never said that. You saw what she did back at the camp. What I said was is she's—" He paused, staring at the inquisitor. Why would he lie at this point? He would see the witch die, so why not tell this man the truth? "That thing she did, she can only do it once, maybe twice, before it renders her unconscious." He grinned. It wasn't a lie, but neither was it the whole truth. "Just don't be in the front row when we find her." His grin slid into a leer as he noticed the other brothers exchanging worried glances.

He held the inquisitor's gaze as the man studied him.

Finally, Anders turned to one of the other brothers and said, "Sergeant, have the men spread out and approach the treeline."

Amused, Torsten watched the men reluctantly moving out, the inquisitor watching from behind. Why did he lie? It wasn't that he was changing his goals. The witch must die before it was too late. No, it was because it was Beadu who told him the secret he withheld. He only had hazy memories of his grandmother, but he knew she and Beadu were close friends. His grandmother was probably the last *saa'myn* the Empire butchered. Her death was the reason Minna's mother sent Beadu into hiding.

The inquisitor, seeing his men safe at the distant treeline, set off across the meadow. Torsten sighed. Beadu likely died in the attack. He regretted that, but it was necessary for the greater good.

Minna

"Minna!"

Minna slowed and looked back. Ulf was bending over, hands on his knees. Trudging back to join him, she looked down the long, open hill they just climbed, but saw no sign of pursuit.

"We trusted him," Ulf said, wincing as he straightened. "Everyone in the camp trusted him. He was a leader."

"That sentry, the one you said someone snuck up on."

"Betrayed. No one snuck up on him. Torsten probably just walked up, told him he was checking to make sure everything was okay. Then he—" They stared at each other.

"We have to keep moving. We're leaving a trail anyone can follow," Minna said.

Ulf turned slowly, taking in their surroundings. He pointed to the highest peak. "I know roughly where we are. That's *Shonum Edemi*, the protector." When he turned back to Minna, he asked, "What did Zaina tell you before we left the camp?"

"She said you know where to go. Do you know what that means?"

"I think she must mean that place we stopped the first night, the shelter. People meet there all the time."

Minna pressed her lips together and rested her hands on her hips. "Back toward Fennig?"

"Let's just try to lose the brothers. We'll talk about where we go tonight."

After a brief discussion, they headed into the rugged terrain to the west. As the day wore on, they traversed a series of rocky ridges, until encountering one too precipitous to climb. Faced with turning south, toward the highway, or north, they headed into the more rugged terrain to the north. The canyon narrowed, then dead ended. Their only choice, besides returning the way they came, was to climb the ridge to the east.

The sun was dipping toward the horizon as Minna finally staggered to the top of the ridge. She bent over, hands on her knees, breathing hard and willing her meager lunch to stay where it was. Ulf, having reached the top long before her, stood in his awkward way, one hand on a hip, staring to the north. Minna straightened on trembling legs, massaging her lower back, and followed his gaze. The ridge rose gradually northward to the shoulders of *Shonum Edemi*. Most of the land lay in twilight, but the snow-capped peak, catching the last rays of sunlight, glowed orange against the deep blue evening sky. A westerly wind lifted a glittering veil of powdery snow from the peak and scattered it toward the east.

Minna turned away, drawing her cloak around herself, and peered down into the shadowy canyon below. They had not seen the brothers since the first time. To the west, across the narrow canyon, a stand of scrubby pines clinging stubbornly to the top of the ridge, were limned by the setting sun. A small group of *lan'and* flitted among the trees, disappearing into the sun's orange glare, strobing across the trunks, then reappearing on the other side. For one panicky moment, Minna wondered if one of them was her spirit guide? How was she supposed to recognize it? How would the one spirit meant for her find her as she traipsed through the mountains? She chewed her lower lip. As important as Beadu made it sound, you would think she would have been a little more helpful. Riddles and half-answers.

The scrubby grass covering the top of the ridge transitioned into a dense mix of evergreens and hardwoods as the ridge descended south toward the highway. She crossed the narrow ridge to the eastern side and looked down. Below, a small stream flowed south from the mountain. Across the stream, forest stretched eastward, across a narrow valley. It was a good place to stop for the night. It would be nearly impossible for anyone to sneak up on them.

"Ulf, I can't keep going." She dropped her pack and bow, and sat heavily, facing the forest to the east, resting her arms on her knees.

Ulf settled beside to her. They sat in silence, lost in their own thoughts.

After several minutes, Ulf asked, "Are you okay?"

No, she wasn't okay. She finally found someone who could help her understand herself, then the Empire and a traitor took her away. Alyn was lost, beyond even the small hope she had of saving her, and she killed— Her breath caught, and she pushed that memory away. But instead of saying all of this, she nodded, staring absently into the distance. "What do we do now?"

"We go where Zaina told us to go." When Minna nodded, he continued, sounding relieved. "They'll expect us. If we don't show up, no telling what they'll think. We can ask them what we should do about your sister."

Minna didn't respond.

"Minna, can you do that thing?"

"What thing?"

"The thing Beadu taught you. I know you're tired, but it hurts."

Minna closed her center, feeling guilty. That was why Ulf was staying so far away from her all day. The whole time, Minna was sure he was angry with her, but it was just that he was too polite to say anything.

"I'm sorry, Ulf. I forgot."

"That's okay."

She knew what he would say, but she had to ask. "Which way is Brennan?"

When Ulf didn't answer, Minna looked up to find him staring into the distance, jaw muscles working. He took a breath and turned toward her, caught her eye and held it. When he spoke, it had the practiced cadence of a well-rehearsed argument.

"Minna, the soldiers who have Alyn will be in Brennan soon. We'll never catch them, even if we had horses." When Minna didn't respond, he continued, "I know you can do that spirit wave thing, but that won't be enough. Besides, we don't have enough food or money, and—"

"I just asked, which way it is?"

Deflating, Ulf turned toward the cliff's edge, sat cross-legged and plucked at blades of grass. They sat quietly as the sun dipped below the horizon behind them, neither able to muster the energy to argue.

She hated to admit it, but Ulf was right. She nearly fainted when she used it at the camp. *I wouldn't be enough.* But Beadu said there were many other spirits. She looked back over her shoulder to the spirits. *If she could find her spirit guide, maybe there was another spirit that could help.* But by the time her spirit guide found her, Alyn would be dead.

As the moon's spectral blue replaced the sun's gold, the mournful hooting of an owl in the forest below broke the silence.

Minna said in a flat tone, "Maybe I should ask the owl what to do."

Ulf chuckled. "My father told me that story, too."

"Great, that's really useful! 'Hey, owl, why didn't my parents tell me the truth?'" She sucked in a breath, pressing her fists against her thighs, swallowing a sob.

She sensed Ulf moving and felt a hesitant hand on her back. Shaking it off, she lurched to her feet on shaky legs. Throwing her arms out, she stood on the rim and shouted into the abyss. "Why didn't anyone ever tell me? How hard would it be?" She paced along the cliff edge, glaring at Ulf. "Look what I learned *in one day.*" The guilt she felt at Ulf's frightened expression fueled her anger. She was tired of having to always think of other people's feelings, of tiptoeing meekly around everyone. "I hid from the world, and when I *did* come to town, I ignored the whispers and the dirty looks. I never fought back when the other children chased me and threw rocks at me." She stopped in front of Ulf, bent over him, and pointed at her chest. "*I* kept to myself so I wouldn't offend *them.* They don't know how lucky they are that I'm—" She felt the whirlwind stir in her mind, the pressure rising. *No!* She gritted her teeth and pushed savagely against it. *I have a right to be angry.* The wind stilled, taking her fury with it. Dropping her arms limply to her sides, she looked up at the *lan'and* who rotated slowly above her, perhaps sensitive to her anguish.

"Minna…"

She spoke in a soft, bleak tone. "Beadu said events intervened. Whatever that means." Lowering her eyes to the moon's pale face, she gestured vaguely with one hand. "All they had to do was explain. Alyn would be home and…" Her breath caught, and she trembled, but she needed to say the words. "… Jason would be alive." Her chin dropped to her chest, and she squeezed her eyes shut. They would build a small house, cozy and warm. They would have a son and a daughter, blond and blue-eyed. Like their father. And as if collapsing into the void once occupied by that small, hopeless dream, she sagged in on herself, folding her arms across her chest and swaying precariously on the precipice.

And then Ulf's arms were around her, pulling her back and lowering her to the ground. Minna melted against him, lay her head on his chest and wept.

Her tears spent, she murmured, "I'm sorry, Ulf. You didn't deserve that. You should be at home with your family. I dragged you out here for nothing."

"Well, technically, it was Marie who made me come with you." The relief in his voice shamed her. "And besides, you needed to meet Beadu, and if I didn't come, you wouldn't have."

Minna sat up and stared at him, sniffling and wiping her face with the sleeve of her cloak. "I never thought to ask you, last night, I was so…"

"Overwhelmed?"

"Yeah, with everything. How did you know where they were?"

"You know my brother, Tamas?" Ulf said, settling back into a comfortable position.

"I know *of* him."

"He's a lot older than us, so you wouldn't have met him before… Anyway, my father doesn't like to go to Brennan anymore, so he lets Tamas do it. Some farmers use our wagons and our horses to ship their produce, and Tamas goes to make sure they get back. I go with him when my father lets me." The note of pride in his voice lifted the corner of Minna's lips. "Somehow, my brother met that woman, Zaina, and got involved with them. Whenever he goes to Brennan, he brings them food, weapons. Stuff they can't get themselves. That's how I met her."

"So, when you ran off after Marie told you to come with me…?"

"Yeah, Tamas lives in town. I just went to tell him I was going. It was his idea to take you to the rebel camp." He chuckled. "Ran into some others that first night, after we left. Remember… that place we spent the night? They use that place a lot because it's out of the weather. I was sure you caught me."

"I was suspicious." Minna sat cross-legged and gazed across the valley. Dozens of small lights moved about among the trees. She threw Ulf a grin and said, "You're an awful liar."

Ulf dropped his eyes and plucked a pebble from the ground. Tossing it over the edge, he said, "I wanted to tell you, but my brother said not to. I guess he was afraid if we were caught, you might let the horse out of the stable."

Minna's quiescent anger surged. "Why didn't they just come get me before... before they took Alyn? Zaina or whoever? Before my father left. They could have told me everything. We would have had all the time they needed."

Ulf cast her a worried look. "I don't know, Minna. I'm not, like, really part of it. I just hear about it from Tamas. My father doesn't even know."

Minna felt her face heat. "Ulf, I'm sorry... again. I just..."

"It's okay, Minna." An awed note entered his voice. "I've never seen you angry before, and I reckon you have more right to be than anyone." He shrugged. "I just... don't want you to be angry with me."

"We hardly ever see each other. You don't know, it could be I get angry all the time."

"Well, *you* don't see *me*." He shrugged, started to say something else, then clamped his mouth shut. Leaning forward, he felt around for another pebble, then sat up, rolling the stone around in the palm of his hand. He glanced at Minna and said, "I see you sometimes, from a distance. I would talk to you, it's just after that time, in the market, I thought..."

"What time? What are you talking about?"

"It was a few days after you tried to tell all the kids about the lights. I wanted to go see you *that* day, but Jason told me you probably didn't want to see a lot of people." When Minna didn't respond, he continued. "Then a few days later, you came to the market with your mother."

Minna gaped at him blankly.

"I said hello, but you just walked away." He tossed the pebble and cut his eyes to her.

Minna shook her head, trying to bring that day to mind.

"I wanted to go see you, but I figured you thought I was like the other kids," Ulf said.

"Ulf. I'm so sorry. I was so upset that day, I don't remember that. If I'd known." She rested a hand on his shoulder and chuckled weakly. "The Mother knows, I could have used a friend."

Ulf nodded. "Me too."

Minna rested her head on his shoulder. After a few minutes, she said, "Part of what?"

"Huh?"

"You said you weren't part of it."

"Oh, yeah. The resistance. They're fighting back against the Empire."

Minna snorted. "I guess we saw how well that's going."

Ulf nudged Minna upright, an uncharacteristic edge entering his voice. "That's not fair, Minna. They were surprised, is all. *Betrayed* and surprised. The Imperials are trained soldiers. We're just learning to fight."

"Why, why are they fighting the Empire?"

"Minna, you don't know what it's like for most *Alle'oss* because you live in Fennig. The Empire leaves us alone. My father says they don't even know we exist." He pointed out into the darkness. "Those people in that camp don't have homes because the Empire burned them or because they had to run so they wouldn't be slaves." He stopped, turning to gaze in the camp's direction. "And now they may all be dead because of that... *nāminu.*"

Now it was Minna's turn to reach out for Ulf, resting her arm across his back and consoling him.

"I'm sorry, Ulf. I didn't know."

"It's easy for people in Fennig to ignore it. They think if they keep to themselves, the Empire will leave them alone. But they won't." He looked at her, swiping at his nose with the back of his hand. "Of all the people in Fennig, you should understand."

Minna leaned her head on Ulf's shoulder.

They sat, leaning into one another, pulling their cloaks tighter, until Minna's teeth began to chatter.

"Let's get out of the wind and have some supper," Ulf said, easing Minna upright. "We can think about what to do tomorrow morning."

Afraid to start a fire, they shared a cold meal. They left their bedrolls when they fled the camp, so they spread her cloak on the ground then huddled together under his.

She stared into the dark, wrapped in Ulf's cloak, surrounded by his scent, wondering what she should do. Why did she want to go to Brennan? Ulf was right. There was little hope of saving Alyn. Was she insisting on going because she didn't know what else to do? Now that she could hide herself, she could go home to Fennig. Maybe her father was already home. If the villagers who killed Jason, and tried to kill her, tried anything, she could take care of herself now. The thought of her mother, who was alone now, almost decided it for her. She would no longer have to worry about hurting her.

Yet, as she lay back-to-back with Ulf, inconvenient thoughts nagged at her. Ulf was also right that the Empire was aware of Fennig now. They would return. Even if they weren't looking for her, could she stand by while they did to Fennig what they did to the rest of Argren? She didn't think so. She would want to fight back, and her parents would suffer their reprisals.

Joining the *Alle'oss* rebels seemed the best option, assuming any of them survived. It would be a difficult and dangerous life, but the brief time she spent with them the previous night left a mark on her. As she drifted off to sleep, she wondered where Alyn was at that moment. Was she afraid, feeling alone and abandoned, wondering where Minna was? Minna told her she wouldn't leave her alone, but Ulf was right. What could she do, even if Alyn was alive?

Chapter 28

Ivan

Ivan paced the deck of the barge, glancing to the quay of the Imperial harbor in Hast each time he turned. The Imperial harbor was south of the bridge. The captain was not happy about bypassing the wharf on the Brochen side of the highway, but she hadn't been happy about much during the voyage. The woman was obviously incompetent or was intentionally slowing them down. Each time he confronted her, she hid behind a tangled mishmash of nautical terms. Reefing, leeward, lufting, wind shadows. Wind shadows?

"I don't see Wolfe's barge. What makes you think he stopped in Hast, Brother Ivan?"

Ivan paused in his pacing and looked at his companion, Brother Victor. "He needs resources. He'll stop here to take advantage of what the Inquisition can provide." Ivan glanced up as they passed beneath the stone arch of the bridge. "He needs horses, provisions. He didn't report to the Inquisition in Lachton, so I doubt he would report in here, but he will have left traces of his intent somewhere. If not, we'll continue on to Lubern."

They stood in silence until the barge pulled alongside the quay. "Take the others and arrange provisions and mounts. I'll report in and meet you in the Dominican house."

"Yes, brother."

Ivan caught the sneer the captain thought she was hiding from him as he was crossing the gangplank. Safely on the quay, he called the dock master over, a lieutenant in the Imperial navy. "I want you to arrest the captain and crew of this barge. Impound the barge and the cargo."

The barge's captain, standing nearby, overheard. "Why you puffed up Imp!"

The lieutenant paled and asked, "Uh, on what charge, sir?"

"Obstruction."

The captain shouted for her crew and fled across the gangplank. The crew, who weren't listening to Ivan's conversation, hesitated for a moment, then sprung into action, frantically trying to cast off the lines.

"Lieutenant!" Ivan shouted, to get the young man's attention. "If they escape, you will take their place."

"Yes, sir." The man shouted for the soldiers standing guard at the fort's gate.

Ivan smirked as the soldiers invaded the small vessel and began corralling its crew. He started walking, ignoring the captain's imprecations.

"Sir. What do I do with them?" the lieutenant called after him.

"Send the crew to the local constabulary. Send the captain to the Inquisition."

"What should I tell them?"

Ivan paused and turned to the dockmaster. "Tell them they are the prisoners of Brother Ivan Teufel. Tell them I will file formal charges when I return to Hast."

Ivan resumed walking, murmuring to himself, "Wind shadows." He was already dismissing the crew's fate from his mind as he passed through the gate, considering what he would tell the Prior. Prior Stenson. How that old fraud managed to wheedle himself into command of the Dominican house in Hast was a mystery only the Malleus could answer.

Still, it wouldn't do to neglect his duty to report in. Technically, he was supposed to be in Brennan. It was only when he caught wind of Wolfe leaving the city that he took it on himself to follow. What could have been so important in Lachton that would prompt Wolfe into such a punishing trip? Why was he in such a hurry and why cover his tracks? Whatever it was, it wasn't Inquisition business. He couldn't prove that Wolfe allowed witches to escape, though he knew it was true. But the mysterious trip to Lachton suggested a much darker mystery. There was heresy here. That he fled when Ivan found him was proof enough. He just needed to discover its shape.

• • •

"But my orders come from Stefan," Ivan said.

"Well, now you have new orders from *Inquisitor* Schakal." The old Prior leaned forward and handed a crumpled sheet of paper to Ivan. "It seems the inquisitor went to Fennig—"

"Fennig? Stefan went where?" At the Prior's annoyed expression, Ivan said, "Sorry, sir. Please continue."

"As I was saying, *Inquisitor* Schakal traveled to Fennig to investigate rumors of a powerful witch, and he apparently found one. He sent to the Malleus asking for support and kicked the hornet's nest. She must be a powerful witch."

"Sir?"

The prior looked at him blankly.

"Hornet's nest? Sir."

"You didn't see the brothers searching everyone crossing the bridge?"

"No, sir. We came in through the harbor."

"Oh, well, the witch has apparently slipped through the Inquisitor's fingers. His message told a rather confusing tale. A village leveled and dozens of people killed." Noticing Ivan's skeptical expression, he said, "Yes, I know. But the Malleus is taking it seriously and has made it a priority to apprehend her. No one may leave Argren without questioning. Every rumor is being investigated. Which brings me to the point. Four days ago, the rangers raided an *Alle'oss* rebel camp. They reported a witch, and several rangers were badly injured when they tried to apprehend her. After—"

"Badly injured? By an *Alle'oss* witch?" Ivan interjected. A Brochen witch capable of the type of magic used by the Seidi was hard to believe.

Irritation flashed across the Prior's face, but then he shrugged. "Yes, it all sounds far-fetched to me as well. Still, we were not there, so who knows? In any case, after the raid, an *Alle'oss* informant confirmed the presence of a witch and his description matched Inquisitor Schakal's fugitive. As we are currently shorthanded, the brothers going to Fennig to assist the Inquisitor were diverted to follow this tip. You and your men will take their place and go to Fennig." When Ivan didn't respond, the Prior bent to a stack of documents on his desk, saying in dismissal, "Your business with Inquisitor Wolfe can wait."

"What description?"

"Hmm?" the prior said without looking up.

"You said the witch in the rebel camp matched Stefan's description. What is the description?"

"Ah. Yes. Not much to go on, but *Inquisitor* Schakal said she was older than most witches, perhaps thirteen or fourteen, green eyes and black hair."

• • •

"We're going to Fennig," Ivan said, pulling on his gloves.

"Where?" Victor asked.

"Exactly," Ivan replied. "Stefan has allowed a powerful witch to escape, and we have been ordered to go to his assistance." How far could Harold run while they were busy chasing rumors? "Any news on Wolfe?"

"Nothing official. He didn't check in, nor did he officially requisition a horse or provisions through the Inquisition quartermaster." Victor grinned. "However, one of the stable boys reports seeing a rather disheveled man in an inquisitor's uniform, talking to four other brothers."

"That's him. The four other men? His escort, maybe?"

"The boy didn't recognize them, but Sergeant Henrik Matison requisitioned four horses yesterday. The destination was listed as Kartok, in Argren."

"Sergeant Matison. So, the rest of them have cast their lot with the heretic."

"Yes, sir. It appears so."

"And they're going to Kartok?"

"Yes, sir."

Victor waited quietly while Ivan considered. A side trip to Kartok would cost them four days, and that was assuming they spent no time investigating. And it was unlikely Matison would have revealed their actual destination. But they did requisition horses, so they weren't planning to leave the Empire. If they were, the quickest way was to board a ship in Lubern and cross the Southern Sea. If he stayed in the Empire, Ivan would find him. "Unfortunately, our business with Wolfe will have to wait for our return from Fennig." He faced Victor. "I trust you have procured horses and provisions."

"Yes, sir."

"Good, let's be off."

Chapter 29

Minna

Minna was dancing with Jason again. He led her confidently around the hill above Fennig, his smile leaving her as breathless as the dance. She knew it was a dream. And though she knew it would end in horror, she lay down each night, anticipating these few precious moments. As they spun slowly to a stop, Jason pulled her close, gazing down at her. As always, she thought he might kiss her, but he stepped back. Minna knew what came next. Knew he would transform into a corpse and turn to dust, but she wouldn't allow herself to look away. It was the penance she set for herself.

Instead, this time, an arrow flew out of the night and pierced his neck. His eyes flew open in surprise, and blood gushed from his open mouth. Minna reached out and took a step toward him, but recoiled when he transformed into an Imperial soldier. She lifted her hands to her face, to block out the sight, and found her hands drenched in blood. The scene shifted abruptly. She stood in darkness, surrounded by faceless men in white uniforms. Her mind screamed for her to run, but she was rooted to the spot. Suddenly, the soldiers lunged at her, grasping and pulling her one way and another. She heard screams and realized it was her.

Someone took her hand, and the scene shifted again. The echoes of her screams faded, replaced by the soft chirr of a mountain bluebird. A cool breeze, carrying the earthy scents of the forest, plucked at her hair. She opened her eyes to find herself standing in the forest glade, on a day like the one when Alyn first saw the spirits. Her sister stood facing her, smiling serenely, golden hair shining in the bright sun. The *lan'and* whirled around them. Minna wanted to speak, but no words would come. Alyn gave her a sly grin and glanced up at the spirits. When she returned her gaze to her sister, she squeezed Minna's hand as she faded. Minna tried to throw her arms around her, to pull her back, but her arms passed through her as if she were smoke. Just before Alyn was gone, she said, "You promised, Minna."

Minna clawed her way up out of the darkness and lay gasping, soaked in sweat, her heart thrumming. Ulf's face hovered over her, worry creasing his brow. She struggled to extricate herself from his restraining hands and lurched to her feet. Facing west, she stumbled a few steps toward the cliff's rim and squinted into an icy wind that blew in overnight. The wind lifted her sweat soaked hair, chilling her and clearing the last vestiges of sleep from her mind.

"Minna?"

She turned back to find Ulf watching her, the same worried expression on his face. "Bad dream," she said, unnecessarily. He nodded, but his concerned expression remained. "Bacon and eggs for breakfast?" Minna asked, forcing a grin.

They shared another unsatisfying meal of hard biscuits, tiptoeing around the subject of where to head next. But, having eaten and preparing to leave, they could no longer avoid the question.

"I'm going to Brennan." Minna stood, feet apart, hands on her hips.

"Zaina told us where to go." Ulf said immediately, as if he were waiting for her pronouncement. "We *have* to go there. If we don't show up, no telling what they'll think. Besides, what are you going—"

"You can go and tell them what happened. I'm going to Brennan." Though she wavered the night before, Minna woke up resolved, and had been girding herself for this moment. She couldn't expect Ulf to risk his life, but her life was her own, and she would not give up on her sister. She hesitated, looking around. "You just need to… point me in the right direction."

Ulf threw up his hands. "It will take us two weeks to walk to Brennan." He pointed to the clouds scudding across the sky from the west. "The weather is going to get worse, and we don't have enough food."

Minna thrust her chin out. "I have my bow. I can hunt."

Ulf glanced at her bow, then sagged, letting his head drop. When he looked up again, he licked his lips and said, "Minna, the brothers who have Alyn will be in Brennan soon. It's probably already too late to catch them." He took a step and reached a hand out toward her. "I'm sorry."

Minna stared at him, then shook her head. "I have to go. I have to be sure."

"Minna."

Minna sighed, resignation dulling her tone. "I know there's no hope, Ulf, but I have to go, anyway."

Ulf stared at her so long, Minna worried about him. Finally, he sighed and said, "Okay, let's go." He started walking, brushing her shoulder as he passed, heading south, along the spine of the ridge toward the highway.

"Where?" she said, spinning around to watch him.

"Brennan," he yelled over his shoulder, striding away with his lanky gait. "I'm not going to let you go on your own."

She would have gone on her own, it was true, but as Minna watched him walking away, something loosened inside her, leaving her feeling wobbly and warm. "Wait," she said and ran after him. He stopped and turned to give her his lopsided smile.

As they walked, Ulf asked, "So, what did you and the old woman talk about?

"Old woman? You mean Saa'myn Beadu?"

"Yeah, that one. What did you talk about?"

Minna returned his smile and said, "*Saa'myn* stuff."

"Secret *saa'myn* stuff, I assume."

"*Very* secret."

He looked at her, one brow rising. "Well, some of it must have been useful."

"What do you mean?"

"You didn't kill me when you blasted those soldiers." He grinned. "Thought I was a goner." He lifted a hand and sighted along his extended fingers. "But you went AHHHH and blasted them."

Grinning, Minna punched him in the arm. "I did not sound like that."

"No, you're right. It was more like," He raised the pitch of his voice, "AHHHHH."

"Funny," Minna said.

"How did you do it?"

"I'm not really sure. Beadu said 'tell the spirits what you want'," Minna said in a rough imitation of Beadu's voice. "I had no idea what she meant, and I still don't know what I did. But—"

Ulf grabbed her arm and dropped to the ground, dragging her with him.

"What?"

"Shh!" He pointed down into the narrow valley.

Minna crawled forward until she could see over the edge. The ravine was still in shadows, but the brothers' white uniforms were visible.

Ulf tugged her back. "Come on, we have to move."

When they were far enough from the edge, they stood and started running south along the top of the ridge.

"Ulf!" When she had his attention, she said, "We have to get off this ridge. There's no cover up here."

Crossing to the other side, she peered down. The drop was steep, but not too steep and the stone had weathered unevenly, leaving cracks and a series of narrow terraces.

"You're not thinking of climbing down there, are you?" Ulf was standing next to her.

"Only choice," she said, "And we have to hurry." She looked back over her shoulder and said, "I'll go first." Looking north, along the ridge, she said, "Hold on."

The scrubby grass that covered the top of the ridge extended another twenty yards north, then the rocky bones of the mountain emerged. Minna ran toward the boundary. They wouldn't leave tracks on the rock, so it would be impossible to track them. She just needed to give the impression they went that way. She found an exposed spot of earth at the edge, took a few steps back and then ran, making sure to step on the dirt. A few yards beyond, she kicked a pile of pebbles across the surface, then found a small stone, placed it in line with the footprint she left, stepped on the stone and pushed off, leaving a scuff mark on the hard stone. It wasn't much, but maybe enough to give them pause.

Edging over to the eastern rim, she walked carefully along the rim until she made it back to where Ulf stood waiting anxiously. "Okay, try to do what I do," she said. She looked over the edge, planning the first part of her descent. Stripping off her cloak, she wrapped it around her pack and dropped it over the edge. Next, she strung her bow and hung it across her body. Then, giving Ulf an encouraging smile, she lowered herself to the ground, rolled onto her stomach and felt with her toe for the first terrace.

•

Minna waited at the base of the cliff, sucking the tips of her fingers, chaffed raw by the rough dolomite, as she watched Ulf negotiated the last few feet of the descent. Above him, the top of the cliff remained unoccupied. Though the climb down wasn't difficult, her arms trembled with fatigue.

Ulf dropped beside her, pale and panting. "Are you alright?" she asked.

Instead of answering, he snatched up his pack, grabbed her hand, and pulled her into motion. They splashed across the ankle-deep stream and sprinted across a narrow meadow to the forest beyond. Minna glanced back, expecting the brothers to appear. When they made it to cover, they paused, catching their breath and watching the top of the ridge.

As Ulf was buttoning his cloak, two men appeared, looking down into the valley. They ducked behind a small spruce and watched as a third man, wearing a maroon cloak, came into view.

"Torsten," Ulf spat.

The men turned as one toward the north. Torsten moved off, disappearing beyond the rim of the cliff.

"We better go," Ulf said and set off toward the south.

With a last look at the top of the ridge, Minna followed.

Chapter 30

Alyn

Since the second night, the night she called the spirits for the first time, Alyn noticed that only the young soldier, who she learned was named Eckehart, would have anything to do with her. The others rarely looked at her directly, but she caught them giving her sidelong glances and whispering among themselves. Awash in the spirits' glow, she watched them over the rim of her bowl the next evening, trying to understand what changed. They acted as if they were afraid of her, but that was absurd, wasn't it?

The next morning, while Eckehart prepared to leave, she glanced at the other soldiers and whispered, "Why do they treat me differently now?"

"Shhh," he warned her, then lifted her into the saddle. Once they were moving and Alyn was, once again, confined to her dark world, Eckehart spoke.

"It would be best if you looked frightened."

At first, Alyn thought she misheard through the thick leather of the hood. But no, she heard him right. "But I am frightened."

"That may be, but you don't *appear* frightened."

Alyn almost laughed. "What possible difference could that make?"

He didn't answer at first, and Alyn felt him fidgeting. Finally, he said, "The witches we bring in are always frightened or angry. They weep or rage or are in shock, barely aware of what is happening. You smile and laugh. You're always looking off in the distance, as if you are watching unseen things." She felt him shaking his head next to hers. "You frighten them because they don't understand you."

They thought her a witch. That was why they took her from her home. "They are afraid of me?"

"They are terrified of you."

It was ridiculous, of course. What could she do if they decided to harm her? But learning that they feared her, unfounded as it was, set her eyes prickling. If they were not the implacable monsters they seemed, perhaps she was not as powerless as she thought.

"What about you? Why are you not afraid?" she asked, unashamed of the quaver in her voice.

He was quiet for a long time, then he said, "I don't see evil in you."

She shook her head. "Why do *you* do this?"

He didn't answer.

Each day, Eckehart helped her onto his horse before placing the hood over her head. She rode, sitting sideways, resting her weight on his chest when she grew weary. Eckehart occasionally spoke softly to her, updating her on their progress, though he refused to answer any more questions. With little else to occupy her time, she sought refuge in her center.

At first, she was just grateful for the relief her center provided. Though the pain, fear and anxiety were still there, she could examine them dispassionately, as though they belonged to another person. As the days passed, she wondered at the curious sensation of being able to observe the workings of her own mind. What did it mean? Something inside her reached out to the spirits when she called them. The same thing that responded to Minna. In the forest glade, when Minna described calling the spirits into her center, she said, 'I felt really small… and alone.' It made little sense to Alyn at the time. She turned it over in her mind, convinced it was all related, but the more she grasped after its meaning, the more it slipped away.

When they stopped each night, she emerged from her center to find her anxieties waiting for her. Though she was not immune to them, she had seen them from a distance, knew the shape of them, and they were no longer her master. She sat quietly, watching the men, wondering at the worried glances they gave her. While she sipped the broth, she called the *lan'and*, watching them dance around her, pondering the strange sensation of joyful familiarity.

As they descended from the heights, they moved into ever more alien terrain that left Alyn gaping each night. One day, she found herself in the middle of a vast sea of grass with only a shadow that might be trees below the mountains to the east. She was relieved to see the *lan'and* were not limited to the trees. They skipped along the top of the grass, dropping out of sight and reappearing like fish leaping in a lake.

One afternoon, they stopped, and Alyn heard the voices of other men. One of them insisted they remove the hood. She felt Eckehart fumbling with the leather thong, then the hood was drawn off, leaving her squinting in the midday sun. There were four different men on horseback, wearing white uniforms under their cloaks. One of them leaned toward her, peering at her with intense gray eyes. His brow furrowed as he searched her face.

"She came from Fennig?" he asked Eckehart, while staring into her eyes.

"Yes, sir."

"You accompanied Stefan to Fennig?"

"Yes, sir. Inquisitor Schakal captured this one. He tasked us with bringing her to Brennan while he remained in Fennig to continue his investigation."

"Can I help you, Inquisitor?" It was the soldier who had been so rough on her the first day.

The man with the gray eyes sat up, turned toward him and said, "We've had reports of a fugitive witch. I was just checking if this one fit her description."

"And does she?" the soldier asked.

"No, the fugitive has black hair."

Minna. Her sister escaped. The smallest ember of hope that flared within Alyn was doused by the hard expressions turned toward her as Eckehart drew the hood over her head. What could her sister do against Imperial soldiers? It would be better if Minna found a place to hide and stayed there.

· · ·

One morning, Eckehart failed to replace the hood. He said nothing. He simply helped her onto the horse and left the hood in his saddlebag. Despite her rising anxiety, she stared around at the foreign landscape. The other soldiers rode ahead of them, sometimes as many as fifty paces. In the afternoon, a smudge appeared on the horizon. As they grew nearer, the smudge slowly resolved into a city. A dark haze hung above it, thinning as it rose and was caught by the wind. It looked to Alyn as if the city was smeared across the sky. Soon, the westerly wind brought an awful odor. Nothing in her experience helped her to identify it. Eckehart noticed her discomfort and spoke for the first time in days. "This is Brennan. Our destination. You can smell the city a long way away. We're lucky; if this were summer, we would have smelled it before we saw it."

"What is it?" Alyn scrunched up her nose, blowing out, trying to expel the smell.

"Some of it is coal smoke. That's a kind of rock that burns. That's where the smoke comes from. Some of it is what you get when people have not enough care for hygiene. It's garbage and sewage and animals and people. Too many people."

Alyn was quiet for a time, trying to imagine that many people. "Why don't they keep it... clean? Don't they care?"

Eckehart laughed. "I imagine most people do care, at least the people who have to live in it. When you're poor and trying to survive, you don't have a lot of time and energy for such things."

"Is everyone poor?"

There was an edge in his voice as he said, "No, but the rich care little for the poor as long as they don't cause trouble."

Alyn couldn't make sense of that. Not everyone in Fennig had as much as others, but no one would be left to live in their own filth. "Maybe they should cause some trouble."

Eckehart chuckled. "Maybe so. Anyway, it's not so bad. After a while, you get used to it."

Alyn found that hard to believe.

• • •

As they neared the city, details became visible. An immense stone wall surrounded the central part of the city, broken up by square towers at regular intervals. People visible along the top of the wall were dwarfed by the structure. Alyn gaped at it. How could humans build such a thing? Outside the wall, a ramshackle collection of buildings pressed up against the highway. The first they encountered, nearly a league from the wall, were so decrepit, Alyn wondered how anyone could live in them.

Soon, they were among a line of people and wagons waiting to enter the city. One of the soldiers rode in front of their group, shouting, "Make way for the Inquisition! Out of the way. Get to the side of the road." People cowered away from the soldiers, but gave her hard looks. When she met their eyes, they hurled insults, touched their lips with two fingers of their right hand, and turned away. She heard the word witch more than once. Eckehart shifted behind her, and a moment later, he held the hood in front of her. "It's best if you have this on when we arrive." She pulled it on and held the reins while Eckehart tied the leather thong.

He took the reins and spoke softly in her ear. "When we arrive, I'll take you to the Inquisition's prison. I don't know for sure what will happen there, but there are rumors."

"Won't they kill me?" She had come to terms with the fact that they would kill her, and though it frightened her, she was more afraid of what would come before that moment.

"Maybe not. Some witches aren't killed. I don't know for sure how they decide which ones will live, but there are rumors that there is some sort of test. If you pass, you live."

Her heart thrummed. She might live. "Live to do what?"

Eckehart paused before saying, "I don't know."

They rode in silence and Alyn noticed that, now she was wearing the hood, she heard no more insults.

"Remember, it would be best if you looked frightened when we arrive."

"I should look frightened to make them feel safer?"

"No! If the guards in the prison are frightened of you, it will be worse for you. There are rumors they will give you something that makes you insensible. The guards are small men, bullies. If they believe you are frightened of them, it will make them feel powerful and they will treat you better."

"Thank you, Eckehart."

"You're welcome. Remember, if you are alive, there is hope."

The sound of people and animals diminished and the sound of the horses' hooves on the cobbled street echoed as if they were inside. When they emerged, she heard many voices, so many, they blended into a dull roar. They rode for what seemed a long time, stopping often, the soldiers shouting for people to clear the way. Eventually, they left the sound of crowds behind, and rode in relative silence for some time. There were shouts between her escorts and others, then clanging and creaking. The horses walked forward into what sounded like another tunnel, then stopped. Eckehart dismounted and helped her to the ground. He whispered in her ear, "Remember, when I remove the hood, act afraid." She nodded. They crossed cobbled pavement. Eckehart steadied her when she stumbled on the uneven ground. They passed through another echoing passage and emerged onto grass. They stopped. Words were exchanged, a door opened, then they were inside. They traversed so many stairs and made so many turns that Alyn lost all sense of direction. Eventually, Eckehart pulled her to a stop. She felt him leaning forward and heard the thuds of his fist on a wooden door. There was a slight creak, and she heard a man say, "Yeah?"

"Prisoner from Fennig. Accused witch captured by Inquisitor Schakal."

"Oh yeah? Where is the Inquisitor then, and when did you escort Stefan, anyway, Ecke?"

"Inquisitor Schakal remained in Fennig to investigate the village and question its inhabitants. We were assigned to the Inquisitor because Fennig is so far into Argren, he wished to have extra protection."

Alyn heard a grunt, followed by a clack and then a door creaking open. Eckehart led her forward. The unknown voice said, "Well, let's see her then."

Eckehart untied the thong of the hood, gave her arm a squeeze, then pulled the hood from her head. She stood in a small, dimly lit room. The only furnishing was a small trestle table in the center. Besides Eckehart, there were two other soldiers. One of them, a slovenly man, stood with his thumbs hitched in his belt, leering down at her. The other sat at the table, regarding her coolly. Under the cold scrutiny of the guards, her fear wasn't an act. She shrank back against Eckehart, her arms across her chest.

The slovenly guard nodded at her. "Now, now. No need to be fearful. S'long as you don't cause us any trouble, we'll treat you well. You cause us trouble, and, well…" He smirked at Eckehart. "Cause you any trouble, did she, Ecke?"

"No problem at all. Docile as a lamb." He removed the manacles and pulled her gently away from the door. Their eyes met, and Eckehart gave her a small nod. He looked at the guards and said, "She's all yours." With that, he walked out the door, and his footsteps receded down the hall.

Alyn looked from one guard to the other, rubbing her chaffed wrists. They studied her silently. The slovenly guard's face took on a speculative expression. He glanced at his companion and said, "She don't look so frightful, does she?"

Rather than answering, the other guard stood and opened a door in the opposite wall. He lit a torch from a lamp and stepped through the door. The other guard motioned for Alyn to follow him, saying, "Now, I know you're scared, but you just follow Brother Siegfried here and he'll show you to your room. Nothin's going to happen to you now."

Alyn edged around the opposite side of the table, keeping an eye on him, then slipped through the door. Siegfried was walking down a long, dark hall. Doors on each side emerged from the shadows momentarily as the torch passed. Alyn rushed to keep up with the receding light. Furtive movements through the small, barred windows in the closed doors revealed there were other prisoners. Siegfried stopped at an open door and turned toward her. Alyn stopped short of the door, leaned forward and peered into the cell.

"Inside," Siegfried said.

She walked cautiously in, examining the room. A narrow window, high on the back wall, let in the late afternoon sun, leaving the cell in semi-darkness. The cell was five paces wide and six paces deep. There was a sleeping pallet with a thin blanket on one wall, and a small desk and chair on the opposite wall. A hole in one corner emitted a foul odor. There was no source of heat, and cold air flowing down from the window swirled around her bare ankles. When Alyn turned back to the door, she found the slovenly guard blocking it, a black shadow against Siegfried's torch.

"Like I said, you don't cause us trouble, we won't cause you any. You get one meal in the evening unless you give us reason to not feed you. If you're good, you can go outside for an hour each week."

He stood, watching her. Alyn held her hands clasped at her waist, shoulders hunched, trying to look small. She nodded and said, "Thank you."

This appeared to be what he wanted, because he nodded and slammed the door. She could hear him talking and laughing as the two guards walked away. When the door at the end of the hall closed, she went to the cell door, stood on her tiptoes and looked out the small window. She called softly, "Can anyone hear me?"

It was silent for so long, she thought no one was listening, but then she heard, "Quiet, wait until night."

Her heart sped up, and a smile lifted the corners of her mouth. Padding over to the sleeping pallet, she sat cross-legged, wrapped the thin blanket around her shoulders, and sank into her center.

Chapter 31

Harold

Harold hoped to sense someone as he approached the small house outside Fennig, but of course, he didn't. He wasn't sure exactly what happened when Stefan arrived in Fennig, but the fact the Inquisition was looking for the black-haired witch in Hast was suggestive. He got a sense of it when they encountered the four brothers a day after they left Hast. The first time he noticed them in the distance, they were descending from the Breakheart Pass. It wasn't long after he sensed the witch. She felt familiar, and she was certainly powerful. He half-hoped, half-dreaded it might be her. He insisted they remove the hood so he could see her. As soon as the matted blond hair came into view, he knew it wasn't her. He peered into her oddly placid face, thinking there might be a resemblance, but it was five years since he saw the girl with the black hair, and he never saw her up close. He couldn't be sure if they were related. For one mad moment, looking into the eyes of the guard the girl was riding with, undoubtedly Eckehart, he thought of trying to free her. He scanned the other members of her escort, all hard men, glowering at him. Something was going on in that group. A fight would be bloody and unpredictable. Reluctantly, he watched them replace the hood and ride toward Hast. Who knew, she might have a chance.

The door of the small house bore evidence of recent repairs. New boards were fitted poorly with what must have been the remains of the original door. "Fenton, Raif, watch the horses. Sergeant, with me."

He paused on the front porch and stared at the bench beside the front door. Five years before, he stood in the forest across the road and watched the girl with her father sitting together on that bench, talking and laughing as they worked at some task. He assumed this little girl could not possibly be the witch. She was far too young to project the power he sensed, and he concluded the witch was still in the house. He waited, watching the pair engrossed in their conversation, the girl telling a story that had her father laughing. He smiled, lost in the memory. He couldn't hear what they said, but he found himself being pulled into their happiness, watching her animated descriptions and her father's reactions. It wasn't long before he was forced to conclude the girl was indeed the witch. He tried to remember if any of the witches he encountered before were as remotely powerful as this little girl. There were none. Harold knew his duty, and it was unambiguous; this girl was a danger to the Empire. He should have approached the house, arrested her and taken her back to Brennan. Yet, he didn't. Instead, he took the first step on the path Karl set before him.

Coming to himself, he glanced at Henrik, who was waiting patiently. He took one last look around the porch, then lifted the latch on the door and entered the house.

Other than a toppled bench next to the table, most of the room appeared undisturbed, as if the occupants merely stepped out. The door to a root cellar was open, and there were unmistakable signs of a struggle in the cellar.

"Looks like they hid in the root cellar when Stefan arrived," Henrik said.

"If it had only been Stefan, it might have worked. Unfortunately, they had a sister with them."

"Someone fought back but was overcome. Not much blood. I doubt anyone died. Not here anyway."

Harold hoped to find the parents. The Inquisition usually left them alive if they didn't resist. Their absence, given the state of the house, was disappointing, but perhaps they fled with their other daughter.

They searched the small bedroom that obviously belonged to the girls. A shaft of sunlight shone through the room's one window, illuminating the dust set swirling by the opening door. Nothing seemed out of place in the tidy room. Most of it was taken up by a bed covered by thick patchwork quilts. A collection of dolls sewn together from old clothing, with woolen hair, watched him with their button eyes from one end of a shelf above the bed. The other end held a collection of materials used for making arrows; flint, a coiled length of sinew, twigs, and a small knife. A small, child-sized bow and quiver was propped in one corner of the room opposite the bed, and a basket filled with fabric and yarn occupied the other. Two small trunks nestled against the center of the wall. One of them held dresses, hairpins, a sewing kit, a partially sewn shirt and a hairbrush. The blond hairs on the brush confirmed his belief that the girl with the brothers they encountered was the sister of the black-haired girl. The other trunk contained leather tunics and pants, a collection of arrowheads, flints, and a knife with a broken handle.

Henrik chuckled. "Never had a sister, so I'm no judge, but it's hard to imagine a family could have two sisters so different."

Harold smiled absently. As he gazed around the cozy room, he had the sense their differences meant little. But perhaps it was only what he wanted to believe.

Next, they searched the larger bedroom on the opposite side of the house. The room held a larger bed, covered by similar quilts.

"Looks like someone left in a hurry," Henrik said.

Two drawers of a small dresser were open and empty. A pair of woolen socks, still rolled into one another, and a thick woolen sweater lay on the floor beside the bed.

Harold pulled the other two drawers open. "Men's clothes, still here."

"Not a good sign."

"Perhaps."

Nothing else was out of place. Harold stopped in the doorway, taking one more look around the room, when his eyes fell on a book peeking out from under the sweater. It stuck out in the small rustic house, where there were no other books of any kind. He brushed the sweater aside and turned the book so he could read the handwritten title on the cover. It said, "Love Letters" in ancient Vollen, a language used only within the Church and the Seidi. Curious, he flipped open the cover and found a dedication on the inside.

To Ragan with all my love, Deirdre

Harold stared at it. Could it be? He supposed there might be another Deirdre in the world, but Deirdre was a Vollen name, meaning sorrow in ancient Vollen. He didn't know anyone named Ragan, but it didn't sound like an *Alle'oss* name. The idea the Malefica was somehow connected to the black-haired witch was too unlikely to believe. He stood and looked absently around the room. There was nothing else that was out of place for an *Alle'oss* house. Could this be the friend Deirdre asked after? One of the lost sisters? He picked the book up, placing it in an inside pocket of his cloak. A riddle for later.

Though they came to Fennig five years before, they never came closer to the village than the small house. He had seen many *Alle'oss* villages as an inquisitor. He found them pretty and well kept, but you would have to call them quaint, tucked away in their mountainous settings. Fennig did not match that description. It reminded him more of a small Imperial city, more orderly than the typical, sprawling *Alle'oss* village, the few streets arranged in a grid and the buildings resembling small Imperial buildings. He wondered about the history of the place. There were a handful of similar towns in Argren, but they all had a much larger Imperial presence. As they neared the top of hill leading to the square, he noticed damage to the buildings at the edge of the village.

"Whoa, something happened here," Raif said.

Part of a building had burned, and many windows and doors were boarded up with newly cut planks. More evidence of hasty repairs. He couldn't think of a way so much damage in such a wide area could occur at one time. Another riddle.

In the village square, a handful of people were going about their business.

They paused in the middle of the square. "Bit quiet for an *Alle'oss* village, isn't it?" Henrik mused.

The few people they saw hurried away when they caught sight of them. He was used to that, at least. Looking around at the buildings that cozied up to the square, he identified one that looked like a tavern.

"Fancy an ale, sergeant?"

"Aye, that I would."

They tied their horses to a hitching post and entered the tavern. A few people gathered in small groups at tables around the room, and two men stood at the small bar at the back of the room. Every eye in the room turned toward them as they entered, lingering beyond what simple curiosity would dictate.

Harold motioned Fenton and Raif toward a table near the door. "Sergeant."

They approached the bar, a crackle from the fire in the hearth the only sound besides their footsteps. One of the men at the bar turned away as he approached, but the other, a large man with a spectacular red beard, stared frankly at them.

"A brandy for me, and ales for my men," Harold said to the man behind the bar, returning Red's attention.

The barkeep filled a wooden mug from a dusty bottle and dropped it onto the bar, saying, "Three Imperial pennies." He filled mugs from a cask.

When Harold opened his cloak to retrieve the money, exposing his uniform, there was a gasp from Red. "Aha, another one!" He punched the man behind him on the arm and said, "Told ya. Told ya that other one sent for help. They'll get her yet."

The other man scowled at Harold and turned back to his ale.

Harold sipped the brandy, studying the large man. "Another one?"

The man beamed at him, beads of ale glistening in his mustache. "Aye, another inquisitor. The other fella got here days ago. Been asking around for the witch." He frowned, scratching his chin. "Ye ask me, she's long gone."

"You're talking about the black-haired witch, I assume."

The man slapped the bar, then turned to punch the other man on the arm again. "Told ya, Erik!" He turned back to Harold. "That's her. Minna. She's been causing trouble around here for years."

Minna. He finally had a name.

Red continued. "Me and some of the boys finally had enough. Cornered her and that boy, Jason. She nearly destroyed the whole place, but we chased her."

Harold glanced around the tavern, gestured with his mug and asked, "Destroyed the whole place?"

Red puffed out his cheeks and Erik snorted, saying, "It weren't near as dramatic as all that. Agmar here has a way with a story."

"You talking about that damage up the hill, at the edge of the village?"

Agmar gave Harold a delighted smile. "Thas right! You saw it, huh? That other fella didn't even notice til I showed him. You shoulda seen it. She rose up, right off the ground, lightnin all around. When she looked right at me... well, I still see those eyes some nights." He shook himself and then lifted his arms, fingers splayed. "Then she lifts her arms and screams some spell, then... boom. The next thing, the whole place is on fire and everythin scattered around."

Harold returned Erik's smirk and asked, "Did anyone die?"

Red frowned. "No, no one died. We's just lucky, I guess." He took a gulp of his ale, foam clinging to his whiskers, dripping on to the bar. He gave Harold a knowing look and said, "It's not because she didn't try, see."

Harold frowned. "If she was able to do all that damage, how did you 'chase her'?"

The other man at the bar, Erik, turned and watched Agmar with interest. Agmar looked uncomfortable. "I spose she stopped to see to her friend, that boy, Jason, I mentioned." He nodded, as if reassuring himself.

"Gave us time to regroup, see? Then we rushed her, and she run off. Haven't seen or felt a sign of her since, though we been lookin for her. That's why I say she probably run off."

"The boy, Jason, he's alive?"

Erik nodded. "Yeah. Was a near thing from what I hear. Took a rock to the temple." He turned a sour look on Agmar before continuing. "Seems to be fine now. That other inquisitor…" His face scrunched up for a minute as if he was thinking.

Agmar interjected. "Name's Stefan."

Erik nodded. "That's it. He's been trying to talk to the blacksmith's boy, but the family won't let him in."

"The boy's the blacksmith's son?"

Agmar nodded, frowning. "Been friends with the witch for years. You ask me, he got what he deserved."

"That's right," Erik said, throwing a glare at Agmar. "A *good* boy. Be a good blacksmith when his dad's done. Not a bad bone in his body."

Agmar glowered back at him.

"Is there an inn in town?"

"Sure is, it's one block east of the square. Ask for Brana, it's her place."

Agmar smiled. "You won't find that other inquisitor there, though."

"No?"

"No, he took Marie's house." For some reason, Agmar seemed to find this funny. "Thas the big house on the west side of the square. She's madder'n a wet hen." He guffawed.

Harold watched him laughing, then asked Erik, "Is that funny?"

"Marie and Agmar, here, been goin at it for a long time about Minna."

Anger flashed across Agmar's face. "We proved her wrong, din't we? She was wrong about that girl. Everybody listen to her, we'd all be dead, eventually."

Erik straightened, an exasperated expression on his face. "Agmar, I don't know how many times we have to have this argument. If you'd left her alone, nothin would have happened. It's cause you cornered her and hurt her friend, she done what she did."

Agmar's face reddened, but before he could launch, Harold overrode him. "There was a woman with the inquisitor, a sister. Has a tattoo on her face. Is she staying in the house with Stefan?"

The two men exchanged a look, then Erik spoke. "Seen her. When they got here. She'd come in here, share an ale. Kind of liked her, spite her being a *witch*." He glared at Agmar.

Agmar shrugged and looked uncomfortable. "I suppose you'd call her a *good* witch?" A range of emotions crawled across his face, then he took a drink of his ale and stared at the casks stacked against the wall behind the bar.

It was obviously a recurring theme with the two of them. Harold said, "You said she would come in here. She hasn't come in recently?"

Erik answered, "No, see, something happened. There's all kinds of rumors, but no one knows for sure. Her and the big man, the sergeant, they just disappeared."

Harold caught Henrik's eye. "Disappeared?"

"Aye," Agmar said. "That inquisitor fella, he's saying they went for help, now, but that's not what he said at first. Had a bunch of us out looking for something. Told us we were lookin for the witch but said to keep an eye out for his sergeant."

"No one's seen the woman since?"

"Not a sign."

Harold drained his mug, wiped his mouth on his sleeve, and said, "Where's the blacksmith located?"

• • •

Fennig's inn was really more a large house than the inns Harold was used to, but it was cozy. The fire in the parlor created a warm, homey ambiance, and the food was the first home cooked meal he had since Karl left. When he arrived, the owner, Brana, and a woman he learned was the displaced Marie, were sitting in the parlor, knitting and sharing a lively conversation. Initially, they were friendly, but when they saw the Inquisition uniforms, they became quiet and suspicious.

When he informed Brana he wanted rooms for himself and his men, Marie sniffed." Imagine that, an inquisitor staying at the inn." She lifted her chin slightly, as if daring him to say anything.

She continued to bait him during the evening meal, but when he didn't rise, she gave up, though it was clear her opinion of him had not softened. She sat across from him now in the parlor, knitting, casting baleful looks his way from time to time. With nothing else to do, he leafed through the book he found in Minna's house. His ancient Vollen was a bit rusty, there was a lot that he couldn't decipher, but he understood enough to tell that it was filled with love poems. It was naïve, occasionally clumsy, but it was such an exuberant expression of a young person's first love, raw and overwhelming, that he found his eyes watering. A memory of Karl laughing as Harold tried to teach him the stilted, formal dances of the Volloch came unbidden to mind. He held his fist to his mouth, squeezing his eyes shut, unwilling to share the moment with Marie. Once he had his emotions under control, he glanced in her direction, finding her staring at him, her knitting forgotten in her lap.

He cleared his throat and focused on the book, flipping through the pages. He nearly decided to retire for the evening when he noticed an inscription on the inside of the back cover. The hand that wrote this was not the same that wrote the poetry. The poet's writing was neat, while this was scrawled across the page, difficult to decipher. He held the book near a lamp, squinting at the text.

H,

You won't find a better ally than Marie. Tell her you have a message for Keelia.

R

Harold sat back, staring at the inscription. He leaned closer to the lamp, studying it again to reassure himself he read it correctly. What did it mean? He sat back again, his gaze settling on Marie, who had resumed knitting. She glanced at him, a small furrow appearing between her brows when she found him watching her. Could H refer to him? He snorted. It was absurd, yet the message was so specific. He did have a message for

Keelia, and Marie sat a few feet from him. He looked back down at the book. R. He flipped to the front cover and read that inscription again, which was written in the same hand as the poetry.

To Ragan with all my love, Deirdre

Ragan. Could the mystery woman and the sister who Deirdre was looking for be the same person? He looked at Marie again and found her watching him, needles clicking as she knitted. Worth a try. He cleared his throat and asked, "Marie, do you know a person named Ragan?"

She fumbled her knitting, jabbing her thumb with a needle. Gasping, she dropped her knitting into her lap and sucked her thumb. She looked at Harold with narrowed eyes, then pulled her thumb from her mouth, and said, "I don't believe I've ever known anyone named Ragan. It doesn't sound like an *Alle'oss* name."

"What is Minna's mother's name?"

Marie stared at him but didn't answer. He was about to ask her what harm it could do to tell him when she answered, "Vada. Vada Hunter."

"Do you know where Minna and her parents are?"

Marie gave a small shake of head. "I wouldn't have any idea."

Harold smiled, nodding. He opened the book to the back cover and held it out. She hesitated, then stuffed her knitting into a small leather satchel next to her chair and took the book. Holding it at arm's length near the lamp on the table beside her chair, she squinted at it. Finally, she handed the book back and said, "I can't read this. It appears to be in a language similar to Vollen, but it isn't Vollen."

Harold flipped through the pages. "It's ancient Vollen, a language only used by the Church and the Seidi today."

"What does it say?"

"I found this in Minna's house this morning." He lifted the book briefly. "I've never seen it before today. Yet, the inscription on the back cover says, H, You won't find a better ally than Marie, and it's signed Ragan. My name is Harold." He met her eyes. "It's a remarkable coincidence, don't you think?"

Her eyes narrowed again, and she said, "You took it from the Hunter's house?"

Harold nodded. "I hoped to find her parents. When I found the door recently repaired and no one home, I investigated. I found this book with, apparently, a message for me, so... yes, I took it."

She sniffed, her hands folded in her lap, her chin lifted. "How do I know it says what you say?"

Harold chuckled. "It's true it's in ancient Vollen, but there are words that are the same. Surely you can read your own name and the word ally." He lifted his brows. She nodded and Harold could tell she was curious, despite what she said.

She held out her hand and Harold handed the book to her. She looked at the inscription again. "There's more. Something about a message and Keelia. What does it say?"

"It says to tell you I have a message for Keelia."

Marie closed the book in her lap and looked at Harold. "Well, do you?"

"As a matter of fact, I do." He stood, retrieved the note from a pocket of his cloak hanging on a coat rack near the door. Taking his seat again, he handed it to Marie.

She turned it over, examining the name on the front: To Keelia, Malefica Dierdre. Her only reaction was a slight widening of her eyes. She turned the note over and held it near the lamp so she could examine the wax seal. Looking back at Harold, she said, "A note from the Malefica?"

He nodded. "She gave it to me, personally. I don't know exactly what it says, but the gist of it is that Keelia should trust me."

They looked at one another, Marie still holding the note near the lamp. She shook herself slightly and held the note out to Harold, saying, "No one has seen Keelia for near two weeks, poor girl. I wouldn't know where she is."

Harold didn't take the note. "I think that you do." When she started to say something, Harold raised his hand. "I know you have no reason to trust me, but if you can get the note to Keelia, she can make up her own mind."

Marie hesitated before slipping the note in the satchel with her knitting. She opened the book in her lap and flipped through the pages. When she saw the inscription on the front cover, her hand went to her mouth. She stared at it, then closed the book slowly and handed it back to Harold, her eyes shimmering in the fire's light.

Harold took the book. Interesting. Apparently, Marie did know Ragan. He watched her pick up her satchel and head up the stairs to her room, then stared into the fire. It would be nice to sleep in a bed again. He flipped through the book of poetry, thinking of Karl. Eventually, he rose in the silent house and headed to his room.

Chapter 32

Minna

Ulf pointed to the east and said, "That looks familiar."

Minna followed his gaze through a gap in the trees. In the distance, a rocky escarpment rose above the hilly, forest covered terrain. Water arced into space over the edge, spreading out as it fell until it disappeared as a misty shower behind the intervening hills. It was a memorable sight.

"The highway should be close," Ulf said.

"Finally."

"I know." Ulf stared forlornly into his nearly empty pack. "I have every confidence you could feed us, if you had the time to hunt, but… do you think we have the time?"

"I've seen plenty of game, but I don't think a fire is a good idea. Not sure I'm hungry enough for raw squirrel, yet." Minna looked at the distant waterfall. "How long before we get to Hast?"

"A week. Maybe." He returned the pack to his back. "Not sure how that helps. We don't have any money."

"The Mother will provide."

"The Mother and Father don't have to eat." Ulf's lopsided grin always brought out Minna's smile. "Least, not in my da's stories."

"One step, then the next." Minna fell in beside him as they began walking again. "Your da still tells stories of the Mother and Father?"

"Oh, yeah." He adopted an older man's voice and wagged his finger. "Don't forget the old ways, Ulf. Someday, you'll be happy you didn't."

"The old ways," Minna mused.

"The old ways," Ulf answered.

Days of anxiety and fear, close calls and little sleep, and the small, intimate moments that friends share. It had only been nine days since they left Fennig, but it seemed a lifetime. Listening to Ulf reciting the *Alle'oss* vocabulary she set him to memorize the night before, Minna couldn't help marveling at how quickly their friendship had grown. Though they didn't speak of it, she knew he felt the same.

It was three days since they last saw Torsten and the brothers. They fled in a generally southwest direction, toward Hast, following a winding path to obscure their trail as much as possible. Rolling hills and stands of beech, birches and maples gradually replaced the steep rocky ridges and evergreen forests. The occasional open meadow presaged the vast open spaces Minna saw in the distance from the top of the pass. At first, they avoided these open spaces, choosing instead to take the long way around through the forest. Now, weary and hungry, a rising sense of urgency drove them to throw caution to the wind and take the shortest route.

A half hour later, they stood atop a steep slope, peering uncertainly down at the Imperial Highway. Fat, fluffy snowflakes drifted lazily in the still air, laying down the first feathery layer of winter's blanket. The air was heavy with the ashy scent of a fire that swept through this part of the forest recently. Only a crow's harsh complaint disturbed the silence.

"So, there's the highway," Minna said, her words coming out as small puffy clouds. "What do you think?"

"Don't see anyone, but we can't see very far."

To the west, the highway emerged from a deep, narrow cut, then curved to the east, before passing by the bottom of the hill and disappearing as it curved back to the north.

They were silent for a time, then Minna caught Ulf's eye. "What do we do? Just walk up the road to Hast? Doesn't seem wise."

"No, I've a better plan. Come on." He stepped up to the edge of the slope, leaned out, and peered down. The fire reduced the underbrush to a thick layer of sooty ash and left blackened, skeletal remains of scrubby trees clinging to the slope. He glanced back, then eased over the edge.

"Careful," Minna said, watching him gingerly navigate the first few feet. With each step, a small gray cloud bloomed around his boots.

Taking hold of a charred branch, Minna eased over the edge. As soon as she settled her weight on her foot, it slid on the loose upper layer. With one foot on the top and one foot sliding down the slope, her legs spread apart.

"Whoa," she muttered under her breath. She bent at the waist. The reed-thin branch she was holding onto bent, then snapped, throwing her off balance. She threw her weight backwards, arms pinwheeling, then sat, bringing her feet together. And then she was sliding down the steep slope, picking up speed as she went.

"Look out," she shouted too late. Ulf was just turning when she plowed into the back of his legs. He landed on top of her, and then both of them were sliding, raising a powdery cloud behind them. Minna wrapped one arm around Ulf's waist and craned her neck, trying to see where they were going. Just before they reached the bottom, they hit a bump that launched them, spinning through the air. They hit the ground in a ditch beside the road, tumbled in a tangled mess, and came to a stop in an explosion of ash.

Ulf rolled away, leaving Minna lying on her back, coughing and flapping her hands at the ash settling on her. Rolling onto her hands and knees, she took inventory and was relieved to find no serious injury. She got to her feet, swiped at her face, then bent over and rubbed her butt. "Ow!"

"You okay?" Ulf asked.

When Minna looked up, she caught him staring at her.

"What?"

A wide grin grew on his face.

"What?"

He pointed at her and said, "Your face. It's... uh...."

"What about my—"

Ulf chuckled.

She wiped her cheeks and looked at her hands. They were black with soot.

"Oh, that's better," Ulf choked out, working up a healthy chortle.

"Funny." She lifted her palms toward him and advanced, wiggling her fingers.

"No!" he grabbed for her wrists, but weak with laughter, he couldn't stop her from clapping her hands to his cheeks.

She stepped back, went to plant her hands on her hips, thought better of it, then stood awkwardly with her hands held out to her side, smiling triumphantly.

"Why, you…" Ulf stared at her in mock outrage.

Ulf was the first to crack. He shook, pale skin reddening under the soot. Minna watched him, a silly grin growing on her face. And then they were both bent over, eyes streaming, laughing helplessly. Straightening to take a breath, Minna snorted. She clapped her hands over her nose. Ulf sucked in a breath and pressed his lips tight against his laughter. They stared at one another, eyes wide. And then they were both bent over again, staggering, great whoops of laughter leaving them breathless.

Ivan

As it turned out, the quartermaster in Hast was not up to the recent demands placed on him. The horses he issued to Ivan and his men were already somewhere in Argren, having been issued by the same man a week before. They were obliged to wait two days while horses were brought from Brennan. All they could do was wait.

Now, a day out from Hast, they rode through the Wollen Cut. The cut was gouged out of the granite escarpment that ran like a ragged scar through the foothills and marked the first significant rise in elevation as the highway climbed into the mountains. It was a remarkable feat of engineering that opened southern Argren to the Empire. Wollen was remembered as an engineering genius, but Ivan suspected his true genius was the ruthlessness required to spend an army of Brochen slaves to complete the project. Did the *Alle'oss* watch with a sense of foreboding as they made their slow progress through the hard stone? If they did, they made no move to stop it. He looked to the top of the rock face bordering the highway. A company of archers atop the escarpment could have kept the Empire at bay for months, though it would only have delayed the inevitable. It was as Daga said; to the strong go the rewards.

At the top of the hill, the road leveled out and turned east. As they rounded the curve, two figures standing on the shoulder of the road came into view. At first, Ivan thought they were fighting, but as he drew nearer, he realized they were laughing.

"*L'oss?*" Victor asked.

Patches of Argren green were visible through the filth on their cloaks. "Probably," he muttered. The boy's hair was red, but the girl… "Brother Tristan, does that female have black hair?"

Before Tristan could answer, the girl looked at them and froze.

Minna

Minna's laughter died instantly when she spotted the brothers. They had black hair, as nearly all Imperials did, but the one in front had a streak of snow white that began above his left eye. Their eyes met for an instant before the man pointed and shouted, "It's her!" They stared at one another for the space of a heartbeat, then the horses surged forward.

Minna grabbed Ulf's hand and pulled him toward the hill they just slid down. When Ulf saw what was happening, he pulled Minna to a stop.

"We'll never get up that hill. Come on!" They raced across the highway, crossed the narrow shoulder, and entered the forest.

The fire leapt the highway, but only cleared the underbrush on this side. The trunks of the widely spaced trees were charred, but the trees survived. Ulf let go of Minna's hand and they wove in and out of the blackened trunks, the soft crunch of the ash beneath their feet barely audible above the rolling thunder of galloping horses coming closer. Minna resisted the urge to look back when the softer ground among the trees muted the hoof beats. She glanced up. The trees were empty of spirits. The men shouted, eager, urging their mounts on, close enough to hear the jangle of the bridles.

At the limit of the fire's destruction, they passed spindly, blackened remains of shrubs. The throaty breaths of the horses were at her ear. And then they crossed the boundary, leaving the ash behind and crashing into a hedge-like stand of living privets. Behind her, the staccato thumps of the horses came to an abrupt stop amid the brothers' frustrated shouts. The ground rose, and they climbed, ducking low to fight their way beneath the tangled branches. They struggled free of the clinging privets and kept climbing through a looser mix of foliage. More shouts, purposeful and controlled, the sound of horses riding away and someone forcing their way through the hedge behind them.

Suddenly, Minna and Ulf emerged into the clear on top of the hill. Ulf turned right and kept going. Minna stopped and pulled her pack off her back. Heart hammering, breath coming in a ragged, smoky puffs, she struggled with fingers clumsy with cold at the leather thongs holding her bow.

"Come on, Minna," Ulf shouted.

Finally, the tie came free. She strung the bow, pulled an arrow from her quiver, as a man burst from the undergrowth. Minna nocked and fired, without thinking, catching him high on the chest. Turning before he fell, she snatched up her pack and fled after Ulf. A bellow of rage behind them as another brother emerged and found his companion. No way to turn and get a shot off before he was on her.

They descended a long slope, Ulf ahead of her, weaving in and out of the hardwoods. Her breath in her ears, a jagged whoosh in time with the crunch of her footsteps in dry leaves. Her heart lurched at the sight of a meadow ahead, covered by the thick, clinging grass as high as her thighs. Behind her, the strangled snarls of the brother getting closer.

She emerged from the trees and slowed, lifting her knees high to fight her way through the grass. Desperate, she looked up to find Ulf waiting for her. She opened her mouth to call for help, then broke into a wide smile. The snow, falling thick enough now to obscure the far side of the meadow, glowed with an ethereal light. Spirits. Minna threw her center open, and the spirits reacted. She called, glimpsed the *lan'and* spiraling toward her, and then she was flying, thrown forward by a heavy blow between her shoulders blades.

She grunted as her breath left her lungs. Her pack and bow went flying, and she landed heavily on her chest, where she lay gasping for air. The *lan'and* poured into her center. For a heartbeat, pain and dizziness vied with the exhilarating rush of the spirits. But Minna was no longer the small, frightened spirit she was that first time in the forest glade, nor was she uncertain as she was at the *Alle'oss* encampment. She plunged into the storm, seeking the stillness at the center. The pain faded, her mind cleared, she opened her mouth and filled her lungs with air.

Before she could rise, a boot appeared beside her and a hand wrapped around her neck, pressing her into the ground. She heard Ulf's wordless shout, saw his boots approaching at a run. There was the clash of steel, and a sword spun away. Gruff laughter, a thud, and Ulf flew backward, landed on his back, and lay still.

The hand tightened on her neck and lifted her to her knees. A sword appeared and was pressed to her throat.

The hand bent her head to the side. She smelled the man's breath and felt his lips moving in her hair. "Give me an excuse. I don't care if they want you alive." He applied pressure to the sword and lifted her to her feet, drawing a shallow cut just below her jawline.

Ulf lay on his back, arms flung wide, not moving. Minna winced at the bite of the sword and peered at the brother out of the corner of her eye. He was searching the tree line. Slowly, she lifted her hand between them and waited.

When the man took a deep breath and opened his mouth to shout, there was the slightest release of the sword's pressure on her neck. The spirit wave hit him on the left side of his chest. He spun away from her, his sword arm flung out, sending the sword flying from his hand. The hand on the back of Minna's neck yanked her off her feet.

She lay staring up into the falling snow, a high clear note reverberating in her mind.

"Minna, watch" Ulf's voice, low and weak, cut through her haze.

"What did you do to me, you *witch*?" Minna rolled over and struggled to her knees. The brother was getting to his feet, a grimace pulling his lips back from his teeth. He stumbled a step, his sword arm flopping limply. With a bellow, he staggered toward her, drawing a dagger with his good arm.

Minna lifted her hand as he loomed over her and blasted him. This time, the wave caught him full in the chest, lifting him and throwing him backward. He landed on his back and didn't move.

Minna tried to stand, but lost her balance and fell to her hands and knees. Her center rang. The note, meeting the dying echo of the first, thrummed. Rising and falling in a slow beat, massaging her mind, and producing a euphoria so powerful, she shivered and nearly swooned. Groaning, she dropped to her elbows, lowering her forehead to the wet grass.

Lost in the sensations in her center, she almost didn't hear Ulf's warning until it was too late. She lifted up and found another brother, the brother with the white streak in his hair, racing toward her. Lurching to her feet, she stepped on the hem of her cloak and stumbled backwards before righting herself and raising her hands. The man stopped, crouching, arms out for balance. He glanced to the side, and before Minna could react, he sprinted to the right. He was on Ulf before Minna's slow mind could recognize what he had in mind. Ulf knelt on one knee, forehead buried in his palm. The brother snatched the shoulder of Ulf's cloak, jerked him to his feet, and pulled him between himself and Minna. A dagger appeared at Ulf's throat.

"Whoa, there," the brother said when Minna lifted her hands. "No need for anyone else to get hurt." He looked past Minna and shouted, "Victor, stop."

Minna looked back over her shoulder. Another brother had come out of the woods behind her. He slowed to a stop, sword held at the ready.

"No need to worry about Brother Victor. Look at me," the brother holding Ulf said quietly.

Minna turned sideways, one hand pointing to each of them, trying to watch both of them. She bit the inside of her cheek, trying to clear her mind, but deep in her center, with the roar of the *lan'and* in her mind, she barely felt it.

"That's good. Like I said, no need for anyone else to get hurt. By the looks of you two, you could use a nice, warm place to sleep. Some food. Now, you just lay down on your stomach, put your face in the grass and tuck your hands out of sight, underneath you."

It was a lie, of course. They intended to kill her, but what about Ulf?

Following her gaze, the brother seemed to guess her thoughts. "What I see is a witch who tricked a boy into traveling with her. He's committed no crime that I can see."

"That's a lie!"

"Ulf, shut up!"

It was probably another lie, but even a slim hope is hope. And it crossed her mind they might take her to Alyn.

She gave Ulf an apologetic grimace and lowered her hands.

"No Minna, you can still get away. Think of your sister," Ulf said.

An arrow struck the brother just above the elbow of the arm holding the dagger. He screeched and yanked his hand away. The dagger flew away, and Ulf dropped to the ground. Minna appealed to the spirits one last time. The wave spread outward, knocking the brothers off their feet. A blast of air from above, filling the vacuum, swirled Minna's cloak and whipped her hair around her head. But she didn't notice as she fell into darkness.

Aron

"You missed." Aron said. He and Zaina peered through a mountain laurel at the edge of the meadow, watching Ulf bending over a prone Minna.

Zaina narrowed her eyes. "Why did I take the shot?"

"Because you're the best," Aron said, giving her his widest smile.

One brow rose as she unstrung her bow. "I didn't miss. If I killed him, he might have killed Ulf in his death throes. Break his arm, his hand goes limp. The boy lives."

Aron watched Ulf helping Minna into a sitting position. "Risky. Wouldn't have been my choice." He grinned at her. "But that's why you're the best."

Minna was on her feet, staring in their direction, while Ulf gathered their belongings.

"Why don't we just go out there and get them?" Zaina asked.

Why not, indeed? Trust. It was the only reason he needed. Had she not earned it? He knew why she confided so little in him. Her plans were a complex tapestry, as delicate as lace. Any misstep — an errant word, an untimely act or a failure to act at the appropriate time — would unravel the carefully interwoven threads. Though she never said so, he knew she feared that if he knew the sacrifices that must be made, he might refuse her. And in his heart, he was grateful for her discretion. Trust. She deserved his trust. She earned it. He believed in her, and her hopes for his people. And though she confided little, Aron surmised much on his own. Conscious of Zaina waiting patiently for his answer, he drew his sword and held it up, the metal dull in the gray light. "Even the best steel must be tempered."

Zaina's gaze moved from Minna and Ulf to the blade. "That what she is, a weapon to be hardened?"

"That... and so much more," Aron said so low Zaina barely heard the words. "Plus, she has an appointment with destiny in Hast she must keep. For all our sakes."

"And what of the boy? Is he expendable?"

Aron returned from his thoughts and gazed at the two young people. "She needs a friend. Someone she can trust and lean on."

Zaina followed his gaze. "They live, right? I mean, why go through the whole charade if they die?"

"Hmmm?" Minna and Ulf started walking cautiously toward them. "Always a chance. Nothing is ever sure." He shook his head and sheathed his sword. "But if she dies, we all do."

Zaina nodded, lips in a tight line, "They're coming this way."

"Yes." He hesitated, but her instructions were clear. Minna must not see them. "Come on, we better go."

"Should we make sure the brothers are dead?"

"No." He turned, trusting that, despite her doubts, Zaina would follow.

Minna

Minna swayed on her feet, watching the tree line while Ulf gathered their belongings. She couldn't see anyone, but someone was obviously there. When she looked back at Ulf, he was holding the sword in his hands. He looked up and their eyes met for a moment, then he dropped the sword and came over to her.

"What do you think?" he asked, looking toward the shadows at the meadow's edge.

"We should go see who it is." When Ulf didn't respond, she asked, "They must be friends, right?"

"Then why not show themselves?"

"Let's go find out."

Ulf took her arm and supported her while they walked across the meadow. No one was there, but the evidence of their presence was clear.

"They went that way," Minna said, pointing. "Two people wearing *Alle'oss* moccasins."

Ulf peered through the trees in the direction Minna pointed. "Should we follow?"

"No," Minna said, standing. "Let's go to Hast."

Ulf nodded and looked out into the meadow. "They must have left their horses nearby. They probably have food, blankets. Things we need."

"Good idea." Minna followed Ulf's gaze. The brother's bodies were nearly invisible, their white uniforms almost indistinguishable from the snow. "But let's go around, through the woods."

Chapter 33

Alyn

Alyn stayed in her center for the rest of the day, mainly to distract herself from the cold and boredom. She emerged late in the afternoon and paced, trying to bring some feeling to her legs. Early in the evening, the door at the end of the hall opened, and momentarily, someone shoved a tin dish and leather water bottle through a flap at the bottom of the cell door. The food was a barley porridge with chunks of some unidentifiable vegetable. It had little flavor, but it wasn't awful. When she finished, she held the empty dish in her lap and stared at it. It was not nearly as much as Eckehart gave her and barely touched her hunger. And this was all she would have to eat until tomorrow evening.

She let her eyes travel over the stone walls of the dim cell, thinking of the cozy little room she shared with Minna. Autumn's chill would be settling in at home. It meant nights, by the fire, listening to her father's stories, surrounded by the comforting smells of home. Bundles of herbs hung up to dry, leather, smoke and her mother's cooking. She and her sister would dash from the warmth of the common room into their chilly bedroom and burrow under their thick quilts. The bed would be toasty from a warming pan, their mother put there earlier. In the dark, they would talk about little things, and big things, dreams of the future, until sleep took them. The memory brought a small smile to her face, but as she gazed around the empty cell, a heaviness settled on her.

She heard a door slam, the sound magnified in the utter silence of the dungeon. Alyn sat staring into space until she began to shiver. She carefully set the dish on the floor, lay on the sleeping pallet and dragged the thin, musty blanket over herself. The shadow that hid the floor climbed the wall as the sun set until the cell was lost in blackness.

She couldn't do this. The trip to get here was difficult. The terror she felt at the start was still too vivid to replay, and the days were long, uncomfortable, and tedious. But at least she was outside among the *lan'and,* and had the mostly silent, but still comforting company of Eckehart. There was a sense of movement. To what, she didn't know, but it occupied her mind. Now that she arrived, the reality of her predicament and what she lost was somehow more real. She felt utterly alone. Where were Minna, her mother and father? Were they alive? Would they ever learn of her fate, or would they live with that uncertainty for the rest of their lives?

"Hey, new girl."

At first, Alyn wasn't sure what she heard.

"Hey, are you awake?"

She stood, wrapping the blanket around her shoulders, and felt her way to the door. Holding onto the bars of the small window with one hand, she called quietly, "Hello?"

"I was wondering about you. Usually, the new girls cry for days. You were so quiet, I was wondering if you were still there."

Alyn rested her forehead on the door, tears dripping off the tip of her nose.

When she didn't answer, the voice said, "My name is Frida."

"I'm Alyn."

"Where are you from?"

"Fennig."

"Fenn... what?"

"Fennig, it's on the other side of *na'lios*. Where are you from?"

"Kartok."

Alyn never heard of it, but didn't feel like asking about it.

"There are three of us, well, four now. The other girls are Tora and Ibbe. Tora is really quiet. She almost never talks. Alva is dreaming."

"Dreaming? She's asleep?"

"Sort of. If you do something, the guards don't like, they make you drink something that makes you dream. Really strange dreams. You don't wake up for a long time. Don't do anything to make them mad at you."

Eckehart was right about that. "Why can you talk at night? Is there no guard?"

"There is a guard at night. We see him sometimes, but he ignores us most of the time. We think he sleeps."

Another voice, softer than Frida's, asked, "Do you know why we're here?"

Frida answered, "I told you already, Tora, we're here because we're witches."

"I *remembered* that," Tora replied. "I just... I thought they were supposed to kill us when we got here. That's what the man said who brought me here."

In the silence that followed, Alyn thought about what Eckehart told her. "The soldier who brought me said we would be tested, and if we passed, they would let us live." When they didn't reply, she asked, "Did they test you?"

At first, there was no response, then Tora said, "I think it must be that woman with the red hair. It was awful."

"Why, what happened?"

"She did something to my mind," Frida said. "Like there was something inside my head, looking around. And then it was like it found something, something that was afraid and tried to get away."

And then Alyn knew what she felt while she was deep in her center, what responded when Minna called to her and why Minna said she felt small and alone. "Your spirit."

"What?"

"Do you two see the spirits? The lights in the trees?"

"Oh, yes! You see them, too?" Tora said. "I told my parents, but they got mad, so I never told anyone else. You see them too? What are they?"

"Yes, I see them. My sister told me they're spirits called *lan'and*. Before the Empire came to Argren, there were powerful women who could talk to the spirits. They were called *saa'myn*. The Empire killed them all and now they're trying to kill us. They call us witches, but we're *saa'myn*."

They were quiet for a time and then Frida asked, "Why do they want to kill us? We don't have any power. We're not salmon."

"We're not *saa'myn* because we're not old enough. They're afraid of us, afraid we'll grow up and be able to fight back."

They were silent for a longer time and then Alyn said, "My sister, Minna, is older. She can talk to the *lan'and*. She taught me how to call them."

"Did they get your sister, too?" Tora asked. "Are they bringing her here? Maybe she can teach me, too."

"I don't know where she is. She went to the harvest festival and didn't come home."

"They probably got her and killed her, like those other girls who were here," Frida said. "After the woman came to see them, they took them away. I think they killed them."

Alyn gripped the bar in the window. "My sister is alive." She nearly convinced herself during her long trip to Brennan that she was happy Minna escaped, that it was better if her sister didn't try to save her. But now, alone in the cold, dark cell, she whispered, "She promised me she wouldn't leave me alone."

"Then where is she?" Frida's voice took on a scornful tone, when she said, "Even if they didn't get her, she's not going to be able to come get you in here."

Alyn had no answer to that. She pressed her forehead to the door and hugged herself. Letting the blanket slip from her shoulders, she wept, shaking with the effort to stay silent.

They were quiet for a long time and then Tora said, "Can *you* teach me to call the spirits?"

Alyn took a deep breath, wiped the tears away and stooped to pick up the blanket. "Yes, I'll teach you. But not tonight." She shuffled back to the sleeping pallet, lay down and sought the comfort of her center.

Ivan

Ivan wasn't sure how long he was unconscious. Under the heavy overcast, it was impossible to tell what time it was, only that it was night. He was shivering, undoubtedly in the early stages of hypothermia, but before attempting to rise, he took the time to catalog his various injuries. The dizziness and throbbing in his head likely meant a concussion. The entire left side of his body ached, but careful prodding proved nothing was broken or torn. Most worrisome was his right arm. Reaching across his body, he probed the wound, and nearly screamed when his fingers brushed the stub of an arrow shaft protruding from his arm above the elbow. He squeezed his eyes shut, breathing through the pain, and willing the muscles in his arm to relax. How did he end up in such a state?

He arrived at the edge of the meadow in time to witness Brother Linton charging the witch. The one for which the Inquisition was searching so frantically. On her knees, the diminutive girl seemed so tiny and helpless next to Linton's bulk, the outcome seemed inevitable. To his astonishment, the witch raised her hand and Linton flew backward, flopping when he hit the ground like a rag doll. When she collapsed afterward, he thought he might reach her before she recovered, but unfortunately, the boy warned her. Still, he might have had her. She appeared ready to give herself up to save the boy until... He gently felt the flesh around the arrow. The shaft must have broken off when he tumbled across the ground. But who shot him? A confederate? Maybe someone the witch and the boy were on their way to meet? If so, why was he alive?

With a groan, he rolled onto his left side, then struggled into a sitting position. He waited, eyes shut, until the worst of the nausea passed. Once he was ready, he climbed unsteadily to his feet and went in search of his companions.

He found Brothers Linton and Victor where the witch threw them, limbs flung out, surprised expressions frozen on their faces. Of the fourth member of their party, Brother Emric, there was no sign, but his absence was evidence enough of his fate. Ironically, it was probably the arrow that saved Ivan's life. When it struck, he spun away and crouched, so he only received a glancing blow of the witch's attack. He shuddered at the memory. It was as if a wave passed through his body, squeezing and stretching his insides.

He gazed down at Victor's cooling body. He and Victor entered the Dominican order together as boys, worked together for years, trusted one another implicitly. He was the only person Ivan ever considered a friend. Perhaps more than any other person he knew, Victor shared his devotion to Domina, the patron of their order. Although each of Daga's sons embodied a virtue the Vollens held dear, as His greatest son, Domina represented His highest ideal: purity. The *Sacramentum Domina*, the canon of his order, was a compendium of the laws of purity and His commandments. It was the third of these commandments to which Ivan's mind turned at this moment, the commandment concerning the sin of anger. To the Dominicans, anger and vengeance were the sole province of Daga. Ivan, and his fellow Dominicans, were merely the instruments of His will. Anger clouded the mind, tempting one to substitute one's own desires for Daga's. Staring at his friend's body, Ivan gave in to temptation.

Throwing his head back, he raged at his god. "Why? Why would you bestow your grace on a Brochen witch?" His tortured muscles screamed in agony, fueling his fury. "What have I done to displease you?" There was no answer. Ivan let his head drop and whispered, "What is it you wish of me?" And in the clarity left behind as his anger ebbed, Daga's will became clear. Victor's sacrifice was a sign Ivan could not ignore. The witch was an abomination. The Malleus may want her alive, but Ivan would see her dead.

Chapter 34

Alyn

Alyn tried to stay in her center, but by the time the door to the guards' room opened, anxiety had her pacing, blanket wrapped around her shoulders. The other girls told her today was the day they could spend an hour outside. It was the first thing she thought of when she woke, and all morning, her eye kept returning to the sliver of blue sky visible through the window. Five days. That was how long she had been in the tiny cell. Not very long, but the thought of being outside left her breathless.

She stopped and listened. The guard the prisoners called Lohkti, after an oafish character in an *Alle'oss* folktale, was talking. Another door, one of the cell doors, opened. She held her hands under her chin, doing the calculations. Ibbe was still dreaming, so she wouldn't be able to go outside. *What did she do to deserve that?* If Tora and Frida each had an hour, she would be outside in a little over two hours. She did nothing the guards wouldn't like, but would they let her out her first week? She resumed pacing, taking deep breaths to slow her heart.

More voices, and then another door opening. Alyn stopped again. This must be something different. The guard said they got one hour alone outside. Holding her breath, she listened, but couldn't make out what Lohkti was saying. She was hurrying to the door when his face appeared in the window. She froze, took two quick steps back, and dipped her eyes. There was the sound of a key in the lock, and the guard pulled the door open.

"Out."

She hesitated only a moment, then joined Lohkti in the hall. Tora and Frida were waiting. They looked like what Alyn imagined. Frida was tall with a large frame, a mane of tawny hair falling about her face. She stood with her back pressed against the wall, head down, glancing furtively at the two guards. Tora's smiling face, surrounded by a tangle of flaming red hair, peeked around Frida, fingers wiggling a greeting. Standing next to Frida, she appeared tiny.

"You girls been good, so you get to go out for an hour today," Lohkti said. "Now, usual we let you out one at a time, but it's frightful cold today. I ain't gonna spend three hours out there, so, since you been so good, we're lettin' you go out at the same time." He stood, thumbs hooked in his belt, chin lifted, peering around at them.

Tora, bouncing on the balls of her feet, squeaked, "Thank you, sir."

He nodded and looked from Tora to Frida expectantly.

Frida said, "Thank you, sir."

Alyn stared at him in disbelief before she remembered to appear meek. She dropped her eyes and said, "Thank you, sir."

Apparently not noticing her hesitation, he nodded and said, "Right. Now, line up."

They followed Lohkti through the guardroom, down a hall, a flight of stairs, and stopped at a small door.

"You two know the routine, so this is for the new girl." He stepped so close to Alyn, his odor washed over her, forcing her to breathe through her mouth. "Outside this door is the prison yard. There's no way out, so don't be gettin' any ideas. I'll be watching the whole time. You can walk anywhere in the yard for the hour, but when I say time's up, you come running. Don't make me come after you or you'll be dreaming. Are we clear?"

Alyn nodded.

"Excuse me. I didn't hear that."

"Yes, sir. I understand."

His gaze lingered on her face before he nodded, turned away, and opened the door.

The yard was rectangular, twenty paces on the long side and ten paces on the short side. The windows from their cells were visible high on the wall on one side. The roofs of neighboring buildings were just visible above a ten-foot wall on the opposite side. It was cold. A chill wind swirled in the yard, tugging at their blankets and sending their hair flying about their heads. It was the most wonderful place Alyn ever saw. She walked into the center of the yard, holding her blanket at her throat with one hand, lifting her face, relishing the feeble warmth the sun could give her. The other girls followed her, standing aside while Alyn turned slowly.

"Let's get over by the wall," Frida said, and walked away without waiting for an answer.

Tora shuffled sideways after her, smiling at Alyn and beckoning with her hand.

They gathered near the wall, where the wind was merely a fretful breeze. Alyn gazed at Lohkti, looking miserable in his thick cloak beside the door and asked, "How long has Ibbe been dreaming?"

Tora pulled the corners of her mouth back and shook her head.

"A week," Frida said. "They gave it to her a couple of days before you got here."

"How does she eat or drink?"

"They dribble that porridge stuff in your mouth," Frida said. "You kind of know what's going on some of the time. It's just all twisted."

When she didn't continue, Alyn asked, "And you don't know what she did?"

Frida frowned. "No more than the other five times you asked."

Tora shrugged. "We don't know, but it must have been bad. Usually, it lasts one or two days." She shook her head violently, sending her hair whipping around her face. "They made me drink it when I got here. I was so scared, I wasn't listening when Lohkti asked me a question. He was really mad."

"He gave it to you just for not answering his question?"

Tora nodded, clenching her blanket under her chin. "It was awful. I dreamed about all the awful things I thought about while they brought me here."

Frida appeared to be ignoring the conversation, studying the cell windows across the yard.

"So, have you found your center yet?" Alyn asked Tora.

Frida sniffed. Tora scrunched her nose and said, "I tried all day yesterday. I don't think I have a center."

Alyn laughed. "Of course you do. That's why you're here." She touched the bridge of the smaller girl's nose. "In here, behind your eyes."

Tora's crossed eyes reminded Alyn so much of her own reaction with Minna that she laughed again.

"Now, close your eyes. Breathe slowly and let yourself go limp. Forget everything outside yourself. The guards. The cell. Us. Forget it all. It's just you and your center."

Tora stood quietly for a minute, then whispered, "What's it like again?"

"It's cool and quiet, like a mountain pond. One of those cool, clear ponds surrounded by ferns. There's a shady spot next to it where you can sit and watch the wind in the trees."

Frida rolled her eyes and Alyn frowned at her, putting her finger to her lips.

Tora stood for another minute. Alyn was running out of ideas to help her. Each of the past three nights, she tried something different while Tora asked a steady stream of questions and Frida scoffed. Alyn was beginning to think Tora's busy mind was the problem. She was about to speak when Tora's mouth dropped open, and her face went slack.

"I feel it."

Frida's brow furrowed. She started to speak, but Alyn grabbed her arm. "Good, Tora! Now, keep it in your mind and… sink into it."

A small furrow appeared between Tora's brows.

"Shhh. Don't force it. Relax into it, like you're falling."

After another minute, Tora shook her head. "I can't do it."

Alyn gripped her shoulder with the hand not clutching her blanket. "But you found your center this time. It took me weeks to do it." Tora grinned. "You'll get it."

"I don't believe any of it," Frida said.

"Come on, Frida. Try it. I know you can do it," Tora said, bouncing on the balls of her feet again.

The bigger girl leaned toward Tora and said, "No. I'm not going to try it, because it's not *real*." Her head swiveled toward Alyn and her eyes narrowed, challenging Alyn to contradict her.

Tora's heels came to a stop, her mouth dropping open. She stared up at Frida, her forehead wrinkling. "Yes, it is too real. I felt it. My center. I felt it."

"I don't believe you." Frida turned until she was facing Alyn, her free hand on her hip. "I don't believe you can call the spirits, either."

Tora's expression was full on outraged now. "Yes, she can." Her expression faltered a bit when she looked at Alyn. "Can't you?"

Alyn looked from Tora's hopeful face to Frida's sneer. "I haven't seen any spirits since we got to the city. I don't know if they'll come."

"Ha! I thought you would say something like that."

"You can try, can't you?" Tora said, nodding, clutching her blanket below her chin with both hands.

Alyn looked up into the empty blue sky. Most days, when she wasn't in her center, she hovered at the edge of despair. It was all she could do to get herself off the sleeping platform to shuffle tearfully about her cell. She longed to call the spirits, to bask in their joyful reassurance. But what if they didn't answer? It would be a devastating blow. One she feared she may not survive.

But if she didn't call them now, she might never be able to. With her mind dulled by hunger and anguish, she was finding it increasingly difficult to settle into her center. Gazing into Tora's hopeful face, she decided it was time to find out, one way or the other. "Okay, I'll try."

Tora started bouncing again, clapping her hands and sending her blanket soaring across the yard with the wind. With a squeak, she took off after it.

Alyn walked to the center of the yard. She turned her face to the sun again, trying to ignore Tora's noisy pursuit. She sank into her center, letting the cold fade into the background, still there, but easily ignored. She lifted her arms, letting her blanket sail away, and called.

Nothing happened.

"Is she doing it?" Tora's small voice.

"Nothing. Just like I thought." A hint of disappointment in Frida's voice.

"Shut up!" Tora complained.

Even deep in her center, Alyn felt the fluttery wings of panic waiting for her to emerge to a devastatingly empty sky.

And then the *lan'and* answered her call. They rose up over the wall and swooped down to chase one another around the yard with Alyn at the center of the vortex. She turned on legs, weak with relief, laughing as her spirit rejoiced. She was a *saa'myn*, and the spirits would come when she called. Even in this bleak place. Somehow, she would teach herself to talk to the *lan'and*, and together, she would rescue herself and her friends. She opened her eyes to find Tora laughing, hopping about, arms waving above her head, blanket forgotten. Frida turned slowly, staring up with her mouth open.

Frida lowered her eyes. "It's true. You *can* do it."

"Hey! You girls, what are you doing?"

Alyn let the spirits go, spinning around to find Lohkti striding toward her. She dropped her eyes and clasped her hands. The other girls did the same.

"Well? I asked what you were doing?"

Alyn peered up at him. "Nothing, sir. We're just happy to be outside, together."

He looked up, scanning the sky. "Well, that's enough for today. Line up."

"But it hasn't been an hour," Alyn said.

He frowned and Alyn realized, too late, she let an edge slip into her voice. She dropped her eyes again. "Sorry, sir."

She felt him studying her until he said, "Line up now!"

Frida and Tora hurried to comply, but Alyn scanned the yard for her blanket. Finding it bunched up in the corner, she ran to retrieve it.

"Hey! I said line up!"

She stopped, looking over her shoulder and pointed, "But my blanket."

"You'll just have to leave it. Now get in line."

She stared at him, hot prickles rising along her back. Setting her jaw, she turned and strode toward her blanket.

"Why, you little…"

She heard his boots on the crushed stone, then his meaty hand wrapped around her wrist. He jerked her around, raising his other hand. She flinched away, but the blow never came. When she opened her eyes, he was staring down at her, his face slack.

"We're not to damage the witches. Least not on the outside. It's dream time for you. That'll teach you some manners." He dragged her across the yard. Tora was holding her blanket in front of her mouth below large, wet eyes, shaking her head. Frida stood frozen. Lohkti pulled the door open and jerked Alyn forward. When she looked back, Tora had her head buried against Frida's chest and Frida was wrapping her arms around her. Their eyes met as Lohkti slammed the door.

Lohkti yanked her up the stairs, twisting her shoulder painfully. When they reached the door to the guardroom, the guard banged on the door. Alyn waited, mind blank, watching Lokhti as if from outside herself. The other guard opened the door and stepped back, surprised, as Lohkti pulled Alyn across the room.

"Got a troublemaker here," he growled.

When they reached her cell, Lohkti threw her to the rough stone floor and slammed the door shut.

Alyn got shakily to her feet, absently examining a scrape on her knee. She limped to the sleeping platform and sat, panting and trembling. Nothing in her mostly idyllic life prepared for what happened to her since being dragged from her home. Small and weak, she felt powerless in the face of anger and violence she could never have imagined. But she was no longer powerless. Though she worried about what they would do to her, the hammering of her heart wasn't from fear. *What gives such small, petty men the right to treat them like this? What did they do, other than being born the way they were? I'll make it through this. I'll find a way, and then I'll make them pay.* The door at the end of the hall opened again. She knew what was coming.

The door to her cell opened, and the two guards entered. Lohkti leered at her, shaking a leather bottle. "Now, this is going to make you dream. Not nice dreams. Not at all. You're not gonna enjoy this, but that's what we have to do, so's you learn your manners."

Alyn edged back against the wall.

"If you take your medicine like a good girl, we'll just give you a little sip."

He stood at the edge of the platform, leaning over her. Alyn thrust herself forward off the wall and drove her heel between his legs. He emitted a strangled squeal, dropped the bottle, and fell on top of her, knocking the breath out of her. Stretched out as she was, her back against the edge of the sleeping platform, she didn't have the leverage to push him off. His hands closed over her arms, pressing down and holding her fast.

The other guard retrieved the bottle from the floor and stood over her, a strange smile on his face. "Now see, that's the behavior we're trying to discourage. I think a sip won't be sufficient. What do you think, Hans?"

"Give it all to her!"

Letting go of one arm, he clamped his hand over her jaw, squeezing until her lips parted. He growled as Alyn scratched at his face with her free hand. The other guard tipped the bottle, pouring the contents over her mouth. She tried to turn her head, but Lohkti held her immobile. Most of the bitter liquid ran down her cheeks and neck, but a good portion went down her throat. Before they finished, a strange, sparkling glow appeared around them. Their faces twisted, eyes bulging, their heads swelling. She was falling down a well. The world became a small circle of light far above her. There was laughter and darkness. And then she dreamed.

Chapter 35

Minna

Ulf's idea for getting to Hast without using the highway involved stairs cut into the face of the granite escarpment. Long before the Empire came, the *Alle'oss* used the stairs to travel between Hast and Argren. From the top of the stairs, Minna gaped at the vista stretched out before her. The tree covered foothills that nestled up to the base of the cliff gradually gave way to the vast open spaces Ulf called the plains. They stretched to the horizon, a blotchy mix of brown and white under a thin blanket of snow. Hast was visible to the northwest on the western bank of the Odun River, a dull brown ribbon in the gray light. The highway emerged from the forest to their right and passed through Hast before veering southwest.

"See all the wagons and people on the highway in front of the bridge?" Ulf asked, pointing.

"Yeah."

"The tax collectors inspect every wagon that crosses the bridge. It can take forever to get across if there is a lot of traffic." He paused, plucking at his filthy cloak. "The problem is you have to give them a good reason for crossing. I don't think they'll believe we're going to Brennan on business."

"How do we cross?"

"We could wait a month and walk across the river when it freezes." Taking in Minna's scowl, Ulf sighed and said, "I might have an idea, but we have to go down and look."

The stairs were narrow and steep. A thin layer of snow over stone worn smooth by countless feet, made for treacherous footing. Minna kept her shoulder to the wall, taking slow, deliberate steps and keeping her eyes on her feet to avoid peering out over empty space. Ulf clomped down the steps with a nonchalance that took her breath away.

"Have you been on these stairs before?" she asked, slightly embarrassed at the quaver in her voice.

"No. My brother told me about them. He said the resistance use them. To be honest, I was a little surprised we found them where he said they would be." Ulf grinned back over his shoulder, drawing a gasp from Minna. "He has a tendency to exaggerate what he knows."

"Just... face forward. And watch your step." She was counting the stairs under her breath, but having lost count when Ulf looked back, she resorted to listening to her breath. Slow breath in through parted lips, then whoosh it out slowly. Slow breath in through parted lips, then whoosh it out slowly.

Twice, they encountered landings where tunnels led into the stone. Inside, stairs led down to another landing, and the stairs cut into the rock face continued in the opposite direction. Minna fairly flew down the last few stairs and stepped onto level ground on shaky legs. She glanced up at the top of the cliff and mumbled to herself, "Never again."

"Huh?" Ulf asked.

"Nothing. Let's get going."

Aware they would be visible from the top of the escarpment, they stuck to the cover of the forest whenever they could. Pausing at the edge of the last stand of trees, Minna gazed out across the treeless expanse. Realizing she let her mouth fall open, she closed it with a snap. The *lan'and*, she was relieved to see, didn't require the forest. They skipped along the snow-covered ground, swooping up when the wind swirled the falling flakes. Minna pulled her cloak tighter. It would be nice to be a spirit.

Once they left the forest, the trail they left in the thin layer of snow would be an arrow pointing their way. Anyone looking down from the heights couldn't help but see it. Though they had not seen pursuers recently, she doubted they gave up. Any hope the falling snow would obscure their tracks was dispelled when she peered at the low clouds. Only a few tiny flakes swirled in the gusty wind.

She caught Ulf's eye and said, "Let's move fast."

He nodded, then set out at a slow jog.

• • •

Two-hours later, Minna trudged to the top of a hill where Ulf knelt, looking to the northwest. Days with little sleep and less to eat were taking its toll. The fast pace Ulf set them didn't last long. With his longer legs, Ulf managed with little difficulty. But for Minna, each step was a struggle against the thick, knee-high grass that clutched at her legs and soaked the bottom of her cloak and boots.

She knelt next to Ulf, puffing out clouds of vapor. "Ulf, I'm not sure how much longer I can go on." She looked up at the sky. "Should we try to find some shelter and rest?"

"We can rest when we're in the city," he said, pointing down the hill. "Hast."

From the top of the bluff, the city spread out before them. Minna's first impression was that it was two different cities. The streets to the south of the highway were cobbled and laid out in an orderly grid. The buildings in this part of the city were primarily cut stone, many of them contained within a towering stone wall. North of the highway was a sprawling, disorganized collection of mainly timber-framed buildings. But what drew Minna's attention more than anything else were the people, a great mass of humanity, clustered around the highway, drifting in both directions.

"All those people."

"I know. That's what I thought the first time. It was scary, but this is nothing. Wait til you see Brennan."

As they watched, a contingent of mounted Imperial soldiers crossed the bridge, heading toward Argren. Ulf pointed to the buildings surrounded by the stone wall. "That's the Imperial fort. The soldiers who attacked our camp probably came from there."

Minna watched the mounted soldiers, having to repress an urge to lie flat on the ground. She glanced at Ulf, who was gazing calmly at the city. Swallowing to wet her dry mouth, she tried to affect the same nonchalance and turned her attention to the bridge. Now that she was paying attention, Minna noted many uniforms. "How are we going to get through?"

"We're in luck." Ulf pointed to the highway to the east of the bridge. A series of enormous wagons, pulled by teams of oxen, were edging to the side of the road, making way for the soldiers heading in the opposite direction.

"What? We hitch a ride on the wagons?"

"If only. No, see the people walking behind the wagons? Those are *Alle'oss* slaves. Most of the slaves work in the mines in the mountains, but some of them, they take to Brennan and other parts of the Empire."

Minna glanced at Ulf, not sure she heard right. He gave her a grim nod, and Minna turned to watch the men and women following the wagons. Even from a distance, their misery was evident. They shuffled along, clutching blankets around their shoulders, heads down. She shook her head and asked, "Slaves?"

"These are probably the lucky ones. The people who work in the mines don't live long." He pointed toward the slaves. "See the men guarding them on the horses, riding up and down the line?" The guards wore blue uniforms Minna had not seen before. "There are only two right now. They have more guards when they're in the mountains, but when they're waiting to cross the bridge, most of the guards head into town. The slaves are usually so weak, it doesn't take much to keep them in line. We wait until the guards aren't looking and blend in. My guess is they barely pay attention, so they won't notice two extra. Once we're across the bridge, we look for a chance to slip into the *Alle'oss* side of Hast. If anyone stops us, we show them our packs to prove we're not slaves."

"Ulf! That's a good plan."

Ulf's eyebrows rose. "You sound surprised."

"Who knew you had such a devious mind?" she asked, punching his shoulder.

"You should ask my mother," Ulf said, putting a hand on the ground to catch himself. "She'll fill you in."

"Ulf, did you steal apple pies from your mother's pie safe?" Minna teased.

The corner of his mouth twitched. "Actually, I prefer her cherry pies."

Minna studied his profile. The left side of his face bore the marks of his encounter with the brother. He was thinner than when they left Fennig. His hair, visible under the hood of his cloak, was matted, and dark circles stood out on the pale skin under his eyes. Yet, not once had he complained. When he glanced at her, she noticed his eyes were a deep blue, almost violet. Of course, she knew that, but in that moment, it was like she was seeing him for the first time.

When he noticed her watching, he asked, "What?"

"Nothing, I just never noticed how blue your eyes are."

His lips tightened, and he looked at the ground before looking back at the city. "I always remembered yours. They're summer green." His cheeks, already red from the cold, flushed a deeper shade.

Minna watched him for a moment longer, then looked at the highway. "You ready?"

"Yeah, we better get going if we want to catch them."

Ivan

After leaving Victor's body, he looked for the horses he left in a gully close to the meadow. Based on the tracks he found next to the highway the next morning, the horses decided the promise of a warm stable and regular fodder in Hast was preferable to waiting. Though he could only manage a slow, hobbling pace, walking kept him warm, and the pain focused his mind. He allowed himself a few minutes of sleep during the warmest part of the day. Each time, it was more difficult to rouse himself. But, finally, he stood on a hill, looking down on Hast in the distance.

There was the usual line of traffic waiting to cross the bridge, longer than usual with the increased scrutiny imposed by the Inquisition. A squad of Imperial calvary were just crossing the bridge, on their way to Argren. He pulled his cloak tighter with his left hand, grimacing as the material caught on the stub of the arrow.

He listened to horses approaching from behind. They were brothers of the Order of Lucian. The Inquisition. When he glimpsed them in the distance, emerging from Wollen's Cut, he redoubled his efforts, pushing himself beyond pain, trying to reach Hast before they caught up to him. But now, with his goal in sight, he admitted defeat. With a sigh, he composed his face and turned to face the riders.

Ivan was surprised to see an *Alle'oss* man with them, sticking out in his maroon cloak, like a mouse among rats. They reined up beside him, the horses shuffling about, snorting and puffing great clouds of mist. They must have ridden hard. Eager for a chance to humiliate a Dominican, no doubt. The unfamiliar inquisitor who led the group stared down at him, no sign of the smirk Ivan saw on his face as they approached. Ivan waited, but instead of acknowledging the inquisitor, he scanned the impassive faces of the other men. Finally, when the inquisitor didn't speak, Ivan sighed and looked up at him. "Inquisi—"

"You seem to be far from home, Dominican," the inquisitor said. He glanced around, turning in his saddle to look back up the highway. "Alone, and far from home."

Ivan swallowed his annoyance and tried to speak again.

The inquisitor cut him off again. "Can I assume you've encountered a bit of trouble?"

Ivan closed his mouth and stared up at the inquisitor, refusing to let his annoyance show on his face. When he thought he gave the man sufficient time to continue, he tried again. "My men and I were attacked by a witch." He glanced at the *Alle'oss* man and added, "A *l'oss* witch." To his annoyance, the man grinned.

"*Ali ērtsi Minna. Ozh'ta ali'ka ērtsi* (It was Minna. It must have been)," he said.

"*Da,*" the inquisitor replied.

"*Ērtsi kīta ni Minna* (Who is Minna)?" Ivan asked and allowed himself some pleasure at their surprise.

The inquisitor took a moment to control his expression before saying, "A witch."

"Black hair?" Ivan asked.

The *Alle'oss* man slapped his thigh. "That's her."

"That witch killed my men, and one of her compatriots put an arrow into my arm." It annoyed Ivan to hear an edge enter his voice. The inquisitor's eyebrows rose, but Ivan didn't care.

"Yes, well, we believe they are heading to Hast," the inquisitor said. He looked Ivan up and down. "You want a ride?"

This time, Ivan let his annoyance show when the man waited, forcing him to reply. "Yes, if it's not too much trouble."

"No trouble." A small smile played at the corners of his mouth. He looked at the *Alle'oss* man and said, "Torsten, give the Dominican a ride."

Ivan watched the inquisitor ride away. He would have to find out that man's name.

Chapter 36

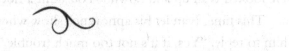

Minna

As they descended the hill, snow began to fall in earnest. Large fluffy flakes tossed about by the wind obscured their approach. They waited in a gully beside the elevated roadbed, watching the wagons rumbling slowly past. When the guard on this side of the road passed, they scrambled up the embankment and merged with the procession.

The *Alle'oss* saw them coming and pulled them into their midst. One of them put her finger to her lips and tugged at the pack Ulf carried. When he resisted, the woman nodded to the guard retreating toward the back of the line. Ulf relented, and the woman took their packs and Minna's bow and tossed them into the back of the wagon. She pulled Minna's hood farther forward, then wrapped one arm around her back. Minna held her breath, resisting the urge to look over her shoulder at the returning guard, but the man passed without comment. Ulf was right about the guards. They either didn't notice there were two more people among their charges, or they didn't care. She glanced back, returning Ulf's smirk.

The woman whispered, "My name is Willa."

"Minna. This is Ulf. The guards don't seem very observant."

"Lucky for you."

"Why don't you run away?"

Willa chuckled. "The only people they take to Brennan are those with families at home. They told us, if we run, or even if we die on the way, they kill our entire family."

Minna stared at her, then gazed at the shambling slaves around her. Some of them appeared as if they would collapse at any minute. How much further did they have to go to save their families? "I'm sorry, I didn't know."

"How could you, dear?"

As they neared the bridge, the immediate fear of discovery faded, replaced by a bored anxiety. They would shuffle forward for a few minutes and then stop, wait until the wagons moved again, and repeat the process. The falling snow muffled distant sounds and seemed to magnify the nearby grinding of the wagon wheels, the clop of the horses' hooves, and the scrape of their feet on the cobbles. Minna bounced in apprehension, peering around the edge of the wagon, anxious to get it over with.

Ulf rested his hand on her shoulder, whispering, "You're supposed to be a slave. Don't draw attention to yourself."

She stopped bouncing and resorted to tapping her fist against her thigh. "Why are we stopping so much?"

"The tax collectors inspect everything that crosses the bridge," Willa said.

Alarmed, Minna clutched Ulf's arm.

"Don't worry," he said. "They're only interested in what's in the wagons. No one pays taxes on slaves."

"They think we're worth less than the coal in this wagon."

"They'll see my bow."

After checking for the guard, Ulf stepped up on the rung of a ladder attached to the back of the wagon, reached into the back and tucked the packs and bow under a canvas sailcloth that covered the contents.

"Don't worry, they don't inspect them carefully," Willa said.

Finally, when the wagon they walked behind was next in line, Minna leaned out and peered ahead. The driver was talking to a man wearing a black uniform who was making notes in a leather-bound book. Two Imperials, carrying halberds, stood behind him while a third lifted the sailcloth and inspected the contents. When one of them looked her way, she retreated to stand next to Willa and Ulf.

To Ulf's questioning look, she said, "Imperials."

The slaves gathered around Minna and Ulf as they moved forward again. Minna kept her head down, taking slow, measured steps, and holding her breath as they passed the soldiers. She peeked from under the hood and found them watching the slaves, contempt written across their faces. One of them said something that made the others laugh.

And then they were past the Imps and onto the bridge. They were going to make it. Minna's heart thudded against her ribs, but the tension that held her breathless drained away. She took Ulf's hand, smiled up at his alarmed face, and froze. Too late, she clamped down on her center.

A hand landed heavily on her shoulder and jerked her around to face a hulking man wearing white. Holding her immobile with a hand on her shoulder, he yanked her hood back with the other and took a lock of her hair between his fingers. His eyes widened, then he turned to look toward the far end of the bridge, exposing a thin, pale scar running from below his ear to the corner of his mouth.

When he looked away, Minna's brain began to work again. The *lan'and* didn't seem to like Hast any more than Fennig, but even though she couldn't see them, she knew they would come. She allowed her center to open, preparing to call. The man's head jerked back toward her. He pushed her toward the back of the wagon, glancing around at the guards. Lowering his face until it was inches from hers, he said, "Keep yourself hidden. The city is full of brothers looking for you."

She was so surprised, she stared at him, taking a moment to process his words. "Me?"

"You're from Fennig? You escaped from an inquisitor not a long ago?"

Minna nodded.

"Is there something I can help you with?"

The brother gave her a warning look, straightened and punched her in the stomach. She bent over, gasping. A hand wrapped around her neck, pressing down and preventing her from standing upright. Dimly, she heard Ulf protesting, followed by a brief scuffle. She tried a shallow breath and was surprised it was painfree. His punch was more to make her bend over than to injure her.

"This girl is wanted for questioning, soldier."

There was a pause and then the other voice said, "A slave is wanted for questioning?"

The hand on the back of Minna's neck lifted her until she was looking up at the mounted guard. He was squinting down at them, his hand resting on the hilt of his sword. The brother's vice-like grip tilted her head slightly to the right.

"This is no slave, you oaf. Look at her. Does she look like these others to you? She must have mingled with the slaves before you entered the city. You don't pay enough attention to notice that?"

"Hey, it's just the two of us here." A peevish note crept into his voice. "I can't watch them all. Besides, they all look alike to me. What do I care if we pick up a few more on the way?"

The brother stepped toward the mounted guard, pulling Minna backward and spinning her around until she was facing the wagon. "Let's ask an inquisitor if they care that a fugitive from the Inquisition almost got away because you're too incompetent to do your job."

She saw Ulf out of the corner of her eye, two of the slaves holding his arms. When she caught his eye, he struggled, but she shook her head as much as she could with the hand on her neck and mouthed the word, 'no'.

The guard was protesting. "No one got away. You got her. Take her then."

The hand on her neck let go, and the man pulled her around by the arm until she faced away from Ulf. The guard was riding toward the back of the line of slaves. The brother leaned in close and said, "If you want to live, follow along." He looked at her hair and pulled her hood up. After studying the result, he shook his head and tried tucking her hair inside. Apparently unsatisfied, he stood, lips pursed, glancing around as if searching for something. Minna looked back at Ulf and shrugged. The man bent close and asked, "Do you know of the Desulti?"

The name meant nothing to Minna. She looked at Ulf, who shrugged.

"I do," Willa said. "There's a Desulti house near my home in Ka'tan."

The brother glanced at the guards, who apparently decided to stay as far as they could from him, then said, "Give me your blanket."

Willa untied the knot at her throat and handed it over. The brother took out a large knife, cut the edge of the blanket, and tore off a long strip.

"Hey!" Minna said.

"Hush," Willa said. "I know what he has in mind."

"Hold still," the man said and begin winding the strip around Minna's head.

"The Desulti are an order of mostly Imperial women who have decided they've had enough of the Empire," Willa said. "Wonder why?" She waited a beat but got no reaction from the brother. "Anyway, they isolate themselves in remote locations, vowing they will never show themselves or speak to anyone outside their order, especially men."

The brother nearly finished wrapping Minna's head, leaving thin slits for her eyes and below her nose. He tucked the end under the wraps, stepped back and studied her, frowning. "Better not move around too much or it might unravel."

"Might work," Willa said. "The women who come into town back home usually use linen, but most people have probably never seen a Desulti. You might want to put her in a bigger cloak, though. They're usually covered head to toe."

The man looked Ulf up and down and said, "I need your cloak."

"Why are you doing this?" Minna asked.

"The Inquisition is looking for an *Alle'oss* girl with black hair." He snapped his fingers at Ulf. "Quick, if we get to the end of the bridge and they see her, there will be nothing I can do."

The wagon moved again, and Ulf handed him his cloak.

The brother motioned Minna to remove her cloak, then drew the larger cloak over her shoulders and buttoned it at her throat. The bottom of the cloak scraped the ground, and Minna's head disappeared inside the hood. She could see him nodding through a small opening.

"Follow my lead. Keep your eyes down. Whatever you do, don't look anyone in the eyes and for Daga's sake, don't speak. Keep your hands inside the cloak. We need to get you off the road, then figure out how to get you out of the city." He adjusted the hood, took her arm, and urged her forward. She heard Ulf protesting behind her and the sounds of the slaves restraining him. The brother led her across the bridge, passing the slow-moving wagons.

Minna glimpsed a mixed group of brothers and soldiers in blue uniforms gathered at the end of the bridge. The brother's hand on her arm pushed her past them, but it pulled her to a stop when a man said, "What you got there, Brother Joseph?"

When he pulled her around, the end of the wrap slipped. She stood still, afraid to breathe, lest the wrap unravel. She was powerless, in the hands of a man she didn't know.

"Desulti, mixed in with the slaves."

There was silence, but for the sound of the men shuffling forward. Minna kept her eyes on the ground and could see the men's feet as they gathered in front of her.

"You sure?" a different voice asked. "Never seen one in Hast, before. Could be anyone under all that."

Another voice joked, "When have you ever seen one, Klaus?"

"Was in Styria. Up in the mountains."

There was some indistinct muttering, then another voice asked. "What's she doing in Hast?"

"Well, I can't very well ask her, can I?" the man they called Joseph said.

"I say we take a look," the joker said. "Always said they must be hiding something under those wraps."

"Yeah, always wondered what they look like. Going off and hiding like they do. Makes you curious, don't it?" There was rough laughter at this comment.

"Besides, for all we know, this could be the witch we're looking for. Who would know?"

Minna was on the verge of calling the *lan'and* when Joseph said, "Which is why I'm taking her to the Seidi house." He put some steel into his voice when he said, "They can handle it."

There was a pause, then the joker said, "Just trying to have a little fun."

"I suggest you pay a little more attention to your duties."

They started moving again, Brother Joseph holding her arm and urging her to hurry. Soon, the clamor around the bridge faded. It seemed to Minna they walked for a long time, taking several turns until she lost all sense of direction. Finally, the hand holding her arm let go, and Minna heard him walking away. She pulled the hood back and peered around through the slit in the wrap. They were alone in an alley so narrow, Minna could have touched the building on each side if she extended her arms. The brother was standing at the end, peering around the corner. She pulled the end of the wrap free and unwound it from her head.

Dropping the material to the ground, she asked, "What's going on? Who are you?" She spun around. "Where's Ulf?"

He lifted his index finger to his lips. "Keep quiet. This side of the river is full of Imperials." He took her arm and led her down the alley. "My name is Joseph. I don't have time to explain now, just... there are people in the Inquisition who want you to live."

Minna jerked her arm free and stopped. "Why? Why are those men looking for me, and why did you save me?"

Joseph looked over her head, mouth working. He took a breath, blew it out and spoke with forced calm. "There was an inquisitor in Fennig recently. He came for you, but you escaped, so he alerted the Inquisition. Everyone is looking for an *Alle'oss* witch with black hair." His eyes lingered on her hair. "Hard to hide an *Alle'oss* with black hair."

Minna put her hands on her hips inside the over-sized cloak and set her jaw. "That inquisitor took my sister. They're taking her to Brennan. I have to go after her."

He lifted his upper lip and drew his brows together. "Gonna save her from the Inquisition? By yourself? What exactly is your plan?"

Minna blinked, gesturing vaguely with her hands. "I… uh… I don't really have a plan. Yet." She gave a brisk nod and met his eyes. "I'm a *saa'myn*. I'll find a way."

"Oh, a *saa'myn*, huh? Gonna tell the inquisitors their futures, are you?" He shook his head. "People trying to keep you alive, and you walk right into the Inquisition's backyard."

Minna's voice rose. "I never asked you to keep me alive, and no one would have to keep me alive if it weren't for you people."

"Keep it down, will you?" They stared at one another until Joseph turned and walked away. "Come on."

She had to hitch the cloak up and jog to keep up. "My friend, the one who tried to stop you. We have to find him."

Joseph glanced over his shoulder. "No, we have to get you out of Hast." He continued, more to himself than to Minna. "Can't get you back across the bridge. That means either Lubern or Brennan. At least while people are still looking. Could put you on a barge, maybe." He stopped suddenly, eyes unfocused. "Maybe." He turned toward Minna and said, "I have a friend in Brennan who might help you."

"Help me get my sister?"

"I don't know about that. But she *can* hide you while we figure out what to do with you. We'll get you out of Hast tonight. It's only fifteen leagues to Brennan. You can walk that in two, maybe three days." He looked at her hair again. "Travel at night, maybe."

"I'm not going anywhere without Ulf."

He stared at her blankly. "Ulf?"

"My friend. He's with the slaves. They're probably still in the city. We can go get him."

"*We* can't do anything of the sort. You can't go anywhere until dark."

"Well, then, *you* can go get him."

Joseph shook his head. Minna, having pushed the cloak back over her shoulders, stood with her hands on her hips and said, "You don't want to make me mad."

She glared up at him until he shook his head and threw his hands up. "I'll check. No promises." He leaned toward her and put his finger near her face. "*Don't* go anywhere."

Minna smiled and nodded. "Of course." Joseph rolled his eyes and brushed past her.

"Get my pack and my bow from the back of the wagon, too," Minna called after him. She watched him round the corner, then slid down the wall to sit cross-legged, the cloak pooling around her. Leaning her head back against the wall, she let her eyes close, enjoying the feathery touch of snowflakes on her face. How long had it been since she slept?

Chapter 37

Ulf

Ulf tried to follow as the brother led Minna away, but the men on either side of him held him firmly. What was Minna trying to say when she caught his eye? It looked as if she was cooperating, and the man acted as if he recognized her. None of it made sense.

Willa threw Minna's smaller cloak over his shoulders, then pushed him forward as the wagon begin to move. "Keep your head down."

"Get on there."

Ulf looked up to find the mounted guard glaring at him. He fell in step with the slaves, edging toward the side of the wagon so he could see what was ahead. As they left the bridge, they stopped again while Inquisition brothers walked along the line of slaves, inspecting each of them. A woman with a blanket wrapped around her, hiding her hair, drew their attention. When she was slow to respond to their demands, a brother ripped the blanket away, jerking her off her feet. They remarked on her red hair, then the soldier tossed the blanket into the slushy snow at the side of the road. They barely looked at Ulf, except to notice his cloak, which, although small for him, was much finer than what the other slaves wore. In fact, they paid little attention to any of the men, pushing them roughly aside to get a better view of the women.

Eventually, the brothers waved them on, and the caravan rumbled slowly through the city. Ulf tried to see into the streets where Minna disappeared. A narrow green space separated the highway from the buildings. A four-foot-high hedge, backed by large elm trees, bordered the highway, as if the Imperials were trying to separate themselves from the ramshackle sprawl to the north. Groups of Imperials moved about on the far side of the green space, but Ulf didn't see any brothers after they left the bridge behind. He waited until the mounted guard passed and sprinted toward the green space, brushing past the hands grasping after him. He struggled through the hedge and crouched behind a large tree, waiting for cries of alarm. When they didn't come, he peeked around the trunk of the tree. A broad walkway of stone pavers separated the green space from the buildings. Across the walkway was a building in the classical Imperial style, with stone columns and a frieze depicting some old battle. Etched into the lentil above a pair of large oak doors were the words *Imperial Military District Administration.* The only people visible were a group of men, deep in conversation, retreating to the west. He dashed across the walkway, ran along the front of the building, and slipped into the narrow street beside it. The street ran the length of the building where it met a wider cross street. He jogged to the intersection and stopped. *Now what?*

Joseph

Joseph walked as quickly as caution allowed. He would have a difficult time explaining his presence if he encountered an inquisitor, especially if he looked as panicked as he felt. Emerging onto the promenade that bordered the Imperial side of the highway, he scanned the road for signs of the caravan. He found them moving away to his left. Glancing in both directions, he stepped onto the green way beside the promenade and jogged after the slowly moving wagons, hugging the hedge and keeping a tree between himself and the guard. Once the guard passed, he kept pace with the slaves, searching for the boy. He had only a vague memory of what he looked like, but he was sure he would recognize him. They thought they were clever, but the two of them stood out among the bedraggled slaves. He noticed them even before she let herself slip.

The boy wasn't there. *Now what?* Did he cause a problem after Joseph took Minna and get himself arrested? He peered back toward the bridge. If the Inquisition had him, he was gone. There was nothing Joseph could do.

He turned back to find one of the female slaves waving at him. When she caught his eye, she pointed back toward a building which housed administrative offices. What did that mean? He shrugged, and she made a motion with her hand that Joseph interpreted as indicating the street on the far side of the building. He considered and dismissed the idea of retrieving the pack and bow, then nodded, waved his thanks and hurried toward the street.

Ulf

Once you left the highway, the city was like a stone maze. The Empire laid the streets out in an orderly grid, but the street names meant nothing to him, and all the buildings looked alike. Lots of stone and heroic statues. Minna disappeared further to the east, but most of the east-west streets were larger with more foot traffic. But there was no other way to go east so, he took a breath and strode confidently onto the wide street. He hadn't gone twenty steps when someone shouted.

"Hey, *l'oss*, what are you doing on this side of the highway?"

Ulf kept walking.

"Hey, *l'oss*, I asked you a question."

Ulf heard rapid steps on the cobbled street behind him, then someone grabbed his arm and pulled him around to face three men wearing unfamiliar uniforms.

"I asked you, Alle'oss, what are you doing here?"

Ulf's mouth opened before his mind came up with an answer. After an awkward pause, he said, "I'm looking for a friend." When the man's stony stare didn't change, Ulf ventured, "He's a brother. Of the Inquisition? Tall." He held his hand above his head. "Scar on his cheek." He traced his finger along his left cheek. "Black, uh… hair." He glanced at their black hair. "Of course. You seen him?"

"A brother, huh? With a scar?" The man smirked at his companions. "Tell you what. We'll show you to the Inquisition. We can ask after your friend, the brother, there, eh?"

Ulf lifted his hands, palms forward. "Oh, that won't be necessary. I'm sure he's around. Told me to meet him somewhere near here." He forced a grin onto his face. "Place is like a maze, isn't it?"

The men took a step back, spreading out to limit his avenues of escape.

Ulf licked his lips, tensing. He might just be able to slip through.

"Ulf!"

Ulf's heart stuttered. He and the men all jerked around toward the voice. The tall brother who took Minna was striding toward them.

"Ulf, I told you to meet me by the district administration building."

Ulf's mouth dropped open. The brother's brow furrowed, and he gave the slightest shake of his head. "Sorry, uh… sir… I was just telling these men how confusing this side of the city is. I was just going to ask for directions."

The brother nodded to the men. "Gentlemen."

"Sorry, brother. We didn't know he was with you. You can't be too careful, you know."

The brother's gaze lingered on them for a moment, then he turned away, dismissing them. To Ulf, he said, "Next time, ask me for directions if you don't know." He stepped aside and gestured down the street. Ulf hung his head, threw what he hoped was a chagrined grimace at the men, and shuffled away.

When he caught up with Ulf, the brother took the back of his arm and guided him across the street.

Ulf stumbled along beside him, trying to keep up. "Where's Minna?"

"Minna. So that's her name." He pulled Ulf into another alley, let go of his arm, and walked ahead. "She was safe when I left her." He looked over his shoulder. "She insisted I come get you." When he looked ahead, he said, "I hope she still is."

Minna

Alone and feeling exposed in the alley, Minna pulled her knees to her chest, and did her best impression of a discarded pile of fabric, heaping the over-sized cloak around herself and pulling the hood over her head. Within moments, her eyelids drooped, but startling at every sound and anxious for Ulf, she was sure she wouldn't fall asleep. She just needed to close her eyes for a bit.

She woke to the click of boots on cobblestones echoing in the small alley. Too many footsteps to be Joseph returning with Ulf. She held her breath, chin on her knees, staring at the small sliver of alley visible through the hood. Legs, wearing the boots and white pants of the Inquisition, appeared and turned toward her. A moment later, her hood was drawn slowly back. Pulse thudding, she slowly raised her head, and found a group of brothers looking down at her, all of them with Ulf's face.

"Wake up, Minna!" they chorused.

Her eyes flew open. Fighting to her feet against the piles of fabric, she whirled around, heart hammering. She was alone in the alley.

From the light, she guessed she only slept for a few minutes, though it was difficult to tell under the heavy overcast. Shuddering at the memory of Ulf in an Inquisition uniform, she lowered her face into her hands and scrubbed vigorously to expunge lingering grogginess. She was facing the t-shaped intersection at the far end of the alley when she lowered her hands.

A single *lan'and* drifted into view. She tensed, instantly awake. The spirit bobbed once, then drifted back the way it came, disappearing from view. Minna watched it go, hitched up the cloak and sprinted toward the intersection. As she neared the end of the alley, the orb appeared as before. Minna slid to a stop. The spirit hovered for a moment, then retreated again. She jogged the last few paces and peeked around the corner.

The spirit hovered in the middle of the street halfway down the block. When she stepped around the corner, it drifted through an iron gate. Minna jogged to the gate and peered into what appeared to be an oasis of green in the desert of stone. A profusion of shrubs in their winter slumber bordered a small park. Snow blanketed most of the ground, but patches of a well-manicured lawn were still visible beneath the single cherry tree in the center of the garden. The *lan'and* was flitting among the bare branches. When Minna stepped up to the gate, resting her hand on the cold iron, the spirit drifted down and hovered on the other side. She lifted the latch and pushed the gate open, wincing at the squeal that echoed in the silent alley. The spirit bobbed once and floated backward, an invitation. She stepped onto the lawn and the spirit flew in spirals above her head.

"*Ērtsu mia and'reoime (*You're my spirit guide*).*"

She knew the truth of the words as soon as she said them, as if she had always known and had only been waiting for the spirit to return. Lifting her arms, she spun slowly, following the spirit further into the garden. Letting her center open, she called. The spirit burst into her mind. Minna's laughter, bright and spontaneous, filled the small garden. The exuberance of the *lan'and* in large groups was overwhelming, but the experience with this one spirit was different; more intimate, more joyful than exhilarating. Her spirit responded, joining the *lan'and* in a swirling dance. There was a familiarity, a relief at reuniting with something long lost.

Minna wept.

Ulf

Ulf was lost again. How Joseph knew where he was going was a mystery. They turned into one stone street after another. He was rushing to keep up with Joseph's long strides, thinking the brother must be lost as well, when he rounded a corner and plowed into Joseph's back.

"Sorry." When Joseph didn't move or respond, Ulf leaned over, trying to see what had the brother's attention. All he saw was a narrow alley, as empty as all the other alleys he had seen.

"Of course," Joseph said. "You two are like a pair of cats."

"You left her *here?*"

Joseph worked his jaw and looked up into the falling snow. Throwing up his hands, he said, "Well, I didn't *want* to leave her here, but she rather insisted I go find *you*."

"Sorry," Ulf mumbled. "Maybe… maybe she's nearby."

Joseph strode down the alley, with Ulf trailing behind him. After a half dozen strides, he stopped and threw his arms out. "Dear Daga," he said.

Ulf felt it too; Minna was shining like a beacon. They sprinted to the end of the alley. Joseph slid to a stop and held his hand up to stop him. Stepping into the cross street, the brother looked both ways, then disappeared to the right. Ulf followed and found him standing halfway down the block, looking into an open gate in a wall on the left side of the street.

Ulf joined him and followed his gaze. Minna stood in the middle of a garden beneath a cherry tree. She faced away from them, reaching up to something Ulf couldn't see.

Ulf stepped through the gate and said, "Minna? You need to—"

She startled and whirled around. His heart lurched when he saw the tears streaking her face, but she laughed and ran toward him, the over-sized cloak flapping behind her. She threw her arms around him. "Oh, Ulf. I found my *and'reoime*," she said and buried her face in his chest, sobbing.

Ulf exchanged a worried look with Joseph, shrugged, and wrapped his arms around her.

Chapter 38

Ivan

By the time Ivan climbed into the saddle behind the *Alle'oss* man, the inquisitor called Torsten, the Lucians were far ahead. They rode in silence for some time. Not that Ivan minded. Besides being a heathen, this man was a traitor, a sin for which the Dominicans held very specific beliefs. It mattered little whose side he served. As they approached the contingent of Imperial Cavalry he saw in the distance crossing the bridge, the man broke his silence.

"You're a Dominican."

It wasn't a question, so Ivan didn't respond. Unfortunately, the man continued.

"I have to admit to some surprise at the tension between you and your Inquisition brothers, Brother....?"

Ivan was tempted to ignore him, but the man was giving him a ride and helped him onto the horse without a hint of contempt. "Ivan. We are from different orders. Orders with different... views on Daga's priorities."

"And yet, you serve the same cause, no? The same gods?" Torsten chuckled and shook his head. "What a luxury it must be. What a lofty position you must stand on, that you might squabble over the nature of the guardians to the Otherworld."

Ivan flushed, caught off guard by the man's knowledge of that contentious, and ridiculous, issue. That he privately agreed with Torsten was beside the point. He would not be lectured on loyalty by a *l'oss* traitor. Exhausted, hungry, and in pain, his temper flared. "Yes, we serve Daga and the Empire. What of you? You would betray your own people? What, for some coin?"

It surprised Ivan to hear the man's laughter. Torsten turned his head so Ivan could hear him over the thunder of the passing cavalry. He gestured to the mounted soldiers and yelled, "What do you see here?"

Ivan watched the men passing, ignoring their surprise at finding a Dominican brother riding behind an *Alle'oss* man. "Imperial Cavalry," he said, feeling he was missing the point.

Torsten waited for the sounds of the hooves to recede behind them before answering. "In a literal sense, yes. But what I see is the first breaths of the coming storm." He pointed toward Hast. "The growth of the garrison in Hast has little to do with one fugitive witch, and everything to do with a few deluded radicals who feel they can hold back the storm."

"The rebels."

"Unlike my countrymen, I've ventured far beyond the boundaries of my homeland. I've seen with my own eyes what remains of the many when a few think they can fight the Empire."

"You would betray your people to save them?"

Ivan felt him tense. He didn't answer at first, but after a few moments, he relaxed. When he spoke, it was with weariness rather than anger. "No, I am not betraying my people. I betray a small number of rebel zealots who refuse to see the truth, so that I might save my family from their folly."

They rode in silence until they crossed the bridge and were level with the fortress. Ivan said, "You can leave me here."

"Don't be foolish. You need to go to the infirmary," Torsten said. "Just tell me where it is."

Ivan hesitated. The truth was, he wasn't sure he could stay on his feet if he were to dismount here. He had been on his last legs before the Lucians caught him, only sheer determination keeping him upright. The gratitude he felt surprised him. The man clearly had no love of the Empire, yet he would extend to a Dominican brother this simple kindness. "Head through the main gate of the fortress." Torsten guided the horse through the traffic towards the fortress without comment. "Thank you," Ivan murmured.

Minna

Ulf gave Minna an uncertain look and said, "So, this *and're*…"

"And rrrre weem," Minna offered.

"Yes, that. Your spirit guide. It's supposed to teach you about the spirits?"

"Something like that."

"Does it… talk?"

"No. Or, I don't think it does. Beadu doesn't seem to ever actually explain things. At least, not in a way that makes it clear."

Ulf frowned, searching the small storeroom they were hiding in. "Is it here, now?"

"No, they don't seem to like cities and they don't like to be away from their own kind for long."

"But it will come back? It can find you, again?"

"Yes."

"Even if we leave the city."

"Yes."

"Um… how do you know? I mean, it seems like Beadu didn't explain much."

"I don't know how I know, but I do. I think that's what Beadu was trying to tell me. She can't tell me everything. I have to learn from the spirits."

"Well, okay then. As long as you're sure."

They sat, shoulder to shoulder, backs to a wall, wedged between casks of ale and crates of produce in the back room of a tavern. The owner was a large woman named Hanna, who glared suspiciously when Joseph arrived with them in tow. She refused to shelter them until Joseph 'turned on his charm' and convinced her to let them stay until night. Joseph left after promising to return.

"I'm sorry about your pack and bow," Ulf said.

Minna gasped and struggled to pull herself up. She lurched toward the exit before she caught herself. Pressing her knuckles to her eyes, she murmured, "Jason made that bow for me."

"I'm sorry, Minna. If I'd known, I would have—"

She held her hands in front of her face, running her thumb over the rough calluses on her fingers. "No, you shouldn't have. If those men found you with a bow, no telling what they would have done." She shook her head. "It's just... it was the only thing I had from him." She closed her hands into fists and let them drop to her side.

"I'm sorry."

Minna nodded, offering him a small smile.

"Was there anything important in the pack?"

"Nothing, except—" She crossed the storeroom to her cloak, draped over crates to dry, and searched frantically through the pockets. Breathing out in relief, she extracted her parents' book and held it to her breast. Dropping next to Ulf, she leafed through familiar pages.

"What's that?"

"A book. It belongs to my parents."

"What's it about?"

Minna's face flushed. "I don't know. The women who ran the school wouldn't let me go, and my parents didn't teach me to read." She waited for Ulf to laugh, but to her relief, he merely reached for the book without comment. Minna handed it to him.

Holding it up to a small lamp perched on a cask beside them, he read the runes written across the cover. "It says, 'Ragan's Journal'. Who's Ragan?"

"Never heard of her."

"Your parents never mentioned her?"

"No."

"Did you ask?"

"Yes. I used to. They always acted like it was this big secret, or they didn't know. My mother started getting angry when I asked, so I just stopped asking."

"Weird."

"Yeah."

He opened it to the first page. "I can't read much of it. It looks a little like Vollen, but different. There're some names, Eaden, Gallia, another name, Deirdre. I can read some words, but not enough to tell what it says." He handed the book back. "Is it important to you?"

"Yes." Why was it important to her? It always fascinated her, but she never understood why. "I guess, after I changed, I felt like I could never have a life in Fennig, that I would have to leave sometime. But I've never been anywhere else, so I couldn't imagine what my life would be like. I heard stories, but they didn't seem real." She opened the book to a random page and brushed her fingertips over the runes. "This seemed real. Someone from somewhere that isn't Fennig wrote it. I don't know, it just made me feel like there could be a life... another life for me... somewhere. If this Ragan did, I mean."

They were silent for a time, then Ulf said, "You could have a life in Fennig, now. Now that you can hide yourself."

She thought of the men who killed Jason, anger and hatred distorting their features. "Maybe. Anyway, now the book reminds me of home. Sitting in my parents' room, holding this book, wondering what great adventures were written inside."

"Now, you can fill a book with our adventures."

Minna laughed. "I can't read, remember?"

"I can teach you to read." Ulf said. "You help me with *Alle'oss*, I'll teach you to read."

Minna cradled the book in her hands, leaning her head against Ulf's shoulder. "I would like that very much, Ulf." Her *and'reoime* left her invigorated, as if she slept for hours, taking the accumulated aches and pains of the past weeks as well, but Ulf didn't have a spirit guide to wash away his fatigue. "Ulf, you need to sleep. We have to travel tonight." She patted her thigh. "Here, stretch out on the floor. You can put your head on my lap."

"Aren't you sleepy?"

"No, I feel great." Minna rested her hand on Ulf's shoulder as he lay his head on her thigh. She thought of the bow making its way to Brennan in the back of the wagon. Perhaps someone like Willa would put it to a good use. She hoped so.

• • •

The storeroom was full of the smells of home, comforting and painful at the same time. Bundles of herbs, smoked meats and sausages hung from the ceiling. The stack of crates on which she leaned her shoulder emitted the earthy aroma of potatoes. It was hard to tell what time it was, but the muffled sounds coming from the kitchen suggested the cooks were preparing the evening meal. Whatever they were cooking made Minna's stomach grumble. Hanna gave them some bread when they arrived, but it wasn't nearly enough. Ulf lay on his side, head resting on her thigh, lips parted slightly, breathing the slow, steady rhythm of sleep.

Minna paged through Ragan's Journal, holding it up to the light from the lamp. The prospect of learning to read from Ulf was so exciting, she wanted to start right away. Ulf had been asleep for a long time. Watching his eyes moving beneath his eyelids, one corner of his mouth lifting, she let him sleep. Whatever his dreams were, they were happy.

Returning to the book, she found the name Ragan on the first page by matching it with the name on the cover. She tried to match the sounds with the runes. The first rune was raido, which made the r sound, and ehwaz made the eh sound. She didn't know the names of the others, but now she knew the sounds they represented.

"Ragan," she sounded out quietly, tracing the name with her finger.

She searched the text for other instances of the runes, marveling at the sloppy handwriting. The same rune looked different in different places. Tiring of that, she let her head fall back against the wall, eyes slitted, images of the last few days drifting lazily through her mind. Her *and'reoime* coaxing her to what was probably the only spot it would be comfortable in the city brought a smile to her face. She straightened. What would happen if…? Careful to open herself the smallest amount to protect Ulf, she sank into her center, called the spirit and waited expectantly. Nothing. Not surprising. She supposed it was like whispering to someone on the far side of a meadow. Sighing, she dropped her chin to her chest and massaged the muscles at the base of her neck.

Feeling another presence in the storeroom, she lifted her head to find the small orb bobbing patiently before her.

"You came," she whispered, a thrill speeding her heart. She closed her eyes and invited the spirit in. It swirled into her center, a warm, happy greeting. "I'm happy to see you, too," she murmured, though she knew the spirit didn't need her to speak out loud. Before, when she called the *lan'and*, they nearly overwhelmed her with their explosive joy. Her guide conveyed a more delicate sense of happiness, familiar and comfortable.

"Beadu said you'll teach me about the spirits." The spirit swooped, then slowed. "What do I do?" She waited, a vague feeling as if she'd forgotten something coming over her. What could that be? The feeling faded and then rose again, stronger than before, and the presence in her mind swooped again. With a start, she realized the feeling came from her spirit guide. Was it asking what she wanted? "You're asking me a question?" A satisfied sense of accomplishment. Shooting the turkey with Jason's bow came to mind, the feeling she had seeing her father's proud

358

smile. "You're using my feelings to talk to me." The same sense of fulfillment.

"Okay, let's see." The only other gift she knew was the fog Beadu created when the Imps attacked the *Alle'oss* camp. She pictured the fog that obscured their flight from the camp in her mind. The spirit swirled and then was gone. She opened her eyes in time to see it disappearing under the door to the alley behind the tavern.

"I guess that wasn't it," she murmured, disappointed. Sighing, she leaned her head on the crate. Her mind was drifting toward sleep, in the pleasant point when dreams emerge from their shadowy places, and she almost missed it. A presence. A spirit, she was sure, but one entirely unlike the *lan'and*. It was so ephemeral that, were her mind occupied in some way more active, she would have missed it. The spirit drifted placidly, seeming oblivious to Minna's presence, projecting no emotion. She extended her awareness toward it. Cold and ethereal, but aware of her all the same. "What gifts do you have for me?" she whispered, trying to restrain her excitement. With the spirit wave, she had to *tell* the spirits what she wanted. She started to picture the fog, but at that moment, a gust of wind shook the door to the alley, startling her and forcing a chilly blast underneath the door.

The presence vanished. What did she do wrong? Frustrated, she rubbed her chilly hands together, searching her center vainly for the spirit. Ulf groaned in his sleep, grimacing and turning his face into her thigh. Minna closed herself, feeling guilty. While she watched him, his hair fluttered, lifted by a gentle breeze. Minna frowned at it and felt a puff of air on her face. She glanced at the door, but this wasn't an icy gust of wind forcing its way under the door. It was a breeze, light, but steady. A gentle rustling caught her attention. She looked up to find the herb bundles fluttering gently in the breeze. While she watched, the cured meats swayed, creaking on their hooks. *What?* The breeze freshened, swirling in the small room, picking up dust and tumbling a stack of linens from a high shelf. Minna's fascination turned to horror when the air suddenly surged powerfully. The herb bundles and sausages were snatched from their hooks and were soon joined by other objects. Minna leapt to her feet, rolling Ulf onto his back. She squinted into the wind, frantically searching her mind for the spirit. The stack of crates on which she was resting her head leaned precariously toward her.

"What the—" Ulf rolled to his feet, turning his back to the wind.

Minna put her hands on a crate, leaning into the stack to hold it upright. A tray of utensils was tossed into the air, the contents clattering around the room.

"Look out!" she yelled above the rising roar.

A cask of flour tipped over, bursting, the contents whipped by the wind into an imitation of the fog Minna was hoping for.

She threw her center open. *Where did you go, you stupid spirit?*

Minna's boots slipped, and the crates tipped precipitously. "Help, Ulf!"

There! She sensed the spirit, not in her center, but in the storeroom. Minna had an impression of breezy curiosity, completely oblivious to the chaos it was creating. "Stop!"

The wind died instantly, and the spirit's presence disappeared. The crates Minna was holding up crashed against the wall, dropping her to her hands and knees. She ducked her head as utensils, sausages and whatever else the wind picked up rained down around them.

"What in—" Ulf started.

The door to the kitchen crashed open, banging against the wall. Minna leapt to her feet, squinting against the light flooding the small room. A woman, obscured by the fog of dust and flour, said, "What are you two doing in here!?"

"It was an accident! I didn't mean—" Minna blurted.

"Oh Daga, what did you do?" It was Hanna, the tavern owner. A man wearing an apron, a cook, peered over her shoulder. Hanna held her hands out, gawping around at the chaos until her eyes came to rest on Minna. "You! What did you do?"

"It was an accident. I…" She took in the mess, shrugging, helplessly. "I'll clean it up?" Hanna stared at her, her horrified expression hardening into anger. Minna, unable to meet her eyes, looked at Ulf instead. A fine layer of flour coated him. While she watched, his surprised face screwed up. His sneeze sent up a cloud of flour and reverberated in the small room. Minna began to giggle. She covered her mouth, but the more she fought it, the harder it was to stop. She bent over, arm across her stomach, the tears filling her eyes caking the flour in her eyelashes.

"WHAT ARE YOU LAUGHING AT!"

Minna snapped upright, the urge to laugh instantly gone. "I'm sorry?"

Hanna disappeared, then reappeared, a broom and dustpan in her hands. She threw them to the floor. "One hour. I'll be back in one hour, and this room better be back to where it was before."

"Even the flour?" Ulf asked.

She glared at him, then left, pulling the door closed with a bang.

When Ulf turned back to her, eyebrows arched, Minna held up her hand to forestall his questions. "I'll explain while we clean." She surveyed the mess forlornly. "I don't think an hour will be enough."

Chapter 39

Minna

As it turned out, an hour was nearly enough. They couldn't salvage everything. The herb bundles were noticeably smaller than before, and a fine layer of flour covered most surfaces. They didn't know where everything was supposed to be, but considering where they started, Minna thought it could be worse. They were sorting the last of the utensils when the door to the kitchen opened.

Hanna entered the room, hands planted firmly on her hips. "It's going to take me weeks to get this back together." Eying the herbs and swiping a shelf with her finger, she studied the flour coating the tip. "Not to mention making up what it cost me."

"We'll... uh... pay for it. Not now," Ulf rushed to add. "We don't have any money now, but we'll come back. Someday." He winced, shrugging at Minna while Hanna's back was turned.

"Someone's going to pay for it, don't worry," Hanna said as she left the room, leaving Ulf and Minna staring sheepishly at one another. When she returned, she held an iron pot balanced on her hip, a towel over her shoulder and carried a lantern in the other hand. She stepped carefully around Ulf and stood in front of Minna. "Close the door, would you?" she said to Ulf, staring intently at Minna's face. "Nice skin. It'll take the dye well." She handed Minna the lantern, lifting her hand until the light fell on the side of her face. Taking Minna's chin between her fingers, she turned her head so she could examine her left temple.

Minna brushed her hand away and took a step back. "What are you doing?"

Hannah tilted her head to the side. "Joseph told me you were a handful." Placing the pot on a crate, she asked, "Do you know about the sisters of the Seidi?"

"Yes."

"Have you seen one?"

Minna nodded, remembering the sister present when the inquisitor took Alyn.

Hanna touched her left temple. "So, you've seen their tattoos."

"Yes."

Hanna gestured to Minna's hair. "An *Alle'oss* girl running around with black hair is hard to hide. But you blend right in if people think you're a sister." She pursed her lips. "My idea, actually. Joseph was thinking you would have to cross open ground at night to get to Brennan, but if people see a sister instead of a witch... you can waltz right past them."

"Why can't I wrap my head again and pretend to be one of those Des—"

"Desulti?" Hanna asked.

"Yeah, those."

"Won't work. It was a miracle it worked before." Hanna leaned toward Minna and peered at her face. "Joseph was probably unaware the Desulti would never travel alone, and only the Murtair wear the wraps. Most people know little about the Desulti, but someone might, and if they did, they'd see right through the disguise."

Minna didn't know what a Murtair was, but it wouldn't matter if she did, so she left it.

"She could just pretend to be a Volloch," Ulf said.

"Maybe," Hannah said. "But she couldn't travel with you, and besides, they might just decide to check her papers because she fits the description. If she has the tattoo, they'll be more likely to leave her alone."

Minna exchanged a frown with Ulf, who was peering over Hanna's shoulder. "How are you going to make me look like a sister?"

"With this." Hanna reached into the pot and withdrew a small paintbrush. "It's a dye made from the roots of the henka plant. It won't be the exact shade of a sister's tattoo, but on your skin, it will be close enough."

"I'll have a tattoo like them?"

"Don't worry, it fades. Lasts a week or two."

"And you can paint a tattoo like theirs?"

"Absolutely, seen enough of them coming and going in Hast." She tapped a crate with her toe and said, "Sit." When Minna hesitated, Hanna said, "We don't have a lot of time. Joseph will be here soon."

"Why are you doing this, after…" Minna gestured to the room.

"Sooner you're gone, the sooner I'll be rid of you." She tapped the crate again. "'Sides, I'm doing it for Joseph."

Minna sat. Hanna picked up a damp cloth resting over the lip of the pot and scrubbed roughly at the flour on Minna's face, then she dried her face with the towel draped over her shoulder. She handed the lantern to Ulf, saying, "Hold it so it shines here." She pointed to the left side of Minna's face. "Hold absolutely still. We won't get a second chance at this."

Minna let out a slow breath and offered her left cheek.

"I'm going to give you the tattoo of a low-level novice. High enough so it's plausible someone as young as you might be out in the world. Besides, the tattoos of the sisters can be devilishly complex. A novice will be easy. Now, hold still."

She dipped the brush in the pot, took Minna's chin and positioned her head so the left side of her face was accessible. After twice trying to brush Minna's unruly hair behind her ear, she held her hair back and asked Ulf to hold it in place.

Dipping the brush once again, she paused, the bristles hovering over Minna's temple, tip of her tongue between her lips, and then she began to paint.

Minna held still, watching Ulf's reaction out of the corner of her eye. When his eyes widened, Minna's head shifted the smallest amount.

Hanna grasped her jaw and held it firmly. "Don't move."

Minutes later, with a cramp forming in the muscles at the base of Minna's neck, Hanna said, "There! All done." She tossed the brush into the pot and sat back, wiping her hands on her apron. "Not half bad, right?" She smiled up at Ulf.

Ulf peered at Minna's face.

"What does it look like?" Minna asked.

"That *might* work," Ulf said.

"What do you mean, might? It'll work, don't worry." Hanna studied the tattoo before adding, "The light's not that good outside now, what with the clouds and night coming on. It'll work." She stood.

"Do you have a mirror?" Minna asked.

"Sorry, the only mirror is in the common room and it's probably best you don't go in there. It's a bit crowded this time of day." She gathered the pot and threw the towel over her shoulder. "Best get ready. Jos—"

The door to the alley rattled on its hinges as someone banged on it. Minna leapt to her feet, knocking the pot out of Hanna's hands. It hit the floor with a hollow clang, splashing dye across the floor.

A muffled voice from outside called, "Hanna, Minna? Open the door."

Hanna, gazing disconsolately at the spreading pool of dye, said, "That's Joseph."

Ulf pulled the door open. Joseph pushed past him, shut the door and brushed the snow from his hair.

"They—" His gaze roved around the room. "What happened here?"

"We'll be discussing that later," Hanna said.

He opened his mouth, shut it, nodded, then said, "They know you came to the city."

"What, how?" Minna asked.

"You didn't tell me the Inquisition was tracking you to Hast."

Ulf glanced at Minna and said, "We forgot about that."

"Well, they tracked you here and alerted the garrison. They're searching the city."

"What are we going to do?"

"They started in the Old City, across the highway, thinking you would be more likely to hide there. We have a little time, but we're going to have to hurry."

"Well, we're packed. What are we waiting for?" Ulf asked.

Joseph glanced at Minna, then did a double take. He reached down and pressed on Minna's chin to get a better look at the tattoo.

Minna brushed his hand away, scowling. "Why does everyone think they can do that?"

"That just might work," Joseph said to Hanna. "The color's not quite right, but most people wouldn't notice. Probably."

They all looked at Minna, who said, "I'm feeling really good about this plan."

"We could sneak out of the city and cross the plains," Ulf suggested.

Joseph shook his head. "There are patrols all around the city now. They'll see your tracks in the snow. If you try to sneak out, they'll find you, and you'll look guilty, even if she looks like a sister." When Ulf spoke again, Joseph cut him off. "And they're guarding the ports and closed the bridge. The only way out of the city is toward the west. Your only chance is to leave looking like you aren't guilty. You'll be on horseback. They won't expect that." He studied the tattoo again. "Keep your hood up, show people glimpses. It looks real enough for that." He looked Minna up and down. "You're a little young for a novice, but you're kind of smallish, so you probably won't be much bigger when you get older, anyway."

Minna pulled back, brows lifting. Ulf, catching her eye, hoisted a blank expression onto this face, the slightest twitch at the corner of his mouth. He covered his mouth with a fist, coughed, and looked at his feet.

Joseph continued without noticing. "More important, the sisters have a certain, let's call it confidence."

"Arrogance?" Hanna asked.

Joseph waggled his head. "Okay, arrogance. They know there's nothing anyone can do to them, and they have the authority of the Seidi behind them. Don't let anyone push you around." He gave Minna a speculative look. "You'll be a natural."

"What's that supposed to mean?"

Ulf bit his lips. "What?" His eyes widened at Minna's glare.

Joseph, still oblivious, said, "Right, you better get going. Have you two ridden a horse before?"

"Ulf's father owns the stables in Fennig," Minna said.

"What about you?"

They hesitated before Ulf said, "She can ride."

Joseph hesitated, then rummaged in a bag he brought. "Here, you'll need these." He held up two cloaks. "If you're a novice, you wouldn't be wearing green *Alle'oss* cloaks." He tossed a dark blue cloak at Minna. "I got the smallest one I could find."

Minna pulled the cloak over her shoulders. The hem pooled around her boots. "Um."

"You'll be on a horse. No one will notice."

"What about our cloaks?" Ulf asked.

Hanna handed Ulf a bag. "They can squeeze them in here. I also put some bread, cheese, sausage and some oats for the horses in there. Enough to get you to Brennan and a bit extra."

"I'm not sure that's a good idea," Joseph said. "If you're searched."

Minna gazed at her green cloak she held in both hands. "We're keeping them." As Joseph started to protest, she said, "My mother made this for me. And besides…", Minna indicated the blue cloak she wore, stepping on the edge and pulling it taut with her foot. "I'd never be able to walk around in this."

Joseph closed his mouth.

"Thank you, Hanna. For everything," Minna said, handing her green cloak to Ulf. "Especially, considering…"

"Good luck. When you come back to Hast, come in through the front door and leave the magic tricks outside," she said, the smallest of smiles softening her face.

Minna's horse was much bigger than Edda, the top of her head was almost even with the horse's withers. She and the horse eyed one another. "You should feel lucky. You won't even know I'm up there." The horse turned away and snorted. The stirrup hung down to just below her chest.

Minna gathered her cloak, preparing to scale the side of the horse, when hands wrapped around her waist.

"Here." Joseph lifted her until she could get her foot in the stirrup, grasp the pommel and hoist herself up.

"Whoa." She gripped the pommel with both hands, peering down at Joseph and Ulf as he adjusted her stirrups.

When he finished, Ulf stood next to Joseph, smiling up at her encouragingly. Joseph rubbed his chin, brows drawn together. "You might want to relax a bit. Look like you've been on a horse before."

Minna felt her face flush. "I'll be fine. Come on, Ulf. Let's get this over with."

"That's more like it," Joseph said, clapping Ulf on the back. "Go to the intersection up here and turn right. That'll take you to the highway. Turn left and follow the road to Brennan."

Minna looked at the intersection and then back at Joseph. "Just ride out of town on the highway?"

"Yeah, what did you think the tattoo was for?" He motioned for Minna to pull up her hood. "Remember, look mysterious. Give them small glimpses of the tattoo."

"Right, small glimpses."

Ulf's horse started walking, and Minna leaned in that direction. Her horse didn't move. Joseph rolled his eyes. Taking the bridle, he pulled the horse's head around and led her after Ulf. "When you get to Brennan, go to the Siren's Song. It's a tavern in the Merchant District. Anyone can tell you where it is. Ask for a sister named Nia. She's usually there on Lachlandis nights. Tell her Joseph sent you and that you're Harold's angel. She'll help you."

"Harold's angel?"

"She'll know what it means. You can ask her to tell you the story."

They arrived at the intersection and Joseph asked, "What's the name of the tavern?"

"The Siren's Song."

"And where is it?"

"The Merchant District."

"I'm supposed to be helping search in the Old City, so I can't come with you. Taking a risk being here. Any questions?"

Minna chewed on her lower lip and asked, "The Seidi, is it a place?"

Joseph stared at her, then blew air through pursed lips. "Okay, crash course. The Seidi is located in the Imperial District in Brennan, next to the Imperial gardens. They test Volloch girls that show signs of Abria's gift... magic... there. If they pass, they enter the Seidi as initiates and move into the Seidi cloister. Eventually, they graduate as novices." He pointed at Minna. "That's you. Novices may leave the Seidi, though usually a sister or an inquisitor supervises them." He stared at the ground, tapping his foot, then said, "They'll stop you on the way out of the city, so you need a good story. Tell them you were with Sister Nara in Kartok. Tell them she sent you home for..."

"Disobedience?" Ulf ventured.

Minna glared at him. "Disobedience?"

"Yeah, disobedience." Joseph said. "That will work, and a bad attitude. People will believe that." Joseph and Ulf snickered.

"Ha, ha. What about Ulf?"

"I'll say Nara sent me with you to make sure you went back."

"That won't work. I'm supposed to be a novice of the Seidi. An arrogant, disobedient novice. Why would I let an *Alle'oss boy* make me obey?"

"She's got a point," Joseph said.

Blank looks all around until Ulf suggested, "Okay, how about this? It's her first time out in the world and Nara sent me to show her the way back. I'm going that way anyway for my father, so I offered to show her the way."

Joseph nodded slowly. "That might work."

"Been regretting it ever since. All the griping and complaining." Ulf grinned.

Minna hitched an eyebrow.

"Just trying to flesh out the story, Min. It's the details that make a story believable."

Minna asked Joseph, "Anything else I should know?"

"Um, the head of the Seidi is Malefica Deirdre. She's a powerful sister. If you get in trouble, use her name."

"Mal…"

"Mal - ef - uh - ka Deirdre." He eyed her and said, "Relax a little. Maybe slump in the saddle a little, like you've been riding all day."

Minna slumped. Her butt slipped forward. When she reached back to push herself up, her hand pushed against the cloak, pulling her further backward. Scrabbling for the pommel, she finally pulled herself upright.

Joseph watched her struggle. "You'll be fine." He continued under his breath as he turned away. "I hope."

Chapter 40

Minna

When they turned onto the highway, the setting sun peeked below the clouds on the western horizon, casting long shadows and forcing them to shade their eyes.

"Do these people travel all night?" Minna asked, watching the traffic on the road.

"They normally stop when it gets dark. I'm guessing they're trying to make up time they lost crossing the bridge. They sleep under their wagons if they have them." He grimaced, gazing up into the snow, which began to fall in earnest as they made their way through the city. "We'll probably have to sleep in the open."

Across the highway, the old part of the city looked peaceful. No sign of the brothers she knew were searching it. Groups of Imps in blue uniforms patrolled the southern border of the Old City on foot. The clops of their horses' hooves on the slushy cobbles suddenly sounded too loud, sure to draw attention to them. Minna tried to slouch impressively, holding her hands in different positions without finding one that felt natural.

"Minna, don't hold the reins so tight."

They were nearing the edge of the city when she saw them: a large contingent of Imperial soldiers and brothers questioning everyone as they left the city. Off to the side, another group sat on horseback, watching the procession, much more comfortably slouched than Minna.

Would a novice hide herself the way the sister in Fennig did? If she opened her center, they would sense her coming, but they were sure to question them, anyway. Minna opened herself to the spirit realms. To Ulf's frightened face, she said, "I'm a novice now, remember? Besides, if this goes bad, I want to be able to defend myself."

Ulf pulled his lips tight, nodded, and said, "You got our story straight?"

"You're my guide boy, leading me back to the Seidi, next to the Imperial gardens. I'm a novice of the Seidi who sees injustice and incompetence everywhere, but no one listens to me. You've been a pain the entire trip, so I'm thinking about ditching you and making my own way."

A small smile flickered across Ulf's face.

"Just trying to flesh out the story," Minna said sweetly.

"Aren't you nervous?"

"Terrified." And she was. Her heart hammered and sweat soaked her tunic, leaving chilly trails down her ribs. She pulled the hood of her cloak further forward, wild escape scenarios playing out in her mind. The jangling of wagon traces, grumbles of the drivers, the clops of the horses' hooves, the shouts of the Imperials, a cacophony, faded behind the whoosh, whoosh of her pulse. Searching the sides of the highway for a way out, she noticed her *and'reoime* pacing them through the elm trees. "How did you know?" she whispered and called the spirit. Closing her eyes, she allowed herself a moment to experience their joy. She took a deep breath, her heart settling into a slow, steady rhythm.

When she opened her eyes, they were nearing the blockade. "Hood," Ulf said, miming pulling her hood farther forward. Minna shrunk within her cloak, slumping in what she hoped was a bored, disobedient pose.

The brothers sensed her coming. They pointed and shouted to one another. Two of the men broke away and approached them while others spread out across the road, drawing weapons. One brother took Minna's bridle and said, "Alright there, let's see you."

"Hands off, brother." Minna turned an insolent frown on him, giving him a glimpse of her face.

His mouth opened and then slammed shut. He peered at her face and turned to whisper to the other brother.

The second brother, an older man with graying hair, craned his neck, trying to get a better view of her face. "What's a novice of the Seidi doing all alone out in the world?"

Minna opened her mouth and froze. What was the name of that sister, again?

The moments dragged out until Ulf snorted. The men seemed to notice him for the first time. Ulf said, "Oh, sorry."

"Who are you?"

"My name's Eric Svenson. I'm from Kartok."

"You're *Alle'oss*. Are you with this... novice?"

"Unfortunately, yes." Ulf hoisted a long-suffering grimace onto his face.

The brother looked from Minna to Ulf, eyes narrowing. "What are you doing together?"

Ulf chuckled. "Well, that's a story." Minna stared at him. Where was this coming from? She hardly recognized the awkward, quiet boy she knew.

The men exchanged a look, then the older one said, "Suppose you tell it."

"Well, I'm going to Brennan, for my father, you see." Ulf leaned toward them and spoke confidentially. "We're in the fur trade. Finest pelts in Argren. Sell a lot to furriers in Brennan." He straightened and waved his hand. "He lets me go to Brennan to arrange..." Ulf hesitated, mouth open, hand frozen in the middle of his gesture.

Minna waited, breathlessly, to hear what Ulf was going to Brennan to arrange.

"Well, it's business things, contracts and such. It's complicated. Not that important to the story."

The older brother opened his mouth, and Ulf rushed on.

"Anyway, I was going to Brennan, and this sister came into town. Kartok. You know it? I'm sure you do. The sister's name was Nara, and she had this one." He hooked a thumb at Minna, opened his mouth and hesitated before turning to look at Minna. "Uh, what was your name again?"

Minna, not expecting to be involved in the story, blurted out the first name that came into her head. "Agatha."

Ulf blinked. "Right. Agatha." He cleared his throat and continued, "They were arguing. In the middle of the town square. Everybody watching. Quite the scene." He chuckled to himself. "Finally, the sister, Nara, tells her to go back to the Seidi." Ulf tipped his head toward Minna and said, "She says she doesn't know the way, so, long story short, Sister Nara asks if anyone can show her." He paused, hand raised. "So, I volunteered, since I was going anyway, you see." He leaned forward and lowered his voice. "Been regretting it, to be honest. A bit churlish, this one."

The men stared at him, then the older brother turned and shouted to a man standing nearby, "Sven, you were with Inquisitor Anders and that l'oss, weren't you? What was the name of the l'oss?"

"Torsten, Inquisitor."

"Right. Find him and bring him here."

Even with her spirit guide in her center, a chill spread from Minna's core. Torsten. The traitor who helped the Inquisition track them. If Torsten saw them, they were as good as dead. She eyed the men on horseback, but dismissed the idea of running. Ulf might have a chance, but even assuming she could stay on her horse at a full gallop, she couldn't outrun experienced riders. She gazed around at the Imperials. Could she fight her way past all of them? Remembering how she swooned in the meadow after using the spirit wave three times, she doubted it. Noticing the brother holding her horse's bridle, squinting at her fake tattoo, she flinched away. Too late, she realized her mistake.

"I think you better come with us until we can confirm this story," the inquisitor said. To the man holding Minna's reins, he said, "Sergeant, take them into custody."

"Yes, Inquisitor," the sergeant said, drawing his sword.

The sergeant's movements seemed to slow, sounds receded and echoed. Alyn's face swam up in Minna's mind.

"Come on then. Both of you, down and keep your hands where I can see them," the sergeant said.

Minna hesitated. "Inquisitor, you have no—" The sergeant, a large man, reached up, grasped her arm and yanked her off the horse. There was a moment of free fall as he let her drop and a sudden, violent stop. She felt a crack in her back and lights flared in her head when her head struck the cobbles. She gasped and squeezed her eyes shut against the searing pain in her back. Something inside her had broken.

There were muffled shouts of bystanders reacting. "Hey!" Ulf's voice, seeming far away.

The violence of the act left her disoriented, her mind overloaded by pain and shock. All except her *and'reoime*, a bright, steadying presence amid the turmoil. She clung to it, allowing herself to sink into her center. The pain in her back and head faded into the background, then disappeared altogether. Carefully, she took a deep, pain-free breath.

Anger. For years, she feared her own anger, afraid of the pressure and the storm, and what it meant for the people around her. But she mastered that fear on the top of the ridge with Ulf. When she met the brothers in the meadow, she had no time for anger. But now, deep within her center, she watched the inferno of her anger and welcomed it. She had a right to her anger and would not deny it. She opened her eyes.

The sergeant loomed over her, leering. "Now, are you going to come along, or do I have to soften you up?" Other Imps were closing in, walking casually, talking and laughing, barely paying attention.

Minna reached out to her spirit guide and felt it answer. A flick of her fingers sent the sergeant flying backwards. He landed on his back ten feet away, his sword skittering across the slushy cobbles. Her center rang, and she steeled herself, expecting the debilitating waves of euphoria, but they did not come. Though the note was the same, it was softer, perhaps because only her spirit guide was in her center. Still, she groaned in response until her spirit guide *sang* a lower harmony that blended so beautifully with her own note, goosebumps rippled across her skin. For the space of half a heartbeat, Minna wasn't sure what she was experiencing, but it mellowed the effect of the spirit wave, leaving her mind clear.

In the stunned silence, Minna struggled to her feet against her oversized cloak. She cast frantically around for Ulf, and found him still mounted, holding the reins of her horse. She crouched, watching the Imperials surrounding her, trying to keep all of them in sight. *It won't be enough.* There were too many. Even if she blasted them all, who else would she hurt?

Catching Ulf's frightened eyes, she shouted, "Hide." He gave her a brief nod, kicked his horse into motion, scattered the brothers converging on him and disappeared between two wagons, heading toward the north side of the city. She was preparing to call the *lan'and,* when a vision of the earlier chaos she caused in the storeroom came into her mind. Wind. Frantically, she reached out to the ethereal spirits and was rewarded when she sensed not one, but many.

"Come now, sweetie. There's no need for—Now!" As one, the men launched themselves at her. Minna lifted her arms and sent a desperate plea to spirits.

This was not the single spirit, playfully testing its limits in the physical realm, as in the storeroom. This was a multitude that, sensing her distress, answered her call. The air exploded into a hurricane, with Minna at its center. Imperials, and everyone else, were taken completely by surprise. The men who were lunging at her were blown into one another, falling into a tangle that was swept along the slick, packed snow. Anyone without shelter was thrown from their feet, boots slipping on the ice and snow. Though she saw them screaming, no sounds rose above the roar. Further from the heart of the storm, the horses fled, their riders thrown or clinging on desperately. One of the immense coal wagons tipped, teetered precariously, then fell on its side, splintering the tongue connecting the yoke to the wagon. Coal spilled onto the ground and was whipped up to become projectiles. Teams of oxen panicked, dragging their wagons haphazardly away from the madness.

Minna's cloak flew out behind her, was snatched by the edge of the storm and whipped around her body. The wind picked up snow from the drifts beside the highway, whipping it into a white wall, leaving her alone in the eye of the storm. She let her head fall back, eyes closed, reached out to her sides, and dipped her fingertips into the icy blast. Her body thrummed with the spirits' song. It was not the euphoric ecstasy of the spirit wave, which rang and faded slowly away. This was a cold, sustained, pulsing note, shivery and exhilarating. Yet, in the part of her mind deep in the tranquility of her center, she sensed her spirit guide's warning. The airy spirits' attention was wavering.

Instinctively, she twisted against the wind, bringing it to an abrupt stop. Silence, deafening in its suddenness, a moment of peace amid the white cloud, which swirled and eddied aimlessly around her. Then the clatter of debris falling to the ground, the shouts and groans of the people caught up in the storm, the bellows of the oxen. As the cloud cleared, floating ice crystals glittered in the sunlight. She gazed around, exhausted and stunned by the destruction. The evidence of the wind's strength was everywhere. Debris littered the ground. Bodies lay around her 100 feet in every direction. She watched people moving about, picking themselves up, staring fearfully in her direction.

Her experience in the storeroom with the single spirit did not prepare her to channel the immense power of the multitude. She felt hollowed out, her muscles spastic and trembling. Her thoughts were slow and sticky, as if embedded in honey. She knew she should flee, but all she wanted to do was to lie down and wrap herself around the deep sense of weary bliss the spirits left her. She was afraid to take a step for fear her shaking legs wouldn't support her. She gazed numbly around at groups of Imperials edging her way. The clatter of horses approaching penetrated the fog, and then the horses skidded to a stop so close they spattered her with slush.

"Minna!" Ulf's voice, sounding as if it came from far away. "Come on, let's get out of here."

Minna swayed, took a step, stumbled, then jerked to a stop. *No, not yet.* They would never get away if the Imps pursued them. Clenching her teeth, she sent a thought to her guide. *"Help me!"* The spirit responded, sending a shuddery wave radiating from her center through her body, sweeping her lassitude away. The sensation of having her strength return so abruptly was almost as pleasurable as the spirit wave. She closed her eyes and groaned a thank you.

"Minna?" Ulf, sounding frantic.

Ignoring him, Minna spun slowly, searching until she spotted the inquisitor lying on his back near a tree twenty feet away. She strode over to him, keeping an eye on the other Imperials. People, drawn by the commotion, were arriving from other parts of the city. Seeing her coming, the inquisitor scuttled back against the tree.

Cloak draped around her and pooling at her feet, Minna gave him her sweetest smile and said, "Inquisitor, if you asked *nicely*, I would have been happy to oblige you. But you didn't." She leaned over him. "You have no right to treat a novice of the Seidi so disrespectfully."

A brother at the edge of her vision edged closer. A flick of her fingers sent him flying.

Minna continued in the same calm voice. "Unless you want to be picking up pieces of these men, I suggest you order them to back off and let us go. If you have a problem, take it up with Malefica Deirdre, but if you don't order these men to make way, I'm going to LOSE MY TEMPER." Minna opened her center wide, sending her spirit guide swirling joyfully through her mind, eliciting grunts of pain and sending the Imperials nearby stumbling away from her. "Inquisitor?"

"Back off! Everyone… let them go," he yelled.

"I don't think everyone heard you. Get up!" Minna stepped back. When the Inquisitor looked at her uncertainly, she yelled, "I SAID GET UP!"

He clawed at the tree trunk, pulling himself upright.

"Now, say it again, so everyone hears."

He took a deep breath and screamed, "No one is to interfere with the sister! Anyone who disobeys will answer to me!"

Glancing around at the Imperials who were watching the exchange, Minna guessed that was probably the best she was going to get. "Good enough. If I see anyone following us, I'll come back." She spun on her heel, hitched up her cloak and stalked away.

Ulf waited, wide-eyed, still mounted and holding her horse's reins. She saw the problem as she approached her horse and sent a message once more to the spirits. *Now, fog.* By the time she made it to her horse, the fog was thick enough that she couldn't see more than ten feet.

"Ulf," she said under her breath. "Help me get on my horse."

Ulf dismounted and came around to Minna, cupped his hands, and boosted her up.

"Come on, boy," Minna said loudly and urged her horse to walk. Fortunately, the horse responded. The Imperials that emerged out of the fog as they passed shuffled quickly away.

"I'll tell Malleus Hoerst about this!" the Inquisitor, apparently regaining his courage now that she was out of sight, screamed, his voice rising eerily out of the fog. "The Malefica will hear of this, and you'll pay for your insolence! Novice Agatha!"

Minna let the fog go as she drew even with a cluster of wagons, jammed together by their team's panicked flight. The drivers, attempting to untangle them, stared at her as they passed. As they emerged from the fog, Minna asked, "Are they coming after us?"

Twisting in his saddle, Ulf said, "No. Can't see much, though." Facing forward again, he said, "I suggest we pick up the pace once we're over that rise up ahead. They might change their minds."

They rode in silence for a few moments. Minna let her spirit guide go and watched it skip across the snow-covered grass in a wide circle around them.

"You might lose your temper?" Ulf ventured.

Minna smirked. "Churlish?"

Ulf chuckled. "Imagine if you couldn't make that fog. Bit of a let-down, having your guide boy boost you onto your horse after calling forth the storm, don't you think?"

They stared at each other, then dissolved into giggles.

"I've never been so scared in my life," Ulf said. "When that brother ran off to find Torsten, I nearly wet myself. I was sure you were going to explode."

"You didn't look scared. You were so good with that story. I was amazed. I couldn't remember any of it."

"*You* were amazing. The way you knocked that sergeant down with just a flick of your fingers. You're getting really good with that thing. And that wind…"

She watched him, staring ahead, brow furrowed, then twisted around and looked back. She could barely make out people cleaning up the mess she created and a group of men in white standing in the highway, looking their way. Not everyone in the wind's path were Imperials. But what else could she have done? Ulf and Alyn would be dead if she let the brothers arrest them. Alyn. She watched Ulf, who was staring into the distance, chewing his lip, his features painted orange by the setting sun.

"Ulf?"

He started and turned toward her. "Um?"

"Do you think there's a chance Alyn is alive?"

"Of course," he said casually.

She thought he would say so, but the offhand way he said it lent it an air of conviction she wasn't expecting. "But, before, you always said it was already too late."

"Yeah, but that Joseph told you that his friend might, *might*, be able to help rescue your sister."

"So?"

"Well, he doesn't strike me as the type to tell you something just to make you happy. If he thinks she might help rescue Alyn, then he must think there's a chance she's alive." He grinned at her. "Right?"

She stared at him. "Yeah." When he turned back toward the setting sun, she followed his gaze. It really was pretty. Her spirit guide swooped by, orbited once, then headed out across the plains. She was a *saa'myn*, descended from women with power, and with her spirit guide's help, she would find a way to keep her promise to her sister.

Torsten

Torsten watched the medic examining Ivan's wounded arm.

"The tip was embedded in the bone," the medic murmured. "But it doesn't feel like it shattered it. I'd say you were lucky."

Ivan barely reacted. He refused the pain killers the medic offered and didn't sleep at all the previous night. When Ivan asked him why he stuck around after bringing him to the infirmary, Torsten equivocated, but the brother didn't seem to have the energy to question him further. In his short time with Ivan, Torsten decided the man was a zealot, a true believer in Daga. But he was not nearly as insufferable as Inquisitor Anders. Torsten couldn't stomach the inquisitor's condescending insults any longer, and he still had a job to do—the Imperials must capture Minna before she provoked them further.

Ivan was telling him, once again, to leave when a roar rose from outside.

Torsten turned and made his way to the infirmary entrance. A crowd raced across the fortress courtyard toward the main gate. The roar died in an instant, as if cut with shears just as Torsten stepped onto the Imperial Highway. Looking to the western end of the city, he had a hard time understanding what he was seeing at first. It looked like a blizzard, but it was only 100 paces across and only extended a hundred feet above the ground. There was only one explanation.

When Ivan stepped up beside him, Torsten said, "It's Minna."

Ivan stared at him. "The witch?"

"My guess is, she escaped."

Ivan began hobbling toward the cloud, but Torsten caught his arm and stopped him. "You're going nowhere like that. You're so exhausted, you can barely walk." He nodded down the street. "Don't worry, I know where she's going."

"Where?"

"She's going to Brennan to rescue her sister."

"Her sister?"

"Yeah. Inquisitor Schakal captured her. Should be in Brennan already."

"But if they get to Brennan, how will we find them?"

"It'll take them until the day after tomorrow to get there," Torsten said. "The girl can't ride well. Inquisitor Anders, the one I was with when we found you, he actually had a good idea about how to catch her. If it's not too late."

"Too late?"

"Go get a few hours' sleep," Torsten said.

Torsten watched Ivan limp back toward the fortress gate, Beadu's words in his mind. "The pivot is whether Minna finds her spirit guide in time. Though it is a slim hope, it is all that we have. Our fate lies with the will of the spirits."

He watched the cloud of snow settling on the far end of Hast. Minna must have found her spirit guide to have produced such a storm. Beadu said she and her sister would be powerful. He couldn't imagine them being powerful enough to make a difference. They would only provoke the Empire and their violent reaction would engulf all of Argren.

He followed Ivan. Of course, Minna was alone, without allies. Her sister was in prison and too young to wield her power, in any case. If they could catch Minna before she had the chance to learn, perhaps all was not lost. Not yet.

Characters

Alle'oss

Minna Hunter	Daughter of Thomas and Vada Hunter, sister of Alyn Hunter
Alyn Hunter	Daughter of Thomas and Vada Hunter, sister of Minna Hunter
Thomas Hunter	Father of Minna and Alyn Hunter
Vada Hunter	Mother of Minna and Alyn Hunter
Ulf Lothan	Son of stablemaster Erik Lothan, brother of Tamas Lothan
Erik Lothan	Stablemaster in Fennig, father of Ulf and Tamas Lothan
Tamas Lothan	Son of stablemaster Erik Lothan, brother of Ulf Lothan
Jason Smyth	Son of blacksmith Gunther Smyth, friend of Minna
Gunther Smyth	Blacksmith in Fennig, father of Jason Smyth
Egan Smyth	Grandfather of Jason Smyth

Aron Hunter	Member of the *Alle'oss* resistance
Beadu	The last *saa'myn*
Zaina	Member of the *Alle'oss* resistance
Marie Ander	Village elder in Fennig, friend of the Hunters and one of Minna's few defenders
Brana Helvig	Friend of Marie, owner of the inn in Fennig
Agatha Ericson	Farmer in Fennig, mother of Agmar, one of Minna's chief antagonists
Agmar Ericson	Farmer in Fennig, son of Agatha, one of Minna's chief antagonists
Mabel	Friend of Agatha
Loden	Friend of Agmar, one of Minna's chief antagonists
Jesper	Friend of Agmar, one of Minna's chief antagonists
Karl Siegling	Friend of Thomas Wolfe
Torsten Junge	Member of the *Alle'oss* resistance
Orla Junge	Wife of Torsten Junge
Lesa Junge	Daughter of Torsten Junge
Fallon Junge	Son of Torsten Junge

Imperials

Brothers of the Inquisition

Harold Wolfe	Inquisitor
Stefan Schakal	Inquisitor, right hand to the Malleus
Hoerst Bernston	The Malleus, leader of the Inquisition
Henrik Matison	Sergeant in Harold Wolfe's escort
Joseph Weidner	Former member of Harold Wolfe's escort
Raif Alundson	Companions-at-arms in Harold Wolfe's escort
Fenton Wynton	Companions-at-arms in Harold Wolfe's escort
Ellgar Gluzman	Sergeant in Stefan Schakal's escort
Eckehart Baumann	Companions-at-arms in Inquisitor Ander's escort, temporarily assigned to Stefan Schakal
Anders Hanke	Inquisitor sent into the wilderness
Torbert Scriver	Inquisitor

Sisters of the Seidi

Deirdre Breasal	The Malefica, leader of the Seidi
Nia Kelly	Deirdre's assistant and friend
Briana Darragh	Leader of Deirdre's opposition in the Seidi

Keelia Darrah	A member of Briana's faction and hero of the emperor's wars
Cara Byrne	A member of Briana's faction who attempts to convince Keelia to join Briana
Carey Walsh	Novice loyal to Deirdre who helped Ulf search for Minna in Brennan

Brothers of the Order Domina

Ivan Teufel	Dominican Brother who pursues Minna to Brennan
Victor	Friend of Ivan Teufel
Linton	Friend of Ivan Teufel
Emric	Friend of Ivan Teufel

Imperials

Luch	Leader of a small gang in the Fallows who confront of Minna
Rat	Member of Luch's gang in the Fallows
Mairt	Member of Luch's gang in the Fallows
Louisa Brukman	Bar maid in the Monk's Habit
Renard Faust	Owner of the Monks' Habit
Xander Mendler	Brother of the Order of Eidolon
Lika	An orphan living on the streets of Brennan

Alle'oss Pronunciation

Consonants in *Alle'oss* are pronounced the same as in English with the exception of r which is trilled unless it is the last letter in a word.

Vowels are pronounced according to the following:
a as in tall, e as in train, i as in neat, o as in poke, u as in too

The macron used in many words does not change the sound of the vowel. It merely increases the length the sound is held.

Alle'oss also has the following dipthongs:
uo as in whoa, ue as in wheh, ua as in whah, ae as in eye, ia as in yah, ie as in yeh, io as in yoh

Stress is normally on the last syllable that ends in a consonant, but if the word has a vowel with a macron, the stress is placed on that syllable.

Ross Allen
Spirit Sight Volume 2

About the Author

Somehow, after spending most of his life in the South, Ross Hightower found himself living in Milwaukee and loving it. One cold, snowy morning, not too long ago, he woke with a story stuck in his head. That wasn't unusual, but what happened next was unprecedented. He wrote it down. That small story grew into his first novel, *Spirit Sight*. While he anxiously waits for its publication, Ross and Debby, his partner of 34 years, are hard at work on a prequel. Some might wonder why it took so long to find their calling in life, but Ross is just grateful he has.

Don't Miss

Spirit Sight Volume 2

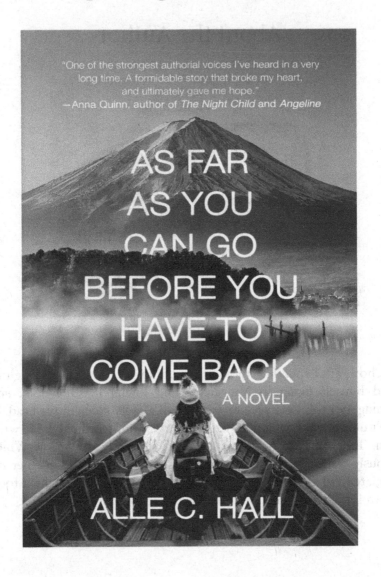

"One of the strongest authorial voices I've heard in a very long time. A formidable story that broke my heart, and ultimately gave me hope."
—Anna Quinn, author of *The Night Child* and *Angeline*

AS FAR AS YOU CAN GO BEFORE YOU HAVE TO COME BACK
A NOVEL

ALLE C. HALL

An Excerpt from
Spirit Sight Volume 2

Alyn

She knew she was dreaming. A small part of her stood aside, watching the same horrors play out over and over, knowing what would happen, but unable to stop it. It's just a dream. But it was more real than a dream, even though it was warped and twisted by the drug. She watched Minna searching for her again. Alyn could see her, knew dark forces were closing in, but no matter how desperately she screamed, she couldn't get her sister's attention. How many times had she watched it happen? How many times would she have to watch it again?

She was cold. Shivering. Awake. She opened her eyes. A bright moon sent a shaft of light through the window, illuminating the cell in a pale blue light. She must still be dreaming. It was so quiet. Even in the darkest nights at home, there were the calls of the owls and nightingales, the howls of the wolves and the yips of coyotes. The dungeon was blanketed in a silence so complete that Alyn clucked her tongue to ensure the drug hadn't taken her hearing. The sound echoed reassuringly in the small cell.

Someone threw a blanket over her while she dreamed, but although she was huddled into a tight little ball beneath it, she was still cold. I'm awake. But the dreams were not done with her. A purple glow surrounded everything, and the edges of objects seemed unwilling to stay where they were meant to be. A dish and water bottle lay beside the bed, undoubtedly left by the guards when they fed her. Her stomach contracted at the sight of the food.

Sitting brought on a wave of nausea, sending the cell spinning and twisting, forcing her to sit quietly while it settled. Sliding onto the floor, she knelt, hands hovering above the dish, unable to bring the warping images of her hands and the dish together. Finally, she closed her eyes and felt her way. Discarding the spoon, she held the dish to her face and licked the crusty remnants of the porridge. It was the same bland meal she had eaten every day since she arrived, but her mouth flooded even so. The plate was nearly clean when her stomach rebelled, threatening to eject its contents. The bowl clattered to the floor as her body convulsed. Instinctively, she sought her center and sank into it, melting to the floor and groaning with relief as her stomach settled. Lying on her back, arms stretched out to her sides, her eyes fell on the window, a narrow slice of moonlit sky. I'll find a way.

The lan'and came to the prison yard when she called, even in this horrid, sterile place. She feared talking to them after watching Minna in the forest glade, but she was a saa'myn and the spirits were her legacy. She was no longer afraid. Closing her eyes, she called, confident they would come. And they did, pouring through the window, glittering purple streaks swirling around the cell as they explored the alien space. Lying on her back, she watched them, a prickle behind her eyes, but she had no tears to shed. She took a long breath, sighed it out, focused on her center and called.

Perhaps it was because Minna prepared her. Perhaps it was because she knew her own spirit so well, having spent so much time in her center. Whatever the reason, the experience was not as traumatic as it was for Minna. The spirits burst into her center, shouting a jubilant greeting. Her laughter, bright and impetuous, echoed in the small space. She lifted her arms, letting them sway to and fro, watching her hands return to their familiar shape as the spirits swept away the remnants of the dreams. Her small spirit, unafraid at the center of the storm, rejoiced. And the spirits spoke to her. Not words. Nothing she could explain, but she understood.

"Alyn?" A small, hopeful voice.

She let the spirits go, and letting her arms fall to her sides, she watched them leave. When they were gone, she stood and walked to the door. "Tora?"

Tora's words came in a rush. "Oh yes! Alyn, we were so worried. I've never seen the guards so mad. It's been days!" Alyn smiled, picturing Tora bouncing on the balls of her feet.

"How long has it been?"

"Five days." Frida's voice.

Five days. "Hello, Frida."

"Was it bad?" Tora asked quietly.

"Yes. Yes, it was awful."

"How do you feel?" A new voice.

"That's Ibbe. She woke up while you were dreaming," Tora said, excitement trilling her voice again.

"Hello, Ibbe. I feel fine. I'm hungry and thirsty," she said, eying the water bottle.

The other girls were quiet and then Ibbe asked, "You don't feel sick?"

"When did you wake up?" Frida's voice. A faint note of accusation.

"I just woke up. I felt sick at first, but I… spoke to the lan'and. I feel much better now."

There was another moment of silence. Alyn grinned, imagining Tora's busy mind filling with questions. When they came, they came in a rush.

"You spoke to them? What did they say? They made you feel better? How did they do it? What was it like? Do you actually, you know, speak? What do their voices sound like?"

"Tora!"

The sound of the door to the guardroom opening ended the conversation.

She scrambled to the bed, pulled the blanket over herself and watched the window in the door. A shadow appeared, lingered for a moment before disappearing. Moments later, the door to the guardroom opened and closed. It was an ominous development. The night guard rarely bothered them. Apparently, the other girls felt the same, as no one disturbed the silence.

Alyn slid to the floor and picked up the water bottle. Pulling the stopper, she poured a drop on her finger and touched it to the tip of her tongue. Just water. Turning the bottle up, she drank it dry, careful to get every drop. It wasn't enough, but it was something. She clambered onto her bed and huddled under the blanket. It took her a long time to fall asleep, but when she did, her dreams were her own.

Note from Ross Hightower

Thank you for reading Spirit Sight, Volume 1. If you liked the story, please consider leaving a review on Goodreads or your favorite online retailer. Reviews are one of the most important ways to spread the word.

If you would like to hear about upcoming books, short stories, and other news from the Spirit Song world, sign up for my newsletter at rosshightower.com.

In the meantime, while you wait for future installments in the Spirit Song Saga, here is a chapter from Spirit Sight, Volume 2. Look for it in the near future.

We hope you enjoyed reading this title from:

www.blackrosewriting.com

Subscribe to our mailing list – *The Rosevine* – and receive **FREE** books, daily deals, and stay current with news about upcoming releases and our hottest authors.
Scan the QR code below to sign up.

Already a subscriber? Please accept a sincere thank you for being a fan of Black Rose Writing authors.

View other Black Rose Writing titles at
www.blackrosewriting.com/books and use promo code
PRINT to receive a **20% discount** when purchasing.

CPSIA information can be obtained
at www.ICGtesting.com
Printed in the USA
LVHW031211080523
746268LV00004B/17

9 781685 130275